In the Crucible

Volume 2: The Mission

In Christ
& Dave

In the Crucible

Volume 2: The Mission

David John Bena

Birch
Grove
Publishing

This book is dedicated to all those who defend our nation. Some wear a uniform; some do not. Some bear arms; some support those who do. Some die; most come home. All are willing to put their lives on the line so that we can live in freedom. I also dedicate this book to the loved ones of those who defend us. They pay the highest price of all. May you be blessed as you read *The Mission.* — David J. Bena

In the Crucible, Volume 2: The Mission
David John Bena

The publisher gratefully acknowledges cover photos by Specialist 3rd Class Joshua Scott, USN; Larry P. Yarham and the A-6 Intruder Association; Raymond Dague; and Melanie Swanson Photography.

Contents

Chukotka

Area 51

China Lake

PRELUDE
Chukotka Peninsula, Russia

CHAPTER ONE
Yanrakinnot, Chukotka

CHAPTER TWO
P'yongyang, North Korea
Yanrakinnot

CHAPTER THREE
Anadyr, Russian Federation
China Lake, California

CHAPTER FOUR
Langley, Virginia
The Oval Office, Washington

CHAPTER FIVE
Yanrakinnot
Moscow, Russia
"Area 51," Nevada
P'yongyang
Port Alsworth, Alaska

CHAPTER SIX
Langley, Virginia
Area 51, Nevada

CHAPTER SEVEN
Yanrakinnot
Area 51, Nevada
Langley, Virginia
Pevek, Northern Chukotka

CHAPTER EIGHT
Area 51, Nevada
Peekskill, New York
P'yongyang, North Korea
Seoul, South Korea

CHAPTER NINE
Oval Office, Washington, DC
Nevada Test & Training Range

CHAPTER TEN
State Department, Washington
Tongch'ang-dong, North Korea
Yanrakinnot

CHAPTER ELEVEN
Oval Office, Washington
Area 51, Nevada
Peekskill, NY
Moscow

CHAPTER TWELVE
Yanrakinnot
Washington, DC

CHAPTER THIRTEEN
North of Area 51
P'yongyang
Seoul, Republic of Korea
Yanrakinnot
Iwakuni, Japan

CHAPTER FOURTEEN
The Oval Office, Washington
The Kremlin
Mys Shmidta, Chukotka
Incheon, Republic of Korea
P'yongyang
Beijing, China

CHAPTER FIFTEEN
Mount Mantap, North Korea
Sea of Japan
P'yongyang
The White House
Over the Sea of Japan
The White House

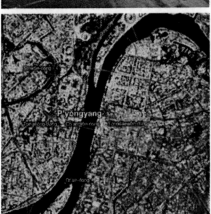

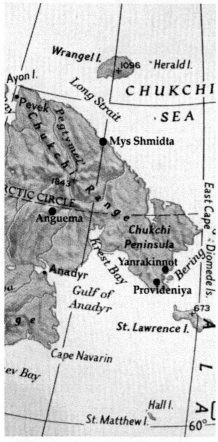

Satellite photos: Washington DC; Area 51,
Nevada; P'yongyang; MCAS Iwakuni,
Japan; Mount Mantap, North Korea

CHAPTER SIXTEEN
North Korean Coastline
Camouflaged Gazebo
P'yongyang
Aboard Clambake Zero Three
Camouflaged Gazebo
Aboard the DPRK Helicopter
P'yongyang
Iwakuni, Japan
P'yongyang
Office of the Chairman, Beijing
Moscow
The Oval Office

CHAPTER SEVENTEEN
The Sea of Japan
Langley, Virginia
Eastern North Korea
Mys Shmidta

CHAPTER EIGHTEEN
North Korea
Area 51

CHAPTER NINETEEN
North Korea-Russia border

CHAPTER TWENTY
Provideniya
CIA Headquarters, Virginia
Uelen, Russia
Moscow

CHAPTER TWENTY-ONE
Mys Shmidta
Pevek, Russia
Amguema

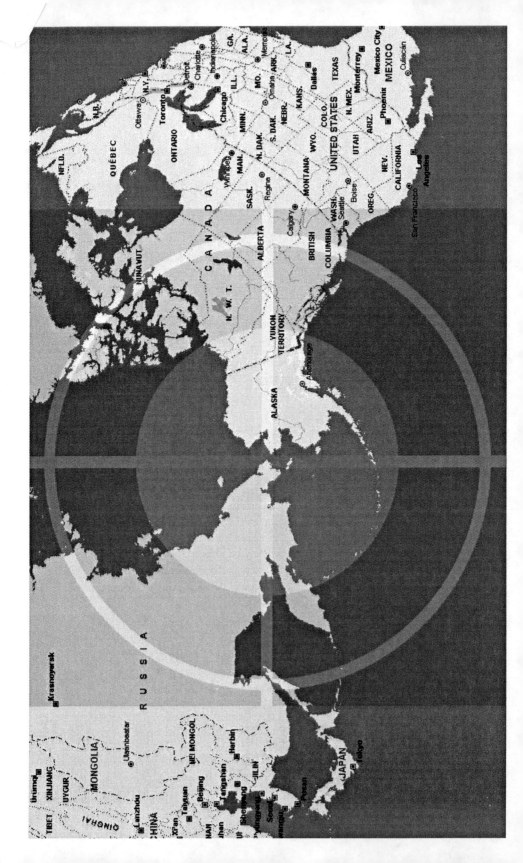

PRELUDE

April 19, 2010 — Over the Chukotka Peninsula, Russian Federation

Sheridan Stockridge, CIA, stood at the hatch of the Piper Chieftain as it descended through five thousand feet. At the signal from the pilot he opened the door and rolled out of the aircraft. The cold air hit him like a hammer, sending chills through his snowsuit.

One. Two. Three. Four. He counted carefully and then yanked his ripcord. He bounced like a ball as the chute billowed out above him, causing pain in his groin due to a poor fit of his straps.

Once he was in a steady descent, he looked around in the setting sunlight. *I see the Bering Sea off to the right. There's the mesa where I'm supposed to land. Let me pull in that direction. I'm freezing! The wind is really howling right now. Hope it settles down before I hit the ground. Okay, let me go over landing procedures.*

Stockridge was bouncing in all directions as the wind beat him around. The gale was variable at about twenty-five knots. *Way too fast. The wind wasn't supposed to be this strong. The sound of it is breaking my eardrums!* Stinging rain pelted his face.

Before he realized it, the ground was coming up fast. As he tried to pull hard to the right, a gust of wind flipped him over. At that point, he hit the earth. His head pounded into a rocky outcropping, breaking his neck. The lights went out permanently for SES-1 Sheridan Stockridge, way before he could prepare himself to meet his maker.

CHAPTER ONE

April 20, 2010 — Yanrakinnot, Chukotka, Russian Federation

"Zach! Wake up!" Bethany punched her husband in the ribs. "There's somebody downstairs in the kitchen."

Father Zacharios woke with a start. He looked at his watch. *Five o'clock. Who could be in our house at this hour?*

He was instantly alert as adrenalin pulsed through his body. Grabbing his rifle, he quietly tiptoed toward the stairs, avoiding creaking boards as much as possible. Father Zacharios, pastor of the Church of the Transfiguration in Yanrakinnot, Russian Federation, had to be vigilant. His former life required it. Forty-six years old and sturdily built, carrying two-hundred-ten pounds of muscle, the five-foot-nine-inch American missionary priest was in top physical shape. Hunting and fishing in this vast wilderness across the Bering Sea from Alaska had forced him to be at his best. The plastic surgery he had undergone in 2008 made him look years younger, but his graying beard and hair betrayed his real age. Father Janos Zacharios, *aka* Colonel Zachary Savage, United States Marine Corps, was ever vigilant.

He silently descended the stairs, rifle at the ready. At the bottom, he peeked around the corner into the kitchen, and then let out a sigh of relief. His friend Leonid sat at the table in silence.

"Good morning, Father," Leonid said in the Yupik language as he stood and bowed. "I did not want to awaken your matushka, so I came in quietly. But I knew you would hear me, sir. You are ever vigilant."

Fighting back embarrassment at the fact that Matushka Bethany had indeed heard Leonid come in while he himself slept like a log, the pastor laid his rifle against the wall and sat down at the table. Leonid sat down across from him. The kitchen was a simple one — a rough wooden table with four chairs on one side, some shelves for pots and plates, a wood stove in the middle, a propane cooking stove, and a small sink. The walls were plastered white. On one wall hung a Russian Orthodox crucifix and on the other a paper church calendar. A baby bassinet sat in the corner. The two windows were covered by drab gray curtains. The wood stove had burned up all its fuel during the night, allowing the frigid arctic winds to blow through the door and window cracks. And so the kitchen was cold at this time of morning. The smell of last night's salmon dinner still hung in the air.

"Coffee or tea, my friend?" Zach asked, looking into Leonid's eyes, searching for his feelings.

"You must come with me at once, Father."

Leonid's nervous about something, too nervous, Father Zacharios thought. He knew and trusted Leonid, nephew of the pastor's former gulag doctor, Peter. Leonid had helped him escape from the Russian secret gulag system two years earlier, and he was one of few in the village who knew that Father Zacharios was actually Colonel Zach Savage.

And Leonid was Father's parish assistant. A big, burly thirty-five-year-old Yupik Eskimo, Leonid was a leader in the village and in the parish. When he smiled, his whole chubby face lit up. When he frowned, his face became a dark, upside-down moon. Today the moon was definitely visible.

"What's wrong, Leonid? Has something happened to Peter?"

"No, Father. Uncle Peter is fine. He has sent me to fetch you. We were out hunting early this morning and found someone up on the mesa. Peter says you need to see him immediately."

"Friend or foe?" Father asked as his adrenalin surged again.

"We think he may have been a friend of yours."

So. Whoever this is, he's dead, the pastor thought as he rose from the table.

"Let me tell Matushka I'm leaving. I'll be right back down."

Climbing the stairs two by two, Zach walked into the bedroom. Bethany was sitting up in bed, nursing baby Tomas. *Still very beautiful at age forty-three,* Zach thought as he glanced down at her. The diminutive blond was dressed in a blue flannel nightgown. The blankets were up over their son's head as he drank his mother's milk. The temperature in the bedroom was close to freezing. It was a small, stark bedroom, typical of other bedrooms around the village. Just a double bed, a bureau, a baby crib, and a crude wooden kneeling bench where Father Zacharios said his prayers. A few pegs on the wooden wall allowed a place to hang their clothes.

"What's up, Zach? I recognized Leonid's voice but couldn't hear the conversation."

"Peter's found a body up on the mesa," Zach said as he slipped into his parka. "Thinks he may be a friend of mine. I'll be back as soon as I can. You'll need to get the stove going this morning."

"Take care, Zach."

Walking back downstairs and picking up his rifle, he and Leonid walked out into the early morning fog. The pastor glanced down the hill toward the sea, shrouded in fog. *Less ice every day,* he thought. *Spring's coming.* They jumped on their snowmachines and headed down the snow-packed road single file, the pastor following Leonid by twenty feet. They moved carefully along the rocky beach road a few miles and then turned left into the hills. They drove an hour as small trees appeared on either side of the curving trail and the temperature dropped with every foot of elevation they climbed.

And then they were at the top, on a rocky, treeless mesa. Father looked across the snow-covered field and saw a gathering of four men. As he and Leonid approached them, he recognized his old friend and mentor, Dr. Peter. He also recognized two of his parishioners. A young

Yupik named Tatak and a Chukchi reindeer herdsman named Muk stood beside each other.

As they pulled up beside the other snowmachines, the pastor noticed a man lying on the ground wearing a parachute harness and some of the parachute wound around him.

"What's going on, Peter? Who is this?"

Peter, Father's gulag doctor and fellow escapee, was eighty years old and very rotund. His face was thin and cracked. He looked intently at the pastor and spoke English so that the others wouldn't understand the conversation.

"I have examined him, Father," Peter said slowly. "I think he hit head when he landed. Neck is broken. Has been dead about twelve hours."

The pastor knelt down and looked at the man's face. . . and recognized him immediately. *Sheridan Stockridge! I don't believe this!*

The pastor glanced at Peter and spoke as he stood up. "This is the man I told you about. Sheridan Stockridge. He was my American handler. The Central Intelligence Agency assigned him to care for me. Peter, he flew the mission I was supposed to fly. He dropped the bombs on Iran."

"So why, my friend, did he come here?"

"I don't know. He was my only contact with America. We've kept up correspondence since I've been here. He's kept me up-to-date regarding my status with the U.S. government. He must have come here to give me a message."

Looking down at the limp body, Father continued speaking quietly, "Now I'll never know what this is all about. And I've lost my only contact with my country."

"Maybe not," Peter handed Zach a piece of paper. "I found this in his pocket."

The pastor looked at the handwritten message, coded the way Sheridan's other mail had been. Slowly deciphering the note, he read silently.

Zach, If something happens to me and I'm not able to speak to you personally, I have left you this note. We desperately need your help. We have a mission only you can perform. Go to the pre-arranged spot and meet my contact there. He's waiting for you. Sherry

The pastor read the note several times before folding it and sticking it in his pocket.

"What does all this mean?" Peter continued the conversation in English.

"It means I have to run down to Provideniya as soon as possible. I have to meet our old friend, James Royal, and someone else this man wanted me to meet."

Thus began a mission which would change the world. . . and nearly kill Zach Savage.

Father Zacharios returned home about noon. Bethany had prepared a lunch of fried walrus and tundra berries, and was making strong coffee as Father Zach walked into the kitchen. Baby Tomas was watching from the bassinet.

Father took off his parka and sat at the table. The smell of the coffee permeated the room.

"So what was that all about, Zach?" Bethany spoke in their native tongue — English.

"The guy who was found dead? Sheridan Stockridge."

Bethany dropped a cup on the linoleum-covered floor, sending glass and coffee flying in all directions. Tomas, frightened by the noise, began to cry. Zach lifted Tomas out of the bassinet and began to comfort him.

Six months old already, Zach thought as he cooed with his son. *This is a most beautiful gift from God.*

Bethany went and got a broom and dustpan, speaking as she began to sweep. "What in the world was Sheridan Stockridge doing here? And how did he die?" Bethany was quickly cleaning up the mess while she talked, tears of grief running down her cheeks.

"He must have gotten tossed around by the wind as he was coming down to earth in his parachute." Zach took a bite of his walrus. "He broke his neck. . . " Zach's voice caught in mid-sentence as he stifled a sniffle.

"Oh, no. That's awful. But what—"

"What was he doing here? It seems he was bringing me a mission only I can accomplish—"

"No! No! A million no's, Zach!" Bethany stopped sweeping the broken glass and walked over to her husband's chair, searching his face. "You're a priest. You're not a Marine anymore! You left that life—"

"Don't get so defensive, Bethany," Zach said as he interrupted her. He took a bite of his berries and put Tomas back in the bassinet. "I know I'm a missionary priest, but—"

"But nothing!" Bethany put her hands on her hips. "And just how do you know that Sherry has a mission for you if he broke his neck on landing?"

"Peter found a coded message in his pocket telling me to meet at the pre-arranged place. . . . Bethany, I owe it to him to go there and find out what this is all about. It was Sherry who worked out my retirement from the Marine Corps and set up our monthly pension, all while I was absent without leave."

Bethany went back to sweeping. "This is insane, Zach Savage! We have a life here. . . a baby. . . a ministry. You can't run off every time someone wants you to go on some mission."

"I might point out to you," Zach said as he smiled, trying to lighten the moment, "that only one person has ever come here asking me to take a mission, and that happened today. It's not like I'm Mr. Force Recon."

"I know. I know. I'm just so worried about this. . . . What happens now?"

"Leonid and I will head for Provideniya tomorrow. If the weather's good, I'll be back by Saturday at the latest, with plenty of time to prepare for Sunday liturgy. Need anything from town?"

"Diapers! Bottles of baby food if you can get them. Some baby clothes — size six months. Can you fit all that on your snowmachine?"

"Think so. . . . Well, I'd better go see old Mrs. Kanchak and give her a pep talk and a blessing."

"Before you go, Zach, let's say a prayer for Sheridan Stockridge's soul."

The two stood beside each other, opened their prayer book and shared in a time of prayer.

Prayers over, Father quickly finished his lunch, slipped on his parka and set out down the road. Bethany sat at the table and thought about what they had just discussed. She felt a cloud descending on them.

As he walked, Zach thought about his ministry. This little village, Yanrakinnot, population four hundred, offered everything he would need in his lifetime. It was a living example of how diverse peoples could live together in peace. Made up equally of Yupiks and Chukchis, with a few Caucasian Russians teaching school and offering social services, it was a self-contained society of brotherhood. The Yupiks, Asian

Eskimos, were the fishermen. They excelled in whale hunting and they were generous in sharing their bounty with the Chukchis — whale, salmon, sea lion, seal.

The Chukchis, natives to the interior of Chukotka, were reindeer herdsmen and hunters. And they in turn shared their bounty with the Yupiks — deer, bear, musk ox, fox.

Although Russian was the official language, the one taught in school, the residents had agreed that the common language of Yanrakinnot would be Chaplinski, a Yupik dialect. Father Zacharios marveled that the village fathers would lay tribal loyalties aside in the interest of harmony.

Yes, this little village of ramshackle huts offers me everything I need, Zach thought. *A place to love my wife and bring up our children, a place to spend abundant time with my Lord God, and a place to share ministry with a people desperately in need of eternal hope.*

Of course there were problems in Yanrakinnot. Alcoholism, for one. It amazed Father how the village could go for weeks without an episode, until someone would bring whiskey in. And the tell-tale signs would appear: family arguments, domestic abuse, church absenteeism. Eventually someone would be beaten severely in a fight. Dr. Peter would patch the wounded. Father would warn people sternly about how somebody would be killed if this continued. And then everyone would calm down and return to peaceful living.

Another problem in Yanrakinnot was frustration that there was so little money in the village. Although the cruise boats now brought tourists into town along with their rubles, poverty was an ever-present fear, bringing with it the hoarding of resources and distrust among residents.

I think maybe the basic spiritual problem in Yanrakinnot is a lack of hope in God. I watch my people fall victim to various addictions as they seek hope in hopelessly false solutions. I preach about it as often as I dare, trying not to sound like a broken record. And I'm making some progress.

Yes, Bethany's right. These people need me here. God has sent me to them. And they are a blessing to me. Can I risk losing all this?

Next morning at seven, Father Zacharios and Leonid jumped on their Arctic Cats and headed south. *Weather's good. We should get there by mid-afternoon.*

Since the thaw was only just getting underway, they took the beach trail down through the Senyavinsky Strait to Rumylet Bay, running on the ice where necessary. As they moved along the snow-covered ice at thirty kilometers per hour, Father had time to say his morning prayers and then to think. He looked at the beautiful mountains to his right, pock-marked by scrub trees and snow. To his left, he observed the strait with its bleak island on the other side. The strait's water was melted in the middle. He kept a sharp eye out for whale spouts.

It is just so beautiful up here, Lord. You really outdid yourself on this part of creation. . . . What I have to know, Lord, is why Sheridan thought that I was so important to his mission. What could he have been thinking about? Not another clandestine bombing mission, I hope. The last one almost got me killed. But it seems to have brought a lasting peace in the Middle East. Sherry said then that we might have to launch another mission like it in another part of the world. But I can't be involved with that, can I, Lord? I'm a priest! Priests don't fly bombing missions. No. It must be something else Sherry meant for me to do.

At the end of the bay, they set off cross-country on what could only be called a rudimentary trail, up and down, hill after hill. The temperature was not bad — about freezing. At noon, they stopped and enjoyed the fish sandwiches Bethany had packed for them. After lunch break, they hit the main road and motored down the trail beside it until arriving at Provideniya Bay about two in the afternoon. They locked up their Arctic Cats in a lot just north of town and walked in. Turning right onto Chabarova Street, they arrived at a tall, drab apartment building. Up to the third floor they trudged and knocked on the door of Apartment 327.

From inside the apartment, someone said in Russian, "Yes? Who is it?"

"A friend with an Arctic Cat," Zach responded quietly, using his code word.

He heard locks being undone and watched as the door opened. As he and Leonid walked quickly into the apartment, the door slammed behind them. It was a typical Provideniya apartment, small, moldy and drafty. The walls were covered with very old, flowery wallpaper. The ceiling was gray with dirt and dust. To the left was a tiny kitchen, and to the right a tiny bedroom. Straight ahead was a living room about ten feet by ten, with the same dingy wallpaper. Floors were covered by old, cracked linoleum. Zach smelled boiled cabbage, a smell which always made him gag.

He noticed two men standing in the living room, his old friend James Royal and a man who looked to be an American. Muk, the Yupik who had opened the door, followed them into the living room.

Father was truly glad to see James Royal again. His mind traveled quickly back to 2008 when James had played a critical role in rescuing him from the gulag, and had subsequently engineered the missionary assignment Father Zacharios now enjoyed.

"So good to see you again, Zach," James Royal said in his soft North Carolina accent as he gave Father a rough hug. "Where's Sherry?"

"Bad news, James," Zach said as he looked down at his hands. "Sherry died on impact after parachuting. His neck was broken."

Silence.

"May God receive his soul, Zach," James responded slowly. "I'm so sorry. . . . What did you do with his body?"

"It is in cold storage. When the ground thaws, we plan on giving him an honorable burial. . . unless you want the body."

"I'll have to get back with you on that. . . . So then, how did you know to come here?"

"Is it safe for us to talk?" Father glanced at the man standing beside James.

"Zach," James said quickly. "This is Simon Longstreet of the Central Intelligence Agency. He came with Sherry to talk with you. It's safe to tell us what's goin' on."

"Okay. Sherry had a coded note in his pocket." Zach looked at the CIA man. "Note said something about a mission assignment for me. Told me to come here. What's going on, Mr. Longstreet?"

"Call me Si," came the response.

The priest looked closely at the CIA man. *Now what have we here? Tall, thin, maybe fifty years old, narrow face with bulbous nose, maybe eastern European, easy smile. Can I trust this guy?*

"I know you probably don't trust me, Father." Simon looked squarely at Zach, seemingly knowing what he was thinking. "I wouldn't if I were you. But I'm a close friend and associate of Sherry Stock—"

"Please," the priest interrupted. "You don't have to call me Father. Just call me Zach."

"All right, Zach. I was an adviser to Sherry when he worked with you a couple years ago. I helped get the A-6E Intruders out of mothballs and ready to fly for the mission to Iran. And I counseled Sherry against flying in your place when the Russians chased you out of America before the mission. He flew that mission. In fact, it's about just such a mission that Sherry and I were sent to find you."

More silence.

"Let's sit down, shall we?" James said, buying time for Zach to think. "Muk, will you go down to the store and get us all some tea? Perhaps Leonid can help you."

As the two Yupiks left, Zach sat down in one of the worn-out easy chairs, while James and Si sat across from him on an equally worn-out sofa.

"Look. I don't know what you're after, Si," Zach said as he fiddled with his pen. "But if it's combat, you need to remember that I'm no longer a Marine officer. I'm a missionary priest, a noncombatant. Surely you're not here to ask me to fly."

"Just hear me out, will ya?" Si replied in his Bronx accent. "This request is coming from so high up in the American government I get nosebleed just thinkin' about it. . . . What do you know about North Korea right now?"

"I listen to the news on KICY from Nome," Zach said. "I know the North Koreans suffered a humiliating international defeat last year when the Chinese put them in their place. And I've also heard that one of Kim Jong Il's sons is being groomed to take over leadership of the country. The 'Dear Leader' is supposed to be dying or something."

"That's pretty good, Zach." Si shifted his long legs on the uncomfortable sofa. "Now let me fill you in on some details, man. Everything I say is way above top secret. Ya got that? But both you and James have a need to know, so here goes.

"The North Koreans think the time is right to snatch South Korea. We've got sources high up in their government who are keeping us informed. They plan on nuking some piece of property owned by the USA in July. We're thinking maybe Guam. . . a sort of shot across our bow—"

"A shot across our bow?" Zach cut in. "A shot across our bow with a nuke?"

"Sounds pretty crazy, I know. But we trust our sources. They're golden. You see, Kim Jong Il is either dead or will kick the bucket very soon. A couple of his old cronies are holding things together until his youngest son, Kim Jong Un, can take over. Jong Un is a chip off the old block, a twenty-seven-year-old whiskey-guzzling womanizer. They are calling him 'The Brilliant Comrade,' but he's nowhere near ready to take over the country. He's neither brilliant, nor much of a comrade. And the cronies know it. So their deal is to bring off a stunning victory in the name of Kim Jong Un, to gain him credibility with the country's leadership and the world's. That victory will be the reunification of all

Korea with ownership by the authorities in P'yongyang. What do ya think of that, Zach?"

"Holy smokes!" Zach looked intently at Si. "That would be terrible. Can they pull it off?"

"Unless America intervenes, they can."

"But what about China? In the past, the Chinese leadership has been able to keep the North Koreans in line. Why can't they do it now?"

"Money. The Chinese smell cold, hard cash. And the money will come from South Korea's vast resources when P'yongyang takes over. . . . Oh, the Chinese will pretend they're trying to keep the North quiet, but secretly they'll support the operation. They sense weakness in the White House.

"And we think the Russians will help as well. They also smell a big pay-off by the North."

"If the American government knows this, why doesn't it trumpet it to the United Nations?"

"Are you naïve or what?" Si sneered as he spoke. "Just who do you think will believe it with no hard evidence? Besides that, the UN is a corrupt organization of wimpy Europeans and Middle East terrorists.

"Zach, we're right back where we were in Iran two years ago. We've got an ugly regime flexing its nuclear muscle, attempting to exploit what it considers a timid American government. We're going to have to resurrect the black ops mission strategy we used with Iran and use it to take out some of the North Korean nuclear capability. We'll send a hard message to them that they can churn, but then they'll burn."

"Are you telling me that you want me to fly?" Zach silently said a prayer as he spoke bluntly to Si.

"I am," Si said. "Sherry couldn't fly this one even if he was still alive. He was too high up in the command structure and knew way too much to risk being captured. The other three crew members from the Iran mission are up and ready. We need you to make a fourth—"

"Let me repeat what I said two years ago to Sherry," Zach said, interrupting Si. "Flying this type of mission is wrong, in my humble opinion. It does not meet the Just War Doctrine. I presume you know the Just War Doctrine?"

"You mean the Just War Theory?" Si folded his arms. "How about giving me your version of it?"

"Humor me, Si, while I remind all three of us. One: The purpose of going to war must be just. Two: War can only be executed after the duly constituted authority orders it. Three: The intention must be to defend national vital interests or correct another nation's stated evil intentions and actions. Four: There must be a high probability of success. Five: War must be a last resort after all diplomatic initiatives have proved futile. Six: The force must be proportional to the threat. That agree with your interpretation, Si?"

"Not bad, Zach." Si bent down to re-tie his boots. "You've got a good hold of the theory. Now let me tell you a couple things.

"One: We're not going to war.

"Two: The action we're contemplating meets every darned one of the criteria you just mentioned. Think about it. Ethicists above my pay grade have already briefed the President on the morality of doing what we may have to do. He's given a buy-off on this. I repeat: he has bought off on the morality of employing a very small number of theatre nukes against North Korea in order to prevent the launching of a whole boat-load of ICBMs by North Korea against us.

"So let me make myself clear. I hear you, Zach. I really do. And with our new leadership, we are not violating the Just War Theory. Even if it costs us something in surprising the enemy, we'll take pains to warn the North Koreans that their actions will bring dire consequences upon themselves. Although we won't admit that we ran the strikes, we'll do everything we can to let them know we're coming for them.

"Zach, we're on the edge of a nuclear war here. If the North launches nukes and actually hits our country, we'll be forced to respond in kind. And then who knows what will happen? But if we can do a preemptive, surgical strike, we can shut them down before they ever get up. We've got no choice. We've got to do it. . . . What do you say?"

"I say I've got to pray about—"

"Well, pray fast, man. It's late April and the North is scheduled to launch nukes at us in July. We need to strike them before they strike us. And you'll need to train for the mission."

"Can you give me a week, Si? If I decide to do this, I have to get someone to cover my parish for me while I'm gone."

"A week." Si sat back and looked at the ceiling. "I'll give you a week to decide. Not a day longer. I'll be right here till then."

"Zach, let me pray for you right now," James said as he stood up and the others followed. He laid his hands on Zach's head and prayed solemnly for the guidance of the Holy Spirit.

On his way back home to Yanrakinnot, Zach wondered about all that had taken place in Provideniya. *How am I going to work this out, Lord? Even more troubling: How am I going to explain this to Bethany?*

CHAPTER TWO

April 20, 2010 — P'yongyang, North Korea

*G*eneral Park Rei Cho and Commissioner Chou Sing Moon sat at the stone table in the garden with Premier Jang Song Thaek. Each was drinking strong black tea. The General was bundled in his winter uniform as the wind howled through the trees. Chou and Jang wore heavy topcoats and fur hats.

"Thank you for meeting me here at my home, gentlemen," Premier Jang said. "It may be cold out here in the garden, but at least we know there are no sound devices, yes?"

I don't know that at all, General Park thought, *so I will say only what cannot be used against me.* To Jang, he responded, "Thank you, Premier Jang. What can I do to assist you?"

Jang Song Thaek, brother-in-law of Kim Jong Il, the Dear Leader of North Korea, was a man of about sixty, with gray, thinning hair and a heavy-set frame. He had been an adviser to Kim Jong Il for many years. General Park Rei Cho, younger by five years and heartier in physical appearance, commanded the vast armed forces of the Democratic People's Republic of Korea (DPRK). Commissioner Chou Sing Moon, one of the Dear Leader's trusted advisers, was about seventy and very frail.

General Park was always careful about what he said around Premier Jang, who secretly shared the governance of DPRK with him and with Chou. The three had been commissioned by the all-but-dead Dear Leader to keep the country 'confident and alive' until Kim's youngest son, Kim Jong Un, was ready to take Kim Jong Il's place as number-one leader of North Korea. He was now in Year Two of a five-year learning curve. Only twenty-seven years old and very fond of alcohol and ladies, Kim Jong Un was learning slowly what it meant to be the dictator of a nation.

General Park did not trust Premier Jang, but sat waiting for Jang to say his piece. *Jang longs to be number-one leader. I see him quietly building a coalition around himself so that, on the death of Kim Jong Il, he can be elevated. Kim Jong Un will meet with an unfortunate accident. Commissioner Chou is also not long for this world. The Dear Leader probably chose the three of us so that we would counter each other's ambitions, but it's not working. Chou is part of the Dear Leader's 'old guard.' And just as Kim Jong Il tried unsuccessfully to move toward a more moderate position in his later years, so has Chou. No. Chou will be murdered by Jang. It's just a matter of time.*

"I hereby call our leadership meeting to order." Premier Jang looked at each in turn. "I want first to talk with you about our wonderful missile program, General Park." Jang shifted his gaze away toward the trees at the back of the garden. "We must continue to heckle the foolish President Remington of the United States. We must continue to challenge him. He is weak. We must exploit that weakness. Therefore I must ask how the latest nuclear tests are going?"

"We are doing well, Premier Jang," the general responded without establishing eye contact with Jang. "Since the near fatal conflict last year with the leaders of the six nations, we are moving again. The humiliation we suffered is over. We should have success this time. Our latest TD-2 missile launch will go from the Musu'dan-ri Launch Pad in less than three months. We are using the launch pad at Tongch'ang-dong as a decoy. The bugs have been worked out. Our TD-2 is set to hit Atka Island in the Aleutian Chain of Alaska on the American Independence Day. Not many people live on Atka Island and not much development. America will not lose much except its arrogance.

"The launch of our TD-2 and its successful destruction of the target will make the point to the foolish Americans that it is time for them to remove themselves from Korea."

"Wonderful," Jang said. "What is your back-up plan in case we have launch problems—"

"We have no back-up plan." The general smirked. "We don't need a back-up plan. You see, we have done all we can to get this one rocket launched. We have no other long-range rocket that can carry a nuclear weapon. We won't have one for another year or so. This one must work.

. .

"And it will work. By launching the one long-range rocket we have, and leaking to the media that we have many others, we can frighten the Americans into believing that we will shower them with nuclear weapons. We have done our homework in deception. Their CIA actually believes we have a number of nuclear weapons.

"Meanwhile, we will build our forces along the DMZ and parade our SCUD missiles. When we tell the world that we have uncovered America's secret plan to invade us from the south, they will have to try and convince the world that they have no intention of invading us. At that point, a provocative move by their soldiers on the DMZ will force us to launch some of our SCUDs. Then we will invade the South to ensure the stability of our peninsula. The American defenses will crumble. They will know they have too few soldiers to counter our massive invasion. They will cry for a truce. We will grant a short truce while we continue to quietly invade, giving them time to remove their forces. In one month after we begin the invasion, the South will be ours.

"And since we will already have claimed that the Americans started it by invading us, we can justify to the world that we must protect our people by unifying the Korean peninsula—"

"This is too risky, General." Commissioner Chou came alive and pointed his finger at Park. "Much can go wrong with your plan. It can all backfire on us."

"I like his plan," Premier Jang said, looking harshly at Chou. Park noticed Jang's face getting red and his temple trembling.

"Premier Jang," Chou now pointed his finger at Jang. "You must not allow this maniacal strategy. I must protest—"

"Chou," Jang said. "I have heard enough of your timid statements. They are slowing us down."

"Well then, let's take it before the cabinet. Surely the Dear Leader will not approve such an irresponsible plan."

"The Dear Leader is in agreement with our strategy, Chou. I just spoke with him this morning."

"Could he hear you, Jang?" Chou stared defiantly at Jang. "Was he even cognizant of your presence in the room?"

Chou is directly challenging Jang's integrity, Park thought. *This is not good. I must intervene.*

But before he could say anything, Jang drew a Glock Thirty from his pocket and put a bullet through Chou's forehead. Chou looked startled and tried to put his hands to his head. But death overtook him before he could do anything. He crumpled and fell to the ground. Blood began to seep into the earth.

Startled, General Park looked quickly from the dead Chou into the eyes of a cool and collected Jang. *How could this animal do such a thing? I feel like strangling him. . . . But I must wait. . . act as if nothing unusual has happened.*

"As I was saying, General." Jang continued the conversation without missing a beat. "I like your plan. It is provocative and risky, but it is brilliant. Meanwhile, our overall strategy continues to be two-pronged.

"Number One: Make life so miserable for the Americans that they will gladly leave all Korea to us.

"And Number Two: Convince our Chinese neighbors that they will benefit from our actions—"

"Premier Jang," General Park interrupted. "What about the Russia card?"

"Yes, yes, General. The Russia card is being played. One of our men spoke with one of theirs at a secret meeting in Vladivostok last week. The Russian leadership is with us. They hope to gain financially as we divide up the bounty from the cruel regime lying to the south of us. They will, of course, continue to outwardly complain about our bravado, but will frustrate the United Nations Security Council in its attempts to censure us. And with Russia competing with China for our favor, we stand to gain much in the way of military equipment and advice, as well as food for our people.

"General, this all hinges on your success with the missile program. I will take care of the international relations. You take care of the military posturing."

"What you say makes sense. Now let me ask you one more question, Premier Jang." The general unconsciously glanced down at Chou. "What about The Brilliant Comrade — Kim Jong Un? Should he not be briefed on all this?"

Jang hesitated before speaking. "My nephew. . . is still learning the ABCs of what it means to lead, General. Leave him to me. Do not speak to him of any of this. Our official plan is to make Kim Jong Un look good and in control. . . and sober. We have given him the name, The Brilliant Comrade, to convey to our people that he is a fit replacement for his father. He will have to grow into the name. I will deal with him. And please know that I am keeping the Dear Leader fully informed, when he is able to listen, so that all decisions still come from him."

"Thank you, Premier Jang. Will there be anything else?"

"You are doing a magnificent job, General. . . . And don't worry about Commissioner Chou here. I understand that his heart has given out. He was quite old, you know. I will have this mess cleaned up. . . . Let's stay in close contact, shall we?"

With that, the General rose, bowed deeply, and walked out of the garden.

I must watch Premier Jang Song Thaek closely, General Park thought as he walked to his military vehicle. *Or I might wind up like Chou. In that short conversation, Jang told me to mind my rockets and let him do everything else. With Jang at the helm, the future does not look good for me or for our new Brilliant Comrade. We will join Chou in death! I must watch closely and build my own coalition. Meanwhile, I must make my own opportunities to spend time with the Dear Leader.*

April 25th — Yanrakinnot

"I've got to help them, Bethany."

Zach and Bethany were lying together in bed. It was two in the afternoon. The liturgy had gone well. And now it was time for a Sunday afternoon nap while Tomas was sleeping. But sleep was not coming. It was decision time.

"Zach, listen to me." Bethany's voice was gentle but firm. Her blond hair blossomed out on the pillow as she lay there looking at her husband. Something stirred in Zach as he looked back at her. *I love her so much. After losing her for eighteen years while I moldered away in the gulag, I don't want to chance losing her again.*

"Zach, you can't fly a bombing mission. You're the priest of this village. Everyone here depends on you. . . . I depend on you. Tomas depends on you. God depends on you, Zach. Your place is here — in Church of the Transfiguration. Don't you see that? Let them get somebody else to fly for them."

"I wish it were that easy, Bethany." Zach laid a hand on her leg. "The world is about to blow up. And as much as I don't want to admit it, they really do need me to do this. There's no one else they can get ready in time, nobody else who is a 'non-person' as am I. They need crew members who are not on the rolls, who don't even officially exist. It's the deniability thing. I'm the fourth crew member. I've got to do it. I can justify it theologically, since I'm not a pacifist. And by flying the mission, I can do a lot to maintain international peace and justice. I think I have no choice with this, kid."

Bethany began to sob quietly. "You may be right, Zach. But I hate the possibility that we won't ever see each other again. We lost each other for so many years. I don't want that to happen again."

"Let's pray about it some more. If I go, I'll need to run down to Anadyr and see the bishop about finding someone to replace me for a while."

"Hold me, Zach. Hold me forever."

Taking the cue, the priest made passionate love to his matushka while their baby boy slept soundly in his crib beside them. Sleep eventually overtook them both as well.

Several hours later, Father was awakened by loud knocking at his front door below. *What now? Can I never get any rest around here?* He ran down the stairs and flung open the door. Tak stood nervously before him.

"Father, a whale has been spotted! We are on the hunt and would like your blessing."

Delighted by the possibility of food for his people, Father yelled, "Bless you? I'll not only bless you. I'll join you on the hunt. When I have been with you before, we have always gotten our whale."

"You will be welcome, Father."

"Bethany," he yelled in English. "I'm going out to help bring in a whale!"

"Be careful, Zach!"

Father and Tak ran down the hill to the edge of the ice where villagers were getting equipment ready. Six metal skiffs with outboard motors, which had been gifts from the Prudhoe Bay Eskimos of Alaska several years before, and five animal skin boats were spread out across the beach. Harpoons, pistols and rifles were being passed out. Ropes were coiled up and placed in the boats. When Leonid saw Father approaching, he gave a shout. All fell to their knees and waited for the blessing, which Father pronounced in a strong, enthusiastic voice.

When he finished the blessing, he called out, "Brothers, if you will have me, I will again join you in the hunt."

All cheered and started clambering into the boats. Father joined the village elder, Mr. Yopskat, in his boat. They headed out into open water in a loose formation, watching for a spout.

Suddenly someone yelled, "Spout sighted!" and pointed to the right. All boats headed right. A minute and a half later, the spout was sighted again, this time much closer to them. As they closed on the whale, they watched carefully. Suddenly, right in front of the boats, the whale popped out of the water. Harpoons were fired, some of which found a home in the whale's flesh. With that, the whale turned and went into high gear in its furious swim for freedom. The boats with harpoons embedded in the whale were suddenly jerked to the right. Father was tossed leftward toward the side of the boat. Only a furious grab by Mr.

Yopskat kept him from flying into the water. As he righted himself, Father gazed at the huge sea creature. He was amazed at the animal's awesome power as it dove, pulling the boats along behind it. The other boats followed, being careful not to get in a position to be lifted when the whale surfaced again. After a minute, the whale reappeared, and immediately men with fifty-six caliber rifles fired lead into the raging animal, beginning the slow process of bleeding it to death. After that, every time the whale surfaced, more lead was pumped into it.

Twenty minutes later, the whale was completely exhausted and gave up the ghost. Several boats came alongside the creature as men tied ropes to its tail. Father reckoned that the whale was about ten meters in length. And then the fleet of boats triumphantly pulled the whale toward shore, men firing rifles into the air in celebration.

When the giant sea creature was finally laying on the beach, the elderly men, who had been waiting on shore, immediately went to work with machetes and axes. Slowly and methodically, they chopped up the whale into large steaks, carved up blubber into huge chunks, and even pulled out and chopped up the largest tongue Father had ever seen. After several hours of hard work, only bones and entrails remained on the beach. The meat and blubber had been divided up and given to each family in the village.

As evening approached, a fire was started on the beach, with Mr. Yopskat in charge. The whale barbecue began. Everyone enjoyed the results of the hunt amidst singing and dancing. Father sat on a chair with Bethany and Tomas sitting beside him, wrapped in blankets. Peter and Leonid sat in the circle of friends with them.

At about midnight, Mr. Yopskat yelled for silence.

"My fellow villagers, you excelled in working well together today as we had victory over Mr. Whale. I must congratulate you on a superior performance. And I would like to publicly thank our priest, Father Zacharios, for his blessing and participation in the hunt. Father, would you close our evening by saying a prayer of thanks that we have food and that no one was hurt today?"

Father said his prayer. Everyone said, "Amen," and all went home.

"Do you see what I mean, Zach?" Bethany said as they walked home. "These people need you and love you. Don't disappoint them."

Next morning, Father walked to Dr. Peter's house.

"Welcome, my son," Peter said as he led Father into the kitchen, a kitchen that strongly resembled Zach's kitchen. Leonid was sitting at the table drinking a mug of coffee. Peter motioned for Father to be seated and then poured a mug for him. Finally, he sat quietly.

Silence.

"And how is Matushka this morning? Not out too late last night?" Peter opened the door for the conversation to start.

"She's doing fine, Peter, as is Tomas. Thanks for asking. . . ."

"Leonid tells me you have been doing some traveling. . . ."

"That's actually what I want to talk with you about," Father said, glad that Peter had broken the ice. "Peter, we've known each other for many years. Saved each other's lives. We have no secrets from each other. And I am eternally grateful to you for getting us out of the gulag the way you did, as well as providing this wonderful village pastorate for me. But I may need to go back to the States. You have probably figured out that Sheridan Stockridge came to call me to an extremely important but dangerous mission. . . ."

Silence.

"I'm really torn as to whether I can do it."

The old doctor stirred his coffee slowly. "Why would you want to leave Matushka, Tomas, and your flock in order to accept a dangerous mission miles from here? Can't someone else do it?"

"That's the problem, Peter. There's no one else who can do it in the time-frame the mission is needed. The only other person who could have done it is dead now — Sheridan. This will be a highly classified mission which is geared toward bringing down a powerful government that threatens the stability of the world. If I don't take the mission, we may very well see nuclear attacks on the United States and a revival` of nuclear proliferation around the world. As much as I love it here with my family, I think I will have to accept the mission. It may take several months to accomplish. . . ."

"I'd like your blessing, Peter."

"Zachary, your commitment to your country has always been very strong." The doctor rose and poured more coffee for everyone. "And now your commitment to God is even stronger. But I see you struggling with these two commitments. Can you serve both God and your country by accepting this mission?"

"You and I have spent many hours talking about the use of controlled violence as a weapon to be used against chaotic and evil violence, Peter." Zach took a sip of his coffee. "Taking that action has sometimes been a necessary evil in our world. I truly believe that in taking this mission, I am honoring God by being a steward of his bounty in curbing chaotic and evil violence."

"Then I bless you in your efforts for all of us, my son. When will you leave?"

"Tomorrow I will go to Provideniya to get details. Then I'll go on to Anadyr to see the bishop."

"Would you like Leonid to accompany you?"

All this time, Leonid had sat silently through the conversation. Yupiks do not speak unless an elder asks for their opinion. Since he had not been asked, he had not spoken. But Father noticed his face lit up when Peter mentioned the possibility of accompanying him.

"Actually, Peter, as much as I would find comfort in Leonid's presence, I think I have to do this myself. And I would much prefer that Leonid keep a protective eye on Matushka while I'm gone."

Leonid's face, which had darkened when Father refused his presence on the trip, brightened again. Without being asked, he responded to Father, "I will be ever vigilant, Father. Just as vigilant as you. Do not worry about your family. I will protect them with my life."

"Thank you, dear friend," Zach said as he laid his hand on Leonid's arm.

Two days later, Father Zacharios said a blessing over his family, kissed Bethany and Tomas goodbye and headed south on his snowmachine, this time without Leonid. The ride was uneventful and safe, giving him plenty of time to pray and think while marveling at the beauty of eastern Chukotka.

Lord, why is this happening? Zach prayed as he rode toward Provideniya. *I thought I could spend the rest of my life ministering here in this beautiful wilderness, loving my wife and bringing up this child you've given us. But here I am, on the horns of a dilemma again, God. Although I'm not a pacifist, I realize that war is hard for you. And it's hard for me. If I launch missiles at nuclear facilities, people will die. Some of them are innocents who just happen to be in the wrong place at the wrong time. I had to kill people in the Iraq War, remember? I didn't like doing it then and I sure as heck don't look forward to doing it now.*

But, Lord, I do understand the whole concept of evil. I do understand that we sometimes need controlled violent force to destroy evil force. That's why we have police. That's why we have armies. I get that, Lord. What I don't like is the fact that I'm being asked to be a part of the controlled violent force. Help me with that, will you?

Clouds were rolling in when he arrived in Provideniya, and by the time he had locked up his Arctic Cat and begun his walk into town, the snow was beginning to fall. A frigid wind howled as he turned into the building on Chabarova Street and walked up the stairs to Apartment 327.

"Welcome, Zach," Si said as Zach entered the apartment.

"Where's James?" Zach asked as he looked around.

"Back in Alaska for a few days. He'll be here next week, hopefully to pick you and me up. Are you ready to head back to the States?"

"On my way to Anadyr to see my bishop right now." Zach sat down in the living room. Si followed suit. "I've got to get permission to leave my parish for two months or as long as it takes. And I have to find a priest to take my place up there."

"Hmm." Si was silent for a moment. "What do you plan on telling your bishop, man? Can you trust him?"

"Bishop Diomid is considered an outlaw by his Moscow superiors, Si. He openly challenged the Metropolitan. The hierarchy tried to replace him two years ago, but after going back into the monastery for a few months, he re-appeared and re-claimed the diocese. His priests all support him. So in effect, we have two Bishops of Chukotka today. One is Archbishop Mark from Khabarovsk, the guy the Patriarch sent in, who has no credibility among our clergy.

"The other is Bishop Diomid, the rightful bishop, who has the loyalty of all the priests. Diomid considers the Moscow government, and by implication, the religious establishment, to be totally corrupt. And my allegiance is to Bishop Diomid. He's weird, cantankerous and unpredictable, I'll grant you that. But he cannot be broken or bought off by the Russian government or by the Orthodox Church hierarchy.

"So don't worry about it, Si. I'll tell him only what I think he needs to know in order to grant me a lengthy vacation and get someone to replace me."

"Well, okay. Just be careful, my man. I don't want the Russians getting involved in this. No way, no how. Now, how about us finding some dinner? When will you head for Anadyr?"

"Tomorrow, if the plane is flying. Let's see if we can rustle up some salmon at the market. It feels like a blizzard's on the way. Maybe we'd better stock up."

And the blizzard was on. The next day was so bad, the flight was called off. Zach spent the day in the apartment with Si and Muk. Muk would go out occasionally, giving Zach and Si time to talk privately.

"So fill me in on the other three crew members, Si."

"Okay. Here's the deal. I don't know how much you heard about the mission to Iran in 2008. What did Sherry tell you?"

"Basically nothin.' He told me they had been successful and that all survived. Gosh, I can't believe Sherry got killed parachuting in to see me."

"I feel the same way, Zach. I'll miss that guy. We were really good friends, him and me." Si sat in silence, looking off into nowhere.

More silence. Then Zach spoke up. "So what can you tell me about the three crew members?"

"Not wanting to sound like a history professor, let me give you the short version, man. When you had to take a powder from the Naval Air Station in California to avoid the Russian mafia, Sherry jumped in and took your place as the bombardier-navigator for the Marine bird. There was just no one else we could find to do it on such short notice. And the schedule was already set up. So in October—"

"Wait," Zach said. "Let me get my dates right. That was October of 2008? I was already in Yanrakinnot by then. Okay, go ahead."

"Okay. On or about October 10, 2008, the two A-6E Intruders and an old Air Force KC-10 flew from China Lake to the Indian Ocean island of Diego Garcia. Several days later, they made the strike. Your old pilot, Bob Shanto, flew the Marine bird, with Sherry as bomb-nav. They hit the secret underground uranium enrichment facility at Natanz and then knocked off Iran's premier nuclear facility near Esfahan. Used earth-penetrating nuke missiles. The Navy crew, Captain Armour and Jerry Casbreau, hit the nuke facilities at Bushehr and Fasa. Same weapons. Bingo. Hit their targets dead-on.

"Both aircrews ejected safely in the desert. Shanto broke his ankle but otherwise was okay. Their airplanes were buried deep by our guys. The aircrews were taken back to the States without the Iranians ever knowing who did it or where they came from. It was the perfect mission.

"The bonus was that President Amadinejad and his senior lieutenant, a guy named Danush Ghadir, just happened to be staying at Bushehr for a photo op. They were killed, man. Poof. Problem solved. The Iranian Mullahs gave up, swore off nukes, and asked to join the world community in promoting nuclear non-proliferation!"

"All I can say to that is, 'Wow,'" Zach said as he stood up and walked to the window. The wind was swirling snow everywhere, but at least the snow had stopped falling. "So Danush Ghadir is dead."

"Danush Ghadir? You knew the guy?"

Zach turned and looked at Si. "Danush Ghadir owned me for two years in Iran back in the early nineties. I was his slave. He tried to murder me."

Zach felt his face flush and his heart rate climb. He took some deep breaths and tried to relax, gazing off into the distance and seeing nothing. Si recognized the problem, a post-traumatic stress flashback, and sat quietly as Zach tried to recover his composure.

Zach finally settled down. "Sorry about that, Si. What happened to the air crews when they got back to the States?"

"Everybody just went home! Aircrews, ground crews — they got paid off and got on with their lives. The aircrews got new identities and moved wherever the heck they wanted. End of story."

"And you say they're ready to do it again? This time in North Korea?"

"They're ready, man. Starting their training in a week. Waitin' for you to arrive. There's still a chance we won't have to do this, you know. China might still be able to shut North Korea down, but—"

"But you're pretty sure this mission is going to go, aren't you?"

"Zach, I'd be lying to you if I said I thought the Chinese could hold the North. Bottom line is I think you've got to fly this mission or we'll all be eating nuclear fallout by late summer."

Silence.

"I'm not sure how to explain my feelings," Zach said as he sat down beside Si on the sofa. "Even though I can agree with you politically, I'm having a great deal of trouble dealing with this in my heart. My Christian faith comes into play here. We're talking about launching nuclear weapons! I have to ask myself, 'Would Jesus approve of such a thing?'"

"Look," Si adjusted his long legs on the couch and scratched his ear. "I'm not much on this faith-in-God stuff, if you know what I mean. I had a Jewish mother and a gentile father. Neither paid much attention to God when I was growing up. Even in college at Notre Dame, I really never engaged when people started talking about God. Kind of avoided the faith thing — still do.

"So I have to go on secular ethical theory here, not what Jesus would or wouldn't do. I think maybe asking the Jesus question may do crazy things to your brain, man. Meaning no disrespect, Father, but Jesus didn't live in a nuclear age. Who knows what he might do if he was walking around today? You sure you want to ask that question?"

"I ask that question about everything I do, Si. That's what faith is all about for me, trying to be like Jesus. At any rate, since Jesus didn't have to deal with nukes, I have to see if there are some principles he taught or things he did that will help me make an ethical decision here. Let me ask you this. On the Iran bombing attack two years ago, how many people died?"

"Jeez, Zach, how should I know? There was very little fallout due to the deep penetration of the bombs. I don't know. Maybe ten thousand or so died. Maybe a few more."

"That's a lot of collateral damage, don't you think?"

"Well, not if you think about how many people Amadinejad would have murdered if he had been able to launch his missiles at Israel. Which I might add, we absolutely knew was his intention."

"I'll give you that, Si. And I know that Jesus never told soldiers to turn in their weapons. He healed them and their families. And he did say that there would be wars and rumors of war. I guess I might surmise from his teachings that war is sometimes the lesser of two evils. When he talked about turning the other cheek, he was talking about one-to-one relationships rather than international politics.

"I guess what I'm really concerned about is the collateral damage, innocent people dying because they're in the wrong place at the wrong time—"

"Which I told you," Si interjected. "We're going to warn the country of dire consequences if they don't turn back."

"That's lame, Si. How many of the common citizens are going to really be warned?"

Si threw up his arms. "Well, listen, man! You want the dead to be Americans and South Koreans — or North Koreans? We've got to make a choice here. I'd advise you to ask your god that.

"Look, I don't have time for a theological discussion, see? I've got to keep a nuclear war from happening. And you're the guy I need to do it. Are you in or not?"

"In." Zach hung his head, got up, put on his parka, and walked out of the apartment into the blizzard.

CHAPTER THREE

April 29th — Anadyr, Russian Federation

*F*ather Zacharios arrived in Anadyr after being marooned in Provideniya for two days due to the blizzard. The Antonov 24 touched down at noon after a rather frightening two-hour flight through bumpy air and heavy fog. As he rode the barge across the bay from the airport, Zach gazed at the city.

So much happened here in Anadyr. Colonel Strasdie tried to murder Peter and me right there on that dock. I can still feel the gun barrel as he held it to my head. And the surprise when his own lieutenant broke the colonel's neck before he could pull the trigger. Lord, you were there all the time. You obviously wanted me around for further mission work or I'd be dead and buried deep by now. But did you save me because you want me to fly some mission to end nuclear proliferation? I wish I could just get a letter from you laying out your plan. But you don't work that way, do you? I know. . . . 'Now we see through a glass darkly, but then face to face.' I guess I have to accept that.

Leaving the barge and proceeding up the street, Zach walked into the Cathedral of the Transfiguration. Once inside, he bowed and then knelt and prayed for a while. He loved the darkness, the candles, and the smell of incense. He felt God's presence.

Then he walked across the bridge to Bishop Diomid's private quarters on Partizan Street. He knocked and waited. After a few minutes, a very large priest, Father Dmitri, came to the door. Recognizing Father Zacharios, he led him through the house to a small office.

Once in the office, Father stood and surveyed the room. It had the same plastered white walls that many buildings in the region shared. But the icons on all four walls were most beautiful. Biblical scenes and Russian saints. The floor was covered with a deep purple Persian rug, with intricate designs of crosses. On the right, against the wall, was a finely-polished prayer desk. And at the end of the room, seated behind a large cherry desk, sat the bishop himself, Bishop Diomid. Thin and short, about age fifty, with long graying beard, twinkling eyes, a simple black cassock and head covering, he looked to Zach to be too frail to have caused so much trouble for the Orthodox Church. But here he was, very much in charge of his diocese.

The priest left them alone, closing the door behind him. As Zach walked toward him, the bishop rose and came out from behind his desk.

Reaching Bishop Diomid, Father Zacharios bowed deeply and placed both palms up toward him.

"Bless me, Your Grace," he said softly.

The bishop made the sign of the cross on Father's palms and said, "May the Lord bless you." Father kissed the bishop's ring and stood.

"Let us pray," Bishop Diomid said. He then prayed softly for about five minutes.

After finishing his prayers, the bishop looked at Father Zacharios. "Please. Sit down, my son." The bishop indicated a chair in front of the desk. As Father sat, the bishop went back behind his desk and sat down.

"I received your message, that you needed an emergency meeting. What is the problem with you?"

Zach swallowed hard. *The bishop doesn't seem upset, just curious. Lord, guide me as to what I should say.* "I need two months off, Your Grace."

"So do I," the bishop chuckled. "But that doesn't mean that I will get them off. And it may be that you may not get them off, either. Why do you need that much time?"

Zach hung his head slightly. And then, screwing up his courage, he began.

"Your Grace, I need you to agree that what I am about to say will be confidential, under the Seal of Confession. I haven't done anything wrong. But what I say is highly sensitive."

The bishop looked at him intently. "All right. This is under the Seal. Is it a confession?"

"Not a confession. I haven't done anything wrong. But for me to tell you why I need the time off, I need to know that you will hold this information to yourself only."

"What? Are you going to tell me you're an escapee from the gulag?" The bishop chuckled again at what he thought was a joke.

"Exactly." Zach stared into Bishop Diomid's eyes. The bishop held his gaze for a moment and then looked away.

"Perhaps you should explain yourself."

"First of all, Your Grace, before I arrived from America to be your missionary priest at Yanrakinnot, you received letters from Metropolitan Jonas and Bishop Kirichi commending me to you. I am embarrassed to tell you that they were forgeries."

"What?" The bishop sat straight up in his chair. "Forgeries? How can that be? I spoke to Bishop Kirichi on the phone about you."

"Let me explain. The Bishop Kirichi with whom you spoke was an agent of the American Central Intelligence Agency."

Father noticed Bishop Diomid's face harden. "Who are you?"

I've got to be careful here, Zach thought. *He's liable to throw me out of his office.*

"My name is Zachary Savage, Your Grace. I started out as a United States Marine. In my early years, I married a wonderful woman and had a baby daughter. I also became a Christian believer, what you might call a 'born again' Christian.

"While fighting in the First Persian Gulf War in 1991, my airplane was shot down by Iraqi gunners. I was captured by the Iraqis but then was sold to the Iranians, the Mujahadin. I was a prisoner in Iran for two years. Then a fellow prisoner helped me escape to Turkmenistan. Unfortunately I was again captured, this time by a crime syndicate. It wasn't long before I was transferred to a Russian crime syndicate named *Dolgoprudnenskaya.* Have you heard of it?"

The bishop scratched his head. "I know of this organization. It is an example of what has happened to our decadent government leadership. Many of those idiots in the Kremlin are members of this organization. Continue."

"I floated around the gulag system for fifteen years, Your Grace. The American government declared me Killed-In-Action. I would have rotted in the gulag had it not been for Dr. Peter and God. Peter saw my faith. He bought me books — books on theology, church history, liturgy, preaching. Some of them may have been from your monastery. I learned how to be a pastor as I cared for the other inmates. But I must admit that I was never really ordained."

Silence.

The bishop broke the silence. "This Dr. Peter of whom you speak. Is he the old man who takes care of your community?"

"Yes, Your Grace. He was the camp doctor at several of my prison camps. Then two years ago, an explosion destroyed our prison, one that is west of Markovo, deep in the wilderness. Dr. Peter and I were able to escape. We were chased for months, across the tundra, until we arrived here in Anadyr. The military leader who was in charge of prisons caught us here one morning as we were preparing to board a vessel to freedom. He was about to shoot us both, had the gun to my head, when, for some reason we have never figured out, his men turned on him and killed him right in front of us—"

The bishop put up his hand to signal that he wanted silence. Then he made the sign of the cross over Zach's head and prayed silently.

After he finished his prayer, he looked intently at Zach and said, "Zachary, that is a miracle. God intervened for you. Alleluia!"

"I agree. He did intervene for me. At any rate, Peter and I then boarded the ship and wound up in Provideniya where an American missionary flew me to Alaska."

"What is the name of this American missionary?"

Should I give him James' name? It could spell disaster. But I do trust my bishop. I'll just have to risk it.

"His name is James Royal."

"I know this man. We have had dealings. He is a good Christian gentleman. Brings help to our people. If only he were Orthodox rather than Protestant."

Father let that comment go by. "James flew me to Alaska, and then I was rescued by the Central Intelligence Agency."

"Praise God," the bishop said as he sighed.

"However, that's not the end of the story."

Bishop Diomid wiped his brow with a handkerchief. He called loudly to his assistant.

"Father Dmitri! It is too hot in here. Fix the problem, please."

With that, Zach heard the banging of pipes, Dmitri trying to cool off the inferno.

After a moment, the bishop resumed the conversation. "I am ready for the rest of the story, Zachary. I truly believe God has been leading you. Even though the decadent leaders of our dear Holy Church do not believe in miracles, I do! What I see happening is that God is at work in you. Just as He has led me to defy the religious authorities who seek to destroy my work, I see God leading you to something very important as well. Continue on. I am interested in the rest of your story."

Zach tried to figure out how best to tell the rest of the story. *Guide me, Lord, to say it just right.*

"When I got back to the United States, I had a rude awakening. I thought I would be welcomed back with open arms. What I found was just the opposite. The American government was not ready for me, not ready to deal with the sensitive relationship it had with the Russian Federation—"

"Why am I not surprised by this?" Bishop Diomid cut in. "The Russian government's decadence has even affected the Americans."

"So I was asked to assist in a highly classified operation, Your Grace. Since I had been a bombardier-navigator, I was asked to participate in a clandestine bombing mission — to destroy much of the nuclear capability of Iran. The American government wanted to do this without being blamed for it. So they used aircraft that had been declared obsolete and they used air crews who did not officially exist. I was to be one of them."

The bishop again raised his hand to stop the conversation.

"You told me you were married and had a daughter. When you returned to your country from the gulag, were you allowed to be reunited?"

"Your Grace, my daughter had died in an auto accident and my wife was dying of cancer."

"May God bless their souls." The bishop once again made the sign of the cross.

"But my wife didn't die! God had me pray for her. She recovered. She is in fact my matushka whom you have met. But it was not all that easy to be reunited with her.

"Your Grace, I was not able to fly that mission to Iran. The Russian Crime Syndicate tried to capture me while I was training for the mission. I escaped with the help of James Royal. The only way for me to survive was to disappear. And God granted me that wish. Bethany was able to join me as we moved here to Chukotka. And so we are here, Your Grace. I am not all I would like to be, but I am loyally yours. I love the Lord Jesus Christ and wish to spend the rest of my life pastoring your people."

"And you shall." The bishop rose and came around the desk. "Your secret is secure with me. I will quietly ordain you so that you are functioning officially. We can do that right now."

"There's something else you should know," Zach said slowly. "It's the reason I need two months off."

The bishop turned and returned to his seat.

"Father Dmitri," he called. "Bring us tea — now."

Turning to Zach, he spoke quickly. "Why do you need the time off?"

"I've had a visit from officials of my government, Your Grace. They want me to fly another mission."

"Fly another mission? Fly another mission? What is wrong with this government of yours? You are a priest, not a military pilot. They should find someone else to fly a mission of dropping bombs. You cannot do it. I will not permit it."

Father Dmitri came in carrying a tray with a beautiful China pitcher, two cups, and a matching sugar bowl and cream pitcher. Zach noticed that the designs were of reindeer — blue designs on white chinaware. The assistant filled both cups with hot tea as the bishop and the priest sat in silence. After the assistant left, Zach continued.

"Your Grace," Zach said after he took a sip of the strong tea. "This mission is of utmost importance. The North Koreans are preparing to launch a nuclear missile attack on American territory. Their purpose is to drive the Americans out of South Korea. Once the Americans leave, the North Koreans will take South Korea. The Chinese are secretly supporting them — as are the Russians."

Again Zach noticed the bishop's anger rise.

"Not the Russians, Zachary," the bishop stated bluntly as he corrected him. "The decadent Russian government. I hate those people. They are greedy, hoping to destroy the world for their own gain. And now you tell me that the Russian government hopes to divide up South Korea with the North Koreans and the Chinese?"

"I'm afraid so," Father said, stirring his tea. "Unless my mission can thwart them. Those high up in my government believe that if several American aircraft were to fire small nuclear missiles into the North Korean nuclear complexes, we could deal them such a blow that they would retreat from their plan. It is a good mission. It will also put the decadent Russian government in their place. Something that has been needed for a long time.

"Your grace, I need two months off so I can train for the mission, drop the bombs on North Korean nuclear facilities, and return to Yanrakinnot. Will you give me permission to do that? Will you assign someone to fill in for me in my parish?"

"Now it is my turn to plan, Zachary," the bishop said. "I believe I need to put you on sabbatical leave." He winked at Zach. "You must return to St. Petersburg for further training in church architecture. I believe you will need to be gone for three months. Meanwhile, I am assigning Father Dema to be the interim pastor in Yanrakinnot. He speaks fluent Chaplinski. And when you return, I will quietly ordain you. You have a great future here in Chukotka, my son."

With that, the bishop rose. "I will make this happen. And I will pray for you each day until you return. Save us, my son."

The final blessing complete, Zach walked back out into a cold drizzle.

As the Antonov lumbered over the Bay of Anadyr on its way back to Provideniya, Zach thought about what had happened on his visit with the bishop. *He agrees with this mission! A Russian Orthodox holy man agrees that one of his priests should fly a bombing mission. He understands the extreme situation in which we find ourselves. He knows the theology of St. Augustine and the experience of Bonhoeffer. He is a recognized Bible scholar and theologian. I must see this as a sign that I am to go forward with the mission. Even if it kills me.*

Same Day — Naval Air Weapons Station, China Lake, California

Retired Master Chief Petty Officer Wendell Gherkie walked into the office of the Commanding Officer of the base and stood at attention in front of his desk. He had been in this very office two years ago. *Same play, different players,* he thought as he stood there. *Different Commanding Officer than before. And the black civilian sitting there looks an awful lot like a CIA man. Suit and tie. Short hair. Tough.*

"Thanks for coming in, Master Chief," the commander said as he rose and shook his hand. "I'm Captain Bob Rubin. This here is Mr. Juan Ramos from Washington."

Mr. Ramos nodded at the Master Chief. "Sit down, Master Chief. I have something I'd like to discuss with you."

"Gentlemen, I'll leave you to your discussion." Captain Rubin headed for the door. "Mr. Ramos, the office is yours for as long as you want it. Good day, Master Chief." With that, the Commanding Officer was out the door.

Master Chief Gherkie sat down in one of the hardback chairs facing Ramos. Gherkie sized him up. Black, very tall and fat. Short hair and thick glasses. His huge chest, biceps, and stomach stretched the material of his suit. *This guy could play offensive tackle for the Bears.*

"So what can I do ya fer, Mister — what was it — Ramirez?"

"Ramos, Master Chief. Juan Ramos. I'm a friend of Mr. Longstreet and Mr. Stockridge. I believe you know them?"

"Might. By the way, you got some kind of identification?"

Ramos took out an ID card and badge and handed them to Gherkie. Gherkie studied each closely.

"Master Chief, we're going to need your services again."

"Let me just ask you what it is I did before that was so important that you'd ask me to do it again—"

"I'm legit, Master Chief. You don't have to play games. You and your men got two A-6E Intruders out of mothballs, fixed 'em up, and then maintained 'em until they flew their effective little missions over Iran. By the way, Mr. Longstreet sends his greetings. He's out of the country or he would have come personally."

"All right, Mr. Ramirez, what is—"

"Ramos. Ramos." Ramos was obviously getting frustrated. "My name is Ramos, not Ramirez, gringo. Let's not get off on the wrong foot. You got anything against black Hispanics?"

"Beat up a lot of 'em growin' up in Chicago, Mon. . . . Just kidding, Mr. Ramos," the Master Chief grunted, obviously embarrassed. "When it comes to ethnic origin and race, I'm color blind. I just got your name mixed up, that's all. A little nervous, if you must know. I will now call you Mr. Ramos."

"Thank you. That is very comforting, Chief."

Master Chief. Master Chief. I'm not a flippin' Chief. I'm a MASTER Chief, you spic!" Gherkie blurted, and then broke out laughing.

"Touché. I think we're going to get along just fine, Master Chief. We're starting out real honest—"

"Okay, let me tell you what this is about. We're going to have to make another clandestine strike. Very soon. But we're going to do it different this time."

"Say on, Mr. Juan Ramos," the Master Chief said as he leaned toward the CIA man, listening very carefully.

"For one thing, we're not going to use Intruders—"

"You're not going to use Intruders. But you're asking me, an Intruder mechanic, to be involved. You stupid or something?"

"Not stupid. Smart. One: We don't have time to get A-6's out of mothballs and stealthed up in time. Two: We need an aircraft that doesn't stick out the way the A-6 does. Everybody knows it's extinct—"

"We don't call them extinct. They're not dinosaurs. We call them obsolete. Got that?"

"All right. Everybody knows they're *obsolete*. So we're going to use an aircraft that's not *obsolete*. We're going to use the EA-6B Prowler."

Silence.

"Let me get this straight. You're going to use my services to make EA-6Bs drop laser guided missiles. And I'll just bet that you expect me to convert EA-6B PROWLERS, two EA-6B Prowlers maybe, into A-6E Intruder platforms. That's the dumbest thing I've ever heard—"

"You too stupid to do it, Master Chief? I can always look for somebody else."

"Don't get your drawers in an uproar, Mr. Ramos. With the right help, I might be able to do it. I'll need a good retired EA-6B Chief to work with me. Just what do you have in mind?"

"Okay. Here's how it goes. We can get one Prowler from VAQ-131 at Whidbey Island and one from VMAQ-3, the Moon Dogs, at Cherry Point. We're gonna have 'em flown to Area 51 near Tonopah—"

"Area 51, huh?" The Master Chief made a whooing sound. "That figures. We're gonna convert Prowlers into Unidentified Flying Objects?"

"Funny. Real funny," Juan said in a deadpan voice. "You really crack me up, gringo. Now get serious. We're putting them into a secure hangar at Area 51. And you and your crew will convert these Prowlers into missile launch pads. Same weaponry as last time in Iran. You'll have to wire the Prowlers for that. Maybe use the HARM circuitry. And you'll need to work on the infrared.

"We want to make the cockpit resemble an A-6E cockpit as close as possible so we don't have to spend a lot of time retraining the aircrews. Same aircrews as last time. Also, we want to keep the ALQ-99 and USQ-113 so we can jam the enemy radar and communications at just the right time."

Gherkie thought for a minute. "Where the heck we gonna put all those black boxes?"

"Hey, you've got the whole back seat! We're going with a two-man crew in each bird instead of four. So tear out the back seats and cockpits and put in the extra black boxes you need."

"I suppose that's possible." Gherkie took out a cigar, licked it down, and lit it.

Juan Ramos looked at him and sighed. "Where have you been? Under a rock? You can't smoke in federal buildings anymore, Master Chief."

"So throw me out. I get nervous. Smoking a cigar calms me down. Don't worry. We'll spray the place before we leave. I brought a little bottle of spray. Always carry it for situations like this. Nobody'll know. You want one?"

"What do you got?"

"Perfectos," the Master Chief said proudly.

"Perfectos? You're kiddin' me, right? I smoke only Cubans. What you've got is like smokin' swamp weed. Give me one."

Juan grabbed the cigar out of Gherkie's hand and took a puff.

"Master Chief, I think this might be the beginning of a beautiful relationship."

CHAPTER FOUR

April 29th — George Bush Center for Intelligence, Langley, Virginia

*A*ll was quiet in the third-floor small conference room of the Central Intelligence Agency. The senior deputy directors of the CIA sat at the long conference table looking at their notes. Their assistants sat silently behind them, waiting for any orders that might come their way. The coffee service had been placed on a wall shelf in the windowless, stark, secure room.

Roland James, staff assistant to Mrs. Thelma Kipp, Director of Science and Technology (D/S&T), smelled the coffee and wanted some. The thirty-five-year-old former Tampa University quarterback, six-feet-four, with sandy, thinning hair, looked like he could still direct his college team to victory. He was also thoroughly addicted to caffeine and needed a cup now. But he was not about to walk over to that coffee urn before any of the directors made a move for it.

He knew his boss would not make a move for it — she was a Mormon. *Mormons don't drink coffee. I have no idea why not.*

He looked hopefully at the other directors at the table.

Curtis Mitchell, Director of the National Clandestine Service (D/NCS) offered no hope. He was a 'super spook.' Such a health freak, he'd probably sworn off coffee years ago.

John Stern, Director of Intelligence (D/I)? Maybe. Roland had seen him drinking coffee before. Why not now? He silently willed Stern to walk to the coffee urn. No such luck. Stern just sat there looking at his notes.

How about Andre Boulant, Director of Support (D/S)? His department had provided the coffee, for gosh sake. Surely he'd go get a cup. No such luck. None of the directors made a move for it. Roland James gave up on getting any coffee and decided to be satisfied with smelling it.

They all just waited. No cell phones were allowed in the conference room. So they waited in silence. It was 1:30 in the afternoon. The CIA Center, a sprawling complex just off the Washington Memorial Parkway eight miles west of Washington, DC, was a beehive of activity as intelligence experts pored over data gathered from communication, satellite, media and human sources. Contingency plans were in place for every potential trouble spot on the earth, and were updated at least weekly.

At the top of this intelligence factory was the Director of the CIA (D/CIA), General Forrest Rogers, USMC Retired. Rogers had survived Beltway infighting for a number of years, having bitten, scratched, and punched his way up to his present position. It also helped that he was married to the sister of the President of the United States of America. The marriage had lost much of its luster five years ago, right after his extramarital affair had been discovered, but the friendship between General Rogers and President Remington had endured. The President trusted Rogers. And everyone inside the Beltway knew the President trusted Rogers, thus making Rogers' position as D/CIA secure.

On this particular day, General Rogers was focusing on North Korea. The former Marine, just short of six feet and as muscular and beefy as he had been when he commanded Marines in the field thirty years ago, walked down the hall alongside his Number Two, Bobbie Turline, Deputy Director of the CIA (DD/CIA). Bobbie, as he liked people to call him, to the consternation of General Rogers, was a 'good old boy' from Oklahoma. Six-three and gangly, the career CIA agent was Rogers' strong right arm on all matters. Bobbie was able to translate CIA jargon and protocols into language Rogers could understand. And Bobbie also knew where all the bodies were buried in 'The Company' — as those in the know liked to call the CIA. The general had learned a long time ago that to lead an organization successfully, one needed to know its history, who the villains were, the buffoons, and the go-to people. Bobbie provided that information to General Rogers and Rogers appreciated it.

"So, what can I expect in the meeting, Bob?" The two were nearing the Conference Room.

"The directors will be briefing you on the latest from North Korea, getting you completely up to speed before your meeting with the National Security Council tomorrow morning."

"Any concerns? Will I get bushwhacked in there?"

"No. I think we'll be all right. DS&T is still arguing with DS on how best to support our operation, but you won't know it. I'd just listen carefully if I were you. We're pretty much ready to go with the plan. You just need to bless it today, and then get the President to give his final approval tomorrow."

They approached the Conference Room. "Okay, Robert, let's do it."

The two walked into the room and everyone rose from their chairs. D/CIA arrived at his place at the head of the table and sat down, silently signaling everyone else to be seated. The DD/CIA sat to his immediate right.

Rogers started right in. "Subject today is DPRK's fanatical desire to shower us with bouquets of ICBMs. I've got to brief the NSC at eight tomorrow morning, and need to go to the White House with a plan. Let's get it together. You want to start, NCS?"

The Director of the National Clandestine Service (D/NCS), Curtis Mitchell, rose and walked to the podium. His aide began the Power Point presentation.

"Let me start with the big picture and then get down into the weeds, General Rogers. Our agents are all over this. As you know, we have moles very high up in the DPRK hierarchy. Here's what North Korea's up to right now. Kim Jong Il is out of it. He's a vegetable.

"The man you see here on the screen is calling the shots — Premier Jang Song Thaek. He's the brother-in-law of Kim Jong Il. A wild radical. Hates us.

"His partner in crime is this man — General Park Rei Cho, Commanding General of the Armed Forces. Another radical, except he's more diplomatic than Jang.

"The third member of the triumvirate is Commissioner Chou Moon Co, seen here at a recent military parade. He's a moderate. Wants North Korea to join the world community. He can be turned. We're putting in an agent to befriend him."

Roland James noticed the telltale sign that General Rogers was getting bored, his drumming of a pencil on the table. *He's missing it,* James thought. *He should be asking more about Commissioner Chou. . . . Oh well, it really doesn't matter. Chou is not long for this world, anyway. He'll be dead before you turn him, you idiot. Why do I put up with these stuffed shirts?*

"That's all good info, Curt," General Rogers cut in. "But the President already knows all this. Get to the good stuff."

"Okay," Mitchell said quickly. "Well, let me review the current strategy of DPRK's leadership.

"One: They want DPRK to succeed on three fronts — nuclear power, space power, economic power — by 2012, the 100th birthday of founding father Kim Il-Sung.

"Two: They want to win the hearts of Koreans around the world — North Koreans, South Koreans, international Koreans — so that all Koreans will agree that the Americans must be ousted from South Korea, thus allowing the entire peninsula to be reunited and stable.

"Three: They want to demonstrate to the world that DPRK is every bit as powerful militarily as the USA, South Korea, and Japan, and that it can dominate them by demonstrating competency in Nuclear Weaponry.

"That's the strategy, sir." Curtis Mitchell established eye contact with the general. "Now here's the way they hope to accomplish it. Here's the good stuff.

"One: They plan an ICBM launch against us sometime during July of this year. We don't yet know where they intend to strike or with how many weapons. But we do know they are capable of lobbing a nuke somewhere into our territory. They believe that just as we've made no military response to their provocative actions in the last several years, that we will react passively even after they send us their little gift. They honestly believe that we are too weak to respond beyond economic sanctions and international pressure.

"Two: They will threaten more nuclear strikes unless we back away from our plans to invade them from the DMZ. I know, I know. We have no plans to invade them. But they will fill the media with accusations, hoping some of it will stick, which it will. They want the world to believe that the USA has it in for them. Listen to this from their state-run newspaper, Minjo Joson:

"We will use nuclear weapons as a merciless means of offense to deal retaliatory strikes against anyone who dares infringe upon the dignity and sovereignty of the DPRK."

Their plan is to put such pressure on us that we will leave South Korea to them. They sincerely believe that their threats, together with world opinion, will force us to fold our cards and drop out if the pressure is strong enough.

"Three: They will put a massive number of troops and SCUDs along the DMZ. Then they'll claim that we provoked them into combat. After throwing some SCUDs into Osan Air Base and killing a few Americans, they'll give us an ultimatum — leave or watch our troops get slaughtered. They firmly believe we will withdraw immediately rather than face the wrath of an American public which has just watched its soldiers die — as in Mogadishu in the 1990s.

"So that's it, sir. It is the opinion of the NCS directorate that only a preemptive strike on North Korea will keep this scenario from becoming a reality."

"Hmm," General Rogers pulled on his nose. "Let's take a short coffee break before we talk about our response, shall we?"

Finally, Raymond James thought as he ran to the coffee urn. *While the general gets his marching orders from the DD/CIA, I can at least enjoy a little coffee.*

As he was pouring the 'black gold' into a cup, Mrs. Kipp approached him.

"Have you gotten the power point ready to go, Roland? We're on shortly. Go check it right now."

I'd like to give you a power point insertion, Roland said under his breath as he took a gulp and retreated to his laptop. *How much longer will I have to endure these idiots? Not much longer, I hope. But Curtis Mitchell knows more than we could have imagined. I'll have to report that. . . . Once Mrs. Kipp is on, the presentation I prepared for her will throw them off a bit. I've got Mrs. Kipp bamboozled. Why not the rest of this bureaucratic buzz group?*

General Rogers finally called the session back to order, after a private discussion with Bobbie Turline, his Number Two.

When all were seated, he began. "Before we hear from the Director of Intelligence, Curt, I want to hear your estimate on how Beijing and Moscow will react to all this? Will they support us if they know the real story of what P'yongyang's trying to pull?"

"Our agents have reported in on both governments," D/NCS responded. "Our estimate? Both the Chinese and the Russians are silently complicit! Although they'll give lip service to our position, they will both clandestinely assist P'yongyang in acquiring the South."

Roland James observed the general's negative body language. *I hope Rogers doesn't buy Mitchell's argument. And I hope Mitchell has only speculation to back this up.*

"That's a pretty strong statement, Mr. Mitchell." General Rogers looked hard at Mitchell. "You got any data to back it up?"

"Sure have, General. We followed a senior DPRK agent, a Kim She-Re, to Vladivostok three weeks ago. He met with a senior Russian agent, a Dmitri Plovnic. We were able to listen in. Plovnic assured Kim of Russia's assistance in North Korea's operation, stating that Kim Jong Il can be assured that although the Russian government will officially object to his actions, Russia will be there for its loyal ally as it reunites the people of Korea. Translation: Russia wants some of the spoil North Korea will reap when it annexes the South.

"General, our agents in the North Korean hierarchy assure us that China is also in it for the spoils. We have taped conversations between Chinese and North Korean agents to that effect."

"So we're in deep kimshee." General Rogers looked around the room. "Thanks, Curt, for having the courage to give us the whole bloody picture. This tells me that our scenario regarding a covert response needs to be put before the President. Care to lay that out—"

Bobbie Turline quickly cut him off. "General, I suggest we go into executive session with only the directors before we discuss a covert operation. We'll brief you fully on the latest. May we dismiss the staff assistants at this point?"

"Ah, yes. Thank you, Mr. Turline," the general said, recovering from his mistake. "Assistants, may I ask you to depart the room for this part of the briefing? Thank you for all you have done to help us get to this point."

With that, the assistants got up and filed out. Roland James left the building and headed for his drop.

April 30th — The Oval Office, Washington, DC

President Russell R. Remington (nicknamed 'R-Cubed' by his fraternity brothers in college) sat at his desk as he chaired the meeting of the National Security Council. It was ten in the morning and the sun was shining in the window, making the President wish he were out jogging instead of chairing the meeting of a group he wished did not even exist.

Remington had now been President of the United States for a year and a half. Tall and trim, with short brown hair, he had a distinctly Reagan look. But physical appearance was where the similarities ended. Remington had run on a ticket of political liberalism and international accommodation.

It started so well, he thought as he sat there. *I battled to get the economy moving out of depression. We're beginning to see some recovery. Then I nearly lost my shirt getting national health going — I'm still dealing with that fallout. And now this North Korea thing. How do I deal with that? This whole mess is getting worse rather than better. I don't have any confidence in this bunch sitting here, not even my brother-in-law. A bunch of hawks, except for State. I wish I could just make it all go away.*

Seated in a semi-circle in front of him were the Vice President, the National Security Adviser, the Secretary of State, the Secretary of Defense, the Chairman of the Joint Chiefs of Staff, the Director of National Intelligence, and the Director of the CIA. General Rogers was briefing the NSC on contingency plans should it be confirmed that the Democratic People's Republic of Korea was actually going to launch a nuclear attack on American soil.

"So that's it, Mr. President. As you can see, the evidence points to the fact, not the possibility, that North Korea will launch a nuclear ICBM at us some time in July. And discussions with the governments of China and Russia to head this off have not been fruitful to date—"

"Not been fruitful?" The President's eyes bored into those of the Director of the CIA. "General Rogers, may I remind you that I am on record as telling the American people that diplomacy is the way we conduct international disputes. How can you, CIA, tell me that discussions with our friends in Beijing and Moscow are not fruitful? International discussions are not the responsibility of the CIA. Let me ask State how we're doing with China and Russia. Hiram?"

Oh jeez, President Remington thought. *Why did I do that? Dr. Hiram Nobely is a slob. Too many years teaching at Harvard. I picked him for State as a favor to the left. But I can't depend on a thing he says.*

Dr. Nobely cleared his throat with a 'harrumph' and sat up straight.

Oh, no. Here comes the college lecture. How do I shut him down?

Wheezing loudly between phrases, Nobely began. "Well, Mr. President. . . there is always. . . room for negotiation. . . . I think that I can call a few. . . people in various countries. . . . I think we can begin to make some progress—"

"With all due respect," Rogers broke in. "We've already worked—"

President Remington put his hand up to stop Rogers. "Let Dr. Nobely speak, General."

"Harrumph. As I was saying. . . we may be able to begin to make some progress. . . . I remember back in the First Gulf War. . . we avoided a prolonged conflict through good, solid, third party negotiations. The Saudis and the Syrians and we talked—"

"Yes. Yes. I know all that." The President stood up and went to the window. "But here's what I want to know about now — North Korea. Hiram, have you had any success with Russia and China on this?"

"Well, we are talking, although neither country has actually taken any action we can discern. . . . But I am not giving up, not by a long shot. No, sir. Not by a long shot."

"Let me get some other input." The President, obviously frustrated, tried again. "Mr. Vice President, how much hope would you give us on successful back-channel negotiations with Russia and China to make North Korea back off this dumb move?"

Vernowsky set his coffee cup down and looked up at the President.

"I'd give it about as much chance as a snowball in hell, Mr. President." The Vice President, seventy years old, and closing out his long career of public service, had nothing to gain by being the President's 'yes' man. "Think about it, Mr. President. Both those countries will profit if we look weak. I don't think they'll lift a finger to help us. They may make noise, but I don't think their hearts will be in it. I personally spoke with Putin last summer over the Georgia debacle. He as much as told me to get lost. He said the era of American swaggering is over, that Russia will again be a nation to contend with.

"And China? Although they love our trade, and even more our debt to them, their long-term deal is to be the dominant player in Asia. No, Mr. President. My estimation is that neither Moscow nor Beijing will help us deal with North Korea. P'yongyang's sure as shootin' going to lob a nuke at us unless we stop them."

President Remington sighed. "So, General Rogers. Is your proposal still a clandestine, pre-emptive strike on North Korea's nuclear weapons facilities?"

"Yes, sir," General Rogers said, clenching his teeth.

"Mr. President." Dr. Nobely fixed his gaze on Rogers. The President returned to his chair. As he sat down, he looked at Nobely.

"I take it you don't agree with a clandestine strike, Dr. Nobely?"

"No, I do not. . . . For one thing, General Rogers plans to obliterate at best four of their facilities. . . . But may I remind you that they have facilities all over North Korea. We hit four of them and they will launch nuclear and conventional weapons. . . all over South Korea, all over our American troops in South Korea. And world opinion will be against us. . . as will the American public. . . . We'll lose credibility. We'll lose the credibility we are just now regaining. . . . And you'll lose the White House. No, sir, I do not agree with any strikes by us against anyone."

"Look, R-Cubed, er, I mean Mr. President," General Rogers said as the president frowned at him. "That's why we're planning a clandestine mission. No one will be able to prove we did it. And we can shut down P'yangyang's communications so they can't give a launch order right away. I think that whoever is leading North Korea, and we know it's not Kim Jong Il, will see that the jig is up, that whoever hit them once can hit them again.

"During the lull after our attack, that's the time to get Russia and China involved. They can both be bribed with concessions from us. Especially if they see that they're not holding a winning hand. Remember what happened with Iran two years ago after we clandestinely hit their facilities? The Russians ended up supporting us! Of course, we had to give in on Georgia. But it was a small price to pay. We can do that again."

"So what you're advocating," the president said as he looked at his hands, "is that we use a couple aircraft not in our inventory and two phantom aircrews to do the job — that we hit four distinct complexes — and that both aircraft will sink into the sea after the attack, with the crews then fading into oblivion. Is that it?"

"That's it, Mr. President," General Rogers said enthusiastically. "We can carry this off. We have everything ready to go. If we don't do this, my fear is that your only option will be responding to a nuclear attack by North Korea."

The President looked hard at Rogers and then looked back at the window. "Keep planning it, General. But do not execute until I tell you. And keep me informed on how it's going."

He then adjusted his tie and smiled at the NSC. "Meanwhile, I'm going to personally call the Russian president. Maybe call in a chit or two. I can't believe it's in the Russians' interest to allow North Korea to launch a nuke. . . . That's it, gentlemen. Thank you for coming."

CHAPTER FIVE

May 2nd — Yanrakinnot

*T*he liturgy had gone well. Father Zacharios had preached about Jesus, the Good Shepherd. In his closing remarks, he explained that there would be a temporary change of shepherds at Church of the Transfiguration.

"My dear people, the bishop has decided that I must represent him back in Moscow and St. Petersburg for several months. I will miss you all terribly. Father Dema of Bishop Diomid's staff will be your shepherd while I am away. I know you will treat him with the deepest respect.

He will be staying with Dr. Peter and Leonid. And I know you will all look after Matushka and Tomas while I am gone."

After lunch and a nap, Father Zacharios and Bethany sat quietly at their kitchen table.

"I wish I didn't have to leave, Bethany," Zach began the conversation. "But I see no other way."

Bethany sat there looking at her hands. "I support you in what you've got to do, Zach. I just feel abandoned out here. I know the people love us. And I know Peter and Leonid will watch over us. But I'm afraid—"

"I understand. I'm afraid, too. We went through this twenty years ago. I flew off and didn't come back for eighteen years. You thought I was dead. I shudder to think that you might ever have to go through that again. But we need to put it in the hands of God and be faithful. I'll pray for you and Tomas each day. And as often as I can, I'll get messages back to you."

The two stood and embraced. Bethany cried in her husband's arms until it was time for him to catch the track vehicle for Provideniya. Choking back tears, Zach again blessed his little family, kissed Bethany and Tomas goodbye, picked up his suitcase and walked to the corner where the vehicle was parked. Peter and Leonid were there, waiting to say goodbye.

"I will pray for you, Father," Leonid said with a sad look on his large, moon-shaped face. "Don't worry about Matushka and the little one. Uncle Peter and I will take good care of them. And I promise that I will guide Father Dema and make sure he makes all his visitations."

"Don't be too hard of him," Father said with a smile. "You're liable to scare him away. He's a cathedral priest, remember? Cathedral clergy don't work very hard. Go easy on him."

"Very well, Father," Leonid said, not getting the joke.

"Thank you for seeing me off, Peter," Father bowed before the doctor. "Once again, I must ask for your blessing."

Peter made the sign of the cross over Father's head. "May Almighty God protect you and your family while you are apart from one another, and may you have success in your crusade. In the name of the Father and of the Son and of the Holy Spirit."

And then, climbing into a seat, Father Zacharios bid farewell to Yanrakinnot. *Will I ever see this place again?* Tears ran down his cheeks as Yanrakinnot fell behind him, out of sight.

The tracked vehicle pulled into Provideniya at about nine that evening, dropping Zach and the other passengers at the market downtown. He picked up his suitcase and headed for the Chabarova Street apartment.

Si and Muk were happy to see him. Muk prepared a dinner of fish soup and reindeer steaks, which they enjoyed with strong coffee. The wonderful smells made the old, ramshackle apartment seem almost tolerable.

After the meal was ended, Zach and Si sat in the living room listening to the radio — Dvorak's Ninth Symphony in E Minor, Opus 95.

"So how will this work, Si? How do I get back to the States and where will I train? China Lake?"

"Okay. It's time for your pre-departure briefing," Si said in a businesslike manner. "James Royal arrives day after tomorrow in his Piper Cherokee with a load of cargo. He departs Wednesday with another load of cargo — you and me. He's going to smuggle us back into Alaska. I think he did that for you once before, no?"

"Yup. Flew me to Port Alsworth, Alaska after a fuel stop in Nome. Same deal this time?"

"Same deal. But on the way, you'll need to shave off that beard and put on some secular clothes rather than that black outfit you've got on. We've got some clothes you can wear. We'll spend a few days in Port Alsworth snapping your photo for a new ID card, passport, and accompanying documentation. Then it'll be down to Las Vegas, where we'll pick up a government vehicle for the training site — Area 51."

"Area 51! Does that site still exist? I heard they closed it to avoid any more UFO freaks from trying to get over the wire to find the hidden spaceship and aliens."

"Area 51 is still active, Zach. The perfect place to train. Good security. Good facilities. Lots of privacy. . . . Anyway, you'll meet the aircrews and maintenance guys. The maintenance crews are there already, working on the airplanes. The aircrew members will arrive a day or so before you do. Once we get there and start training, I'll give you the rest of the brief."

"How about my communications with Bethany? What provision have you made for that?"

"None," Si said with a sad look on his face. "Too risky. This whole operation is way above top secret. Only a few people in Washington even know about it. So, as of today, nobody gets to call, text, email, or send mail. We are going dark until after the operation. Got it?"

"Got it. What you say makes sense. But I surely would like to let Bethany know when I've arrived safely in the States and that all is going well."

"Can't chance it."

Silence.

Three days later, May 5th, Zach was on his way to Alaska.

May 7th — Moscow, Russian Federation

President Medvedev sat at his desk in the ornate office of the President of the Russian Federation. The walls were filled with paintings of Russian leaders, from Peter the Great to Gorbachev, though Gorby's was in a corner where it wasn't readily seen. Plush carpets covered the tiled floor. A magnificent fireplace anchored the office, and a fire burning brightly. Four finely-crafted cherry chairs and end tables circled the hearth. Prime Minister Putin lounged in one of the chairs, listening in to the president's phone conversation.

"Yes, Mr. President," Medvedev spoke into the phone. "We agree with you on this. North Korea is way too provocative and needs to be put in its place. . . . Yes, we will certainly support a United Nations Resolution to tighten economic sanctions. . . . Of course we will try back channel communications to see what it will take to back them away from launching a nuclear missile. It is in no one's interest to allow such a thing. . . . Thank you, Mr. President. I will have my people coordinate with yours."

Placing the phone back on its hook, Medvedev made a face at Putin. "Blah, blah, blah. The President of the United States is the most boring person I have ever met. He is insisting that we intervene with the North Koreans."

"The President is an idiot," Putin said as he spat into the fireplace. "I'm glad you are humoring him. Right now, he is probably bragging that he got the President of Russia to do his bidding with Kim Jong Il. . . . What do we hear from our Intelligence Service Director?"

"North Korea plans to launch their lone ICBM on America on its Independence Day, aimed at one of the Aleutian Islands. Covertly, we have told P'yongyang that we support them. We've shown them the press statements we will allegedly put out condemning the attack and asking the USA to be patient while the world community seeks negotiations with Kim Jong Il. We've also assured them that we will stall the Americans while the North gets ready for its invasion across the DMZ.

"Our intelligence people tell us that the Americans are planning a small pre-emptive strike on North Korea's nuclear launch pads. . . sometime before the North Korean missile is fired at them. We hope this happens. It will devastate the North Korean Premier Jang enough that he will lose face with the cabinet, and provide a moment in time for us to act.

"Before Jang can convince the cabinet to launch their small nukes at South Korea in retaliation, our man General Park will convince the cabinet that Jang has to go. Park will then get Kim Jong Un installed as the new leader, with Park calling the shots and publicly tilting North Korea toward Russia. End results?

"America does our dirty work for us. North Korea loses its nuclear weapons capability and comes under our dominance. We gain hegemony in the area. China looks bad. We look good."

Putin looked into the fire. "Hopefully, this ambitious plan will work. But it is conditioned by a lot of 'ifs.' IF we succeed, we can indeed control the North Koreans and wrest them from the grip of the Chinese. The fact that we own the Commanding General of the DPRK armed forces helps immensely.

"Well, keep working on it, my friend," Putin said as he stood up to leave. "We may reap a harvest from all this. . . or we may reap a whirlwind."

Same Day — Air Force Test Center, "Area 51," Nevada

Master Chief Kendall Gherkie, retired A-6E Intruder maintenance chief, sat in the pilot seat of an EA-6B Prowler in Hangar Three at the northwest end of the secretive Area 51, Horney Airport, near Tonopah, Nevada. Master Sergeant Josiah Washington, USMC, retired EA-6B Prowler maintenance chief, sat to Gherkie's right in the electronic countermeasures officer seat. It was just after midnight and the two were supervising their crews as they converted two EA-6B Prowler electronic countermeasures birds into laser missile platforms.

"So I grew up on the streets of South Chicago, Washington," Gherkie said, keeping a practiced eye on the work force below. "Tough life. My pop was a drunk. My mom worked two jobs. She was gone more than she was around. I sorta thought she didn't like us kids much. Beat us up when she was home. So I in turn beat up anybody who looked at me wrong.

"After I beat one Hispanic kid to a pulp, the judge told me I could either go to jail or join the Navy. I chose the Navy. Turned out to be a good choice. I was dumb but I wasn't stupid. Scored high enough on the AQT to become an airplane mechanic. Joined the A-6A Intruder community when the aircraft was brand new.

"Two Western Pacific tours later, I was a Petty Officer Second Class. Shipped over twice and decided to make the Navy my career. Sea duty was my thing — exotic ports of call, mysterious women, lots of booze. But through it all, Washington, my greatest love was working on the A-6 Intruder radar bomber."

"I hear that," Washington responded. "Keepin' all your birds up and ready is what makes life worth livin.'"

"Yeah, well I excelled at it. Kept getting promoted. Then came the day when I stood at attention while the Skipper made me a Master Chief Petty Officer. Can't go any higher than that as a non-com. That's a day I'll never forget. I bought the bar at the chief's mess. They had to carry me home when it was all over. Hangover lasted three days.

"But before I knew it, I was forty-nine years old and my Intruders were being mothballed down at Davis-Monthan Air Force Base. My thirty years were up, so I figured it was time to retire along with the Intruders. I was stationed at China Lake at the time, so I just stayed on. Took an apartment near the base. Since I'd been divorced twice, my retirement pay was distributed three ways. Didn't leave me much.

"I spent twelve very boring years there in the high desert of California. Frustrating years. Everything I loved seemed to have been ripped away from me. The Intruders were retired. I got too old to chase women. The chief's club was changing and becoming boring due to the de-glamorization of alcohol by the military establishment. Life was just no fun anymore. To tell you the truth, Washington, three years ago I was trying to figure out the best way to kill myself."

"Man, that's not so good. What'd you do to get out of that trap?"

"Funniest thing happened. I got called into the base commander's office at China Lake one day. I was 'invited' to take charge of a highly classified mission — restoring two retired A-6E Intruders so that they could be used to clandestinely bomb some of Iran's nuclear facilities. I'm telling you, it was the best four months of my life. I got to choose my shipmates. Had all the beer I wanted, free of charge. And I got a chance to make a difference, Washington. Our aircrews blew the Iranian nuclear facilities to smithereens. . . . Even killed the president. Can't think of his name — I nicknamed him 'Amana Nutjob.' When it was all over, I had a new lease on life.

"And here I am again, restoring aircraft for another secret mission. Good work. Good pay. Free beer. Life is good. . . . How about you, Washington? What's your story?"

"I'm about as different from you as black is from white, Master Chief," Washington responded after glancing down out of the cockpit to make sure his men were hard at work. "I was raised on the Mississippi Delta. Parents were poor, black farmers. I grew up knowing nothin' except pickin' cotton and goin' to church. I was a good boy, strong in my Pentecostal faith and obedient to my parents. And so, when my old man told me to join the Marines and make somethin' of myself, I did it. Out of boot camp, I got selected for electronics. Did so well in school, I got sent to avionics. Eventually wound up in the EA-6B Prowler community and stayed with it.

"While you were drinkin' beer all over Asia, I was workin' on Prowlers at Whidbey Island and Cherry Point. You ever do shore duty at Whidbey, Master Chief?"

"Whidbey? Heck, yeah. I had a wife and a kid up there. That former wife is still on the island, by the way, married to a retired First Class. I never did like Washington State, though. Too wet all the time. Tried to stay on the East Coast as much as possible. Had several tours at Oceana. In fact, I left a wife and kids there, too. . . . How about you, Washington? Did you ever get married?"

"You bet I did. Met me a female Marine, a BAM, married her and had five kids. Still married to her, in fact. Kids are up and out of the house. We live back in Mississippi.

"But while we were at Cherry Point, we were pillars of the chapel community on the base. I was just a faithful Marine, Master Chief. . . except when I was on a cruise. I developed this habit of fallin' off the wagon at least once every cruise. I was never a woman chaser, mind ya.' My vice was simply sittin' in a bar in some port and drinkin' rum till I had to be carried back to the ship. After which I would feel extremely guilty."

"Why in thunder did you feel guilty about that?" Gherkie looked at Washington incredulously. "Everybody's got a right to get blottoed in port."

"You say that 'cus you're a pagan, Master Chief. I ain't no pagan. I'm a Christian. I got no right to get blottoed anywhere. So when I sobered up, I'd confess my sins to the chaplain and live a holy life — until the next cruise. . . . Anyway, I eventually realized that I shouldn't stay in the Marines if I couldn't control my rum intake. Retired and moved back to Mississippi. Cost of livin' is so low there, we can live on my retirement pay. I figured I was done with the Marines. Just minister at church and enjoy life.

"So it was a real surprise when I got called a couple of weeks ago. Couldn't refuse the offer they made me. Good money and good mission. Can't beat that. So here I am, workin' with you, a pagan Master Chief who makes me drink beer every morning when we get off our shift."

"Am I succeeding in turning you into a pagan, Washington?"

"Nope. Not if I can control my beer intake. Am I succeedin' in turnin' you into a Christian, Master Chief?"

"Keep talking to me, Washington. You're beginning to make sense, much as I hate to admit it."

The Master Chief glanced at his watch. "Okay. Let's take a look at this cockpit before we check the radar. Mr. Ramos will be dropping by at 0100. Let's have it together when he gets here."

"Okay, Master Chief," Master Sergeant Washington said as he gazed into his laptop. "We've converted both cockpits from Prowler to Intruder. Do they look A-6 enough for you?"

"Yeah. I think we got it right. Matches the Naval Air Training and Operational Procedures Manual picture. Plus the EA-6B equipment we're retaining shouldn't confuse either pilot or bombardier-navigator. These crews are Intruder guys, not Prowler guys. We got to make it as easy on 'em as possible. . . . Yeah, this cockpit'll do. Make sure your guys get the other cockpit to look just like this one. And make sure the simulator is an exact replica."

"Aye, aye."

"Okay, let's climb down and look at the radars."

May 8th — P'yongyang

Dirge music played, ending the memorial service for the late Commissioner Chou Sing Moon. Kim Jong Il's double had sat through the service, giving people the impression that The Dear Leader was doing well. Premier Jang Song Taek had just given an exquisite eulogy, laying out all the wonderful things Chou had done for the Democratic People's Republic of Korea. General Park Rei Cho sat through the eulogy, wondering how Jang could honor a man he had only days before shot dead.

Premier Jang is one dangerous character, General Park thought as he watched Jang out of the corner of his eye. *To shoot someone in cold blood one day and then sing his praises the next? Only a warped person can do that.*

Jang took his seat beside Park as the dirge music continued.

"Well, General, we'll miss Commissioner Chou," Jang whispered. "Now it's just the two of us running the country. We'll need to meet more frequently from now on."

So you can monitor my every movement and my every decision? Park thought, convinced that Jang had a tail on him. Aloud, he said, "That is a good idea, Premier Jang. How often would you like to meet?"

"I think weekly for now. As we get into June, we should perhaps meet daily. At my home."

"That can be arranged." *This will make my contact with Moscow more complicated,* Park thought as he rose from his chair and started out of the theatre. *More complicated but not impossible. I think I know how to dispose of Premier Jang. . . when the moment is right.*

Same Day — Port Alsworth, Alaska

The Piper Cherokee, with Glen Sanders in the left seat, James Royal in the right, and Zach and Si in the back, touched down on the gravel runway of Port Alsworth, Alaska, just after noon on Saturday, May 8th, after a rough flight from Provideniya with a fuel stop in Nome. Zach knew Glen, the chief pilot, from the rescue two years before, and was glad to know that Glen was again assisting. On final approach, Zach glanced to his left, looking for Mark and Sandy's house, where he had lived while recuperating from his escape from Russia. The house was gone. A stab of pain hit him as he remembered that it had been torched by the Russian mafia two years prior.

"Si," he said as the aircraft rolled out after landing. "When I escaped here two years ago, I stayed with a great couple named Mark and Sandy. They were a real blessing to me. But the Russian Crime Syndicate got wind of them after I was long gone. Came after them. Mark and Sandy had to be lifted out of here by the Company. Given new identities. And moved to the lower forty-eight. Their house got torched in the process. . . . I messed them up, Si. If I hadn't come here, none of that would have happened to them. I don't want to have that happen to anyone else."

"It'll be okay, Zach. We'll just be here two days. The Russians have no idea where you are. They've probably given up on you. No one here in Port Alsworth will be in danger. We'll just lay low at James' house, get the stuff done to make you into somebody else, and then get on down to Vegas."

An hour later, Zach, Si, and James Royal were seated on James' front porch, which covered the entire front of the upscale cabin. Only forest surrounded them. Zach sat in a comfortable wooden rocking chair, while James and Si sat on rustic porch chairs, all three facing the forest. They had just finished a lunch of burgers and fries, cooked by James' wife, Marie.

"This afternoon, we'll make contact with the Company," Si said as he scratched his knee. "I'll take some photos of you and email them down secure. They'll express-mail your passport, license, and assorted other ID. Two days here and we'll move south."

"Tomorrow is Sunday." Zach gazed into the forest. "I can't chance going to church here. It'll be the first Sunday I've missed church since October of 2008. Kind of saddens me."

"You can worship with us right here, Zach," James said with a smile on his face. "Marie and I and the kids will be your congregation. I'll preside and you can preach. Will that violate your orders?"

"That's very kind of you, James. I'll take you up on the offer. We just can't do communion together. You want to sit in on it, Simon?"

"You know, I told you I'm not much on the religious stuff," Si said.

Not overly defensive, Zach noticed.

"But I might sit in. Never heard you preach, Zach. Don't hit me with hellfire and brimstones or I'll walk out in the middle of your sermon."

"No fire. No brimstones. Just the beautiful story of Jesus, Si. Not to worry."

Later that day, Si took photos of Zach and communicated with his home office. Zach took a nap. James and Marie took the kids for a hike.

Supper was venison stew.

"I love this stew, Marie." Zach gave her a thumbs up. They were seated in the ample dining room, James at the head of the table, Marie at the foot, Zach and Si at one side, while James, Jr., age eleven, and Sally, age nine, sat on the other side. It was an enjoyable meal. But as the conversation continued, Zach became homesick.

What is Bethany doing right now? Probably wondering when I'll contact her. Will I ever see her again? Will I watch Tomas grow up? Please, Lord, protect them for me. I want to be home right now, polishing my sermon for tomorrow's liturgy. Playing with my son until bedtime. Making love to my wife. Lord, bring me safely home.

"Isn't that right, Zach?" Si asked.

"What? What?" Zach looked up, embarrassed. "Sorry. I must have strayed off."

"I was saying that the Russian economy is going to hell in a hand basket. Isn't that right?"

"Uh. Yeah. It's not good, not good at all."

Meal over, Zach turned in early, trying to catch up on missed sleep and feeling too homesick to be much involved in conversation.

The worship service the next morning was one Zach would not soon forget. James led a beautiful worship liturgy. The kids sang a duet. *Those kids have perfect pitch*, Zach thought. Marie played hymns on the piano, hymns he hadn't heard in a long time. It being Mother's Day, Zach gave a sermon on God's love as evidenced by a mother's love for her children. He also gave a testimony about how Jesus became real to him so many years ago when he asked Him into his life. He finished the sermon by noting that thinking about the suffering and death of Jesus always helped him focus on living a Christ-like life.

Each time Zach glanced at Si, he noted that the CIA man was listening intently. *Maybe Si will get it. Maybe this is the first step for him into God's kingdom.*

Tuesday afternoon, the documents arrived from Washington, DC, and plans were made to head south.

"See the passport?" Si was briefing Zach on his new identity. "Your name is Zachary Fuller. You're a technical representative — tech rep for short — for Northrop Grumman Systems Corporation. You live in Farmingdale, Long Island. You're a retired Marine colonel. You're at Area 51 to help with some experimental mods for the new EFA-18 Growler. Memorize all this stuff so well that you actually think you are Fuller.

"Tomorrow we fly to Ted Stevens Airport in Anchorage, where we'll say goodbye to James and Glen and change to a business jet. Then it's on to Las Vegas where we'll stay overnight at Nellis Air Force Base. Thursday we get a staff car and drive to Area 51. Should be there by noon. Any questions?"

"Yeah, Simon. A couple. Will the other crew members be there when we arrive?"

"Yup. They get in today and will start their training tomorrow. Next question?"

"Any chance of James getting a message to Bethany that I'm okay?"

"Sorry about that, champ. I know you want her to know it'll all work out. But you gotta believe she's safe and that she'll do okay without you. It's too dangerous to have any contact with her. Too dangerous for James and too dangerous for your wife and kid. Trust the system, man."

And the next day they were on their way to the lower forty-eight. *We're on our way, Lord. I don't know if I trust Si's system, but I do trust yours. Show me the way.*

CHAPTER SIX

May 12th — CIA Headquarters, Langley, Virginia

*R*oland James sat in his small, closet-sized office next to the large office of his boss, Mrs. Thelma Kipp, Director of Science and Technology (D/S&T) of the Central Intelligence Agency. It was eight o'clock on Wednesday morning, meaning that Mrs. Kipp was at her weekly private meeting with the director and would not be in her office until ten. Being Mrs. Kipp's staff assistant gave Roland access to a lot of classified information. But one bit of information he didn't have as yet was the CIA's plan regarding a pre-emptive strike by the USA against North Korea. He desperately needed that info.

He sat there behind his small government-issued desk. Classified papers were strewn everywhere, evidence of the many issues with which Mrs. Kipp was involved.

I've got to get this mess cleaned up, Roland thought as he looked at the many documents on his desk, on the bookcase, on the floor. *This office is one major security violation and I don't need that kind of scrutiny. Let's see, my first priority is to get these papers sorted and filed correctly. My second priority is to schmooze with Nita and check out Thelma Kipp's desk to see what info I can extract from her. My third priority is to make a drop."*

After he had cleaned his office and filed, passed on, or properly disposed of the classified documents, he decided to take some of the papers into Mrs. Kipp's office and look around.

"Need to take these papers into Mrs. Kipp's office," Roland said to Nita, the private secretary guarding Mrs. Kipp's office. He winked at her and gave her a tap on the cheek. He had been having sex with this secretary for several months. At five-eleven and two hundred fifteen lumpy pounds, and with a face that would stop a clock, the forty-five-year-old brunette was not, in Roland's opinion, a 'looker.'

She's not all that great, but having sex with her allows me access to Mrs. Kipp's office. Besides, we're both single. There's no big deal about us having a secret fling, is there?

Nita smiled at him as he walked into Mrs. Kipp's office and closed the door behind him. Once in the office, he sat in her chair and began looking through her papers. He knew that there was no surveillance camera, so he was not worried about being discovered. After several minutes of searching, he came to what he was looking for, her notes from a previous high level meeting.

She's definitely sloppy on security — leaving this folder right on her desk. I'll have to come in here more often when she's out. Okay. What's this say?

"In order for the USA to maintain deniability, the attack will take place using aircraft not in the inventory by crews not on the rolls. It will be a limited pre-emptive strike. Our hope is that when the leaders of DPRK realize they can be hit and their arsenal devastated, they will back away from launching ICBMs, of which they may have a number. Details on the attack are being worked out and will be briefed when available."

Roland snapped photos of the document. *That's good as far as it goes. But which aircraft? From which bases? When? There is much I've got to learn. But this documentation can be effective. I'll get this to the drop before the day is out.*

Just as he was putting the document back into the folder, Nita stepped quietly into the office. Walking up to him, she put her hands on his shoulder. "Are you pretending to be Mrs. Kipp, Roland?" She was playful as she said it, moving her hands down onto his chest.

"Well, I had to write a note to her, so I sat at her desk to do it," he said as he rose and hugged her. *How do I get out of this? The last thing I need is to be discovered making love to Nita in Mrs. Kipp's office.* "But Nita, as much as I'd like to stay and play, I realize that this is neither the time nor the place."

Nita continued to explore with her hands. "Mrs. Kipp is having her hair done after her meeting. She won't be back for an hour at the earliest.

I've put an 'Out for a Meeting' sign on my desk, held all calls, and locked the door. I am a very efficient secretary, don't you think?"

Oh, what the heck, Roland thought, and let things proceed to an immoral conclusion.

Two hours later, Mrs. Kipp arrived at her office and called for Roland.

He entered and took a seat in front of her desk as he tried to wipe from his mind what had just happened in this office.

Mrs. Thelma Kipp was in her fifties, having arrived at the agency thirty years ago after receiving a doctorate in international relations. She was barely five feet tall and quite chunky. Her graying hair was short and disheveled, and her thick, large-framed glasses gave her a fishlike quality. In spite of her small stature, she was very assertive, a fact that greatly disturbed Roland James. He preferred submissive women. Plus, Roland thought she was way too moralistic. *Maybe because she's a Mormon. I hate all religions, but I especially hate Mormonism.*

"So what happened here this morning, Mr. James?" Mrs. Kipp fixed her eyes on him.

Does she know? Roland's mind was moving rapidly, rolling over possible answers. *Did she smell something in here? Better plead ignorance.*

"To tell you the truth, I haven't been here much of the morning, Mrs. Kipp. I had to help Roger Dempsey get a briefing ready for the D/I. Just got to the office about 15 minutes ago. Not much going on. Has Nita reporting anything unusual?"

Is she believing me? Did Nita tell her about us?

Silence.

"From now on, Roland, get permission from me before you help someone from another directorate. . . . Okay, my priority today is to focus on the North Korea situation. I need you to get the latest satellite photos from D/I as well as agent reports from NCS. I've got to figure out how to suggest we use our technology."

Bingo, Roland thought as relief flowed over him. *Here's what I need to know.*

"Yes, ma'am. What technology are you thinking of using?"

"This may seem like an old fashioned, idiotic idea, Roland," she said. "Someone has come up with the wild idea of modifying two EA-6B Prowlers into old Intruder bombers. Put aircrews in them that are no longer in the military but who used to fly Intruders. The Prowlers would not be in our inventory and the aircrews supposedly don't even officially exist! It's a weird idea, but I like it. Gives us deniability. What do you think of that?"

I can't believe she's telling me this. So how do I keep her talking?

"Intriguing, Mrs. Kipp." Roland made a tent with his hands and stared at the ceiling. "I guess I like the idea. But do we have enough time to do major modifications like that? What date are we thinking about for this mission?"

"My thinking is that we will have enough time. Our intel is that we need to be ready to go sometime in July."

"Hmm. . . . We couldn't be found out if the aircraft and aircrews disappeared after they attacked. I would suppose the best thing would be for them to crash at sea. Would the aircrews go down with their airplanes?"

"Hardly," she bristled. "We don't treat our people that way. They'd eject and be picked up at sea."

"That's a great idea. I guess they'd need to take off from a base in Japan. Iwakuni or maybe Misawa? They probably could get to a few North Korean targets from those bases."

"That was my thinking as well. Probably Iwakuni."

"And they'd need weapons that could be carried the distance and be powerful enough to do the damage necessary." *Got to be careful here. Don't want her thinking I'm getting too nosey.* "Weapons like that are not my specialty, but I doubt we could get our airplanes there with enough fuel if they had to carry that much firepower under their wings."

"We're thinking about nukes, Roland. One-thousand-pound laser-guided bunker-busters, small MADs. The technology's there to do the job. What do you think about that?"

Holy Smokes! They're going to nuke us. "Yes. That might work. But what about nuclear fallout? There are Americans on the peninsula. Chinese to the north. Japanese not far to the east. Depending on the winds, we could cause a catastrophe. . . . Mrs. Kipp, this plan might cause more problems than it solves."

"Back off, Mr. James!" *She's upset that I questioned her judgment.* "Do you think we wouldn't have nuclear and armed forces experts from D/I as well as our directorate working on the concept? Where do you think we got this plan? If you're worried about nuclear fallout, let me assure you that these bombs will penetrate deeply into the earth and the fall-out will be negligible. . . ."

"I'm so sorry, Mrs. Kipp. I didn't mean to question your judgment. Please forget—"

"Just think before you speak next time, Mr. James. You've got excellent potential for leadership in the Company, but you have to learn the art of tact. . . . At any rate, I want you to work on this with aides from the other directorates. I'm going to put together our portion of the plan today and tomorrow. Then I want you to coordinate with the others to fine-tune the plan. Keep me informed. We need to get it all to the director by this time next week so he can brief the President. Any questions?"

"No, ma'am. I'll go to work on this immediately." He stood and walked out of the office, once again winking at Nita as he walked by her. As he put on his suit coat and started for the drop, he laughed to himself.

Kipp not only gave me the plan. She put me on the committee that's fine tuning it. Wait until my contact reads all this!

Two minutes after he left his office, Nita got Rhoda to sit in for her and also left.

May 13th — Air Force Test Center, Area 51, Nevada

Zach and Si had gotten off to a slow start due to bad weather, losing a day in Port Alsworth until the fog cleared enough to take off for Anchorage. They finally arrived in Las Vegas on Friday night, the 12th. Even at eight in the evening the temperature was above one hundred degrees in Vegas.

As they walked down the hall toward baggage claim, Si said quietly, "In a few minutes, we're gonna be met by one of the great ones — Chico Ramos. Old friend of mine."

"Chico!" Longstreet gave him his Hollywood smile as they arrived at baggage claim. "How the heck are ya, Spic?"

"I'll give you a spic, gringo." Chico gave him a rough hug as they bantered with each other.

"Chico Ramos, meet Zach Fuller, fourth member of our air crew. Zach, meet Chico."

"Hey, Chico. Glad to meet you."

Zach observed Chico. A very short, thin man. Maybe forty-five years old. Long scar down the right side of his face. His muscular arms said that although he was small, he was a man to be reckoned with.

"Likewise," Chico responded. "Heard a lot about you. Thanks for comin,' Man. We can use you here."

"So what's the plan, my man?" Si asked as they waited for his baggage.

"Got it in control," Chico responded. "I'll fill you in when we get to the car."

Bags collected, they walked out of the terminal to the curb where a black Mercury Grand Marquis was sitting with a note on its windshield saying 'Municipal Vehicle — DO NOT TOW.'

Once in the car, Chico driving, Si sitting beside him and Zach in the right rear seat, they pulled out into traffic.

"I've got reservations for us at the bachelor officers quarters at Nellis Air Force Base here in town. Tomorrow morning, we'll head north to Area 51."

"We gotta hit the base exchange before we leave," Si said. "Zach's got to buy some clothes and stuff. By the way, how's it going up there at dreamland?"

"Great! Juan Ramos is overseein' the operation. We got your old Master Chief Gherkie headin' the conversion. A Marine Master Sergeant named Washington, EA-6B expert, is helpin' him supervise. We got two Prowlers, one from Whidbey and one from Cherry Point—"

"Wait a minute," Zach interrupted the conversation. "We'll use Prowlers? You're kidding me, right?"

"No time to bring Intruders out of mothballs, colonel," Chico said slowly. "So we're goin' to make the Prowlers into Intruders. It'll work, sir. . .

"Anyway, our guys started by guttin' the cockpits. Then Gherkie took a crew down to Davis-Monthan in our KC-10. Brought a load of parts back from mothballed A-6s. So now they're convertin' the birds."

"Is that even possible?" Zach asked. "Intruders and Prowlers look similar, but their innards have to be totally different. How do you turn an ECM bird into a bomber?"

"We'll give you a good briefin' on that when you get up there, colonel," Chico responded. "We're doin' a bit of jerry riggin' and it's workin' just fine. *Bueno!* We're almost ready to fly. The simulator's already up and runnin.' Your crewmates are startin' their cockpit work tomorrow."

They pulled into Nellis, found the BOQ and checked in. After a bite at the club, they turned in.

Next morning, Zach was up early doing his morning prayer office. The other two slept late. After breakfast, they hit the base exchange and bought several outfits for Zach, plus various toiletries and an electric razor.

By ten o'clock, they were in the Mercury and heading out the main gate. As they drove northeast on Highway 93, Zach thought about what he was getting himself into.

Okay, Lord, what's next? He watched the brown countryside as they drove north. *It'll be good to see Bob Shanto again and get caught up with him. We've gone through so much together. And while I still have questions about the necessity of conducting such a mission, I must admit I'm getting excited about it, Lord. Please take care of Bethany. I really do want to spend my life with her.*

His prayers and thoughts consumed him. From time to time, he glanced out at the terrain, noting the brown rocky hills, the cactus, even a white, dry lake. As they drove up the Pahranagat Valley, the terrain became stark and jagged. Mountains rose on each side. Sometimes he would see a lake off to the left. After passing Alamo and Ash Springs, they turned left off Highway 93 at Chrystal Springs onto Highway 375, the 'ET Highway.'

Si pulled out some sandwiches for them to eat. As they ate, the road took them up into the hills. *More miles and miles of miles and miles. Will we ever get to Area 51?*

Eventually they turned left onto a gravel road, and he saw his first sign of Area 51, a warning that trespassers would be shot on sight. *That's a happy thought. How do the goons know we're the good guys rather than ET freaks?*

The gate appeared almost suddenly, with a white temporary building on its right. As they pulled up and stopped at the gate, two armed guards slowly came out of the building and approached the car. Zach could see two other men at the windows, rifles trained on them.

"State your business, sir," one of the guards said, as the other stood a few yards off, rifle at the ready.

"I'm Chico Ramos. Remember me? I just left here two days ago to pick up my fellow workers."

"Let me see some identification, please."

Chico scowled and presented his ID card to the guard.

"Please step out of the car, slowly with your hands where we can see them, gentlemen." The other guard backed away a few yards where he would have more control of the situation.

Chico's card was scanned by a gadget the guard had at his belt. "State your name and your business here."

"Chico Ramos, tech rep for Northrup Grumman, working on an experimental aircraft. My name and photo are in the box in your office.

There should be two others in there. One for Simon Longstreet and one for Colonel Zachary Fuller."

The guard walked over and checked Si and his ID. Then he did the same with Zach. After looking through the passenger compartment and trunk, going through their suitcases, and running a bomb detector through and under the car, he asked them to remain standing while he went into the guard house. In a minute, he emerged with three ID badges with their names and photos. Handing them the badges, he saluted Zach and headed back to the guardhouse with the other guard.

The three got back into their car and drove on into the base. Zach was surprised at how spread out the base was and how many buildings there were. He was also surprised not to see anyone walking about. *This looks like a ghost base.*

They passed the south end of the runway and hit the main street. Here he could see vehicles parked and some moving down the road. But no people walked in the mid-afternoon sweltering heat.

"Any credibility to the rumor that this is a base for investigating UFOs and space aliens?" Zach quipped.

"Hey, we don't know nothin' about any of that," Chico said, glancing over his shoulder. "I do know there's stuff goin' on underneath us. Supposed to be underground facilities for somethin' we don't know about. There are some places on this base that have fences around them with special guards. May be the entrances to the underground. Kind of spooky, if you ask me. I just focus on our piece of the action. . . . Okay, there's our dorm and eating facility."

They pulled up in front of a white, wooden two story. It looked like an old World War II barracks to Zach. They got out of the car, quickly picked up their baggage and stuff they'd bought at the base exchange, and walked as fast as they could toward the south end of the building. Zach judged the temperature to be way over one hundred degrees, and he was feeling it. His blood had thickened as it had adjusted to the frigid temperatures of Chukotka. So this heat seemed almost unbearable to him.

As they entered the building, Zach noticed they were in a long hallway with rooms on either side. The air conditioning was on full blast. He loved that.

"This is your suite, colonel," Chico said quietly as he opened the door to Suite 125. "This is where you'll call home. The other aircrew members are on this hall as well, but they're probably sleeping right now. We work from 10 at night until 8 in the morning here."

Zach walked into his new quarters. He was standing in a living room about ten feet long and ten feet wide. The walls were paneled with imitation pine, and the floor was carpeted with a cheap gray rug. A brown recliner sat in one corner, with a small brown couch beside it along one wall. A large flat-screen TV covered the second wall. The third wall featured two small windows completely covered with dark gray drapes. And the fourth wall had nothing on it, just the door out into the hallway. He walked through a narrow hallway off the living room, past the bathroom on one side and a small kitchenette on the other, and into his bedroom. The bedroom was the exact size of the living room. There he found a double bed, a small brown bureau, a desk and chair and a sink.

So this will be home for a while.

He lay on the bed and thought about where he was. *Area 51! This place is famous, or maybe infamous. I remember reading the history of this base. Back in the 50s, it was rumored that the UFO and some aliens that were found in Roswell, New Mexico were secretly brought here by the American Government for investigation. It's also been rumored that other UFOs down through the years have been brought here. And I remember the Indiana Jones movie about the Ark of the Covenant being secretly stored here. Lots of rumors; very little substance.*

But what is fact is that the F-117 Stealth fighter was developed here. In fact, a whole squadron of F-117s was stationed here for two years. The pilots flew them at night and parked them in the hangars by day. Two years and no press leaks. Nobody spilled the beans. Twelve airplanes, aircrews and ground crews. Out here in dry Grooms Lake and nobody even knew they were here. Unbelievable. Hey, if twelve airplanes could be here for two years with nobody knowing about it, we ought to be safe with two airplanes here for two months. . . . Well, I'd better give my suite a blessing and say my prayers.

Prayers over and glancing at his new Seiko to see that it was five in the afternoon, Zach donned a Hawaiian shirt, khaki shorts, and sandals, and walked down the hall to the dayroom. The dayroom was a large room in the center of the building, with several couches and easy chairs, some vending machines, a pool table and a large screen TV.

He stood and watched as a professional baseball game was being aired. Still getting used to TV again, Zach's attention was captured any time he saw a television screen. The California Angels were up three over the Seattle Mariners in the bottom of the fifth inning. He noticed all that in the course of thirty seconds.

"Hey, champ," came a voice from one of the couches. "Welcome home."

Immediately recognizing the voice, Zach rushed to the couch as the man arose to greet him with a rough hug. His old pilot, Bob Shanto, smiled from ear to ear. In his mid-fifties, with thinning gray hair and a bit of a beer belly attached to his six-foot-three-inch frame, the Alabaman could still pose for a Marine recruiting poster. He was chisel-faced, and he stood erect. Zach recalled that since his wife and five children had been killed in a horrific car accident ten years ago, he had become a changed man — reclusive.

"Bob, am I glad to see you!"

"Likewise, young Zach. Ya'll sure 'nuff have changed your face. They told us ya'll would look different. But I knew your walk, kid. Kinda wondered if you'd be in a beard and weird black clothes or somethin.'"

"Name's Zach Fuller, Bob. Colonel, USMC. Why would I wear a beard and weird black clothes?"

"Got it," Bob realized he needed to shut his mouth in the day-room about what he had heard regarding Zach's occupation. "Well, my name's Bob Gallagher, Lieutenant Colonel, USMC. So, you outrank me again, ya young stud. . . . Hey, let's get Wally and Jerry up. It's time to catch up."

Bob ran down the hall banging on two doors while Zach waited in the dayroom, gazing at the TV. Zach could hear him yelling, "Get up, you maggots. Ya'll gonna sleep all afternoon? Zach's here!"

In ten minutes, Wally and Jerry were in the dayroom, giving Zach rough hugs and smacking him on the back. He tried to remember what he knew about these brave men.

Captain Wallace Armour, U.S. Navy, Retired. Former Carrier Air Group Commander and A-6 pilot. Divorced with no family except an estranged brother in California. Fell off the side of the earth two years ago so he could fly the clandestine mission. What's he doing now?

And Jerry Casbreau, former Commander and A-6 bomb-nav. Convicted murderer of the man who was having an affair with Jerry's wife. Freed from Leavenworth by Sheridan Stockridge so he could fly as Wally's bombardier-navigator. What is he doing these days?

"It's catch up time," Bob boomed out. "Let's go to my suite for a drink and get Zach caught up on everything."

Ensconced in Bob's living room, they sat sipping their drinks — Bob with a scotch on the rocks, Wally with a gin martini, and Zach and Jerry with cokes. Zach noticed that Bob's room was an exact duplicate of his own — same couch and chair, same TV, which, fortunately, was off.

"So, catch me up," Zach started the conversation. "What have you guys been doing the last two years?"

"I'll start," Bob said. "As I predicted, I settled into a cabin in the woods of western Montana. . . . Just me and my German Shepherd and the bears and wolves."

A cold chill ran down Zach's back as he remembered the wolves with which he and Dr. Peter had had to deal as they were escaping across the Siberian tundra. He once again pictured himself firing Peter's rifle at the largest wolf he had ever seen as it flew off the rock in its attack upon him. Shrugging off the shiver, he concentrated on listening to Bob.

"I got nobody up there in Montana to talk to. Don't really want nobody, actually. Just my dog, Cusser. I'm cool just bein' by my own self. Sometimes I talk to the postmistress at the general store. I go into the village 'bout once a month. She invites me over for supper sometimes, along with her ex-husband, the local cop. Strange arrangement, that one.

"Let's see. Got me a satellite TV. . . . Keeps me up on news and movies. Drink a little scotch sometimes. That's 'bout it fer me. The postmistress and her ex are watchin' Cusser while I'm quote visitin' my sister in Birmin'ham unquote — least that's where they think I am. Got a switch on my phone. In an emergency, they can call me in B'ham. Rings somewhere magic. I don't know. Then it lets me know when a call's come through. I can't be in direct contact with anybody — rules of the road here. But I sure do need to get reports on Cusser.

"Anyway, I was kinda glad when Sheridan found me for this new mission. Can't wait. By the way, my name's not Bob Shanto up there, nor is it here. Name's Bob Gallagher."

"Well, I sure went the opposite direction," Wally said. Closing in on sixty, Wally was good looking, well proportioned, and sported a full head of brown hair. "I decided to settle in St. Thomas down in the Caribbean. I told you I love the sea. I've got a thirty-five-foot sailboat. Live on it, in fact. Except I also own a condo there. Some babes don't like the water."

"Babes? You still chasin' babes, you rascal?" Bob boomed. "You're sixty flippin' years old!"

"Never too old. It's all attitude. By the way, my name is Wallace Johnson, and I'm a retired building inspector. . . . Mind if I replenish my martini?"

"So what about you, Jerry," Zach asked. "What have you been doing?"

"You're not gonna believe this, Zach. I'm a believing Catholic now. Sherry got me set up in an apartment in Milwaukee after the Iran mission. For some reason I can't work out, I stumbled into a church soon after I got there. Before I knew it, I was working at the Catholic rescue mission. One day, the message from the Priest gripped me and I gave my life to Jesus Christ. So now I'm the assistant director of the mission. My name's Jerry DeFrancisco. Because of the, uh, ample retirement Sherry got for me, I'm able to give a lot, anonymously of course, to the work there. Right now, everybody thinks I'm on a hiking vacation in Iceland. But I'm here to fly!"

"So what can ya'll tell us about yourself, young Zach?" Bob asked. "We thought ya'll deserted us at China Lake. Man, was I mad? Then we all heard the Russian mob was after ya'll and we had more understandin.' What's life like fer ya'll, champ?"

"I wish I could be as open as you guys are," Zach said quietly. "But I'm in a bit more complicated situation than you are. Let's just say that I'm with the woman I married back in 1988. We have a young son and we live in another country. Are you ready for this? I'm a clergyman."

A cuss word slipped out of Wally's mouth. "Bob, you and I both have Jesus freaks for B/N's!. . . . Oh well. Maybe they'll be our lucky charms. They've maybe got an in with the Big Guy upstairs?"

"No lucky charms here," Zach said as he smiled at Wally. "Just lots of hard work to make this mission a success, whatever that mission may—"

"Which reminds me," Bob cut in. "We've got a briefing with Juan Ramos and Chico Ramos, the Ramos boys, tonight at 2200. They're goin' to fill us in on the mission. . . . By the way, Zach, we heard that Sherry bought the farm. So sorry."

"Yeah," Zach said with his head bowed. "He was killed parachuting in to get me for the mission. Really sad. He was a good man. We had to bury him up there."

"We'll miss 'im all right. Can't believe he's not with us, gettin' us ready."

CHAPTER SEVEN

May 13th — Yanrakinnot

*J*t had not been a good day for Bethany. Tomas had been sick all night with diarrhea and was throwing up a lot. And Bethany wasn't feeling very well herself.

Mostly I'm just missing Zach. I'm worried sick about him. He's been gone for ten days and I've heard nothing. I'm just scared about all this. I wonder if that's why Tomas is sick.

Plus I'm tired of getting up every morning to a cold house and no husband to start the fire. I'm tired of being both mother and father. And I'm lonesome. I feel like throwing a pity party for myself. I just wish I knew something about Zach.

She heard a soft knock at the door. She knew it to be Leonid's knock. Leonid came by every other morning about this time. She would give him a cup of coffee and they would sit silently together for a half hour in the kitchen. Leonid wasn't much of a talker. And Bethany didn't want to seem like a whiner. If she did, Leonid would tell Peter that he was worried about her. Then the whole village would be at her door, trying to cheer her up. So she just sat silently with him each time he visited. At least his presence was a comfort to her.

Today his moonface was sporting a wide smile. He sat down and accepted the coffee Bethany placed before him. As he smiled, he stared at her.

He's got information for me. Zach?

"Well, Leonid. I thank you for coming to see Tomas and me. How have you been?"

"I am fine, Matushka. I was in Provideniya yesterday."

He's definitely got info. Or else he wouldn't bring up Provideniya.

"And how are things in Provideniya? Have you been visiting with your friend Muk?"

"I did indeed see Muk yesterday, Matushka. He sends you his regards and invites you to come to Provideniya for a holiday. The track vehicle could get you there in just a few hours."

"That's very kind of Muk," she said. *I wish we could just get to the point without all this small talk.* "How is the weather in Provideniya?"

"Much warmer than here, Matushka. The snow is gone in the city. The port may be opening for the season very soon. Sooner this year than last. Some say it is global warming. I think it is just a warm year."

Another knock at the door. *That's Peter's knock. Definitely information for me if Leonid needs Peter to convey it. Hope this is good news.*

Bethany went to the door and ushered Peter in. He sat down across from Leonid and accepted the mug of coffee Bethany presented him. Bethany put a dish of whale jerky between the two men and they began munching heartily.

Tomas stirred and began to cry. Bethany picked him up out of the bassinet and began nursing him. Leonid stared at the top of her breast for a moment as she fed Tomas. Then Peter kicked Leonid's foot under the table and he abruptly looked away.

"Peter, before you leave, can you look at Tomas?" Bethany said, seeming not to notice. "He's got diarrhea pretty badly and his fever is now in its third day."

Peter stared at the baby. "After you have fed him, let me examine Tomas. I may have something in my kit that would help. But I want to check his heart, ears and lungs. It's probably just a spring influenza, but I want to be sure. . . . Matushka, we have a word from Muk."

Bethany felt her heart skip a beat. "What is it, Peter? Good news from Father?"

Peter sat silent for a moment. Then he spoke slowly. "Muk says to tell you that he has word that Father is safe in the United States. He is doing what he set out to do. He will be gone until mid-July. He does not want you to worry."

Bethany let out a sigh of relief as she continued to feed Tomas. "Well, I wish he were coming home tomorrow. But it is good to know he is safe, is it not?" She stifled a tear. *It's not good to let these men see me cry.*

"Matushka," Peter looked into her eyes with a kind expression on his face. "I know this is very hard for you. You love Father passionately. This I know. Leonid and I will watch over you. Leonid will come over every morning to start the fire, if that is all right with you. He loves you as a sister. Would it be all right if he comes over every morning to get things going for you? He'll cause you no trouble."

Bethany saw Leonid's face light up. "Why, that is so kind of you, Leonid. Thank you so much. I accept your offer. Will you be able to stay for breakfast each day?"

"Yes, Matushka. I can stay for breakfast. Is it okay if I bring Father Dema with me sometimes?"

"It is okay if you bring Father Dema every day, Leonid. And Peter, you are welcome also."

"Well," Peter said, smiling. "It sounds like we will have a daily coffee klatch. Three men, one woman, one little boy, and God."

"What a beautiful sentiment, Peter," Bethany responded. *Things are looking up*, she thought. *At least I'll have some good company each day.*

After Bethany completed the feeding, Peter examined Tomas. While he was slightly worried about the buildup of fluid in Tomas' lungs, he said nothing as he gave Bethany some antibiotic pills. He said he would check him tomorrow when he came for breakfast.

Later that day, Mrs. Topchat came over and spent an hour with Bethany. Thus began a steady flow of villagers into the home of the pastor's wife, all carefully orchestrated by Dr. Peter.

Same Day — Hangar Three, Area 51, Nevada

The four crew members were sitting in the hangar ready room in their forest green flight suits. The ready room was a large conference room with ten airline-type seats in two columns facing a white writing board. In the back of the cavernous room were two flight simulators. Four desks also dotted the walls. There were no windows in the room. No pictures on the walls. Just an institutional gray everywhere. On one side was a coffee-maker on a table, with white mugs and the usual creamers and sugar packets. Incandescent lights along the ceiling provided a bright atmosphere.

Two men entered the room, one large and black, the other small and Hispanic. They walked to the front of the room and the short one walked to the podium.

"Welcome, gentlemen. In case you've not already met us, we are the Ramos brothers, Juan and Chico. I'm Chico, the white Spic and this is my bro Juan, the black Spic."

The four airmen chuckled.

"We work for our friendly Company and our job is to get you ready for your bombing mission. Which is kind of interesting since we're both afraid of flying. But that's the Company for you. Its logic escapes me."

More chuckling.

"Our third partner, to assure diversity in the Company, is a Caucasian Jew named Simon Longstreet. So there you have it — a fully diverse CIA team. . . . But wait a minute! You guys don't pass the diversity test. You're all white guys. And you're all old as the hills. Where's the diversity in that? I'll bet you don't even know what a *sopapilla* is. You probably think it's some kind of metamucil."

"Eh? What'd you say?" Juan shouted. "I don't hear so good no more. You say something about eatin' strudel?"

By this time, all four crew members were rolling in laughter.

"Okay. The politically incorrect show's over," Wally called as he tried to recover, his smile literally covering his entire face. "We get it. You young studs are going to get us old ferds ready for the mission. I think this might be more fun than we bargained for. So where's Si, anyway?"

"Should be comin' in the room shortly, sir," Juan responded. "He had to take a phone call."

On cue, Si walked in, wearing a yarmulke. "So, Goyim, you want I should be at your beck and call already!" More laughter.

Frivolity over and everyone at ease, Chico began the briefing while Juan started the power point.

"Gentlemen, you have been made aware that the DPRK is threatening world stability. We know for a fact that they fully intend to launch an ICBM on us on July 4th as a beginning volley to push us off the Korean peninsula so they can take over South Korea. Our government is looking at various options in order to stop the North Koreans. One of those options involves you. Just as you, with the exception of Colonel Zach Fuller, stopped Iran in its tracks two years ago, you may need to go into action again, this time against North Korea."

"This," he pointed to the white board "is a Taep'o-dong 2C/3 Intercontinental Ballistic Missile, nicknamed the TD-2. The North Koreans have rigged up a nuclear warhead on it. After several failures, they are now ready to launch one or more of these missiles at us, and our intel is giving strong indications that they want to do it on Independence Day.

"That's where you come in. You're going to blow these missiles up early in the morning of July 4th, along with a few other North Korean nuclear sites and secret research centers. You'll use the same thousand-pound laser-guided missiles you used in Iran."

Chico let that sink in for a moment as the crews gazed at the power point picture of the TD-2. "But we're going to use a different launch platform this time. The EA-6B Prowler." An airborne Prowler appeared on the screen.

"Si, can you bring the Master Chief and the Master Sergeant in?"

Si walked out and was back in a minute with the two men, both of whom were in khaki work clothes.

"Gentlemen, I would like to introduce you to our two magic makers. Retired Master Chief Wendell Gherkie. You may already know him."

"Hey, Master Chief," yelled Bob. "How ya'll doin?' Are we here 'cus you spent all your bucks from the last time and need some replenishment?" The other crew members showed their appreciation for the Master Chief by yelling similar good-natured insults his way.

"All right, sirs, settle down, will ya?"

Decorum returned to the room. "Master Chief Gherkie is supervising the operation. And let me introduce retired Master Sergeant Washington, expert on the EA-6B. Gherkie and Washington have banded together to convert two EA-6Bs from ECM birds into missile platforms. They have reconstructed the cockpits so that they look very much like your old A-6E cockpits. They've retained some gear from the Prowler, which will be of great assistance to you.

"Later, you can take a look at the simulators in the back of the room. They're working copies of the cockpits you'll park your butts in every night for the next couple months. The Master Chief and the Master Sergeant have a combined team of EA-6B and A-6E retired ground crews. They're top notch and will not only convert your aircraft. They'll maintain them and keep them in an up-status for you. Let's give these guys a round of applause."

The aircrews politely applauded as the two exited the room.

"So here's the plan. Tonight you'll read up on the EA-6B. Study time. And you'll fool around in the simulators, getting used to them. Tomorrow night, I'll give you a good briefing on your bastardized aircraft. Then it will be simulator time. Pilots will start with takeoffs and landings. B-Ns will play with the radar, the infrared, and the laser system. Three nights of sim time and you'll take your first actual flights.

"Oh, and I know you're gonna love this. Your exercise program starts tonight. The tread mills are in the next room."

Groans could be heard from all four crewmen.

"And we'll take a class in land and water survival to get you refamiliarized with escape and evasion. Plus some time on the pistol range. . . . So, you sirs ready to rock and roll?"

"Let's roll," Wally shouted on behalf of the others.

May 14th — CIA Headquarters, Langley, Virginia

Friday morning, Roland James mused as he sat at his desk. *Nothing important happens here on Fridays except the usual Friday afternoon personnel crises. Why do people around here have to wait until Friday to announce their impending divorces, financial woes, and kid problems? Just makes for a lot of weekend work. Wish I could get out of here by noon.*

Just then, Nita poked her head in the door. "Mrs. Kipp wants you, sweetheart."

"Thanks, Nita." *I wish she'd keep the 'sweetheart' stuff for when we're alone in her apartment tonight.* Roland got up and walked to Mrs. Kipp's office. After knocking, he walked in. Sitting there with Mrs. Kipp were the Director of Intelligence (D/I) John Stern and his staff assistant Roger Dempsey.

Roland James sat down in an easy chair beside Roger. Mrs. Kipp was seated behind her desk. She had one of those chairs that could be adjusted for height, and Roland noticed that she had her chair up so high, she towered over the others. *Her little legs are probably swinging in the breeze under her desk,* he thought as he smiled at her.

"Roland," Mrs. Kipp began the conversation. "Thanks for working with Roger in doing part of the fine-tuning for the North Korea operation. Dr. Stern and I would like you to give us an account of where you stand on it. We'd like to have it wrapped up by Monday."

The adrenalin flowed as Roland began to speak. "We've pretty much narrowed down the targets to four: the nuclear reactor at Kumho-Chigo, the Chonma-San uranium enrichment site, and the launch pads at Taechon and Yongjo-Ri—"

"Those are your targets?" Dr. Stern raised his arms in frustration. "What about Yongbyon and Musudan-Ri? Why aren't they on the roster? Yongbyon is the heart of the North Korean nuclear weapons program and Musudan-Ri is the launch site known to be fitted for TD-2s. What's going on here, Mr. James?"

Gotta be careful here, Roland thought quickly. *Gotta carefully pull the wool over his eyes.*

"Dr. Stern," he began, hoping that Roger, whom he had already convinced regarding target selection, would chime in. "Our advanced technology leads us to believe that the launch pad at Musudan-Ri is a decoy. Their military has used it a number of times. We believe it is unlikely they will use the site for the real thing and that we'd be wasting a missile on it. And as for Yongbyon, we don't think an aircraft can get close enough to drop a bomb on it. The site is one of the most heavily defended in the world.

"The targets we've selected, sir, cover a good range for intimidating DPRK, and we believe the TD-2 will launch from Taechon. Satellites have picked up activity there which can be interpreted as getting ready for a major launch. Also, I think they will launch not one but two ICBMs at the same time. We believe the other ICBM will be launched from Yongjo-Ri."

"Do you concur with that, Roger?" Dr. Stern looked at his assistant.

Come on, Roger. Back me up on this.

"I think Roland's estimate has some credibility, sir. The data looks pretty good for the targets he's selected."

Killing me with soft agreement while covering your own butt. Thanks, Roger!

Silence reigned as Mrs. Kipp fiddled with a pen and Dr. Stern looked at his notes.

"I presume you have the technological data to back up your conclusions?" Dr. Stern turned toward Roland.

"We've made some educated guesses, Dr. Stern," Roland answered as flatly as he could. Inside he was bristling. *That idiot is challenging me right in front of my boss. I've got to convince him to back off.* "I believe the data will back us up. And we've vetted this with the other directorates. There is agreement on the targets."

He's not convinced. I can tell that. Let me try another approach.

"You know, Dr. Stern, Mrs. Kipp feels that we probably won't need to launch our strike at all, that the North Korean leadership may be so intimidated when it's leaked that we're thinking about a pre-emptive strike on them that they'll back down before it becomes necessary to bomb them. . . . So in the end, it doesn't really matter what targets we put up, does—"

"Roland," Mrs. Kipp cut in. "My feelings are not germane here. It doesn't matter how I feel. We want the best targets possible in case we have to launch a strike."

Silence. *I've just been cut off at the knees by Thelma. I hate that witch woman.*

"I want your data by close of business today," Dr. Stern said in a matter-of-fact voice. "I may have to do some massaging of those targets."

Then turning to Mrs. Kipp, he said, "How about the aircraft and air-crews?"

"I've talked with Curt Mitchell at NCS. He says his folks have the aircraft and aircrews mated up and beginning their training at an undisclosed airbase. We should have no trouble getting them ready."

"Are these the crews we used the last time?"

"Almost," Mrs. Kipp said. "The two pilots are the same. They're old like us but still absolutely flawless in their airmanship. They've both gotten new names and identities and their former names now have 'deceased' after them in military files. One of the bombardier-naviga-tors was on the last mission. He's listed as a murderer, pulling a life sentence in a maximum detention center in West Virginia.

"The other bombardier-navigator didn't make the last trip, although he was slated to. Got into some trouble with the Russian mafia. Had to get out of Dodge before we made the strike. He's listed as a deserter in military files. He's been living somewhere in eastern Siberia, serving as a priest or minister of some kind. He also has a new identity now and has come out of Siberia to fly the mission.

"All four are sterling. And they'll fade back into the woodwork after the mission. If they die, there's no trail leading back to us. Their finger-prints have been removed from all files and they'll be carrying no ID's. People won't even know what country they're from. We're encouraging them to grow their hair a bit long and sport modest beards so they won't look like American fighting men."

This is good info, Roland thought. *I've got to get it written up and dropped. Sure hope Stern doesn't change my target selection. That would mess everything up.*

"Okay," Dr. Stern said as he rose from his chair. "I'll massage this plan over the weekend. Roger, you'll bring the data and work with me."

"May I assist?" Roland looked sheepishly at Stern.

"Mrs. Kipp." Dr. Stern spoke as he walked out of the room. "I won't be needing your aide for this anymore."

Ouch! That hurt.

After Stern and Dempsey left, Kipp and James sat quietly. Finally Mrs. Kipp looked at Roland and spoke.

"You have embarrassed me for the last time, Mr. James. Monday, I'll see about having you transferred out of here. Pack your personal effects and take the rest of the day off."

With that, she called security. "Can you send someone down here right now to monitor a clean-out, please? Thank you."

Then she turned to Roland. "Remain seated until security arrives." With that, she reached for her computer and began typing. *I'd like to reach across her desk and strangle her right now, but I saw it when she pulled the forty-five out of her desk and laid it in her lap.* It was a long two minutes until security arrived.

Roland cleared out his desk and walked out of the building after turning in his badge. As he made his way to the car, he did some thinking.

I've got to frame this right with my contact. Maybe it's good that I'm being transferred. I've probably gotten as much done here as I could. I'll call in a few chits and get something maybe even more lucrative, some place where I can continue getting info to pass on.

He got into his white Mitsubishi Lancer and drove to the Connecticut Avenue post office. After finding a place to park, he walked in and dialed the combination to his mailbox. Quickly he inserted the information for his contact. Then, looking around and seeing no one, he walked out.

The drop wasn't supposed to be until five, but who cares? Dropping my info three hours early won't hurt anything.

Returning to his car, he drove back to his apartment in Chevy Chase and collapsed for a nap.

Fifteen minutes after he left the post office, Nita arrived, dressed in a burka. She opened James' mailbox *(glad he sleeps heavily. It was easy to find the combination in his pants pocket),* removed the documents, put them into her burka, and inserted a new set of documents into the box. Glancing around and seeing no one, she quietly walked out of the post office.

An hour later, she was meeting with her own contact, showing him what she had found, telling him what had happened in Mrs. Kipp's office, and receiving instructions as to her next action.

That night at seven, Roland James arrived at Nita's upscale apartment in Ballston.

I don't want to eat. I want to make love. I need it after what I've gone through today!

Seeing Nita dressed in a provocative skirt and blouse, he told her that dinner would have to wait. He led her into her bedroom and made love to her in every creative way he could think of. All his concerns and sorrows were washed away as he fulfilled his desires. Nita complied with his kinky wishes.

Later, the two sat and talked while enjoying the dinner Nita had cooked.

I feel so much more relaxed now. Maybe Nita will console me.

"It was just so horrible, Nita. Your boss sold me down the river."

"I'm sorry, sweetheart," she replied softly. "Thelma can be a real witch sometimes. How did it all turn out in the end?"

"That's the trouble. It ended horribly. I'm being transferred on Monday. I had to clean out my desk while a security agent monitored me. Humiliating! My credibility is shot. They'll probably give me some wimpy job in hopes that I'll quit."

"That's just not right, Roland," Nita said as she stroked his arm. "After all you've done for them. It's not fair. . . . Hey! You know what? Maybe I can help find you a new job. I used to work over at the Department of State. Got to know some of the higher ups pretty well. Want me to talk to some people there?"

"State." Roland gazed at the ceiling. "That sounds interesting. . . . But won't they check me out with Thelma the Witch?"

"I can take care of that. I'm her executive secretary, after all. I can speak for her without her even knowing I've spoken. Want me to try?"

"Nita," Roland said, looking at her with a broad smile. "You are terrific."

"It's the least I can do after the way my boss treated you. . . . Now, how about some dessert? I've made strawberry upside-down cake."

"Great! I love that. You're just too good to me, Nita."

Nita went to the kitchen, served up two bowls of cake with strawberries and walked back into the dining room.

Dinner over, Roland decided to reward Nita by making love to her again. Once again, she gladly acquiesced.

After he left, Anatoly came out of the spare bedroom.

"That guy's hormones are unbelievable," he said in Russian.

Nita responded, "I hate him and can't wait to be taken off this project, Anatoly. I wish I could just stab him through his groin area."

"Soon you will be able to reward him in that very manner. But now we still need him. . . . Where can you get him assigned?"

"A while back I had a lurid affair with the executive assistant of Dr. Hiram Nobely, Secretary of State. He's married and so will do whatever I ask him. I think I will call him and demand that he hire this wonderful Roland James, a man with great potential but one who was misused by the hawkish CIA. He'll hire him in a minute. Then we can see what's cooking at State regarding North Korea. James will tell me everything when we have what is called pillow talk. And I'll keep going to his drop right after he does to substitute the info we want P'yongyang to have."

"Good plan," responded Anatoly. "I shall report this."

Same Day — Far East Command HQ, Pevek, Northern Chukotka

Dmitri Plovnic, Russian Army major and executive officer of the Far East Military Command, also secretly in the employ of the Russian crime syndicate *Dolgoprudnenskaya*, sat in his stark office along the waterfront of the city of Pevek. It was two in the afternoon. He was listening intently over the phone. Five feet nine, blond-headed, and in perfect shape, the forty-five-year-old Russian from St. Petersburg had been stationed in Pevek for ten years. He had been hired by *dolgoprudnenskaya* to monitor the movements of his former commander, a Colonel Strasdie, whose death he had helped arrange when Strasdie became a liability to the crime syndicate. Plovnic was now the executive officer to his new commander, Colonel Broshnev, also a syndicate employee. Except that Broshnev didn't know that Plovnic was a fellow employee of the syndicate.

Plovnic had a number of duties in addition to being the executive officer of Far East MilCom. One was to monitor Broshnev. Another was to operate as a clandestine international agent for the Russian government. He was actually the chief *Dolgoprudnenskaya* operative east of the Urals. Broshnev definitely didn't know any of those facts. No one did except his superiors in Moscow, one of whom was speaking to him on the phone.

"We have a special mission for you, Dmitri," the caller was saying. "We have found out that one of the American crew members who will possibly fly a nuclear pre-emptive strike on DPRK actually lives in your territory. We have to find out who he is and where he is training."

"Hmm. . . . Plovnic said as he glanced out the window at the ships entering Chaunskaya Bay. Spring had come early to the north. Most of the snow was gone and the bay was clear of heavy ice. *Something about this sounds familiar.*

"You've got to give me more to work on than that. Searching for him will be like looking for a needle in a haystack. Have you got anything else?"

"Well, we have heard that he lives in eastern Siberia and that he is a priest. There's something shady in all this. Why is an American priest living in Siberia? Does he have papers?

"He has now escaped Siberia and is in America training for the mission, Dmitri. But perhaps he has left family members behind. Perhaps someone in his congregation may know where he is. If we can get that information, we can sell it to the Russian government. They are very intent on keeping up with these developments. See what you can dig up."

Plovnic thought for a moment. *Can it possibly be the American that idiot Lieutenant Beronovski had us free two years ago? The one who escaped from Strefograd gulag? The one I saw in the Anadyr warehouse? If I'm not mistaken, our agents in the USA tried to nab him but failed miserably. Did he come back here and join his queer doctor friend?*

"Yes, I'll nose around. I'll get on it right away."

CHAPTER EIGHT

May 14th — Area 51, Nevada

*T*he four airmen sat in the ready room, listening to Chico Ramos give them a briefing on the aircraft they would be flying. It was close to midnight. For the remainder of the evening, they would go through cockpit familiarization and begin working in the flight simulators. Before being released at eight the next morning, they would also each log three miles on the treadmills and lift weights.

Zach was in a yawning mood as Chico droned on.

"Okay, gentlemen. Let me bore you with some facts. This is an A-6E Intruder." He pointed at the screen.

"Can you repeat that?" Wally said in a deadpan voice as he folded his arms. "Did you say that's an RA-5C Vigilante? Can we see several other photos? Maybe a shot from the top and one from the bottom? I want to make sure I know what an A-6E Intruder looks like so I don't get it mixed up with a P-47 Thunderbolt or a Vigilante, for crying out loud."

"Funny. Real funny," Chico responded. "I do realize that you guys have logged lots of hours in the A-6E Intruder and know it like the back of your hand. Sorry to insult your intelligence. Just hear me out."

All four folded their arms and looked bored.

"The A-6E Intruder is fifty-three feet long, fifty-three feet wide and sixteen feet high. Pictured here is one from Marine All Weather Attack Squadron Two and a Quarter.

"Now this slide shows you an EA-6B Prowler. Notice the resemblance. The Prowler is a derivative of the Intruder. Sixty feet long, same width, and a foot higher. The Prowler is seven feet longer because it's got an enlarged cockpit — holds four people rather than two.

"Pilots, listen up. Center of gravity's different in the Prowler — farther aft. We've had a few Prowlers crash over the years due to the fact that at high angles of attack, fuel migration causes additional shifts in CG with the result that the aircraft has a slightly negative longitudinal static stability. It'll feel different when you fly it. Pay close attention to that when you fly the simulator. Our training syllabus will help you get used to flying the Prowler. Some changes have been made to the aircraft to help you out — leading edge strakes, fin pod extended, ailerons added, reconfigured flaps and slats.

"Okay. Engines. The Intruder had two Pratt & Whitney J52s with ninety-three hundred pounds of thrust each. The Prowler has two advanced J52s with ten thousand-four hundred pounds of thrust each. The Prowler's five thousand pounds heavier than the Intruder, so it gets two thousand pounds more thrust. Got it?"

The two pilots were now watching carefully. The bomb-navs were still slightly bored.

"Top speed for the Intruder? Five hundred sixty-three knots. Top speed for the Prowler? Same. Combat cruise speed for both empty is four hundred-eighty knots. Service ceiling for the Intruder? Forty thousand feet. Service ceiling for the Prowler? Thirty-nine thousand feet. Rate of climb with the Intruder?

Seventy-six hundred feet a minute. Rate of climb for the Prowler as we've got it configured? Ten thousand feet per minute. Faster climb!

"Okay. Let's talk avionics."

The B/Ns got interested.

"We've put together a cockpit in the Prowler that highly resembles the Intruder's — both sides of the aircraft. The backseats are gone, now filled with strapped down black boxes.

"Pilots, you still have the Vertical Display Indicator — your yellow brick road slaved to the B/N's crosshairs. And you've got a heads up display. You will have no trouble converting to this cockpit configuration.

It *is* an A-6E pilot's cockpit. Oh, and we rigged up the terrain avoidance system you had in the Intruders two years ago. You'll need that.

"B/Ns, you've got everything you had in the A-6E, plus some. We've removed the old A-6E ECM and put in some other stuff for you. Jerry-rigged two pieces of equipment from the Prowler. One is an updated ALQ-99 radar jammer. We've invented an automatic mode, which means you just monitor the system while it drives the enemy crazy. One minute, they'll see you. The next they'll see twenty of you. The next you'll be twenty miles from where they last saw you. The next they'll just see snow. You get what I mean? We've also kept the Prowler's USQ 113 for voice and data link jamming. The 99 and the 113 are going to save your lives. As well as drive the enemy crazy, they'll keep him from talking with anybody about the problem or passing you off to somebody else. You will effectively shut down the enemy's air defenses.

"We've also kept the Prowler's INS/GPS navigation system. It'll keep you accurate and right on the money. Offensively you'll have what the Intruder had — good tracking radar, infrared, laser guided bombing, and a truly integrated offensive system.

"Let's look under the airplane. Five stations, just like the Intruder. See here? For the Navy crew, this is what you'll carry. A fuel tank on the center station. A jammer pod each on the outside stations. And a one-thousand-pound nuclear laser-guided bunker-buster, GBU-16 derivative, on each of the inside stations.

"Marine crew, yours will be configured just a little different because we'll have an extra target for you. So you'll have the fuel tank on the center station. One each nuke laser GBUs on Stations One and Two. A conventional GBU on Station Three. And a jamming pod on Station Four."

Zach yawned loudly.

"Am I keeping you awake, colonel?" Chico said to Zach as he frowned.

"Sorry, Chico," Zach said, wiping his hand across his face. "I've still got a little jet lag. Can we take a coffee break?"

"Yeah, let's take fifteen minutes," Wally responded quickly. He was as bored as Zach. "Let's get the preliminaries out of the way so we can start flying, Chico! We didn't come here to sit around on our butts and listen to lectures."

May 17th — Peekskill, New York

Kim Myong Chol stood looking out the window of his condo in Peekskill, New York, twenty-five miles north of New York City. It was six in the afternoon. Set on top of a hill in a religious school turned condo building, his location afforded him a magnificent view of the Hudson River and to the south the Indian Point Nuclear Station Unit 3. The nuclear power plant was the focus of his gaze.

So, he thought. *After all these years of waiting patiently here in this god-forsaken and decadent land, I will have my vengeance. The time has finally come to pay the Americans back for the atrocities they have committed against us, the way they have humiliated us and subjected our people to starvation by keeping us out of the community of nations. Now it is time for the people of America to suffer for a while. I am just grateful that after being a sleeper here for so many years, I can contribute to our finest hour.*

The short, non-descript Korean restaurant manager, age forty-seven, read again the instruction he had received earlier in the day.

Your cell is to go into action the afternoon of July 4th. Agent One will approach the north fence as practiced successfully. Number Two will likewise approach the south fence. Number Three will prepare to move from her security position inside to the reactor control area. At precisely 1:35 New York time, Number One will throw his satchel charge into the fence to create a diversion. He will then run through the blast area firing his rifle until he is shot down. At 1:37, Number Two will throw his satchel charge into the south fence and immediately sneak through to the spent fuel cell rod pool number two, where he will throw two grenades into the pool. At precisely 1:39, Number Three will leave her position, move to the reactor control room and set off her nuclear satchel bomb. Most of the plant security guards will be absorbed in the Independence Day picnic on the banks of the Hudson. Since the plant has just gotten a 'Satisfactory' on its triennial Operational Safeguard Response Evaluation, many of the best security agents will have been moved to another plant to prepare for the OSRE there. The plant's guards will be completely unprepared for your attack. Please congratulate your cell and let them know that their hard work and planning will result in the deaths of two hundred thousand Americans and will convince the decadent American political leaders to withdraw from the Korean peninsula. Your deaths will not be in vain. Your family members in DPRK will be well compensated.

Kim Myong Chol smiled as he re-read the instruction. *Yes. This is as I've imagined it would be. Cesium-37, that rascal radioactive isotope, will spread radiation everywhere for miles. I only wish I could be around to see the devastation. . . .*

Well, I'd better get my cell together so we can drill this operation each day until it is perfect.

Meanwhile, across the continent in Oceanside, California, Yu Sun Shin received a similar message about San Onofre Nuclear Generating Station Unit 2 near San Clemente. The noose was tightening.

Same Day — P'yongyang, DPRK

General Park Rei Cho, Premier Jang Song Thaek, and Minister of Intelligence Pak Dong Sung sat on Jang's Garden patio drinking tea and enjoying the warm, fresh air. It was early afternoon and the sun was shining, making it a beautiful day in P'yongyang. General Park was wearing his combat uniform and Jang and Pak were both in khaki suits.

Minister of Intelligence Pak was speaking. "I'm afraid that our contact in the American Intelligence community who was giving us the information has been fired." He bowed his head and kept his eyes averted as he spoke. A young man not yet forty years old, he had been moved up the ladder quickly because of his intelligence, practicality and ruthlessness. But he knew his position at this point was threatened.

"How could you let this happen, Minister Pak?" Premier Jang looked at him and scowled. "Did you not vet him thoroughly? It is quite unacceptable that he would be fired. Our intelligence is now cut off at a critical time!"

"I apologize, Premier Jang. It's my responsibility. I am at fault and will find a suitable replacement."

"Will you fly to Washington DC and notify the director of the Central Intelligence Agency that you have made a terrible mistake and must now nominate another DPRK spy to take Roland James' place?" Jang's sarcasm cut through the air.

Park noticed Pak do a double take when he heard Jang give the name of the dead agent. *This one is certainly naïve. Does Pak not realize that Jang has his own people watching every move he makes? I'm afraid I know where this conversation is going.*

"Please, sir," Pak tried to negotiate. "I have others in the CIA. I can get one of them to take James' place."

"Do you think I'm stupid, Pak?" Jang's face was taut as blood vessels began to protrude from his temples and neck. "Do you think you have the power to quickly move one of your agents into a position to take up where James left off? No. We have lost valuable information because of your stupidity."

Pak continued to bow his head and gaze off into the garden. "I am sorry. I'm responsible for this strategic blunder. How can I make it up to you?"

Without another word, Jang pulled out his Glock with silencer and put a bullet through Pak's head. As Pak fell out of his chair, Park mused, *there goes another one. Jang will now have to plan a beautiful eulogy for the honorable hero Minister Pak Dong Sung.*

Jang put the pistol back into his pocket and looked at Park. "I'll get a new Minister of Intelligence immediately and get the information flowing again."

Park refused to look at the now dead Pak.

"I understand that the last documentation from our contact in the CIA was that the Americans have changed their plan," Park said as he surveyed the documents Pak had brought, sitting on the table. "They will now attack us with a whole fleet of their famous stealth bombers and fighters. At least, that's what they want us to think. They want to frighten us. I don't buy that they will actually attack us. They don't have the fortitude. I believe this to be a bluff."

"Good insight, General," Jang responded. "We'll just have to do a press release for Minjo Joson and KNCA News Agency. We will let the world know that we're aware that the latest American war games are provocative and dangerous to the Korean peninsula. We'll insist that the world community condemn their aggressive acts. And we will warn of the dire consequences if they don't immediately refrain from their foolish plans. That will put more pressure on the timid American president. Our public relations people and psychologists will come up with just the right wording. Meanwhile, I want you to assume that they will attack with their stealth bombers and fighters. Plan your air defenses accordingly."

"I will comply, Premier Jang. . . . By the way, I notice on my schedule that you and I have a meeting with the Dear Leader tomorrow morning. What is our agenda?"

"Leave the agenda to me, General. We both know that the Dear Leader's hearing is not what it should be. So we will have a prepared script to read him and then have him sign off on our plan. . . . Now, let me get this mess cleaned up. We will meet tomorrow at the Dear Leader's home."

General Park rose, bowed, and left the premises. *Jang seems to believe the phony information we were given,* Park thought as he walked to his car. *It will be my job to keep him convinced that what the documents say is actually the American plan. The trap is falling into place.*

May 18 — New York Times article

North Korea Again Declares Its Independent Spirit
By James Sampson, Staff Writer

Once again, the government of the Democratic People's Republic of Korea (DPRK) is showing its independent spirit.

As if flaunting its growing nuclear weapons program, Dear Leader Kim Jong Il yesterday was quoted in Minjo Joson, "We have recently learned that the corrupt American government is reinforcing its positions on our peninsula. We will no longer tolerate such actions. President Remington and his lackeys should be aware that DPRK has the means to grievously punish the United States should that country continue to harass us. We have the weapons to defend ourselves and the Korean peninsula. Let the Americans be hereby warned. We are ready to use our army and our vast arsenal of conventional and nuclear weapons to push them off our peninsula and free the peoples to our south who been enslaved by their American masters."

Of course, we all have heard bombastic comments before from Kim Jong Il. But he must be taken seriously. He has overseen a complete renovation of his nuclear arsenal since the mid 1990s. Since their apparent scolding by Beijing in August last year, P'yongyang has burst back on the scene by announcing the development of ICBMs capable of hitting US soil. In January, they launched an ICBM that landed a projectile off the eastern shores of the Hawaiian Islands. Last summer, they threw out inspectors of the International Atomic Energy Agency and reactivated their plutonium-producing reactor at Yongbyon, according to the Associated Press.

Neither the American government nor the United Nations Security Council has been able to contain Kim. In spite of U.N. sanctions, North Korea motors on in developing nuclear weapons, ballistic missiles, and other unconventional weapons programs. While Beijing and Moscow continually encourage North Korea to return to six party denuclearization talks, P'yongyang now insists that only the removal of all American Armed Forces from the Korean peninsula will entice DPRK to stand down its weapons development programs.

President Remington must maneuver carefully. The DPRK has a one-million-man army sitting on the DMZ and has Seoul squarely in its gunsights. If the North Koreans chose to come across the border, there would be little Washington could do short of launching its own nuclear arsenal.

Which leads to the speculation that President Remington may indeed be building up his conventional forces on the peninsula. This year's planned Key Resolve/Foal Eagle war games in July and August reportedly will be the largest ever, including South Korean, American, Australian, British, and even Japanese forces, as South Korea begins to look like an armed camp.

Interested people want to know whether Kim's accusations of American bullying on the Korean peninsula have some credence. But how far can this game of 'chicken' go before North Korea, Japan, South Korea and part of the North American continent become a great conflagration of retaliatory thermonuclear attacks?

There is speculation that Kim Jong Il is grooming his youngest son, Kim Jong Un to take his place as he struggles to recuperate from his recent stroke.

Reports are that Kim Jong Un is a chip off the old block, just as belligerent and determined as is his father. In fact, Kim Jong Un's recent press statement is chilling, "The DPRK is determined to sacrifice all rather than become a lap dog of the decadent West. Koreans around the world are hereby called on to come to the defense of the Korean peninsula. I will settle for no less than the total extraction of American troops from our peace-loving peninsula. And we now have the means to make that happen. Or we will gladly die trying."

Chilling, indeed.

May 19th — Seoul, Republic of Korea

President Lee Myung-bak sat restlessly at his desk in the Blue House, official residence and executive offices of the President of the Republic of Korea (ROK). It was a spacious room, covered with ornate light blue carpeting. The Presidential desk sat at the end of the room, a polished birch wood piece. On the desk sat a computer keyboard and large desktop monitor. There were also knickknacks from various foreign governmental figures. A wooden elephant from Thailand, a brass wallaby from Australia, and a gold liberty bell from the USA.

On the walls around the desk were large photos of Lee and his friends. A 'grin and handshake' with the CEO of Hyundai Cars and

Lee when he was CEO of Hyundai Construction. A 'grin and stand together' with the mayor of Tokyo when Lee was mayor of Seoul. A shot with the pastor of Somang Presbyterian Church receiving Lee as an elder in the church along with Lee's wife, Kim Kyung-sook as a deaconess. And a photo of Lee bowing before the Pope when the Pontiff visited the Republic of Korea in 2009.

In front of the desk were four birch straight-backed chairs which matched the desk. And at the other end of the office, a long conference table, once again matching the desk, with eight chairs around it.

The sixty-nine-year-old president was tall by Korean standards, and paper-thin. He wore a black western style suit with white shirt and medium blue tie. The nervous look on his face told his Prime Minister, Han Seung-Soo, seated in one of the straight-back chairs, that all was not well this morning.

Han, older by five years, shorter, heavy set, and wearing almost matching apparel, was a friend of Lee's, who in fact nominated Han for prime minister after Lee was elected president. Lee and Han saw many things alike. Both were Christians, Han a devout Roman Catholic and Lee a Presbyterian. And they had the same feeling about DPRK — fear.

I wonder if this meeting is about North Korea, Han thought as he sat in front of the desk waiting for Lee to address him.

The president looked at Han and spoke. "Have you seen today's *New York Times* article on Kim Jong Il's provocative statements? And those of his son?"

Han had indeed seen the article. His aides spent each early morning scouring the major newspapers for articles related to the Republic of Korea.

"The writers of the *New York Times* are idiots, Mr. President," Han replied. "The article of which you speak simply enables Kim to become even more belligerent. It is reckless journalism and we should protest it to the President of the United States."

"The President of the USA has no power over the public media, Seung." Lee moved quickly to addressing Han by his first name. "But I will protest anyway. In fact, I've called you in so you can listen in on my conversation with him on the hotline."

"Did you read the article in *Minjo Joson,* Myung?" Han also moved to a first name basis with his president. "It is even more inflammatory than the *Times* article. It is obviously a press release written by Kim's people. Why can't we convince the world media that Kim Jong Il is a vegetable and that the leaders running the country use a double for him at State Affairs—"

"We've put it in our papers but the liberal media refuses to pick it up. It is a scandal. . . but the fact is that this article is a message for us, Seung. They're coming for us. DPRK is preparing to invade the South! All the work I put into trying to engage them through investment. . . for nothing. They don't want to invest with us as partners. They want to own us! They want to take our resources and collectivize them, to be the big shots on the peninsula. And they obviously have Beijing convinced that it is good business for them as well. I don't have a good feeling about this. That's why I have a call in to Washington."

As if on cue, the phone rang and Lee picked it up.

"Yes, I'll wait," he told his executive secretary as he punched in 'speaker phone' so Han could listen in.

"Hello, Mr. President," Lee said in English. "It is so good to speak with you. How is your family?"

"And my best to you, Mr. President," President Remington answered politely. "My family's well, thank you. And yours?"

"Doing well. Our oldest grandson leaves for college this autumn. He will attend Stanford. Nuclear engineering. So glad you could assist in getting him admitted."

"Glad to help a fellow Presbyterian, Mr. President," Remington said with a chuckle. "So why do I have the honor of a call from you, sir?"

Han frowned at Lee, who frowned back.

"I am very concerned about the latest article in your *New York Times*. I think you must know the one of which I speak. It is provocative to a great degree. I believe it will further fuel North Korea's flexing of its muscles. . . and I don't understand the writer's comments about this year's war games being the biggest war exercise ever. I don't like my country being described as an armed camp of foreigners. This will not go down well with the leftists in our country. Can you comment on this?"

"Untrue! This year's Key Resolve exercise is actually smaller than it's been in years. I've got my people working on getting a retraction from the *Times*. Unfortunately, the news media is picking it up and spreading it to the world. Heads will roll over this, let me assure you, Mr. Lee. The *Times* has a right to be liberal, but it has no right to make up facts as they go along. . . . How can I help rectify this with you?"

"My intelligence people believe something is going on up north." Lee was handed a note from Han and read it aloud to the American president. "Are you aware that Kim Jong Il has lost control of his country? And that some radicals have taken over? My hunch is that Kim's brother-in-law, Premier Jang Song Thaek, is in charge now. He is dangerous, Mr. President, more dangerous than Kim Jong Il. He just might invade us to see what he can get out of it. Are you aware of these things?"

"Mr. Lee, as much as this worries you, let me assure you we are on top of the situation. I have personally been in contact with the President of the Russian Federation and have received assurances that he will use his back channel influence to contain P'yongyang. And I have a similar call in to Beijing. . . . It's obviously not in our national interest to see you invaded. You are our closest ally. I think we can use negotiation to contain the North Koreans. Every few years they experience a drought and need food for their people. You know that. We'll start quietly channeling some food and supplies to them. I guarantee the food and supplies will shut them up."

"I appreciate your assurances, Mr. President." Lee read another note from Han. "But I must remind you that I live less than one hundred miles from the DMZ and that many of your Americans, both military and civilian, live here with me. Seoul is the number one target of the North Korean government. If the DPRK decides they will attack, we will all be vaporized in minutes. That will not go over well with the American people. And let me also remind you," Lee continued reading Han's note aloud, "DPRK now has intercontinental ballistic missiles capable of hitting American soil, maybe even the North American continent. I would advise you to put this crisis at the top of your agenda."

"Absolutely. Hey, I'm for you, not against you. We'll protect your people and ours as well. We've got every intelligence asset on this crisis. . . . Tell you what. Let's be in weekly contact on this, okay? And maybe your intel people and mine can meet daily to share info. What do you think?"

"Thank you, Mr. President. I appreciate that."

"Hey, I gotta go now. But let's talk this same time next week. So long, Mr. President."

Lee realized he was now holding a phone connected to no one.

"I think I've just been given what the Americans call the brush-off, Mr. Prime Minister."

"I quite agree, Myung. That was definitely a brush-off. And a poor one at that."

"All right. Let's begin reviewing our contingency plans for assassinating the top leaders of North Korea, specifically Premier Jang, and also the commanding general, Park I think his name is, as well as all three of Kim's sons."

"That is a wise decision, Mr. President," Han said as he stood. "I'll bring the appropriate people in two hours from now if that will work for you."

Standing with him, Lee said quietly, "Let us pray about this, Han. We need guidance from our Holy Father. Would you lead us?"

CHAPTER NINE

May 19th — Oval Office, Washington, DC

"*W*hat the heck do we do now?" President Remington threw up his arms as he dropped the phone into its cradle. He was seated at his desk, with the Vice President and the Secretary of State standing in front of him.

"We're in a hurt locker," Vice President Vernowsky said as he scratched his neck. "I think we need to move forward with the planning of a clandestine attack on the Commies' nuke facilities. And, Mr. President, we need to be ready to actually make this surprise attack on North Korea if necessary. Not just a bluff, but a real commitment."

Seeing Remington's frown, he quickly added, "We can do this without claiming it was us who did it. Deniability and all that. But the point will be squarely made. The Commies will back down once they see their beloved nuclear weapons program up in smoke. Let's let 'em have it!"

"I don't much like that language of calling the North Koreans 'commies,' Mr. Vice President." Remington looked hard at Vernowsky. But Vernonwsky returned the stare back at Remington.

He's not backing down, Remington thought. *He's not going to let me intimidate him.*

Finally, the President lowered his eyes and shuffled some papers. "Mr. Vice President, I see your point. Take personal charge of the operation. Make sure it's well planned with complete deniability from us. But do not allow those airplanes to leave the USA without my express permission. Have you got that?"

"Got it," Vernowsky said, stepping back a foot. "I'll contact D/CIA and get up to speed on—"

"Mr. President, I must protest," Dr. Hiram Nobely, Secretary of State, wheezing as usual, interrupted. He unconsciously moved right between the President and the Vice President. "I'm making progress with the esteemed ambassador of the Democratic People's Republic of Korea. . . . He assures me that Kim Jong Il has no plan to attack us. . . or launch an ICBM at us. All Kim wants is respect. He simply wants the recognition that. . . . we have prevented him from having—"

"Are you kidding, Nobely?" Vernowsky shoved him out of the way. "You believe that bombastic slob of an ambassador? He's connin' you!"

"Back off, John." The President stood up from his chair. "Everyone has equal voice in this office. And let's not become school boys shoving each other around."

Vernowsky backed off, but continued to glare at Nobely.

"Do not allow this crazy plan to bomb DPRK, Mr. President. . . . I am making good progress. . . . It's on the United Nations Security Council agenda for next Tuesday. . . . I'm sure we can work all this confusion out. . . . I think you're right to have back-door negotiations with DPRK. Food and technology. That's what we need to assure them of. . . . They just want our help, Mr. President. . . . But they don't know a face-saving way to ask for it."

Vernowsky sighed audibly. "I can't believe I'm hearing this garbage."

The President walked to the window behind his desk and looked out. He stood there silently. The VP and State stood fidgeting in front of the desk. The VP could smell coffee brewing in the anteroom. He wanted some right now more than he'd ever wanted anything in his life.

"Okay," Remington said turning toward them. "We'll follow both approaches. Prepare for both eventualities."

As Nobely started to interrupt, the President put up his hand to stifle him. "Not now, Hiram. I've decided what we'll do. Both approaches until we have a better intel picture of all this. And I'm getting a call into Beijing on the hotline. Surely they can shut down this foolish North Korean rhetoric."

At Remington's request, Dr. Nobely left the office, wheezing a sad farewell. Vernowsky lingered.

"He's a blundering idiot with no international credibility," Vernowsky said as he stood there and looked down at the President, who was now seated behind his desk. "I hope you realize that. He needs to be put out to pasture."

"I know, John," Remington looked up at the Vice President. *Although Vernowsky's an ardent hawk, at least he tells it straight. And I can trust him. I'd better listen.*

"He's also a stinkin' sieve when it comes to keeping classified info quiet." Vernowsky continued his attack on Nobely as he sat down in front of the desk. "Here's what I suggest. Let Nobely talk to the North Korean ambassador until he's blue in the face. Even encourage him to. Now, we have to assume that the ambassador is pumping him for all he can get out of him. Probably complimenting him up the butt. You know how that game works. Nobely's a pushover if you tell him how smart he is.

"Okay, so let's give Nobely bogus data. You tell him you really heard what he was telling you and that you've changed your plans. Let Nobely pass that on to the Commies, er, I mean North Koreans. We'll know if he's passing it on when our own people in P'yongyang report what Nobely's told the ambassador. Then we can fire State with prejudice and get someone in here who will truly represent you. What do you think?"

"As entrapping as your suggestion is, John, I guess I agree with you. We'll let State destroy himself. What do you suggest we tell him?"

"That we're going to mount a major air attack on North Korea's nuclear arsenal, and that we're going to do it on July 10th. Let him know that we think the North Koreans are going to cross the DMZ on July 20th and so we're going to hit them first.

"And that the Key Resolve exercise is actually the means by which we'll invade the North. They don't know that we're aware of their plan to launch a nuke on the 4th. So we'll actually launch our little attack as originally planned on the 3rd. Surprise the heck out of them.

"And we'll allow the South Koreans to do their assassination thing the same day. Cut them off at the knees. They'll fold. And the Chi-Coms and Ruskies will sit there with their pants down. They'll have no choice but to support the collapse of North Korea."

The President of the United States looked at the Vice President with a glazed look in his eyes. "Permission granted to move forward with your plan. But do not allow those airplanes to leave US soil without getting my explicit permission."

"Yes, sir," Vernowsky said as he got up and left the room.

This is a nightmare, Remington thought as he sat there tapping his pen on the desk. *I don't think I can go through with all this. Why is this happening on my watch? I thought my administration would just be about health care and stimulus packages. Somehow I've been co-opted into dealing with an international crisis. And I'm stuck until I can solve it in a non-violent way. I promised that. But at the cost of our position in South Korea?*

Nobely was met at the Oval Office hall elevator by his executive assistant, Franz Rochelle. A native of France and one-time professor of political science at the University of Paris, Rochelle had become a naturalized American citizen. Tall, thin, and in great physical shape, Rochelle enjoyed immense popularity among the elite of Washington.

Rochelle had served as Secretary Nobely's executive assistant for two years. He wore an expensive brown double-breasted suit which highlighted his physique. Always one to catch the eye of the women, he was intimate with any number of government workers, both senior and junior, including Thelma Kipp's executive secretary, Nita.

Standing beside the elevator with Rochelle was Roland James.

As Nobely shuffled up to them, he glanced at Roland James and then said to Rochelle, "Whom do we have here?"

"My new assistant, Dr. Nobely," Rochelle replied happily. "This is Roland James. He's just come over to us from CIA."

Rochelle let that sink in. *The idiot Nobely's going to love what I tell him now. He'll be so happy, he'll kiss me.*

"Mr. James knows where all the bodies are buried at the CIA. He's already been of great help to us. And he thinks like us, Mr. Secretary. Not one of those CIA hawks."

Nobely smiled. "Fine. Fine. Glad to meet you. . . . What's your name? James?. . . . Well, in these trying times, we certainly need you. Welcome aboard."

May 25 – Five Hundred Feet over the Nevada Test & Training Range

"Okay, good buddy," Bob said over the aircraft intercom as he sat in the left seat of the EA-6B Prowler turned missile launch platform. "We're level at five hundred feet. Speed four-fifty on the way to five hundred. Followin' the yellow brick road."

The yellow brick road was Bob's vertical display indicator, which was a screen with a highway in the sky, giving directional, attitudinal, and other pertinent information. Directional information came from the bombardier-navigator's slew stick and computer.

Zach sat in the right seat, gazing into his radarscope. "Roger that. Twenty-four miles at two-seven-five before we hit the initial point. . . . From my side, Bob, this Prowler acts just like the old Intruder."

"Yeah," Bob said as he added power. "But this aircraft has more oomph than the old Intruder. It'll scat! Even with the stealth technology fabric and goop pumped onto the fuselage and wings."

Zach glanced out the right side of the Prowler and could just make out the mountain formations in the distance. It was 0100 on a night without a moon. *No problem. We can take off, fly the mission, and land without ever seeing the ground. Amazing. This airplane's got everything.*

"Okay, Bob. Come right to three-two-zero. We're at the Initial Point. Plan calls for us to descend to a hundred feet for ten miles."

"Three-two-zero, a hundred feet. Speed five hundred. Terrain Avoidance comin' on."

Terrain Avoidance was like an altitude cruise control that kept the aircraft at one hundred feet above the ground no matter where they went. Bob monitored the Terrain Avoidance carefully as the Prowler bounded around in the turbulence, keeping to the heading.

Zach had the target, a large oil tank, in his cross hairs. Locking it up, he went to FLIR — Forward Looking Infrared. "Okay. I can see the target on the FLIR. Climb to a thousand feet."

"Roger, one thousand feet. Terrain Avoidance comin' off."

"The detector head's got a laser lock-on. I'm going into attack." Zach toggled the Attack switch on his stick.

Bob looked at everything carefully. As aircraft commander, he was responsible for anything that came off his airplane. Convinced, he responded, "Lookin' good, Zach. I'm committin' to the attack." He hit the Commit button on his stick, which allowed the computer to release the missile at just the right millisecond.

The missile blasted off its wing pylon and headed toward the target Zach had lasered. Bob pulled hard left and started a one hundred-eighty degree turn as they scurried away. Zach watched on the FLIR as the missile hit the oil tank square in the center.

"BOOM!" Zach yelled. "We hit it dead on!"

"Whisper more of them sweet nothins' in my ear, Zach. And give me an escape headin.'"

"Oh yeah," Zach said as he looked at his flight plan. "Sorry about that. Come left to one-two-zero and climb to five thousand feet."

"One-two-zero and five, aye."

Zach called Control and announced they were departing the target area of the training range.

"We're comin' along just fine, Zach. Turn your oxygen off." Bob removed his oxygen mask and lit a cigarette.

"Wish you wouldn't smoke while we're flying, Bob." Zach looked across the cockpit as he turned his oxygen off. "That's a flight violation, remember? Someday we're going to be blown away when you light up."

"Yeah, well, I can't really walk outdoors for a smoke right now, can I?" Bob took a long drag on his Lucky Strike. "Anyway, as I was sayin' before ya'll so rudely interrupted me, we're comin' along just fine. This is, what, our fifth flight? Kinks are worked out. Ya'll haven't lost your touch. And I think I can still handle this beast pretty good."

"Pretty good? You're brilliant in the cockpit!" Zach called to him. "You were born to fly airplanes."

Bob pulled the power back a notch. "Yeah, I guess I know that. That's probably why I miss flyin' so much. It's a shame to have a talent and not be able to use it. Just wish I hadn't had that heart attack. Lost my license to fly. . . . Did I tell you about the offer I got from a rancher up there in Montana this past winter?"

"No, I thought you didn't mix with the people up there, except for the postmistress."

"Yeah," Bob said with a smile on his face. "Well, she let slip to this rancher that I was some kind of a pilot. So he asked me if I'd teach him to fly. On his ranch. Which is huge. We won't even need to file any flight plans. Nobody'll know we're flyin.' Which means I can fly without a license while I teach the rancher to fly. What do ya'll think about that?"

"I think it's insane, just like everything else you do," Zach smiled back at Bob. "And I think you will take him up on his offer when you get home. Right?"

"You betcha."

Twenty miles from the field, Bob and Zach put their oxygen masks back on, turned on the oxygen, and called the tower for permission to land.

"Roger, Clambake Zero Three," the tower controller called. "Cleared to land Runway Three Two Right. Winds three-zero-zero at ten. Altimeter two-niner-niner-five. Call gear down."

Bob and Zach landed about ten minutes before Wally and Jerry touched down. After parking their aircraft in front of the hangar so they could be towed in, both crews walked into the ready room, got cleaned up and sat in their chairs enjoying soft drinks. Using their hands to describe the flying, they de-briefed one another on their flights.

Juan Ramos walked slowly into the room. All eyes turned toward the big man.

"Bob, your phone went off while you were flying. It's not good news. About your dog."

Bob took the phone and went into the head. The other three looked at Juan, who shook his head slowly while showing a sad face.

A minute later, Bob returned with his head bowed.

"Cusser's dead," he said, choking back tears. "He got out last night and chased down a wolf. Bad move. The whole pack got him. Postmistress's ex found 'im this morning, all torn up. Nothin' he could do but bury 'im. . . . I'm sure gonna miss that dog."

"So sorry," Wally said as he stood and put his hand on Bob's shoulder. "I know that dog meant a lot to you."

"How about if I say a prayer, Bob?" Zach stood and put his hand on Bob's other shoulder.

"That's a bit over the top," Wally said, looking hard at Zach. "Let's keep our prayers to ourselves, shall we? Praying for dogs is a bit much for me."

"Shut up and let him pray." Bob glanced at Wally. "He's my B/N and he can pray if I tell 'im to. And I'm tellin' him to right now."

"Sorry, Wally," Zach replied in a soft voice. "I didn't mean to insult your spirituality. Would you like to leave for a moment while I say a prayer?"

Wally looked at Zach with his hands on his hips. Then he slowly stepped back and lowered his hands down to his side. "Well, go ahead and say some words if your aircraft commander tells you to. I'll just shut up and listen."

Wally put his hand back on Bob's shoulder, closed his eyes and bowed his head.

Jerry stood up and put a hand on Bob's shoulder as well. Juan just looked incredulously at the foursome.

Zach gave a heartfelt prayer, thanking God for the gift of His creatures and especially for Cusser. He also asked for comfort for Bob as he did some mourning for his dog. And he ended by asking protection for the crew members as they flew their missions.

When the prayer was over, they all sat down and were silent.

Finally Wally spoke. "I was off base on my remark, Zach. I am hereby naming you our detachment chaplain. You pray any dad-blamed time you want to. And keep rattling your prayer beads for our mission and our safety. I don't want to do anything to make the guy upstairs mad at me right now. And we can use all the help we can get."

Juan walked to the front of the room, looked at the four crewmen one by one and said in a nonchalant way, "Well, alrighty then, gents. Now that we've had our prayer meeting, let's talk about dropping bombs. Specifically, your bombs. . . on target. Ready to go?"

"Do it, Juan," Wally replied. "Get us smart real fast."

"*Si, senors,*" Juan tried to lighten the mood. "*Que pasa?*"

"We're up for learning about our mission, Juan. Lay it on us."

"*Si,*" Juan said, leaning on the podium. "So far, you've just been practicing flying and bombing. Your bomb scores tell us you're ready for the next step. To learn and practice your specific routes for the July 3rd raid. Let's talk about that."

Note pads came out. The four crewmen glued their eyes on Juan Ramos and his Power Point presentation.

"Once again, Captain Wally and Commander Jerry, you'll be known as the Navy Team. Colonels Bob and Zach, you'll be known as the Marine Team.

"For the Navy Team, watch my screen. Here's your first target — the Tongch'ang-dong launch facility."

"You're kidding us, right?" Jerry giggled. "The place is called Tongch'angs-dong?"

"Funny," Juan said in his usual deadpan. "It's a new facility, geared toward launching the TD-2. Intel says it's one of the two places from which the launch might take place in July. As you can see, it's close to the water on the northwest end of North Korea and not far from the China border. Be careful not to stray over the border! You'll come in from the east, go feet dry, climb the hill and bust the complex.

"After you cream Tongch'ang-dong, you'll head north and then east low level through the valleys and hit the mother of all nuclear facilities, Yongbyon. Major complex sixty miles north of P'yongyang. It'll rattle the capital city. Yongbyon's got it all — two nuke reactors, R&D, fuel fabrication. You're going to hit the newest reactor they just got up and running. In the process, the bunker buster will take out their other reactor and then fly through the ceiling of their underground labs. One big mess. A little more collateral damage there, but once again, because the complex is away from populated areas, not too much. Nuclear fall-out will not be major because the bunker-buster will be in the bunker. Mushroom cloud won't be that big. Fallout will be concentrated.

"After you hit the second target, you'll stay low and exit out the east side of the country over the Sea of Japan, go one hundred-twenty miles out to sea and eject. If you run out of gas first, try as hard as you can to get out over the water. We don't want one of our aircraft crashing on land where it can be found and identified. Fuel's going to be tricky, I'll give you that. Any questions on your targets?"

Wally piped up. "How serious is the fuel concern?"

"It's a serious obstacle. We'll talk about it as we get into the planning. You'll be able to refuel in-flight down south before going low level, but you'll have to really pull back on the power to save gas before you get near the target. We think you can make it barring unforeseen problems."

Hearing no further comments from the Navy team, Juan turned to the Marines.

"Marine Team," Juan said. "You will take out the other major launch pad. See it here? Musudan-ri on the northeast coast. You'll hit it from the south at the same time the Navy Team's hitting their first target. As with the western missile launch site, this one sits just off the water. You'll be launching your missile while you're still feet wet.

"After you pulverize Musudan-ri, you'll do a right one-eighty and then east and north low-level over the sea till you get to your second target, the Ch'ongji high explosives and R&D site. See the buildings here to the south of town? The big one is called the East Sea Light Electric Factory. Nothing light about it. Chemical weapons, surface-to-sea weapons, even SAM-7s. Your bunker buster will take out everything above ground and below, and the high explosives stored there will take out the rest of the complex. Collateral damage might be a little higher here, maybe a few thousand. Questions?"

"Okay so far," Bob said. "But we've also got a conventional bomb aboard. What do we do with that?"

"Classified right now. The target for your conventional laser guided missile is over here on the south side of Mount Mantap. See it here? Can't tell you what it is right now. You may not be ordered to hit it. But if you are ordered to hit it, you'll make a hard left after hitting the Yong-dok complex and head into the hills. It's about fifty miles inland. After you hit your targets, you'll also exit east out to sea one-hundred-twenty miles to this point here and eject. Any questions?"

Hearing none, he began to wrap up. The screen went blank.

"We're going to use both the enhanced ALQ-99 and the USQ-113 to help you get in and out without being shot down. We'll assist you with a little satellite jamming. With the jammers/deceivers you've got, you'll have the enemy radar guys so confused they won't know which end is up. And when you blast their communications and data links, they'll be shut down until you finish your work. Tomorrow night, we'll have a class on how to use them, when, what altitude, etcetera.

"Okay. That should wrap it up. Go ahead and jog three miles on the treadmill and we'll call it a night."

As the aircrews filed out of the ready room, Zach was pensive.

It's looking more and more like we'll actually fly this mission. I need to be prayed up and I need to pray fervently for both aircrews. And I need to pray that we don't actually have to do this. Boy, do I miss Bethany and Tomas! I think I'll write to them when I get off work in the morning.

Wally sidled up beside Zach and whispered, "Zach, you got a minute after work? I need to talk with you about something."

"Sure, Wally. Drop by my suite when you're ready." To himself, he thought. *So much for writing to Bethany.*

At nine that morning, after chow, Wally tapped on Zach's door.

"Come on in, Wally," Zach said as he opened the door. Wally glanced left and right and quickly walked in.

"Okay," Wally said quietly. "Here's the deal, Zach. I've got what I'd call a spiritual problem here."

Zach motioned Wally to sit in the lounge chair while he sat on the couch. Some Sixties music was playing quietly on the radio. Zach recognized 'You Just Keep Me Hanging On' by the Supremes.

"Well, can I say a prayer for wisdom before you let me know the problem?"

"Fire away," Wally responded, bowing his head and closing his eyes.

Zach prayed and then looked into Wally's eyes. *Lord, help me to help Wally as best You and I can.*

"I think all that religious stuff you've been spouting is getting to me, Zach. All I can think about is getting things right with the big guy upstairs. You've got me reading a Bible! I've never read the Bible. Thought it was for religious nuts.

"And the funny thing is that I am agreeing with what Jesus says in there. Zach, I want to change my life. Stop chasing women who care about little except my money. Start praying and living for God. . . . Oh man, I can't believe I'm sayin' this. . . . So, what do I do now, chaplain?"

"Wally, I know that in your heart you're a good man. I'm not surprised to hear that you want to become a believer. Let me ask you a few questions."

"Go. I'm all ears."

"Okay. These women you've been chasing for so long. Are you truly sorry you've offended God and His design for you?"

"I'm saying I'm sorry and I'm believing it."

"Okay. So right here, right now, and out loud, tell God you're sorry for your sins."

Wally hesitated. Then he bowed his head and spoke. "God, if you're up there, I'm sorry I screwed up so many times. . . . Please forgive me."

"That's great, Wally. According to the Bible, you have just taken the first step to salvation. It's what the Bible calls repenting. You've repented of your sins. . .

"Now for the second question. Do you believe that God loves you so much, He sent His Son Jesus to shed His blood for your sins and bring you into a relationship with Him?"

"I heard you talking about that in your chapel service. I just have a hard time believing God can love me after all I've done. I personally am not sure I'm worth it."

"Wally, in God's eyes, you worth it. Even if you don't feel you're worth it. Just believe the Bible. Listen to John 3:16, 'For God loved the world — that's you — so much, that He gave His only Son, so that all who believe in Him — once again, that's you — shall not perish, but will have everlasting life.'

"That's what we call salvation, Wally, and that's what God wants to give you free of charge — eternity in heaven. When you believe in what Jesus did for you, you can be confident that when you finally die and close your peepers on this earth, you'll open them looking into the loving eyes of Jesus. . . . So let me ask you that question again: Do you believe that God loves you so much that He sent His Son Jesus to shed His blood for your sins and bring you into a relationship with Him?"

"I do."

"That's right, Wally, let's you and me receive Jesus into our hearts. Repeat after me."

Wally looked at Zach as tears welled up in his eyes. "All right. I'm ready to do this."

"God, thanks for saving me for heaven."

Wally repeated the phrase.

"Based on my repentance, I receive Jesus as my Lord and Savior."

Wally repeated the next phrase.

"Come into my life and change my heart. I want to live for you."

Wally repeated that phrase slowly.

"Amen. . . . That's it, Wally. You are now in a relationship with Jesus your Savior."

"All right! Man, this is great! Thanks, Zach. I feel completely clean for the first time in years. What's next?"

Zach pulled a booklet out of his briefcase. "Read this from cover to cover. Follow the Bible readings. Apply the principles to your life. And let's meet for an hour every other day to go over it."

Wally looked through the booklet. "Suppose I can do that. . . . But one thing, Zach. Let's keep this just between us. I don't really feel up to talking about my conversion to the others."

"I understand your position. And I will respect that. But hopefully, you'll soon feel bold enough to share your faith."

"I'll work on that, chaplain. I truly will. . . . Well, I'd better be going. We both need some shut eye. How about it if we meet day after tomorrow — same time?"

"Works for me. Congratulations on becoming a believing Christian, Wally."

Wally grinned from ear to ear as he left.

After he was gone, Zach prayed fervently for Wally and his new way of living. He prayed for the safety of Bethany and Tomas. And he ended with his daily conclusion:

"Lord, if there's any way for us to avoid firing those nuke missiles, make it happen. In Jesus' name, Amen.

CHAPTER TEN

May 28th — Office, Secretary of State, Washington, DC

*R*oland James sat at his desk in his new office. It was the typical government office of an up-and-coming executive. White walls with an autographed 12″ by 14″ picture of President Remington above his desk. Below it an autographed picture of Hiram Nobely, Secretary of State. Various other patriotic pictures on the walls. Cherry veneer bookcases on one wall, full of law and history books and classics he'd rented. A desk covered with the same veneer, cheap but better looking than the gray metal monstrosity he'd been issued at the Company. A vase with flowers sat on the desk, with sweet-smelling lilacs. At the front of his desk, was a brass nameplate, with the inscription "Roland James, Special Assistant to the Secretary of State." Two fabric-covered chairs with an end table between them were positioned near the wall opposite from his desk.

Having been in the office for two weeks now, Roland was already thinking about changes he would make. *I really want to get rid of those cheap, patriotic photos on the walls — get some good quality prints up there instead.* He stood and looked out his window at C Street Northwest. *Friday noon. Why aren't people out there jogging and milling around?* Then he remembered. *Memorial Day Weekend. Everybody's already left town to avoid the traffic jams. Memorial Day. What a stupid idea Memorial Day is. Memorializing a bunch of soldiers who didn't know enough to avoid getting done in by their enemy? Typical of this country, though. That attitude is why the USA is so weak. Memorializing the stupid. Well, it won't be long before my country cuts this one down to size. I can hardly wait!*

Franz Rochelle, Executive Assistant to the Secretary of State, poked his head in and smiled at Roland.

"*Mon ami*, let me take you to lunch, no?" The Frenchman smiled. "To celebrate the American Memorial Day."

"Sure, Mr. Rochelle. Thanks for asking."

Roland grabbed his suit coat from his chair, threw it on and hurried along behind Franz. *I love the treatment they're giving me here*, he thought as he caught up with Rochelle and walked to his left. *The executive assistant to the Secretary of State taking me out to lunch? And all I have to do is keep filling him in on the workings of the Company. Heck, when I run out of stuff I know, I'll just make it up as I go along. This Frenchman's got about as much brainpower as a pig. He'll believe anything I tell him. Can't wait to fill Nita in on this job she got me. Tonight's the night. I just wish I didn't have to look at her face. She's not all that bad from the neck down.*

Franz led him to the elevator, where they boarded and descended to the third floor. As they approached a door and walked in, Roland noticed the sign on the door. **Senior Executive Dining Room.** *Holy smokes. I'm going to eat with the muckity mucks. I can't believe it.*

The waiter led them to a small private dining room off the main room where Hiram Nobely sat wolfing down a lobster salad. Roland smelled the lobster and his mouth started watering. He glanced around. *Plush. The carpet's so padded, it feels like a mattress. And look at the table set-up. Straight out of Paris. I'm gonna love this.*

"Welcome. . . . welcome," Hiram said in his wheezing voice, barely looking up from his salad. "Glad you two could join me."

Franz and Roland sat to the left and right of Hiram. The waiter brought each of them a lobster salad.

"Hope you don't mind fish, gentlemen." Hiram asked for a second salad. "I don't eat meat on Fridays. . . . Spiritual discipline."

I thought they dumped that concept with Vatican II, Roland thought, but of course he said nothing.

"Ah, we will enjoy the lobster, I'm sure, *monsieur,*" Franz replied. "The French cooking here is second only to Paris. *N'est-ce pas?*"

They sat silently while they ate their salads.

The waiter removed the salad plates, whisked the table clean, and then brought more rolls. Hiram put three of them on his bread plate, plus several huge slabs of butter. As he spread butter all over one of the rolls, Hiram looked up at Roland.

"Mr. Rochelle tells me you have been very valuable to him. . . . So glad to hear that your vast experience at the. . . hallowed halls of the Central Intelligence Agency has been a definite benefit to State. . . . Thank you so much."

Roland blushed. "Glad I can be of service, Mr. Secretary."

The waiter came back with three plates, each with a monstrous lobster tail, a bowl of melted butter, an ear of corn, and a slice of watermelon. He placed a plate in front of each diner and began to walk out, only to be interrupted by Hiram.

"George, pour me another glass of chardonnay. And pour my friends some as well."

The waiter went out for the wine.

Roland tasted the first bite of buttered lobster tail. *This tastes as good as it smells — heavenly. I wonder if they serve seconds.*

Hiram pointed a fork at Roland. "There's something I want your advice on, Mr. James."

Hiram stuck another forkful of lobster into his mouth and began seriously munching. The waiter came back in with the wine and filled each of the three glasses.

"How can I be of service, sir?" Roland responded. *How do I eat the corn? Hold the ear and plow in with my teeth? Is that proper etiquette? How's Franz doing it?*

Noticing Franz daintily slicing off the kernels with his knife, Roland began to do the same, until Hiram picked up his ear of corn with both hands and did the buzz saw routine with his teeth. *Now I'm really confused. Think I'll just skip the corn and stick to the lobster tail.*

"I've been briefed by the President," Hiram said between large bites, "that his *quote* pre-emptive strike *unquote* on our North Korean friends will be a massive attack by several squadrons of our latest airplanes. . . . But earlier I was led to believe that we would do a quiet, clandestine attack using only a few airplanes, none of them claiming to be from. . . the United States of America. . . . I'm wondering which it will be so that we can plan appropriately. . . . What did you hear over at the Company?"

Before Roland could respond, he looked at Hiram's plate and saw that it was empty. *How did he eat a whole lobster tail, an ear of corn, and a watermelon wedge in that short a period of time? Plus all three rolls. I'm only on my third bite of lobster!*

Composing himself, Roland said, "I don't know where this massive strike idea is coming from, Mr. Secretary." He was thinking while he was speaking. "That's totally different than what we were planning at CIA. We were talking about taking two EA-6B Prowlers, converting them to missile platforms, and using them to hit some nuclear facilities in North Korea. The pilots would fly the aircraft into the sea after the attacks so that no one could blame the USA. The idea behind our plan is, or was, that the North Koreans would cave in on their nuclear weapons ambitions once they experienced the fact that they could be hurt badly before they could even fire a nuclear weapon."

"And what was the timing of your attack, Mr. James?" Hiram waved at the waiter, holding up his plate and pointing toward the kitchen.

"I believe we didn't have a specific date yet. Sometime in July was what I heard."

Another plate of lobster tails and corn appeared from the kitchen and was placed before Hiram, who immediately dug in.

"And Mr. James." Hiram slathered another roll with a huge slab of butter. "Was there ever any discussion, of running your mission out in the open? Maybe even warning DPRK about it ahead of time?"

"No, sir," Roland said, taking another bite of lobster. "None."

Hiram looked at Franz. "Mr. Rochelle, we are either being sold a bill of goods by the President of the United States of America. . . . Or he has taken a completely different tack than CIA has suggested he take."

"Why would he not take CIA's advice, *monsieur*?" Franz drained his wine glass and motioned for more.

"Because he doesn't trust General Rogers, the director of the CIA, that's why." Hiram smiled as he downed another large bite of lobster and then did the buzz saw trick with his corn. "President Remington has no intention of launching a mission against DPRK. That's why he's changed the plan. . . . By leaking that he will conduct a massive bombardment attack, he is banking on the fact that Moscow and Beijing will convince our North Korean friends to back off. . . . It's a brilliant strategy, Franz. . . . He keeps Rogers and CIA busy doing their little mission plan. He confuses the intelligence communities of several nations as they all try to figure out which type mission he has planned. . . . And after he's gotten the full attention of Russia and China, he negotiates with the big boys to come to a practical settlement. It's brilliant. . . . Now, how do I get credit for it?"

Roland dropped his fork. *What? Nobely's going to try to take credit for it? How can I get in on this?*

Picking up his fork and clearing his throat, Roland said, "Mr. Secretary, I think that that is the strategy I heard you talking about last week. You talked about keeping the diplomacy going. Keeping all options open. Surprising the North Koreans into a settlement that might include a payoff for them. I think the President borrowed your strategy, sir. . . and it is brilliant statesmanship, if you ask me."

"You like it?" Hiram looked affectionately at Roland. "Glad you realized so quickly that it is actually my strategy the President is claiming as his own."

Then turning to Franz, Hiram continued, "Here's your homework assignment for this weekend, Mr. Rochelle. Number one: How do I officially get behind the President's new plan? Number two: How do I get General Rogers into a position where he appears before the President as a mindless hawk? Number three: How do I let the world know that I was the brains behind the President's new plan?

"I'd like you to brief me on your ideas first thing Tuesday morning. And please include Mr. James here in your weekend homework assignment."

"*Oui, oui, monsieur.* We shall have it ready for you *toute suite* Tuesday morning."

Hope this doesn't mean we have to work tonight, Roland thought as the cheesecake arrived.

That night in Nita's apartment, Roland had his way several times with Nita as she complied with his wishes.

As they lay together in bed, exhausted, Roland turned to her and said, "Yeah, Nita, my new job at State is going great! I went to lunch with the Secretary of State today. Just the Secretary, his exec assistant and me."

That's really romantic after-talk, Nita thought. *Now this bozo's going to bore me with his great accomplishments after one week as a State peon. How long must I endure this stuff? Maybe I should tell him how much hotter Franz Rochelle is in bed.*

"Sounds good, Roland," she replied, stroking his arm. "Are they trying to pry CIA secrets out of you yet?"

"Yeah," Roland said, sitting up in bed and taking a sip of scotch. "But I'm taking them on a wild goose chase. They won't get anything true out of me about CIA. . . . One thing I need to ask you about, though."

"One thing?" She sat up beside him, covering her body self-consciously. *Here it comes. He's going to pump me for info and I'll give him the lies we want him to have.*

"Yeah." Roland took another sip of his drink and lay back down. "Nobely seems to think that our pre-emptive strike plan is actually just a bluff — the threat of a massive attack by our stealth bombers and fighters if the North Koreans as much as lay a finger on their missile trigger finger. Have you heard anything about that at the Company?"

"A lot has changed since you left, Roland." *I think I can get him to believe this.* Nita lay back down and began stroking his arm romantically. "You know, one of the dumber things Thelma Kipp does is to leave her door open when she's on the phone. I can hear everything she says! And she's been on the phone a lot with Dr. Stern. He's changed the whole scenario, Roland. What Nobely told you is the new plan. It's changed. The threat of a massive strike will be leaked so that the North Koreans will shiver in their boots and shut down their plans to hit us or to invade the South. Good plan, if you ask me. But I'm just an executive secretary. What do I know?"

"Yeah, good plan," Roland said. "But what about the plan we were working on — with the EA-6B Prowlers?"

"That plan has been thrown out, Roland. It's done."

"Hmm." Roland took another sip. "I'm meeting with the executive assistant tomorrow to form a State response. We'll support the new plan."

"Is the executive assistant, Franz whatever his name is, aware of the new plan?"

"Seems to be. I'm not sure how to take that guy. He's seems kind of slick to me. I'm not sure I can trust him."

You idiot. Of course you can't trust him. He'll use you and lose you. "Yes, I think you can trust him."

"Is he the one you had the affair with, Nita?" Roland looked into her eyes.

Nita flinched. "Not an affair. A fling. A one night stand. He took advantage of me when I had too much to drink. That's all. . . . You're not jealous, are you?" She smiled at him and winked.

"No, but I do think of the two of you, you know, together, when I see him."

"Well," Nita said softly, kissing him on the cheek. "Don't let it affect your behavior around him. It was just one of those little things that happen sometimes. Won't happen again, I'll tell you that."

"That's what I like to hear."

"Ouch." Nita put her hand to her head. "Roland, I've had this killer headache all day. And now it's back. Do you think we can call it a night?"

"Sure, Nita. Sorry. I've got to get up early tomorrow anyway."

Roland got dressed and left the apartment. When he got to his car, he got his laptop out. *That new plan sets us up for a victory,* Roland thought. *The President's too weak to carry through with his threat. He still thinks he can negotiate himself out of this. Oh, he'll threaten, all right. Meanwhile, we'll stuff a nuke down his throat and then pour across the DMZ before he can figure out what happened to him. This is excellent.*

Roland quickly typed out his report, printed it on his portable printer and drove to the drop.

Ten minutes after he left the drop, Nita showed up, took out his report, and put hers in the box and went home.

May 29th, 2010 — Tongch'ang-dong Launch Facility, DPRK

Premier Jang Song Thaek and the future Brilliant Comrade Kim Jong Un, youngest son of our Dear Leader Kim Jong Il, stood on a platform looking down on the new control room of the Tonch'ang-dong Launch Facility. They were deep in the woods of northwestern Korea. A jubilant General Park Rei Cho, Commander of Forces of the DPRK, was showing them around.

"Gentlemen, we have everything ready," Park said loudly as he stood there with them. "We have practiced and we are ready for our patriotic launch of the TD-2."

The Control Room was deep beneath the earth just to the west of the launch pad. It was a room about the size of a basketball court. On the walls were screens showing 'live' the platform from which the TD-2 would launch above them at Tongch'ang-dong, as well as the platform from which the TD-2 with the nuclear warhead at Musudan-ri would launch. There also were live shots of the DMZ Checkpoint Charlie and the runway at Osan Air Base, Seoul, South Korea. At twenty consoles scattered around the control room sat white-coated scientists and technicians quietly going over procedures on the intercom. The floor, walls and ceiling were polished gray concrete.

"And how will we launch our TD-2s if the Americans do a preemptive strike and blow this all away?" Kim Jong Un said with a defiant voice. Kim was tall for a Korean, almost six feet, and developing the paunch of his father. He was dressed in the typical suit worn by Korean officials.

As he heard the question, Park hesitated. *This one will take much teaching in diplomacy,* Park mused. *He is obstinate and too confrontational.*

Before General Park could answer, Premier Jang took over.

"Relax, nephew," Jang said with just a hint of impatience. "Our intelligence people high up in the American government have assured us that the Americans think we will launch on July 20, and so they plan to frighten us by threatening a launch of their stealth bombers and fighters on July 10. But we will launch on July 4, their Independence Day. We also have a few surprises for them on their own soil, thanks to our sleeper cells. They will be so confused by all this and by our subsequent SCUD attacks on their Osan and Kunsan Air Bases, they will not launch a strike against us—"

"How do we know they will be all that confused, uncle?" Kim cut in. "They have a formidable ICBM fleet. They will likely retaliate by launching their nuclear arsenal on us."

"Please," responded General Park. "Let me explain, Brilliant Comrade." *Perhaps calling him by his future title will shut him up enough to listen.* "We have excellent intelligence. The American president is weak. In his private meetings, he denies the seriousness of the threat. He has promised his constituency that he will be able to negotiate peace everywhere in the world. And he actually believes that. He sees himself as the Great Peacemaker.

"Meanwhile, we are already providing information to the world that the Americans are being provocative in planning their large war games so close to the DMZ, that we have interrogated their spies and found that the Americans actually plan to invade us. The world is beginning to distrust America's actions on our beloved peninsula. Some of their allies are even speaking of canceling their participation in the war games.

"And the Chinese and Russians will respond to our July 4th strikes by quickly calling an emergency meeting of the Security Council of the United Nations before the decadent Americans can respond militarily. Then our allies will tie the USA up in diplomacy for as long as possible, advising them not to respond militarily but to allow the Security Council to get to the bottom of the problem.

"After two days, we will claim that American soldiers penetrated the DMZ, giving us no choice but to counterattack. As we pour across the DMZ with air, tanks, and infantry, backed up by long-range artillery, we will demand that all Americans leave the peninsula immediately or face dire consequences. The American president and his advisers will see the futility of staying. And the president is afraid to launch his nuclear forces. They will withdraw. The victory will be yours, Brilliant Comrade."

Silence.

Finally, Kim Jong Un looked straight into the eyes of Park and said, "If this works, I will make sure you are decorated for your illustrious execution of our plan in saving the Korean Peninsula. But if this plan does not work, General, I will personally see that you are blamed and executed for your attempted coup. Do you understand me? This had better work well."

Park averted his eyes as Kim spoke, glancing at Jang instead.

"Nephew. Nephew." Jang pointed his finger at Kim. "You must not speak that way to our people. It is most inappropriate. Surely General Park knows the risks involved in this operation. He is a dedicated, loyal warrior who has served your father well over the years. I believe an apology from you is in order."

"Apology?" Kim put his hands on his hips and looked at his uncle. "You are dreaming. We apologize to no one."

Then, turning to Park, he said, "Remember what I said, General. Do not make a mistake on this."

Turning back to his uncle, he said, "I've seen enough. Get the helicopter ready, Uncle. I have an engagement back in P'yongyang."

As the three walked silently out of the control room, Park's mind was moving a mile a minute.

So, I must report that I will not be able to prop up Kim Jong Un as my puppet. I must assassinate him as well as Jang. I can, however, control Un's brother, Kim Jong Chol. But he's so effeminate, I'll need to work with him on taking on a tougher exterior.

June 1st, 2010 — Yanrakinnot

The *Spirit of Oceanus* arrived in the bay off Yanrakinnot with the first group of tourists to arrive for the season. It was noon and lunch had just been served aboard the two-hundred-ninety-five-foot cruise ship. It was jacket weather. A fine mist was falling, a menace but not a showstopper for the tours. All one hundred passengers debarked by inflatable 'Zodiacs' and headed for adventures in and around the village. Some tours would start at the reindeer herds, some at the whaling museum, and some would take track vehicle rides into the mountains. All would return to the village to spend time buying souvenirs before enjoying a wild game barbecue and native dancing on the beach in the evening, if the weather allowed.

Andrei Rubtzova and Julian Taft came ashore on their own small inflatable. After securing the raft, Andrei pulled a photo out of his shirt pocket and studied it.

So. Let me see if I can find this woman. If she is the Matushka, she should be in the Pastor's home. . . unless she has fled. I'll just nose around on my own.

He and his fellow crew member entered the village, not following a tour. They were an interesting pair. Andrei Rubtzova was a tall, middle-aged Russian, with dark hair, large face and nose, and not a bit of fat on him. He was dressed in the blue work clothes of the *Spirit of*

Oceanus crew. He was, in fact, an engineman. His crewmate was a New Zealander who had been with the ship since its transfer from New Zealand to Russia a year before. Much smaller and heavier than Rubtzova, the blond-gray-headed Julian Taft was the Chief Engineman of the boat and was also dressed in matching blue clothing. The two had become friends when the tour started a week ago, so Julian was happy to oblige Andrei by joining him on a self-guided tour of the village.

Rubtzova walked up the dirt street, followed by Julian.

"This is not the prettiest village in all Chukotka, Andrei," Julian remarked as he looked from shack to shack. Paint had long ago faded from most of the small wooden and plaster dwellings, which were built with no particular pattern or style up and down the main street.

"Julian, this is your first Chukotka village. They all look like this! These people are Yupiks and Chukchis. They are stupid and their homes reflect their stupidity. Get used to it!"

"Do I hear Russian prejudice coming out of you?" Julian smiled and winked.

"Just objective observation, Julian. These people are idiots. They have no common sense. Trade them a few bottles of vodka for their furs and watch the fireworks. In fact, I may do that tonight before we leave, just for fun.

"But there is one building in the village that's always kept beautiful: their church. They are devout when it comes to keeping their church up, I'll say that for them. I think it's up this way."

The two continued up the hill, took a left turn, and arrived at the church building. The sign in front of it said in Russian, 'Church of the Transfiguration.' The exterior was of large stone construction, with a gold, wooden rounded cupola bearing a Russian Orthodox cross at the top.

They walked into the building and stood in the darkness. Candles were lighted along one wall, casting long shadows through the building. The scent of incense still hung in the air from the Divine Liturgy that had been celebrated two days prior. Ornate ornaments hung from chains. Beautiful icons of Biblical and Russian saints adorned the walls. And at the far end was the Iconostasis.

"I say," Julian said, pointing to the large partition. "That is really lovely. I've never seen anything quite like it."

"It's the Iconostasis. Every Orthodox church has one. It's a partition. Separates man from God. On our side, which is the larger side, we have man's territory. This is where we all gather for worship."

"But no pews?" Julian looked around. "In our churches in New Zealand, we have rows of seats for people to use while worshiping. All I see here are some benches along the walls."

"We stand to pray, Julian. It is our way. . . . As I was saying, through the doors in the partition, the priest goes over to God's side. On that side, the priest prepares the holy bread.

"You see the icons on the partition? Most all churches have the same designs. See on the left? That is the Virgin Mary and the baby Jesus. That's called the 'Incarnation.' Now if you look to the right, you see Jesus coming back to earth. That's called the 'Second Coming.' And on the doors, you see the four Gospel writers, Matthew, Mark, Luke and John. And you see there? That is the angel announcing to the Virgin Mary that she will become pregnant with Jesus. And finally, I'm sure you recognize that one: The Last Supper."

"You certainly know your religion, Andrei Rubtzova. You could lead a tour of churches. I didn't know you were so religious."

"Knowing about religion and being religious are two entirely different things, Julian. I grew up in an atheistic nation. It was forbidden to be religious unless you were old. So with that forbidden challenge, I found out all I could about our national church. But I certainly do not live by its tenets. Too ancient to be relevant. . . . But its churches are beautiful and mysterious. I always look at the local church whenever I can."

"May I help you?" They heard a voice in broken Russian. A man entered the church.

Who might this be? thought Andrei. *Maybe I can get some information from him.*

"Hello," Andrei responded with a smile. "We are from the ship. Just admiring this beautiful church. Are you the Father?"

"Not the Father," the Yupik answered, walking up to them. "I am the administrator, Leonid."

"And where is the Father?"

"Out visiting the sick. Would you like to have a consultation with him?"

Got to be careful here. I don't want this guy getting suspicious of me. "I was told by a friend in Anadyr that a wonderful priest named Zacharios was here. But I may have this village mixed up with another. Is your priest named Zacharios?"

"Our priest right now is Father Dema," Leonid answered curtly and crossed his arms.

He's suspicious. Better change the subject. "Well, I must have the wrong village. No, I do not need to consult with Father Dema. . . . By the way, is the house next door where he lives? It's nicely maintained."

"The house next door is the priest's house."

"Nicely done. Both church and priest's house. . . . Well, we'll be going then. Thanks so much for your help. . . Was it Leonid?"

"Yes. Leonid. Thank you for seeing our church."

Andrei and Julian walked out of the building under the watchful eye of Leonid.

Tonight, when the barbecue takes place on the beach, I'll sneak back up here and have a look at the house. I think this Leonid is holding something back.

Then turning to Julian, Andrei said, "Julian, I have a photo permit. We can take pictures. Will you take one of me in front of the church?"

The rest of the day for Andrei Rubtzova and Julian Taft was spent walking about, taking photos, and engaging the village folk in conversation. At about three in the afternoon, they rode their inflatable back to the ship to pick up a few things. On the way, he thought about the answers he had received to his questions in the village.

Yes, Father Zacharios is our American. The villagers told me he's on special assignment to Moscow and St. Petersburg — a lie, no doubt. And that the Matushka is at home with their little son. Father Dema is a substitute while Father Zacharios is gone for three months. This all fits nicely. I can report that he is our man. And once I have taken a photo of Matushka, my job here will be done.

Leonid found his uncle at the doctor's office.

"Uncle, something strange happened a little while ago."

"What is that, Leonid?" Peter asked absent-mindedly as he took inventory of his medications in the cabinet. The doctor's office was an addition built onto the home of Peter and Leonid. It contained one room, with an old gray sofa near the door for people to wait, a desk where Peter could do his paperwork, a cabinet for medications and instruments, and at the far end of the room an examination table behind a white cloth partition. The place smelled of methyl alcohol and varmint repellent. The old doctor was dressed in typical village attire, a colorful flannel shirt, baggy brown trousers, and black rubber knee boots. Leonid was wearing similar clothes, but his muscular physique stretched the fabric around his chest and shoulders.

"Some men came to the church from the ship," Leonid said slowly, continually glancing out the window. "One was Russian and the other maybe British. The Russian made me feel suspicious of him."

Peter carefully put down his inventory list, closed the cabinet and beckoned Leonid to be seated on the sofa. They both sat.

"Tell me, Leonid. What made you feel suspicious?"

"He had a sinister look on his face, even when he smiled. He asked about Father Zacharios, claiming that someone in Anadyr referred him here. He also wanted to know about the priest's house."

"What did you tell him, Leonid?"

"I told him the truth, uncle. But I did not answer more than his specific questions. I told him that we did not have a Father Zacharios here. I did not explain why. And I told him that the house next door to the church is the priest's house, but I did not say who lived in it."

"And where did the two men go when they left the church?"

"Uncle, it looked to me that they traveled around the village taking pictures, buying souvenirs, and talking to people. I discreetly followed them."

"Hmm," Peter said. "It sounds to me like these men might be spying on us. They have probably been asking our villagers questions about Father Zacharios. Surely you know what this might mean."

"Yes, Uncle. It is what we have been afraid of. Matushka may be in danger."

"Here's what you must do, Leonid. Get my Ticca rifle and hide it in the church. Tonight, while the tourists are down at the beach, keep watch on the house. I'll go down to the beach and keep an eye on the two men you have described to me. Protect Matushka and the baby with your life, Leonid. Don't hesitate to shoot anyone who threatens them."

"Yes, Uncle."

In the evening, with daylight lasting well after midnight, the party went on in spite of the misting rain. Peter quietly watched Andrei Rubtzova and Julian Taft walk through the crowd. He watched as Andrei traded a villager a bottle of vodka for a pelt. Then he watched him do it again three more times with three different villagers.

Very soon, before these villagers get drunk, I will buy their bottles for hard cash. I'll give them no choice but to sell me their vodka. Then I can avoid a tragedy.

Peter watched as Andrei Rubtzova left the pelts with Julian and went off alone. He followed a safe distance behind Andrei as he went up the hill toward the church and house.

Leonid was sitting on the stoop in the shadows in front of the church when he saw Andrei approach the house. He watched as Andrei peeked into one of the front room windows where Matushka was probably sitting, nursing Tomas. Leonid knew this because he himself had often peeked into that very same window to secretly watch Matushka nurse Tomas. Leonid watched as Andrei walked around to the back of the house. It was then that Leonid hurried into the church and picked up the rifle.

Leonid quietly walked to the back of the house. Andrei was there, prying the window with a screwdriver.

"Stop!" Leonid sighted in on Andrei, about twenty feet away from him.

Andrei jumped. Then, looking down the barrel of Andrei's rifle, he seemed to calm down.

"It's all right, Leonid," he said quietly. "See my camera? I'm simply trying to get a good picture of the beautiful woman and her baby. Doesn't she look beautiful in there?"

Leonid did not shift his aim from Andrei. "You have no right to pry open that window, nor do you have permission to photograph Matushka. Back away from the window—"

"Surely I mean no harm," Andrei interrupted. He slowly backed away from the window. "Please put the rifle down. Someone may get hurt."

"You must stay right where you are until the constable comes."

Just then, Bethany came to the window and opened it. As Leonid glanced up, Andrei drew his knife and threw it at Leonid. Just in time, Leonid saw the knife flying at him, moved quickly to the right and fired twice at point blank range.

Andrei Rubtzova crumpled as blood began to flow from his chest. Bethany shrieked and ran from the window. Peter came around the corner. Leonid fell, the knife deep into his left leg.

Peter quickly examined Andrei. *Dead.*

He moved to Leonid. "Let me help you inside, Leonid. You have been wounded."

To Bethany, he called through the window, "Matushka, help me get Leonid into the house. He's been wounded."

Bethany timidly unlocked the back door and assisted Peter as he dragged the still-conscious Leonid up the steps and into the house. Tomas cried from the living room where Bethany had placed him in the bassinet.

They laid Leonid on the floor and Peter began ministering to Leonid's wounded leg.

"What? What happened, Peter?" Bethany was finally able to speak. She was breathing heavily as she stooped over Leonid and held Tomas tightly.

I have to be careful not to make her unduly frightened. Peter looked up at Bethany. "That man was trying to break into your house. Leonid caught him in the act. It looks to me that the man tried to knife Leonid and Leonid defended himself. . . and you."

"Dear Leonid. Thank you so much for saving me!" Bethany stroked Leonid's head. "There's no telling what might have happened had you not been here to protect me."

Leonid lay there with the typical stoicism of the Yupik. He allowed his uncle to clean the wound and bandage it.

Just then, the constable burst through the front door. "What is going on in here? I heard shots fired." The Chukchi police officer, a roundish, short, bald-headed man with a yellow ski hat and matching yellow coat looked around before focusing his eyes on Leonid.

"It's okay, Rut," Peter said with a soothing voice. "A man tried to break into Matushka's house. He stabbed Leonid. And Leonid defended himself. The man is lying dead in the backyard."

"It's true, Rut," Bethany chimed in. "I saw it happen."

Rut bowed before Bethany. "I'm glad you are not hurt, Matushka." Then, turning to Peter, he asked, "Is the dead man one of ours or is he from the ship?"

"From the ship. I think he's a crewman."

"I could have predicted something like this when we first allowed the ships to come in here. Even though we make much needed money, it is also much trouble. . . . Well, I'll go down and get the captain. What can I do to assist you?"

"I'd like it very much if you will remove the dead man from my backyard," Bethany said as she looked at the constable.

"I will do so immediately, Matushka. I am so sorry this had to happen to you. I'll patrol your home regularly from now on."

"Thank you so much, Rut," she replied as she led him to the back door. She watched Rut throw the dead Russian over his shoulder and head down the hill toward the beach.

Back in the house, Bethany began again to stroke Leonid's head. He was now seated on the sofa beside her. Peter was cleaning up the blood.

"Peter." Bethany motioned for Peter to sit down in the chair next to the sofa. He sat down. "You don't think this has anything to do with Father's mission, do you?"

"I'm afraid it may, Matushka. Leonid, tell Matushka about this afternoon."

As Leonid slowly explained the encounter in the church, Bethany's eyes grew dark.

She's getting frightened, Peter thought. *But maybe that has to happen now.*

"What do we do, Peter? If this man is a spy, the fact that he has been killed will surely get back to his superiors. And they will send someone else for me."

"I don't want to sugarcoat this, Matushka," Peter said quietly. "But I believe you are in danger. When Father left on his mission, I fashioned a plan should this sort of thing happen. We have a few days to act on my plan, because I believe it will be several days before his superiors realize he's missing and can react. Meanwhile, both Leonid and I will stay here with you and keep watch. Tomorrow I'll let you and Leonid know the plan."

Back aboard the ship, the captain listed Andrei Rubtzova as 'killed while breaking and entering.' He told Julian Taft to put him on ice until they reached Provideniya.

CHAPTER ELEVEN

June 4th, 2010 — Oval Office, Washington, DC

*O**kay, I've got to play my cards close to my chest or the stuff's gonna fly,* President Remington thought as he sat at his desk. He glanced at the National Security Council members as they gathered for the Friday morning meeting.

The Vice President telling an off-color joke to the Secretary of Defense. The National Security Adviser stoically going over her notes. The Director of National Intelligence whispering sweet nothings to the Director of the CIA.

Those two hate each other. The Chairman of the Joint Chiefs of Staff trying to hear what the Director of National Intelligence is whispering. And the Secretary of State glowering at all of us as he wheezes his way through life. What was I thinking when I put these guys together? This isn't a team. It's a brawl waiting to happen.

"Okay, ladies and gentlemen." He sat up straight. "Let's bring this meeting to order. NSA?"

The National Security Adviser, Dr. Jane Logan, cleared her throat and stood. As she stood, the President mused to himself, *I thought she would be more objective when I plucked her from teaching at the University of Maine. But she's made a hard right turn. Why? She's from my home state, for gosh sakes. I should have checked her out more thoroughly rather than rely on Senator McIver's advice.*

"Mr. President," the NSA began her remarks. "I suggest we move directly to the North Korea problem. This problem is not going away, sir. It's intensifying. Thank you for inviting General Rogers of CIA to sit in with us this morning. General Rogers, can you give us an update on the intelligence your agency has gathered?"

"Yes, ma'am," General Rogers said, standing as the NSA sat down. "Mr. President, DPRK is continuing to work on two launch pads. Our satellite intel shows that they are readying for TD-2 launches. They're also reinforcing their troops along the DMZ, including bringing up infantry units, tank units, and SCUD battalions. Plus they've increased training sorties with their newest MIGs, provoking our air defenses on a daily basis.

"Our HUMINT estimates that they are readying a nuke attack on us for July 20th to be followed immediately by a grab for the whole peninsula."

The President bowed his head and clicked his ballpoint pen continuously as silence descended upon the group.

Here's where the hoodwinking begins. Hope we can sell this.

Finally looking up, he said to the Secretary of Defense, "What's our plan to counter their intentions, SECDEF?"

"It's as we've been planning, Mr. President. The Chairman of the JCS has alerted our units to do some enormous saber rattling. In three weeks, we'll send a squadron each of F-22 Raptors from Hickam and Elmendorf out to Misawa in Japan, along with in-flight refuelers.

"At the same time, we'll send ten B-2 Spirits from Whiteman out to Anderson Air Base, Guam. That's the most B-2s we're ever sent anywhere at one time and it's over half our entire B-2 force. It will be noticed! Our aircraft will start operational and training flights as soon as they restage at the bases—"

"Mr. President," Secretary of State Nobely interrupted. "Do you not see the danger in all this?. . . . We've just heard that the North Koreans are being provocative. . . . And so we are becoming provocative? Does this not concern you? When two sides are being provocative toward one another, war is often the result. . . . I must object, sir. This is not a time for provocation, but a time for renewed efforts at negotiation. . . . The North Koreans will not be cowed just because we put massive aircraft and aircraft carriers in their immediate vicinity, Mr. President. . . . Indeed, they are already positioning their forces to face us."

Here comes old blow bag. Let me cut him off at the knees.

"Okay, Secretary Nobely," the President looked at him with disdain. "What progress have you made in the negotiation department? What specifically have you accomplished?"

"Negotiation, my dear sir, is a slow process, but it yields long term results. . . . While I cannot give you specific accomplishments. . . I can tell you that at State, we are talking at the highest levels. . . to representatives of the P'yongyang government—"

"That's nuts, Mr. President," Vice President Vernowsky cut in. "Those Korean Commies will keep Nobely talking right on through their invasion. . . . May I remind you, Mr. Nobely, that the Japanese did exactly that as they attacked Pearl Harbor. I thought you were a history professor, for gosh sake."

"Cool down, John," the President said as he swept down with both hands. Then, turning to the Secretary of State, he continued, "Mr. Nobely, let me explain again that your desire to negotiate is very important to us. And as you know, I am also negotiating back channel with government leaders in Asia and Europe. But we also must do the saber rattling to get P'yongyang's attention or they may very well nuke us, thinking that we're weak. We have to have a credible military threat before they'll listen to us.

"By the way, SECDEF, in line with that threat, I want three carrier task forces on the scene within the month, to join the George Washington already in those waters. Put two in the Sea of Japan off the North Korean eastern coast, and two in the Yellow Sea off the North Korean western coast. If we have to, we'll actually use these forces against P'yongyang."

The Secretary of Defense glanced at the Chairman of the Joint Chiefs of Staff, got a thumbs up from him and replied, "Yes, sir. We were anticipating the carrier battle groups. We'll have the Reagan, the Stennis and the Lincoln join the George Washington by July 1st."

"Okay," President Remington responded. "We all know what we need to do. Any questions?"

State rose to speak but the President cut him off. "That's all. Thank you for coming. . . . Mr. Vice President, can you, National Intelligence and CIA stay for a moment? I want to talk with you about coordinating the intelligence effort."

The room cleared, leaving Vice President John Vernowsky, National Intelligence Director Sandy Lindquist, and CIA Director Forrest Rogers. The three stood in front of the President's desk.

"So," the President looked up at the three. "We now know for certain that Nobely is the sieve that is somehow getting our information to P'yongyang. And he doesn't even know he's doing it. P'yongyang already knows we're planning a buildup and that we think they're going to launch a nuke on July 20th. By tomorrow, they'll know which units are being called up and where they'll be going—"

"And they'll be smug because they think we don't know that their actual plan is for July 4th," the Vice President said, smiling. "So let's tighten the noose without them even knowing we're doing it."

Man, I hope we don't have to really do this, President Remington thought as he looked from person to person. "General Rogers, fill us in on your plans so far."

"We've converted the Prowlers into missile launch platforms out at Area 51, sir," General Rogers responded. "Our crews are training for their specific missions. Targets have been identified and are being refreshed each day.

"Three weeks from today, the aircraft and support personnel will quietly arrive at our Marine Corps Air Station at Iwakuni, down near Hiroshima. They'll simply come in as an EA-6B Prowler deployment. The Group Commander out there is an old Prowler guy and has been made aware of the general nature of our business. He'll provide cover for us at Iwakuni.

"We're set for the mission to launch on the evening of July 3rd. Using low level flying and their excellent radar and radio jamming, both aircraft will hit their targets simultaneously, one aircraft on the east coast of North Korea and one on the west coast. After hitting their attacks, they'll eject from their aircraft at designated locations out to sea. The aircraft will sink into the sea never to be seen again and the airmen will be picked up by a submarine.

"No one will be able to blame us for the attack, but the right people will know we did it. We'll hit them so fast, they'll be thrown into disarray. Then we'll fry their communications with a shot from one of our satellites. They'll be dead in the water. We're relying on the South Koreans to take out their top leaders on the same night. . . . Cut their heads off."

"That's where my back channel communications with Moscow and Beijing come in," the President spoke confidently. "I have a fairly high confidence level that those governments will convince North Korea to stand down before we ever have to take this gruesome action. They'll strangle P'yongyang by withholding equipment and supplies until they cry 'uncle.' I've got this on good authority."

"I hope you're right, Mr. President," National Intelligence Director Lindquist said slowly, whisking the blond hair from her eyes. "But just in case we get no support from them, we're prepared to go with this plan, are we not?"

Lindquist is beautiful, Remington thought as he gazed at her. *There's nothing I'd like more than a dalliance with her. Do I dare come on to her? Maybe plant a seed?*

"Uh, yes, I am prepared to go with this plan, Miss Lindquist." He shifted his gaze to the CIA Director. "General Rogers, you keep Vice President Vernowsky informed on the secure phone each and every day. But do not allow those aircraft to leave American airspace without clearing it with me.

"Okay, John and Forrest, you may be excused. Sandy, can you stay back a moment? I need to ask you about what your people have found out about terrorist cells working in conjunction with DPRK."

Vice President Vernowsky and General Rogers left together, heading toward the Vice President's office.

Meanwhile, riding in a white Lincoln staff car toward the Department of State building, Secretary of State Nobely was in deep conversation with Executive Assistant Franz Rochelle and Aide Roland James. James was seated in the front passenger seat, Rochelle in the back seat behind the driver, and Nobely in the seat of honor, the right rear. The driver, an elderly Asian whom Nobely trusted implicitly, listened in on the conversation while he navigated down Constitution Avenue through the noonday traffic.

"Well, Mr. Rochelle, I think we're on track with the President. . . . We will do some saber rattling. I want to go with your plan. . . to leak to the press that I abhor North Korea's provocative actions. . . and, er, will

not tolerate them. Meanwhile, I will let the DPRK ambassador know.
. . that we will give them time to stand down. . . . We'll continue our
conversations together. I'll get some time on the phone with my counterpart there in P'yongyang. . . . He seems quite open to doing some
horse-trading."

"*Tres bon*, Mr. Secretary," Franz said. "And how shall I frame the
saber rattling?"

"Leak it to Smith at the *Washington Post* that I have convinced the. .
. President of the United States to send two squadrons of Raptors from
Alaska and Hawaii, ten Spirits from Missouri. . . and, let me see, three
carrier task forces, the Reagan, the Lincoln, and the Stennis, to deploy
to the Japan/Korea area. . . and that I believe it is in DPRK's interests to
negotiate with us. But if not, I can't be responsible for the consequences.
. . . You know, frame it like that."

"Where in the world will all that military equipment fit out there,
Mr. Secretary?" Roland James looked incredulously at him.

"Son, this is highly classified, but I can tell you. . . . We've got room
for every last airplane and every last ship over there. The F-22s will be
up in Misawa, a base four hundred miles north of Tokyo, perfect for
our fleet of Raptors. . . . And the B-2s will be down at Anderson Air
Base in Guam, ten of them, Mr. James. That's over half the fleet, you
know. . . . Took me awhile to pry those out of the Secretary of Defense.
And the carriers? Two task forces will be east of Korea and two will be
west. . . . That's where we'll have them, Mr. James. . . . A real dog and
pony show.

"And they'll never fire a weapon, son. We won't need to use them
for violent purposes because I will do what I'm famous for. . . horse
trading with the big boys. Yes, I'll get this whole thing settled without
a bomb being dropped or a missile being launched. . . . I've got some
good ideas of what North Korea needs. Yes, I'll settle this. . . and look
good and strong while I do it."

June 6th, 2010 — Area 51

Remembering D-Day, 1944, the aircrews sat in the ready room listening
to Juan Ramos give them more specifics on the mission. It was ten-
thirty in the evening and their workday was just beginning.

As Zach sat there daydreaming, he thought back to earlier in the
evening. *Well, the church service seemed to go well in here. Not a bad place
to hold a service. Just about every air and ground crew member showed up. I
thought Jerry did a good job on the readings. Hope I did okay on the sermon.*

"Today is D-Day, gentlemen," Juan said in his gruff voice, interrupting Zach's daydream but only for a second. "Even though none of you were born on D-Day 1944, you sure look like it to me. You are really old! You know that, amigos?"

Jerry threw a glove at Juan while the others booed him.

"All right. Can't you take a joke? You gringos are all alike." Then getting serious, Juan continued. "Tonight I'm going to give you a rundown of *your* D-Day, July 3rd, 2010. Then you're going to study. . . . He stopped talking and looked at Zach. "Colonel Zach? You with us?"

"Uh, sorry, Juan. I must have strayed off."

"Quite all right, colonel." Juan smiled at him. "I strayed off during your sermon, so now we're even." Everyone laughed.

"As I was saying before Colonel Zach strayed off, I'll brief you on your mission profile and details. Then later tonight, you'll study the whole mission and go over it together. Finally at 0230, you'll fly a practice profile. Got it?"

Heads nodded.

"Okay. On July 3rd, both teams will take off from Iwakuni at 2330 as part of a four-plane section. Once at altitude, the lead EA-6B aircraft, flown by the Wing Commander, followed by our Navy Team, will break off from the section and head west. You'll refuel in-flight, and then, just west of Chejudo Island — see it here on the chart? You'll descend to one hundred feet above the water. The lead EA-6B will give you the kiss off and head back to Iwakuni.

"But you will head north northwest as low as you can handle it, up the Yellow Sea and then north northeast up Korea Bay. Because you've got to carry your missiles on exterior ejection racks rather than on interior fuselage racks, you won't be completely invisible on radar, not totally stealthy. So the lower you can go and the least amount of time you spend running your radar, the less likelihood you'll be picked up by enemy radar. I'd advise you to just stay with GPS until you get within target range.

"Another thing: While you're heading north, you'll need to pull the power back so you can save on gas. Low and slow as you go north. Just remember that you've got to hit your first target as close to 0235 as you can.

"Speaking of target range: When you get thirty miles from your first target, climb to two thousand feet and turn on both your ALQ-99 and USQ-113. We've got the enemy's emitter characteristics in the CPU and it'll automatically jam. You don't have to do anything with it except turn it on. Same goes for the 113. You'll drive the enemy controllers dizzy with all the tap dancing they'll find on their scopes and you'll fry their voice comm and data links. We'll give you a little help with a satellite strike. What we've got to do is fool their Surface-to-Air Missile, the SA-10A Grumbler. The enemy has them strung around the launch pad.

"So, getting to the target: When you hit the IP, head west to your first target, Tongch'ang-dong. See it here on the chart? Remember that you've got to hit it as close to 0235 as you can. Hopefully the weather will be good and you can hit it with the FLIR. If not, use your radar.

"As previously briefed, turn starboard coming off target and head into the valley for target number two, Yongbyon. See it here? Same deal on target number two. Once you pulverize that one, follow this flight-planned route at low level. Come out on the east side at this point here, just south of Hungnam.

"Then it's one-hundred-twenty miles east over the water. Eject at that point. If for some reason you still have one or both bombs on your aircraft, turn on the positioning device before ejecting so that we can later locate your aircraft in the water and pull the bomb or bombs off it.

"Now we've got this neat phone for you. It's the SG-2520 satellite phone. It's even got a GPS in it. Once you land in the water and crawl into your life raft, turn that hummer on and punch in your code. A rescue crew from the sub will be sitting in a boat waiting for your call. If you land in the prescribed area, they'll pick you up quickly and take you aboard the sub. If you don't quite make it to the ejection point before you have to punch out, the rescue team will pick up your coordinates when you switch on your phone. The sub'll come for you.

"Now, if for some reason you have to eject over land, use your phone GPS for navigation and get to this point on the chart. . . . See it here? Coordinates are already in the phone. Stay there. Don't move unless you absolutely have to. Call on your SAT phone and the good guys will come for you. Got it?

"Now let me change the focus. If you do have to punch out over land, we've got a couple weapons you'll be carrying on your person. First off, you'll be carrying this Yargin Pya, MR 443. This is a Russian semi-automatic with a seventeen-round magazine. Nine millimeter. If you've got to shoot an animal or a person at long range, this'll do the job. It kicks. When you're on the range, you'll have plenty of time to get used to firing it.

"Second, you'll have this baby here. It's a Glock 36 Slimline semi-automatic. Cute little bugger, isn't it? It's a forty-five caliber and can put a big hole in anybody you have to shoot at close range. Magazine holds seven rounds. You'll have time to practice firing it to get used to it.

"Now," Juan continued. "Marine Team. Similar mission—"

"Chu Hoi!" Bob stood, shouting the word for 'Surrender' and waving his white handkerchief. "We need a break, Juan. I smell coffee and want some — now! And I need to make a head call."

Wally stood. "Yeah, let's take a break, Juan. Gentlemen, take ten."

The four crewmen walked to the coffee table and loaded up while Juan stood at the podium going over his notes.

"Well, ya'll," Bob said quietly as they huddled and drank their coffee. "A whole boatload of if's in this mission, if ya'll ask me. We screw this up in the least and we'll be either target practice or fish bait. Ya'll think this thing is actually do-able?"

"What's the matter, Marine? Can't hack it?" Wally looked at Bob and smiled, but he was only half joking. "There are always if's in this business. But a mission's a mission. It's dangerous but do-able. It's a typical Navy mission, Jarhead. You want to fly for Delta Airlines or you want some real action?"

"I'm just sayin'," Bob said, countering. "I can hack anythin' the Navy can hack. But let me tell ya'll. Zach and me — we're gonna watch this one real close. I don't mind dangerous. I'm just not too in love with suicide."

Meanwhile, Zach and Jerry just stood there listening to their pilots square off.

"You'll feel more confidence once we start flying the profile, Bob," Wally said as he refilled his cup. "Now, make your head call so we can get back to the briefing. We can't start flying the profile till we finish the stupid briefing."

"Marine Team," Juan was back giving the briefing. "After you take off and climb to altitude, you'll be number two with the other EA-6B as you break off from the other two aircraft. You'll head north one-hundred miles, in-flight refueling along the way. After refueling, you'll descend to one-hundred feet. The EA-6B will kiss you off and head back to the Kune.

"You'll head north to your first target, Musudan-ri. Same info as I gave the Navy crew for your little journey north into the mouth of the tiger. Remember: hit target number one as close to 0235 as possible. Then hit target number two, and hit target number three only if ordered.

"Egress? Go east, young men. Go feet wet at Yongch'ong-dong. See it here on the map? Eject at one-hundred-twenty miles off the east coast. These coordinates. Same rescue procedures."

"Okay," Zach said. "Now it's time for me to fly this hog."

Bob and Zach were flying through the mountains north of Area 51. They had finished the briefing with Juan, had practiced the flight in the simulator, and now were actually flying the route. They were just coming off Target Number Three.

Zach reached across the cockpit with his left hand and grabbed the control stick.

"Ya'll got the aircraft, Zach," Bob responded. "Here's the part where I have the heart attack and you've got to get us out over the water. . . . That's it. Take it real easy pullin' that stick back. . . . Okay. You're at a thousand feet above ground level. Good. Hit the terrain avoidance for one thousand feet."

"This is almost fun." Zach glanced across at Bob. "Now I get to zig along through the valley. What a great aircraft!"

"So easy even a B/N can fly it." Bob chuckled as he monitored closely. "Not that ya'll will actually do this. 'Cus I ain't plannin' on havin' one of them heart attacks again. . . . Here we go. Simulate feet wet at this point. Keep her straight a hundred and twenty miles. Let's just say you've done that. Now simulate ejecting us both. . . . Yup, we got that part down well. How ya'll feelin' about flyin' this low?"

"Probably over-confident, Bob. It just feels comfortable. The self-trimming aspects of the aircraft really help with stability. Very little need to trim. Okay, you've got the aircraft back."

Zach removed his hand from the stick and Bob took control.

"Let's call it a night, young Zach." Bob turned toward home. In fifteen minutes they were on final for a full stop on Runway One Four Left."

June 7th, 2010 — Peekskill, NY

"Not good enough," restaurant manager Kim Myong Chol called out. "We need to do it again."

Kim and his three team members were up in the woods above Peekskill in an area he had laid out to resemble the Indian Point Nuclear Station Unit Three. He had been meticulous in setting the dimensions of the simulated walls, spent fuel cell pool Number Two, and reactor control area. Of course he couldn't actually build these items, so he put signs on posts to show where they were. His team had been practicing once a day for a week.

"Pak, you were a minute late getting to the pool, a whole minute."

"I'm thought I was right on time, Mr. Kim," Pak responded indignantly. It was a hot June afternoon and all three team members were sweating.

"You were one minute late. Now the whole team must suffer for your carelessness. We will go through the whole thing again. Everyone set your watches again. Set them to 1:25. Three-two-one-set. Now go back to your positions and go through it again, this time exactly on the dot."

As the three jogged away, Kim watched them. *We must not let the Dear Leader down,* he thought. *We must shine brightly as we gain glory for our leader. We are one month away from glory.*

At precisely 1:35, Son Song Chol, a twenty-two-year-old computer programmer dressed in traditional black warrior clothing, threw his simulated satchel charge at the simulated north fence and called Kim. When it 'blew a hole in the fence,' he ran through, heading south until engaging imaginary guards running toward him. He fired repeatedly until he was shot and killed. He lay there with a satisfied look on his face.

At 1:37, Pak Cho Sung, a thirty-year-old taxi driver dressed in the same type outfit, threw his imaginary satchel charge at the simulated south fence and called Kim. When it 'blew a hole in the fence,' he snuck through and headed northeast toward spent fuel cell Pond Number Two, arriving at exactly 1:41. He again called Kim to report that he had arrived at precisely 1:41. He then climbed up and threw his two grenades into the imaginary pool. He counted to five and watched them 'blow,' imagining the holocaust he would cause.

Meanwhile at 1:39, Sunni Thai Sey, thirty-two-year-old security guard at Work Station Fourteen, left her post and ran toward the Reactor Control Area, arriving there at 1:42. She called Kim and then pushed the button on her 'nuclear satchel bomb.' She imagined how her heroic action would restore the glory of the Democratic Peoples' Republic of Korea.

Kim, standing to the west of the 'facility' undercover at the simulated bus stop, smiled. *Yes. We did it perfectly. We will restore the glory of DPRK. We will be true to our Dear Leader.*

Same Day — Moscow

The Office of the President of the Russian Federation was quiet and dark. President Medvedev was turning lights off as he prepared to leave for the weekend. It was nine in the evening. He would pick up his wife and be at their dacha by midnight.

As he walked out the door, he was met by Prime Minister Putin.

Oh no. Not now, Vladimir. I'm already late. Can this wait?

"Before you leave, my friend," Putin began. "We should go over the Korea initiative one last time. I have new information."

"Come in, sir. Let me get a light on." Medvedev turned on the lamp on an end table and motioned for Putin to be seated.

Putin never sleeps, he thought. *He prowls these halls just looking for someone to talk to. If I'm not careful, he'll keep me here all night.*

"What is the new information, Mr. Prime Minister?"

"We have heard from General Park," Putin spoke as he sat down in one of the chairs in front of the fireplace. Medvedev sat to his right. "Park has decided that Kim Jong Un is not fit to share leadership with him. He will make sure Jong Un is in the assassination plan. Park says he will groom the number two son to be his partner."

"The effeminate one? How's he going to pull that off?" Medvedev forgot about his wife and the dacha.

"He says he can bring Kim Jong Chol along. . . get him some speech therapy. . . teach him to walk like a warrior. Park says it can be done and that Jong Chol will glory in the attention."

"So," Medvedev said. "Do we trust Park with this new twist?"

"We have to trust him, Mr. President. Our hold on North Korea is centered in the Commanding General of the Armed Forces of the Democratic Peoples' Republic of Korea. I think we can work this change into our plan. After General Park takes over and props up Kim Jong Chol, we'll have the two of them here for a grand reception. Even give son number two a high award for valor in saving his nation from disaster.

"Now, do you mind if we go over the scenario again just to make sure we are on the same page?"

"Yes, sir," Medvedev said resignedly. "Let me call my wife and let her know I'll be a little late."

CHAPTER TWELVE

June 8th — Yanrakinnot

Major Dmitri Plovnic got off the inflatable with other passengers from the cruise ship. He looked like a tourist rather than the chief operative of the crime syndicate *Dolgoprudnenskaya* and a clandestine agent for the Russian government. He had left Pevek to personally see to this project. A diminutive figure, with thick glasses and a light growth of blond hair on his face, he blended in with the tourists, sporting a checkered, blue flannel jacket and a black ski hat.

It was a pleasant day in Yanrakinnot. At noon, the sun was bright, and the snow was melting fast. People were wearing light jackets. Plovnic had signed up for the reindeer farm excursion but had explained to the tour operator that he might miss some of the tour so he could visit his cousin who was teaching at the school.

As his tour group walked up the road leading to the farm, his thoughts were traveling a mile a minute.

So. My agent was shot here in this village. For breaking and entering? I doubt that. There must be something here he was investigating. Something or someone. I'll start my search at the church. I just have to find it in this hodge-podge of buildings.

His tour group continued up the hill. Then he looked to the left.

Ah, there it is. So now I'll just stop for a moment, let the group move forward, while I quietly turn left up this street.

As the group disappeared up the street, Plovnic turned left and walked slowly toward the church, pretending to admire the homes along the way. Once at the church, he checked the door and found it unlocked. He walked in and looked at the beautiful interior, once again acting his part as a tourist.

Now, where would the priest's house be? Probably next door. Let me just walk back outside and look around.

Plovnic walked out of the church in a nonchalant manner. He looked left and looked right. To his left, about twenty meters from the church, he saw what had to be the priest's house. He walked slowly along the road toward it, and passed it. Then he saw the Orthodox cross on the front door.

That's it! Now how do I get in there? If the priest is at home, I want to seem harmless.

Plovnic walked up to the front door and knocked. From inside, he heard the "May I help you?" coming from a woman. *No priest in the house or he would have come to the door.*

"I'm from Bishop Dionid's office in Anadyr with a message for Father."

The door opened. "Come in, please," came the woman's voice.

Plovnic entered the kitchen and took the seat offered to him. He looked closely at the strikingly beautiful middle-aged woman standing in front of him holding a baby. *This is the matushka. But is it the matushka I am seeking?*

"Would you like a cup of coffee, Mr.—"

"Ramshovski, Madame. I thank you for the coffee." He watched carefully as she put the pot on the stove. *American-accented Russian. I think I've hit pay dirt.*

"What message do you have, sir?" The woman sat down at the other side of the table. "Father is away for the day, tending to the mission church up the valley."

"When will he be home? The bishop told me to give the message personally to Father Zacharios. If he won't be too late, I can wait."

Something caught his eye off to the left. But before he could move, the rifle butt hit him squarely on the temple. Plovnic went down.

Leonid and Peter looked down at him. Peter checked for vital signs.

"Good job, Leonid. He's out cold but still alive."

"Thank you, Uncle," Leonid said as he smiled at Bethany. "As soon as he said he had a message from Bishop Dionid for Father, I knew he was lying. . . . What do we do with this man now?"

"I'll take care of him," Peter said as he pulled a needle out of his medical bag. "I'll inject him with a sedative and dump him down by the pier. . . . Matushka, it is time to put our plan into action. Get everything ready for your journey. Leonid, you do the same. I want you both on your way in one hour. It's too dangerous for you here, Matushka."

Bethany pulled an envelope out of her pocket.

"Peter, I've written a note to Zach, letting him know why I had to leave. Can you give it to him when he returns? And tell him I'll be waiting for him."

Peter took the letter and smiled at her.

"You are a brave woman, Matushka. You and Leonid will do fine. Leonid knows the way. Tomas has recovered from his flu, but I will tell everyone that you had to take him to the hospital in Anadyr and that you will be gone for several weeks for treatment."

Leonid headed quickly out the front door, saying over his shoulder, "I'll be back in one hour, Matushka. Please be ready. We need to make twenty miles before dark."

Peter lifted Plovnic and put him over his shoulder. "I'll also be back in one hour to see you off, Matushka. And I will have your snowmachine filled with petrol."

"Thank you so much, Peter. . . . Well, I'd better pack everything."

At two that afternoon, Leonid and Peter stopped in front of the house with two snowmachines, both with trailers attached. Peter packed Bethany's gear in the trailer, rigging a makeshift crib in the trailer for Tomas.

"Goodbye, my dear Peter," Bethany said as she hugged the old man. "Please pray for us."

Peter said a prayer for traveling mercies. Leonid slipped onto the lead snowmachine as Bethany tied Tomas into the crib and started hers.

"Stop frequently, Leonid," Peter said as he shook his nephew's hand. "Women with babies need to stop more frequently than men. . . and be on your best behavior. Your map is well-drawn, with stop locations. Just follow the route and you'll be there before you know it."

"Thank you, Uncle. I won't let you down."

About five that afternoon, Plovnic awakened, shivering. He was lying in a snow bank near the dock. After brushing himself off, he jogged in place to get his blood flowing, all the while cursing about being duped by a stupid Yupik.

He walked back up the hill to the church. Being careful with each step, he approached the house from the rear. He tried the door. Locked. He walked slowly to the front door. Locked. Seeing no one, he peeked into the front window.

Room vacant. Just as I suspected. She has gone into hiding. This is bad, very bad. There's no way I can find her now. It's time to go back to the ship. I've got to be in Pevek in two days. I'll just have to come back later and figure out where this matushka has gone.

Leonid, Bethany, and Tomas traveled northwest, through mountain passes, across frozen rivers, up and down hills. They slept in tents along the way, Leonid following the map and the instructions given him by Peter.

On the third night, they sat by the fire enjoying the heat. Bethany had fried some deer meat and heated some beans. And now she was feeding Tomas. Leonid tried not to stare, but he couldn't help himself.

I love Matushka, he thought as he watched. *Since my Materina died, I have felt so alone. And I now have the same feelings for Matushka that I had for Materina. But Matushka belongs to Father rather than to me. And I am a Christian. I must behave myself. . . . But suppose Father never finds us. Maybe there is a chance for me. Look how beautiful she is as she feeds Tomas. Maybe my day will come.*

Bethany sat feeding Tomas, seemingly clueless about Leonid's feelings. But he did notice that she stood up and walked into the tent to finish the feeding.

The next night, while they sat by the fire, Leonid picked up his log and put it down beside Bethany.

How will she feel about me sitting right beside her? She doesn't seem angry. She just smiled at me.

Confused by Bethany's smile, he took her hand. Bethany looked at Leonid for a moment, and then quickly withdrew her hand from his. As she stood up to leave, Leonid called, "My Matushka, I am so sorry. I, I love you, Bethany. . . ."

Bethany looked down at him, staring coldly into his eyes. Then her eyes softened. She sat back down beside him.

"Leonid, you have done so much for me." Bethany took his hands in hers. "And I love you, too. But not the kind of love that is romantic, Leonid. I am already married to Father. And we love each other very much—"

Leonid bowed his head and pulled his hands away. "I am a sinner, Matushka. I am so sorry. It's just that since my Materina died, I've been so lonesome for a woman. . . . And you've been so good to me, I began to think of you the same way I felt for her. . . . I'm so, so sorry. I am a sinner and don't deserve to live."

Bethany didn't say anything for a few minutes.

Will she forgive a worthless sinner like me? Why did I do such a stupid thing? I want to kill myself.

Bethany spoke gently. "Do you remember when we talked about Jesus dying for our sins? He has taken your sins and my sins to the cross, Leonid. Because you have confessed your sinfulness, God forgives you in Jesus. And I forgive you, too, Leonid. . . . I think you just got confused with all the stress, don't you?"

"Yes, my Matushka. I got confused. I will not bother you again."

"I know you won't, Leonid. I trust you. You're like a brother to me. So let's keep what happened tonight between the two of us and God, all right?"

"Yes, Matushka. You are very kind to me. Kinder than I deserve."

Bethany arose and looked down at him again. "Let's have our night prayers. I'll get my prayer book."

And she no longer fed Tomas in his presence.

Two weeks later, they arrived in the northern port city of Mys Shmidta on the Chukchi Sea. Leonid led them to the apartment of an old doctor, a friend of Peter's. After eating and spending time getting to know one another, the doctor showed Bethany her new apartment, right next to his. Leonid moved in with the doctor.

June 11th — Washington, DC

Roland James arrived at Nita's apartment at nine in the evening. Using the key she'd given him, he let himself in. Nita met him in the hall with a kiss and a hug.

"How was your week, Roland?" She playfully touched him.

"Terrific, Nita." Roland playfully fondled her. "But not as terrific as it will be with you tonight!"

Without another word, he led her to the bedroom, where she acquiesced to all his cravings.

Afterward, as they sat in bed together sipping drinks, Nita decided it was time to pump him for information.

"Your clandestine news releases are hitting the target, Roland. The *Post* is saying that the Secretary of State is behind the effort to encourage North Korea to resume negotiations with the USA. And that he is letting the North Koreans know that if they don't negotiate, they'll face dire consequences. Good job!"

"Thank you, Nita. I've discovered I have a knack for this stuff. The Secretary personally congratulated me at the staff meeting this morning."

"Is he really having any success talking with the North Korean ambassador or is it just spin you're putting on it?"

"If you want to know the truth, I don't think the Secretary's getting anywhere. I've gotten the impression that the North Korean ambassador is just leading him along, making a fool out of him."

"So why don't you tactfully tell the Secretary?"

"Are you crazy? I'm on top of the world right now. You think I'd sacrifice that? Besides, I have a suspicion that the North Korean authorities are right this time. Don't you think the Americans have screwed this whole thing up? They should have left the Korean Peninsula years ago. Maybe this whole thing is a way to restore proper hegemony to the nations of Asia, and to get America out of where it should never have been in the first place."

"You really believe that, Roland? It almost sounds like you favor the North Koreans over America."

"You know I do. . . . Okay, Nita." Roland looked hard at her. "Let's cut the crud. You know I favor the North Koreans because you've been following me."

He's on to me. I knew it would happen sooner or later. Plan B.

"What are you talking about, Roland. Why would I follow you?"

"Who do you work for? The Company, right? You've been setting me up, haven't you?"

Nita tensed, subconsciously pulling the covers up over her breast. "I work for the Company, yes. But I'm not following you. Are you paranoid or some—"

"When I left the post office yesterday, I waited around the corner. I saw you walk in. I've seen you there another time. No way that's a coincidence. . . . I don't like being followed. You know too much now, don't you? I'm going to have to waste you, you witch."

The knife came out from under the covers with such lightning speed that Roland had no time to react. Nita plunged it into his groin and jumped out of bed. As Roland screamed in pain, Anatoly rushed in and finished Roland off with several pops from his blackjack.

"So you got your wish, Natasha," Anatoly said, panting as he began to wrap Roland in a blanket. "You wanted to stab him in the groin and you have done so. Congratulations. On the negative side, we have lost him as a contact. I'll have to report this."

"I had no choice, Anatoly. He had me made and was about to kill me! I executed Plan B as we had briefed it. Report that."

"I will do so," Anatoly responded as he flipped Roland over his shoulder. "I'll make sure this body is never found. You clean up the blood and prepare to disappear."

On Monday, Franz Rochelle noticed that Roland James was not in his office. When he still hadn't arrived at noon, Franz called Roland's cell phone and left a message. He also called his apartment and left a message. No response. By four, Franz was getting worried. He called Roland's coded secret number. No response.

On his way home that night, Franz stopped by Roland's apartment. All dark. Newspapers were strewn around his door. Franz found the Super, showed his badge, and got the Super to open the apartment door. He walked cautiously in and flipped on the light. Everything was in order. He walked through every room in the apartment, looking under furniture and in closets. Clothes were all there. Suitcases under the bed. Food in the cabinets. He listened to the voicemail. None but Franz's message.

Something's up. If I don't see him tomorrow, I'll have to report that he is missing.

On Tuesday morning, Franz began the process of reporting that Roland James was missing. No next-of-kin. No other address than the apartment. He called the police to report a missing person. They checked hospitals and morgues, talked to neighbors. They talked to his former employer at CIA. Nothing. Roland James had disappeared.

In the afternoon, Franz had a meeting with Secretary of State Nobely. He sat in an overstuffed chair in the large, plush office as Nobely sat at his desk.

"He has disappeared, *monsieur.* I cannot explain it. It is possible that he has come to a tragic end."

"Have you considered the possibility," Nobely said, rubbing the end of his pen in his ear, "that this James. . . might be an agent of the Company? Do you think the Company may have gotten what they wanted from us. . . and then whisked him away?"

"No. No. Not possible." Franz looked incredulous.

"Yes. . . yes. . . possible," Nobely wheezed. "Didn't you notice that he knew an awful lot about the Company for someone so low in grade? I think. . . General Rogers is behind this, a set-up. . . . Feed us bogus information, then have James disappear. . . . We start an investigation, and are then embarrassed when it is revealed that we have allowed a foreign agent into our midst. . . . Well, let's not play into their hands. Call off the investigation, Franz. . . . Tell them James called from his mother's death-bed in, say, Missoula, Montana. . . . In a week, we'll terminate his contract. . . . Case closed."

"*Oui, monsieur.*" Franz got out of his chair and walked out of the office.

That same afternoon in the Oval Office, President Remington met with the Vice President, the Secretary of State, the Director of National Intelligence and the Director of the CIA. Subject? North Korea.

The president sat silently behind his desk, forcing the others to sit uncomfortably and wait for him to call the meeting to order. Secretary of State Hiram Nobely shuffled and wheezed in his chair to the far right of the President's desk. Director of the CIA, General Forrest Rogers, sat close beside Nobely. The Vice President sat in a stuffed chair just to the President's left. He was gazing out the window. And the Director of National Intelligence, Sandy Lindquist, sat to the President's far left, looking at her notes.

Almost time to spring on Nobely, Remington thought. *If we do this right, we can back him into the corner and force him to resign.*

"Okay, let's bring the meeting to order." The president looked from face to face. "This whole North Korea debacle is getting out of control. And it's been complicated by the fact that someone's been leaking close-hold info to the Press. . . . I need you to know that I launched an investigation into this, as well as into the possibility that someone high up is secretly negotiating with North Korean officials without my permission."

The room was silent. Remington again looked from face to face.

"That's treason," Vice President Vernowsky said. "The perpetrator ought to taken out and shot. Who is it, Mr. President?"

"Easy, John." Remington raised his hand. "We don't shoot traitors anymore, at least not in my administration. . . ."

More silence, except for Nobely's wheezing. General Rogers, who had been writing something in his notebook, put his pen down.

"Hiram," Remington said as he turned and faced the Secretary of State in the chair to his right. "We've tracked down the leak to the *Post.* It was one of your younger aides, a man named Roland James. What do you have to say for yourself?"

Nobely looked disdainfully at General Rogers. "What do I have to say for myself?. . . . I would say for starters that I thought this country had freedom of the press, and that no journalist is to give up his sources. . . . I would say that whoever forced a journalist to reveal a source is the real traitor. . . . And I would be willing to bet that the really guilty one here is none other than. . . than General Rogers. . . . Mr. President, I have reason to believe that General Rogers tried to set me up by moving this — what's his name? Roland James? — into my department. If this James leaked anything to the press, it was at the instigation of the director of the CIA. . . . That's what I have to say for myself." With that, Nobely sat back with a smile on his face.

"Nice try, Hiram." The President stared at Nobely. "But your statement has no credibility. We've also found out that you, Mr. Nobely, have been negotiating with the North Korean ambassador, passing on to him close hold information from our NSC meetings, and offering him food and even weapon concessions. All without consulting with me about it. That is consorting with the enemy, Mr. Secretary."

"Don't you think I know what you're trying to do, Mr. President?" Nobely moved forward in his seat. Remington noticed that his face was red and that sweat was pouring from his forehead. "You and your brother-in-law, Rogers here, are trying to destroy me so that I will get the blame for your hawkish failed policies with North Korea. . . . Well, I won't stand for it. No, sir, I will not stand for it."

"I'm afraid you will stand for it, Nobely," Remington said as he continued to stare at the Secretary of State. "We have you on tape negotiating with the ambassador. And your own driver has reported your orders to Roland James to leak info to the press. It's all right here in this dossier. And if that's not enough, we have photos of you in a hotel with a certain prostitute.

"We've got enough to hang you, Nobely. Now what do you say?"

Nobely sat back in his chair, silent for a moment.

Hope he takes the bait, Remington thought as the silence lengthened.

"This is a blatant violation of my freedom of privacy." Nobely's voice became measured. "I cannot continue to be a part of this frame-up by all of you. . . . It is quite obvious that your intention is to destroy my character. . . . And you're doing it all illegally. The frustrating part is that I can do nothing to stop you. . . .

"So my integrity forces me to distance myself from this corrupt Administration. . . . You shall have my resignation by close of business tomorrow. I shall simply go back to my office now, call my staff together, and let them know that my health is failing. . . . I'll tell them that if I can no longer. . . do the honorable job I've been doing with my usual brilliance, then I shall not do it at all. . . . I shall put my affairs in order so that the new Secretary of State can sit down at my desk with everything he or she needs to function well."

"That's not the way it's going to happen, Nobely." The President pulled a sheet of stationery out of his desk drawer. "Here's your resignation. You can sign it right here in front of your peers. You will not return to your office. I'll make the announcement that you collapsed in our meeting and the doctors found that you had a serious stroke and therefore cannot appear publicly. We'll set you up in a quiet house near Harvard where eventually you'll be allowed to teach a few classes in your wheelchair. You'll also sign this form stating that you will never divulge classified information or any information from State or our NSC meetings. If you violate this agreement, I will make sure you go to prison for the rest of your miserable life. Now sign these papers and get out of my sight."

Nobely grabbed a pen and signed the resignation and form. As the President pressed a button under his desktop, a security agent came in and escorted the former Secretary of State Hiram Nobely out. And that was the end of his public career.

CHAPTER THIRTEEN

June 15th — In the Air North of Area 51

"**M**issile away," Zach called as the missile blasted off the right wing and started down the laser beam, headed for the freight car serving as the target. Bob pulled hard left and descended to one hundred feet.

"Okay, Zach, I'm headin' into the valley for the escape route. You with me?"

The two crewmen were on a rehearsal hop over the rugged terrain of Nevada's Cactus Mountain range. It was 0236 and the night was clear. They had been flying every night for several weeks and had regained their old crew coordination. They anticipated each other's every move — important for any low-level bombing mission.

"Good," Zach responded as he looked into his radar scope. "Terrain Avoidance is working, not that we need it in this bright moonlight."

They wound through the valley for five minutes.

"Unbeknownst to you," Bob said, glancing at Zach, "my protocol calls for me to have a heart attack. . . right now. Aircraft is trimmed up. Power's at ninety percent. You've got it, kid."

He took his hand off the control stick. Zach immediately reached over and grabbed it with his left hand. "Okay, so now I climb to a thousand feet actual, switch Terrain Avoidance to a thousand feet, put this hummer into autopilot and get the flock out of here!"

He started a slow climb as he kept his eyes moving between the terrain outside and the radar scope and instruments inside. "I need to head east to the sea."

Two minutes later, Zach called "Feet wet," indicating that he was simulating that they were now over the sea. "We're burning jet fuel like an inferno. Since I can't reach the throttle, I've got to get us as close to the ejection point as I can before we run out of gas."

"I'd talk ya'll through this if I wasn't passed out with this horrendous fake heart attack, but I might comment that you're doing great. And it looks like we got enough gas to get there."

Five minutes later, Zach announced that they had hit the ejection point. "I'm about to simulate ejecting you and making myself the aircraft commander for two seconds. Any last words?"

"Get me out of this coffin," Bob called.

"Okay," Zach responded. "Say good bye, marine!"

"Good bye, marine!" Bob yelled as Zach simulated the dual ejection.

Bob broke into the exercise. "You did good, Zach. I'll give ya'll an A for that one. . . . I've got the aircraft back." When he said that, Zach took his hand off the control stick and Bob took control. "But just remember: I ain't got no intention of havin' another one of them heart attacks, so don't get too rambunctious about becomin' the aircraft commander. . . . no way, no how."

Suddenly the cockpit went dark.

"Electrical failure," Bob yelled.

Zach quickly grabbed his flashlight and shined it on the instrument panel.

"I'm deployin' the ram air turbine. . . . now."

Red cockpit lighting returned.

"What's going on?" Zach said over the intercom.

"For some reason, our generators have failed. I'll try recyclin'." Bob recycled and stowed the RAT. Again the lights went out.

"Redeployin' the RAT." Lights came back on.

"Okay, good buddy," Bob said in a calm voice. "We'll land this hummer with the ram air turbine only. Give me directions to the field."

"Roger. Come right two-one-eight-zero." Zach's voice took on a clipped, professional tone. "Fifty-three miles."

Suddenly the lights went out again.

"Complete electrical failure," Zach stated as he ripped off his mask.

Bob did the same and yelled, "Get the Trouble Shootin' Checklist out."

Zach retrieved the checklist, pointed his flashlight toward it, and began shouting check items at Bob, who responded to each item.

"We've got about ten minutes on the back-up battery, kid," Bob yelled back. "I may have to make a no flaps, no slats landin'. . . . dicey. Ya'll got the field?"

"Field straight ahead at ten miles." Just then the back-up battery went dead.

"Okay," Bob yelled. "So I make a no flaps, no slats landin'. . . . Hey, it's problems like this that prove I need to be the one who makes the big bucks. . . . I'll overfly the tower flappin' our wings. The moonlight's bright enough to show us off to 'em. Then I'll carefully come around and land this sucker. Long rollout."

Bob flew the prescribed profile. At the one-eighty, he blew the landing gear down. At the ninety, he slowed slightly while keeping the aircraft well above stall speed. He greased the Prowler onto the runway and then used aerodynamic breaking on the long rollout.

As they sat there at the end of the runway watching the fire-rescue trucks arrive, Zach smiled at Bob. "YOU may be an old ferd, but you fly good for an old ferd. Thanks for saving our bacon."

"Thanks, kid. But I hope this never, ever happens to us over North Korea!"

Seeing that there was no need for fire-rescue, those vehicles left and a tow-motor arrived. Hooking up to the Prowler, the tow-motor dragged the aircraft back and into the hangar.

"Why do you think the RAT stopped working, Bob?" Zach was still trying to figure out what happened.

"I've seen it before. I'll bet a million bucks that the RAT blades fouled. Glad ya'll were fast on that check list. That could have been a catastrophe. So now the Chief'll have to figure all of it out, and maybe make another run to Cherry Point for spare parts. We've only got these two aircraft. . . . Gotta keep 'em up and runnin.'"

"Have you seen their spare parts inventory, Bob?" Zach smiled. "Trust me. They won't need to make another run."

The crew climbed down from the cockpit and headed for the Ready Room, where Wally and Jerry were already ensconced in seats enjoying cokes.

"Heard you had a little electrical problem," Jerry yelled as Bob and Zach walked in and sat down beside them. "The Chief's going to be mad at you for breaking the aircraft. He'll sick Master Sergeant Washington on ya. Figures the Marines would screw it up."

Bob rose up, glared at Jerry and began to respond angrily. Just then, Simon Longstreet and the Ramos boys walked in.

"Break it up, gents," Si said as he looked from face to face. "Tension's building too high right now." He walked to the lectern.

"Bob, you did an outstanding job on that emergency. Thanks for saving the aircraft. The Chief'll will run down the problem and get it fixed pronto."

Bob sat back down.

"The reason the Ramos boys are here right now," Si continued, "is to alert you that word has come down from on high. We're cleared to fly to Iwakuni."

"Hallelujah," Wally said. "Finally, we can quit practicing and do this for real. We've been getting on each other's nerves all week. . . . So when do we leave?"

"Scenario calls for us to take off in five days — June 20th. Father's Day. We go at 2100. The KC-10 will be pathfinder and gas passer. The two Prowlers will be in trail formation. First stop will be Kaneohe Bay Marine Corps Air Station on the beautiful island of Oahu. But don't get your hopes up. There will be no liberty. Just park the birds in a secure hangar, have a meal and hit the rack.

"Next night, after dark, we do it again, this time landing on the lonely isle of Wake after crossing the International Dateline. Same routine — secure hangar, food, sleep.

"Third evening, we do it one last time, finally landing at Iwakuni Marine Corps Air Station on the island of Honshu.

"Now until Sunday, you'll stop flying, do simulators every night, and keep up your conditioning. We'll all go to the pistol range one more time. The maintenance crew will get these birds in tiptop shape for the ocean crossing. Everybody will take Saturday and Sunday nights off. . . . Any questions?"

"Yeah," Wally responded slowly. "Since we're leaving on Sunday evening, I'd like the chaplain to lead both air and ground crews in a voluntary worship service here in the ready room on Sunday morning. Gotta make sure the big guy upstairs has decided to take the trip with us. That okay with you, Zach?"

"Thanks, skipper. I'll get something prepared."

That Sunday evening, Si, Juan, and Chico joined the ground crews as they boarded the KC-10. The aircrews climbed into their cockpits. And the force headed west, Japan-bound.

June 16th — P'yongyang

General Park Rei Cho, Commander of the Armed Forces of DPRK, sat on a stone bench in the garden of Premier Jang Song Thaek, secret leader of DPRK. It was cool for mid-June and General Park was happy to let the sun warm him. He was attired in his gray, summer battle dress uniform. On the other bench sat Premier Jang, wearing his black suit and bowler cap. The two had been sitting quietly for two minutes, listening to the chirping of the birds.

Finally, Premier Jang broke the silence. "So, General, our man Roland James has disappeared in Washington, DC. Why did you not bring the new Director of Intelligence with you today? He must explain this great failure."

"I did not want you to shoot another Director of Intelligence, Premier Jang. So I told him to stay at the office."

"Someone must pay for this intelligence disaster! I will not tolerate it!"

I must get him away from always trying to make someone pay, Park thought.

"Premier Jang, our intelligence people tell us that James may have run away. But I am suspicious. No one can find any clues as to where he might have run. I suspect foul play. Perhaps the CIA discovered who he is and killed him."

"My thoughts exactly, General," Jang said as he calmed down. "Our people who were keeping a tail on him reported that he was having a torrid love affair with a secretary in the CIA. She might have discovered his real identity and had him killed. Do you know anything about that secretary?"

I've got to be careful here, Park thought. *Jang is good at sensing when someone is lying to him.*

"Our intelligence has discovered that she is the executive secretary to one of the directors at the CIA. No sign of her being an operative. . . . I think she may have become suspicious and told her boss. Then the CIA operatives maybe interrogated him before killing him. We'll never find his body. I'm sure of that."

Jang was quiet for a moment. "If he has been interrogated by the CIA, how much could they have gotten out of him?"

"Our intelligence people think he probably told the CIA, if he was interrogated, that he worked for us. But there was very little else he could have told them, except that he dropped a lot of intel to us. They will then know that we have been aware that they are saber-rattling with their fighters and bombers, and that we know there is no sub-stance to it."

"So, General, you are telling me that the Americans have gained nothing by catching James, and that our July 4th plan is secure."

"Of course, sir. They still think we will make our attack on July 20 rather than July 4. We fed that info to James in order to deal with just such an instance as this. Since they may now know that we have the intel on their plans, they will increase their threat that unless we back off of our plan, they will annihilate us. It means nothing. Our sneak attacks on July 4th will throw them into such confusion that our plan will work flawlessly."

"All right. Let's continue with our plan, even though we don't have intel updates from James. Have our intelligence operatives try to get other sleepers in the American government on this immediately."

With that, Park sensed the meeting was over. Standing and bow-ing, Park left the garden and walked to his car.

Jang bought what I said, hook, line and sinker. This operation may succeed after all. I'd better review the assassination plan.

Same day — Seoul, Republic of Korea

President Lee Myung-bak sat at his desk in his office. Prime Minister Han Seung-soo sat in one of the straight-backed chairs in front of the desk. Beside him sat the Intelligence Director of the Republic of Korea, Yu Sun-shin. Compared to Lee's sixty-nine years and Han's seventy-two, Yu was just a child at fifty. But he was a very 'smart' child. He knew the intelligence business better than anyone in the country. Edu-cated at Harvard and recruited there by the American CIA, he had the knowledge and the experience to remain one step ahead of his North Korean counterparts. Of medium height and build, he was almost indistinguishable from either a farmer or an engineer — perfect for not sticking out.

Prime Minister Han turned in his chair and looked at Yu. "Mr. Yu, please give your estimate to the President."

Yu took some papers out of his briefcase, sorted them and began. "Mr. President. Our intelligence confirms that P'yongyang will launch a nuclear attack on the American island of Atka in Alaska. They plan on launching at 9 a.m. July 4, Washington DC time. That is 11 in the evening Korea time. An hour later, their sleeper terrorists will take out two nuclear power plants in America, one in New York and one in Cali-fornia. These actions are geared toward striking terror in the hearts of the American population so that their government will readily remove their armed forces from the Korean Peninsula when they see that the odds are stacked against their staying."

"Does the American Government know all this, Yu?" The president looked sternly at his intelligence chief.

"Indeed, sir. We have made this information available to the CIA. They are dealing with it on two fronts. Their FBI is on the hunt for the sleepers who plan on taking out the power plants. And the CIA is supervising a clandestine air strike against certain targets in North Korea the early morning of July 4th, our time."

The president sat quietly for a moment. "What kind of clandestine strike? We have been hearing that the Americans will saber rattle with B-2s and F-22s, but we have heard of no strike. I have been on the phone with the American president several times in the last few weeks. He has said nothing of a strike."

"This is your official notification, Mr. President. Even with the scrambling of communications, the CIA felt it was too dangerous to tell you this over the phone. The leaked information that the Americans will saber-rattle with their fleets of bombers and fighters is simply a smoke screen. The actual strike will be by two American bombers in the early hours of July 4th. They will hit quickly and then disappear. No one will be able to prove it was the Americans. And the strike will be a complete surprise to the North.

"As the American aircraft are making their strikes, we will have the opportunity to assassinate the leadership of the North. Our forces will take out Premier Jang, General Park, and all three sons of Kim Jong Il. We have a constant tail on each of them and have learned their movements. We know that the three sons will be at a secret family meeting with their father in the mountains, making it simple to take out all four of them. Jang and Park will also be easy to take out because their security men actually belong to us.

"As soon as they are wiped out, there will be time for a new government to quickly assemble under the leadership of our undercover man, Vice-Marshall Han Fo Chi. Marshall Han will have a forged letter from the Dear Leader naming him the interim Premier of the cabinet. He is already trusted by the military and has risen to Vice Marshall.

"Since the ICBMs will have been destroyed by the American aircraft, and hopefully the attack on the American nuclear power plants will also have been averted, Marshall Han will command their armed forces to stand down. The Chinese will not have time to do their dastardly deeds and will have to accept the new arrangement. . . . This may be the beginning of a whole new way of life on the Korean Peninsula, Mr. President. Do we have the go ahead with our assassination plan?"

Lee sat silently. "The operation is approved, Mr. Yu."

June 22nd — Yanrakinnot

Dmitri Plovnic, Chief Eastern Operative of the *Dolgoprudnenskaya* crime syndicate, hit the north edge of Yanrakinnot at dusk. He was tired and hungry. He had taken several spills with his all terrain vehicle and had gotten lost twice. But here he was.

I need food and a place to sleep. First things first. I don't want to be seen, so I'll have to steal some food from a house where nobody's home. Then maybe I can curl up in the church for a few hours of sleep. Tomorrow I'll get down to the business of finding out where the matushka is.

Plovnic parked his ATV in a clump of trees and waited for dark. *Now to find a house to break into.* He used the darkness to conceal his movements as he walked down the street. Dogs barked, but that was not unusual. The noise of the barking never brought a face to a window. Spying a house with no dog outside, he walked around to the back. He quietly checked the back door. It opened. He walked into the kitchen. Nobody stirred. Quickly he grabbed as much jerky as he could carry and put it in his pocket. He also grabbed a pitcher of water. Then he made his way back to the ATV and enjoyed his stolen food.

Dinner over, he made his way to the church. Looking around and seeing no one, he quietly walked in. Nothing. No one. He walked through the iconostasis and lay on the carpet in front of the altar. Without saying a prayer, he fell asleep immediately, waking with a start sometime during the night when he sensed someone there with him. Looking around and seeing no one, he fell asleep again. But the whole night was given over to short periods of sleep and long periods of lying awake listening. He just sensed a presence he could not understand.

Something's weird here. I know there's no such thing as god, but there might be ghosts. . . . This is the last time I'll sleep in a church.

Next morning, Plovnic was up and out before dawn. He walked to the priest's house and looked in the back window to the living room. A lantern was burning on a table.

Something is different in there. . . . I wonder if another priest has come.

As he stood there looking in the window, he saw the priest come down the stairs.

That's not Savage. Too short and fat. Maybe I'll try him in an hour and do some picking of his brain.

But as he turned away from the window, he jumped. He was looking straight into the face of Peter, who was holding a rifle on him.

"Do not move," Peter said gruffly in Russian. "Who are you and what do you want?"

"You don't need to point that rifle at me, old man," Plovnic said slowly, keeping his hands close to his pockets. "I am harmless. I'm simply trying to bring a message to the priest. . . . from the bishop in Anadyr."

"You deliver messages by peeking into windows?"

"Well, the last time I was here, someone knocked me out with a club and dumped me down by the dock. So of course I'm more careful this time. . . . I simply want to speak to the priest, or his matushka, and deliver the message."

"Your manner is familiar, sir," Peter said as he watched Plovnic. "I have seen you before."

"That may be possible. Did you see me the last time I was here trying to deliver the message?"

"Another time. Two years ago. In a warehouse in Anadyr. You and your lieutenant saved us from being shot by Colonel Strasdie. You were there. You work for the crime syndicate, don't you?"

"You have a good memory, doctor." Plovnic nonchalantly slipped his right hand near his pocket. "Yes, we saved you. There was no need for that insane colonel to kill you in cold blood. We don't work that way. And now I am no longer with the crime syndicate. You see, I am trying to amend my life and so have begun working for the Bishop of Anadyr and Chukotka. That's why I am here. Let me show you the message."

Plovnic reached into his pocket as if to retrieve the message, but instead brought out a Glock with silencer, moved quickly left and fired three times into Peter's chest. Before Peter could fire or say a word, he was down and out.

Pity. I would like to have interrogated him about the matushka. Now I've got to bury his fat body instead. Got to hurry. It's beginning to get light.

He walked back to the church, found a shovel in a closet, then went back and dragged Peter up the hill. After searching Peter's pockets and finding his street address, Plovnic unceremoniously buried the doctor on the hill that looked down on the village of Yanrakinnot.

Distasteful task over, Plovnic jogged through the dawn's early light down to Peter's house and went through it with a fine tooth comb.

Nothing here. Nothing at all. The matushka has vanished off the side of the earth and I have no clues about finding her. When I get back to Pevek, I'll put out an All Points Bulletin for her. Somehow she's got to turn up in a village in the peninsula. She can't hide in the woods forever. Now I've got to get out of this village before I'm seen.

Putting everything back exactly as he had found it, he opened the door and peeked out. Seeing no one, he slipped out and jogged back to his ATV. Pulling it out of its camouflaged position, he fired it up and headed out across the tundra.

Same Day — Marine Corps Air Station, Iwakuni, Japan

The KC-10 with two Prowlers in trail got clearance for a straight-in to Runway Zero Two at Marine Corps Air Station Iwakuni, Japan, on the southwest end of Honshu Island. It was still dark at five in the morning as the jets roared over Hiroshima Bay at low level, heading for touchdown. The first to land was the KC-10, which was directed to park on the Base Operations tarmac. A minute later the Navy Prowler touched down, followed thirty seconds later by the Marine Prowler.

The two Prowlers found a 'Follow Me' truck waiting for them at the north end of Runway Zero Two, and were escorted to a hangar on the southwest corner of one of the American flight lines. The pilots shut their birds down and then all four crewmen climbed down from their cockpits, stretched, and walked into the hangar as the Prowlers were towed in and the large doors came closed. Zach surveyed the situation as they walked in.

Cooler here than the Nevada desert. That's for sure. I see a few outlines of mountains to the east where the sun is coming up. And the same guys in black battle attire doing security duty for us.

"These guys look just like the ones who did security back at Area 51, Bob," Zach whispered as they were escorted into the second floor ready room. "Can they be the same guys?"

"They're CIA, kid. You been livin' under a rock or somethin'? This whole operation's a CIA affair, remember? Startin' with Si and the Ramos boys."

"Sure. I should have understood that. For some reason, I had the impression that I was working for the Department of Defense."

"Forget that. DOD may not even know we exist."

"That's really comforting," Zach answered with some sarcasm.

The four crewmen sat in the ready room seats and were offered cold drinks. Zach noticed that this ready room looked almost exactly like the one in the hangar in Nevada — same battleship gray paint, same pipes along the ceiling, same air-conditioning blasting through the room.

A few minutes later, Si, Juan, Chico, and the twenty ground crewmen all walked in. Everyone grabbed a soda and sat down quietly while Si walked to the podium.

"On behalf of the First Marine Aircraft Wing Commander, welcome to Iwakuni, gents. The Commanding General would have loved to greet you personally except that he don't know we're here and we're gonna keep it that way."

Laughter from the crowd.

"So here's the deal. There's a supply building right behind us that's been fitted as a barracks and mess hall for us. This will be our home until a few days after July 4th. No one is to leave these premises. You will be shot on sight if you try to leave. We need the utmost security on this operation. And of course, there are no working phones and you have no cell phones. There will be no communications with anybody back home, same as Area 51. Our workday will continue to be 2200 to 0800.

"Ground crews, you'll have until the morning of July 3rd to get these birds in perfect flying and bombing order. They will not fly till then. We've brought enough black boxes and maintenance gear to answer any write-ups the air crews may have from the Trans-Pac.

"Aircrews, this ready room will be yours until you fly. Although we were not able to bring the simulators, you'll have some time each night to sit in the cockpits and go over your flight plans for the night of the 3rd.

"Everybody, we will muster in the mess hall every night at 2200 for a sit brief, an intel brief, and any other hot poop you need to have. By the way, we have people back in the States monitoring and watching over your families. If anything is up with your family, we'll render assistance and let you know about it."

Zach heard that statement and thought, *Yeah. Sure. You're taking care of families back in the States. But what about my family in Yanrakinnot? I'll just bet nobody's taking care of Bethany and Tomas. But I'm sure glad Peter and Leonid are there to protect them.*

His thoughts were interrupted by Si's nasal voice. "Before we break for a day's rest, I have the room assignments for everyone. Morning chow is ready right now. Let's go eat and then get some sleep."

After the meal, Zach sat on a chair in his bedroom, a small sleeping space with a camp cot, a chair and tiny desk without computer, and a small chest of drawers. A lamp on the desk provided the only light to the windowless room. On the desk were some books — a copy of *Moby Dick*, *A Complete Guide to the Koreas*, and some maps of the Korean Peninsula. He thumbed through *Moby Dick*.

Somebody must have raided the base library closet to get us all a book to read. I remember reading this one when I was still in high school. I surely am glad I only have to live here for eleven days. This place could make me claustrophobic — brings back too many gulag memories.

His mind drifted back to 1993, when he was first incarcerated in a gulag in Dnepropetrovsk, Ukraine.

I woke up on a narrow bed, with a paper-thin mattress beneath me. As I looked around, I saw that I was in a room that reminded me of a jail cell. About 8 by 8, no windows, a door at one end with bars in the upper half for observation. In the corner of the room was a 'honey bucket' for going to the bathroom. The walls of the cell were dank cement block. The cell was cold. I just sat there on my bed, saying my prayers and trying to remember how I had gotten there. But nothing came to mind. I sat for hours, not able to focus on any thoughts.

Zach felt a chill as he relived that awful time in his life. *It was awful. How did I survive? The freaking doctor who diagnosed me as paranoid with violent delusions, who administered haloperidol like it was candy. The terrible convulsions that resulted, the uncontrollable rolling of my head, my muscles twitching, my language becoming a babbling stream of noise, the nightmares. . . . I've got to get out of this room!*

Zach jumped off his chair and ran out of the room. He nervously sat in the TV lounge. He sat there for the rest of the day, dozing and waking, determined that he would spend as little time as possible in his sleeping space.

I can't wait for July 3rd. Give me strength, Lord.

CHAPTER FOURTEEN

June 25th — The Oval Office, Washington, DC

*P*resident Remington sat at his desk, deep in thought. Sitting in their usual spots in front of the fireplace were Vice President John Vernowsky, White House Chief of Staff Rory Candostino, and Special Assistant and personal adviser Verona Myer.

Remington stared at his desk, refusing to make eye contact with any of them, as they waited for the President to speak.

This thing is going to hell in a hand basket, Remington thought. *I'm losing my base of support on the left without gaining anyone from the right. The left thinks I'm selling out to the right. The right hates me. I'm getting isolated. . . . And this bunch here. They're at each other's throats, and mine, anytime the subject of my new pick for State comes up. . . . Oh well, I might as well get this show on the road.*

"I've called you in here this morning because I trust the three of you above everyone else. We've got a real problem. I had to get rid of Nobely. He's lucky I didn't have him shot. The extreme left is suspicious of the 'stroke excuse,' but haven't yet demanded that an investigation be launched. Now I'm getting flack from the left because I chose a moderate for Secretary of State. The activist movie guy from Hollywood is demanding that I choose another person. He's threatening to get Congress involved in an investigation of the new secretary. I'm getting phone calls, emails, text messages, and faxes from around the country demanding that I change my decision."

"You should listen to these people, Mr. President," Verona Myer said. "These are your friends. They can get you re-elected. If you betray them, you're done. Can't you see—"

"Verona, sometimes a president has to do what his base does not approve of—"

"That's crazy talk, Mr. President." Verona tried again. "We're making a giant step to the left in this country. Don't back down because of some idiot in P'yongyang. Don't listen to the freaky right."

"Mr. President? If I may?" Vice President Vernowsky stood up.

Much as I hate to admit it, John Vernowsky is making more sense than everybody on the left put together. What a nightmare.

"Go ahead, John," Remington motioned to his vice president. "Speak to us. Verona, can you give way to the Vice President?"

Verona crossed her arms and frowned.

Vernowsky began his lecture. "With all due respect, Mr. President, this is not a political campaign we're dealing with here. We ought not be counting votes for two years hence—"

"It's not two years hence, Mr. Vice President," Verona cut it. "It's this November. We mishandle November 2010, and 2012 goes out the window!"

"Verona, please. Let Vice President Vernowsky finish."

Vernowsky gave Verona a frown. "As I was saying, we're not doing politics here. We're trying to avert a world crisis. We're trying to stop a nuclear attack. Let's not bow to politics.

"Look, you chose a very competent man to replace Nobely. He's neither right-wing nor left-wing. Horace Finlay is just who you need for this time. He's got good international credentials. You vetted him with the leaders of Congress. He's going to be confirmed. Don't let the kooky fringe push you off the road."

"I take personal offense to that remark, Mr. Vice President." Verona stood and put her hands on her hips. She had been advising the president for some years, having become his confidante when he had run for the Senate. She had a doctorate from Cal Poly and was very proud of her leftist credentials. One of the news networks had retrieved a speech she had made in the late 1990s during which she called capitalism the scourge of the world and socialism the only hope for America. This revelation had caused great embarrassment for Remington, but not enough to distance himself from her. "Our friends on the left are not kooks. They're law-abiding citizens trying to remake this nation after the disaster we inherited—"

"Whatever, Verona," Vernowsky said casually as he blew her off. "Mr. President, I implore you. Don't change your mind on this. The left will forgive you if you stay the course. If you change the course and select another left-wing Secretary, the right will never forgive you. And the independent vote is absolutely turning to the right."

"Mr. President, may I offer a middle way?" the fifty-year-old Chief of Staff Rory Candostino, a rangy politico from many campaigns, piped up. "Stay with Horace Finlay for State. We're too far down the road to change that. And in fact, your poll numbers are up since you nominated him. So throw a bone to the far left by making your Saturday radio talk appealing to them. Talk about how Finlay has given assurance that on his watch, only negotiations will be used in foreign policy and that, in his opinion, military force is not a viable option in the North Korean crisis."

"Brilliant, Rory," the president said, brightening. "As usual, you've got a good sense of the pulse of where we are right now. . . . Okay, so that's the way we'll go with this."

As Verona started to speak, the Chief of Staff cut her off. "Mr. President, we're way behind on today's schedule. You're due at the Sierra Club national luncheon."

"Right, Rory. Thank you, Verona. Sorry, I couldn't take your advice this time." The president rose and headed in the opposite direction from Verona. "John, follow me for a moment, will you?"

As the Chief of Staff assertively ushered Verona Myer out the official office door, the President and Vice President went out the side door through the kitchenette.

"So what's the story on our aircrews, John?"

"They're in Iwakuni, sir. Their aircraft and munitions are at the ready. Unless we make some progress with Moscow and Beijing, we're prepared for the surprise attack the early morning hours of July 4th. All is going well. P'yongyang is convinced we're going to threaten a major attack on July 10th, so they think they'll be the ones to launch the surprise attack on us! I think we've got them, sir, if we have to attack."

They two loitered in the kitchenette.

"What about the sleepers who are scheduled to blow up our nuclear plants in California and New York?" The President fiddled with the American flag lapel on his jacket flap.

"The FBI's got the leaders in their cross-hairs. We'll stop 'em cold before July 4th."

"Okay. Thanks, John. Do not launch those aircraft for North Korea until you have cleared it with me. And if they do launch, I want direct access to them. I need complete freedom to call off the attack. You hear me?"

"Yes, sir. I'll relay it to General Rogers."

"Good. Not to mix business with pleasure, but when you talk to him, let him know I expect him in the White House tomorrow night for the ball game."

Same Day — The Kremlin

Friday evening, ten o'clock. President Medvedev went through his office spaces turning off lights. *Why does my staff not follow my example on saving energy? They've all left for the weekend without turning off a thing. I'll have to do a memo on that next week.* As he was about to turn off the one remaining lamp, he noticed a person pop through the door.

Putin. Oh, no. It's going to be another long night. The eagle roams, looking for a kill.

"Good evening, Mr. President." Vladimir Putin, the bookish, slight Prime Minister of Russia said.

"Good evening, Mr. Prime Minister. And how are you doing this fine June night? Ten o'clock and it's still light outside. I love this time of year. I was about to take a walk in the park."

Putin chose not to talk about the weather. "Do you have a moment? We need to talk about North Korea."

"Of course, sir. Come into my office. Coffee?"

"If it's not too much trouble. I realize you have dismissed your entire staff for the evening. When I sat at this desk, I never let my personal staff leave until I did."

Which is why they all hated you, Medvedev thought, although he would never say such a thing. "No trouble at all. I have one of those new coffee makers. Water's always hot and ready to brew. And good coffee beans from our friend in Venezuela."

Medvedev hit the switch for the coffee and began turning on some lights. "Please sit down here by the fireplace, sir."

Putin sat in his favorite spot, right in front of the fireplace. Since it was a warm, late June evening, no fire burned. "What have you heard about the operation?"

"Well, I am sick of calls from President Remington, if that's what you mean. I have agreed to have our UN ambassador harangue the Security Council with a demand that DPRK stand down from its nuclear weapons program or face sanctions."

"That's good, Mr. President. It will divert attention from what's really happening. And it will get the American president off your back. . . . What about Beijing?"

"Our people tell me that Beijing is giving Remington the big brush-off." Medvedev handed a cup of coffee to the Prime Minister, and then sat down beside him. "Since America is so far in debt to them, they feel they can treat the American president any way they wish. And they wish to insult him by continually putting him off on the red phone."

"How are the Americans doing on their plan to attack North Korea?" Putin took a sip of the piping hot coffee.

"They have their two attack aircraft at the Marine air base in Japan, ready for the July 4th strike. Our agents have sighted the aircraft.

"The American president is still hoping to avert the crisis in the UN. But I think he will agree to the American attack when he sees the inability of the Security Council to do anything and the reluctance of Beijing to rein in Kim Jong Il. In order to save his country from a nuclear attack by North Korea, he will launch the pre-emptive strike.

"Meanwhile, General Park is on target to humiliate China's man, Premier Jang, for not preventing the American strike. He will do this at an emergency meeting of the cabinet right after the strike. He will propose that Kim Jong Chol replace Jang, and he has cultivated the cabinet to the point where they trust him.

"At the same meeting, he will expose the Americans as trigger-happy cowboys who did not need to launch their nuclear attack, thereby taking their credibility away in eastern Asia. Once the new leader is established, North Korea will tilt our way. . . . And with that, Mr. Prime Minister, we will again establish hegemony in eastern Asia, to the dismay of the Chinese."

"Let's go over the plan carefully, Mr. President, just to make sure we have not miscalculated anything."

Yes, it will be a long night, Medvedev thought as he poured Putin and himself another cup of coffee.

June 29th — Mys Shmidta, Chukotka

Bethany Savage looked out the window of her apartment and surveyed the port of Mys Shmidta to the east.

The ice is melting fast, she thought. *The port may open any day. Then I'll have to be ever vigilant. I think those seeking me will come in by ship, as they did in Yanrakinnot. Hopefully this black hair and makeup will fool them. And the pillow I wear under my dress to make me seem fat. But mostly I'll stay in the apartment while the port is open. Leonid can buy what I need. . . . Oh Zach, where are you?* Tears began to flow down her cheeks as she sobbed. *I miss you so much. Come back to me soon.*

As she dabbed at her cheeks, she looked around her small apartment, a one-room efficiency with a bathroom. It had the typical moldy, flowered wallpaper on the walls and brittle, cracked linoleum on the floor. She had brought one of Zach's crosses, and it was the only item on the wall. The bed was an old couch that opened up into a bed. She had a small crib for Tomas that Leonid had found in a store. She also had a small icebox for storing a little food, a camper's propane gas stove with a pan of tomato soup and a coffee pot sitting on it warming, and a sink with a single spigot that produced cold water. Beside the sink, a table and two chairs served as her dining room. On the table were two plates, spoons and knives, cups, and a loaf of black bread and cheese.

There was a knock at the door, causing Bethany to jump, and Tomas, snuggling in her arms, to cry. She tried to clean the tears off her face as she headed for the door.

Noon. Leonid is here for lunch. He knocked again — three quick knocks, a pause, and then one knock. It was Leonid's code to let her know he was at the door.

Bethany opened the door and tried to smile.

"You have been crying, Matushka," Leonid said as he glanced at her. She closed the door behind him as he entered the apartment.

"Please sit, Leonid. I'm sorry you saw me crying. I just miss Father so much." She saw Leonid's moonface fall. He sat down and prayed silently.

She spooned hot soup into his bowl and filled his cup with coffee. "Leonid, you are doing such a wonderful thing in taking care of me. And I am never lonely when you are here."

She saw his face soften and turn upward. "But Father is my husband, none the less. I love him with a different love than I love you. I love him as my husband and it hurts me when I can't see him, when I worry about whether he is alive. I love you as a dear friend, Leonid. And that is a beautiful love."

Leonid touched her hand as she sat down. "Thank you, my dear Matushka. Your love is so kind. Thank you for returning my love."

They ate in silence, Leonid breaking large hunks off the loaf of bread and dipping them in his soup. He ate the cheese by separate chunks.

"People are saying that the port will be opening on July 5th, one week," he said slowly between bites. "And then it may get dangerous for you, Matushka. You must stay here in the apartment for the two months the port is open. I'll keep an eye on the docks. I'll look for the man who came into your house in Yanrakinnot, the one I whacked with Peter's rifle butt. I will never forget his face."

"Hopefully Father will join us by then," she said. "Peter will have told him where we are. Perhaps he'll have a new assignment from the bishop. I doubt we would be safe returning to Yanrakinnot."

"That's a great pity." Leonid took a slurp of his coffee. "There are wonderful people in Yanrakinnot. But there are also good villages in the interior made up of Chukchi reindeer herdsmen. We will move to one of those when Father comes for us. We'll start a new life. And Peter may be able to join us if he can find some medical relief in Yanrakinnot."

Bethany sat silently for a few minutes. "Leonid, Peter will not be able to join us. He must stay in Yanrakinnot and take care of his people. Perhaps after we are settled into a new village, you will want to return to Peter—"

"I cannot. . . . bear leaving you, Matushka. Where you go, I will go. I want to watch Tomas grow up. I will be his Godfather."

"And you shall if that is your wish. You have already been a second father to Tomas. You are deeply loved in this family."

Satisfied, Leonid ate the rest of his meal in silence. Bethany let Tomas crawl on the floor as she finished her meal.

Lord, bring Zach back to me safely, she prayed silently, stifling a sob.

Leonid noticed the sob. His face fell again.

July 1st — Jayu Park, Incheon, Republic of Korea

Lee Myung-bak, President of the Republic of Korea, walked along a tree-lined path beside Prime Minister Han Seung-soo. Intelligence Director Yu Sun-shin walked behind them. Plain-clothed security guards walked several paces to their front and rear, just out of hearing.

They were walking through the beautiful Jayu Park in the city of Incheon, a port city about fifteen miles southwest of Seoul. All three were casually dressed in blue windbreakers with baseball caps pulled down over their heads. They walked in silence until they approached the tower with General MacArthur's statue at the top. Lee stopped and turned back to Yu.

"Yu, I have brought you to Freedom Park because of its historical meaning. Our ties with the United States of America are tight. General MacArthur saved us from Communism almost sixty years ago, and the Americans have kept us safe ever since. We owe them our gratitude."

"Yes, Mr. President. I know that and deeply respect our debt to America."

Lee resumed the walk, saying little. They climbed the hill and looked at the soaring bronze open arches of the Centennial Monument. As they gazed up at its towering height, Lee continued, "As you know, this monument represents the Amity and Trade Treaty signed by the USA and Korea way back in 1882. Our ties with the Americans go back many generations. For most of that time, we have been subservient to them and dependent on them. But it is different today. Today we have a chance to pay back some of that debt by saving them from the rogues of the North."

Prime Minister Han broke into the conversation. "Mr. President, the American president has certain weaknesses. Yu and I are not sure that he has the gumption to go ahead with their clandestine nuclear strike on the weapons of the North. If we do not succeed in our assassinations and the American strike does not come, we will risk our entire nation. The North may go ahead and launch an invasion at the DMZ, fire SCUDs at Seoul and even here in Incheon. . . . It could be the end of us."

Lee resumed his walk, followed by Han and Yu. Down the hill they walked, and after some moments finally arrived at Seokjeongru. They looked across to the port and in the distance to the Incheon International Airport.

"Yes, we could lose all this," Lee said quietly. "But it is worth the risk. We must pray that President Remington has the courage to allow the two American aircraft to make their strikes. We must have our assassination teams in place to do their work effectively. And we must have everything in order for Marshall Han Fo Chi to take over as interim Premier. . . . We must succeed. The world is depending on us. Do not mess this operation up, Director Yu. You have my permission to go forward with the plan."

Same Day — P'yongyang

General Park Rei Cho sat quietly on the garden patio of Premier Jang Song Thaek. The Premier and The Brilliant Comrade, Kim Jong Un sat across the concrete table from him. It was three in the afternoon and Kim Jong Un was getting restless. He was throwing a party at five and needed to supervise the set-up at his immaculately furnished penthouse flat on the other side of P'yongyang.

"Let's get on with this, Uncle," Kim said as he shifted on the uncomfortable concrete bench.

"Patience, Nephew," Jang said quietly. Then, turning confidently to Park, he said, "General, give us a rundown on the preparations for Saturday night."

"All is ready, Premier Jang," Park said as he pulled some papers from his briefcase and spread them on the table. With no wind blowing, the papers sat motionless in the afternoon sun. "The Americans fly daily their bombers and fighters off our coast hoping to intimidate us. And we are aware that they are bringing four of their aircraft carriers into easy flying range of our launch pads and indeed the capital. But even with all that, we are ready to launch Saturday night—"

Kim Jong Un cut into the conversation. "It is an insult for the dirty Americans to fly so close to our borders and to sail their carrier boats here. We should challenge them. General, you are to send MIGs into their formations, force them to avoid hitting our aircraft. Let's make them think twice about saber-rattling so close to us."

Park began to speak but was interrupted by Jang.

"The Brilliant Comrade is right, General. They won't fire on us if we don't fire on them. And by challenging them, we will create a brilliant diversion while we ready our launch. In fact, let's send some of our ships within sight of their carriers. Not too close. The captains of those ships don't need permission from the President to fire on us if we get too close. But we can continually threaten them, play with their minds, show them we're not afraid of them. And we'll complain to the press and to the UN that their provocative actions are part of their Operation Key Resolve effort to trick us into attacking them. Let's especially intensify our efforts on Saturday, all day. Keep them busy while we prepare to launch the ICBM. See to it, General. . . . You have done well, Nephew, in coming up with this idea!"

This is foolishness, Park thought as he watched Jang slap Kim on the back. *Does Kim not see that Jang is using him? Oh, well. Let them carry on. In four days, they'll both be history.*

"I agree, Brilliant Comrade," Park said slowly. "You have learned well. And your brilliance is already helping us succeed."

Just then, Kim jumped out of his seat. "See to it, General Park. And do not make a mistake on this launch or on the invasion to follow. I am holding you personally accountable. If you can't do it right, I have people who can. Do you understand me?"

Before Park could respond, Kim turned to Jang. "Enough of this talk. I have things to do and people to see, uncle. Please see that my car is ready right now."

Jang made eye contact and stared at Kim before speaking. "Brilliant Comrade, may I remind you that I have been given the responsibility of training and supervising you until your father says otherwise. I will not have you talk to me in this manner."

"Please, Uncle," Kim said quickly. "We don't air our differences in front of the workers. Please have my car ready by the time I get to the front of your house." With that, he trudged out of the garden.

After he was gone, Jang looked at Park apologetically. "You must excuse him, General. He is still not ready to lead, is he? He will need continual supervision by me for some time to come. . . . For now, I'll let him cool his heels in the front yard while he waits for his car. In fifteen minutes, I'll call for his car. And if he comes back here complaining, I might just shoot him in the foot." Jang laughed heartily as he finished the sentence. Park joined him in the frivolity.

You are creating a monster, Premier Jang, Park said to himself. *But that's okay, you'll soon spend eternity together. . . . in hell."*

July 2nd — Beijing

The Chairman of the Chinese People's Republic, President Hu Jintao, sat in an easy chair in a nondescript office in Zhangnanhai, seat of government for the nation. Sixty-eight years old and slightly paunchy, the intelligent technocrat managed his country of 1.3 billion people in a quiet, low-key manner. Hu knew he had other means of enforcing his will if the humble approach didn't work. . . . He was, after all, also Commander-in-Chief of the People's Liberation Army. Hu was dressed in a black business suit, but was already thinking of retreating to his farm in the country north of Beijing as soon as the workday was over.

Facing Chairman Hu in an identical easy chair was Vice President Xi Jinping. Xi was much younger than Hu, only fifty-seven years old, but had the same personality. He was a frugal, hard-working, down-to-earth technocrat. Trim and athletic, Xi was a master at ping-pong and had a photographic memory. In a word, he was Hu's alter-ego. Xi wore an exact duplicate of Hu's suit and even wore the same maroon tie and gold tie tack.

"We need to proceed carefully with this P'yongyang business, my friend," Hu said to Xi. "Our man Premier Jang has the situation well in hand, but so much can go wrong."

"I've read the report," Xi said slowly. "The Americans are being provocative in dealing with the North Korean 'menace' as they call it. They have four aircraft carrier battle groups surrounding DPRK, their carriers Ronald Reagan and Abraham Lincoln in the Sea of Japan, and the John Stennis and George Washington in the Yellow Sea and Korea Bay. Their aircraft are already doing patrols dangerously close to our borders. We've had to challenge them with our interceptors the last two days.

"Plus they have put two squadrons of Raptor fighter jets in at the northern Japanese base of Misawa and ten Spirit bombers into Anderson Base on Guam. The buildup is way beyond the normal annual war games they play in South Korea. Our intelligence sources tell us that the Americans think P'yongyang will launch a nuclear strike against them on July 20th, so the Americans are threatening a massive raid on North Korea on the 10th unless DPRK openly stands down from its plan. These American aircraft carrier groups and US Air Force planes are placed here to show P'yongyang that they are serious."

"And. . . . are the Americans serious, Xi?" The president stared out the window at the willow trees blowing wildly in the wind.

"They are not. Not in my opinion. The American president is weak. He is pleading with Moscow to put pressure on Kim Jong Il. He's even trying to plead with us, but we don't have to listen. Soon we will be able to tell him what to do, or threaten to withhold from him our financial support. He'll soon be in our back pocket.

"And we're prepared to find financial markets that are not dependent on the USA. Here's how. When P'yongyang makes its surprise nuclear ICBM launch on July 4th, everything will fall into our lap. The Americans will leave the Korean Peninsula in disgrace and we will gain control of Seoul's economy. The Americans will be forced to trade with P'yongyang since so much of their economy depends on Seoul. And with Premier Jang in charge of P'yongyang, we will own Seoul. . . . This is a sound business plan, Mr. Chairman."

"But what if the Americans decide to launch a nuclear attack of their own? P'yongyang has no defensive capability when it comes to nuclear arms. Will we have to engage our troops and equipment against the Americans?"

"The Americans will not retaliate. They will be fearful of launching a nuclear retaliation with their own American troops living only one hundred miles away from the blasts. And they have nowhere near enough troops to attack on the ground.

"Plus, the media is already convincing the world that America is the provocateur here. Russia will convince them to take the Korean attack before the Security Council for a 'quick' punishment of P'yongyang. By the time that gets on the docket, the SCUDs will be flying and the troops will be headed south across the DMZ. The whole war should be wrapped up by August. I repeat, sir, this is a sound business plan."

"I trust you, Xi," Chairman Hu said as he smiled at his young companion. "I trust you because I know you will someday sit in my seat. You have everything to lose if the plan goes bad. So you will not allow it to go bad."

Xi smiled broadly. "Thank you for your confidence, sir. I will not let you down."

CHAPTER FIFTEEN

2330 Hours, July 3rd — MCAS Iwakuni, Japan

"*A*nd so it begins," Bob Shanto said over the intercom to his bombardier-navigator, Zach Savage, as they started engines on the flight line of the Marine Corps Air Station Iwakuni, Japan.

"You cannot believe how glad I am to get out of that dreary bunk in the supply building," Zach said to Bob as they began their taxi toward Runway Zero Two. They were the last aircraft in the flight. "I have this claustrophobia problem and that small room drove me nuts!"

"I hate to tell ya'll this, good buddy," Bob said, glancing across the cockpit at him. "But do you recall that a submarine's gonna rescue us after we fire these missiles? How big do ya'll imagine your sleepin' space is gonna be in that sub?"

"Thanks for reminding me of that wonderful nugget of info, old man."

Just then, they heard Electronic Countermeasures Officer Number One (ECMO-1) in the lead bird come up on the radio. "Iwakuni Tower, Prowler 24 with a flight of four for takeoff at ten second intervals."

"Prowler 24, you are cleared with a flight of four for takeoff Runway Zero Two Left. Winds zero-five-zero at ten. Altimeter two-niner-niner-four."

"Two-niner-niner-four." Dash One and Dash Two lined up for takeoff and started their roll. "Dash One's rolling."

Zach watched as Dash One began its roll down the runway. He counted to ten and watched as Dash Two began its roll. He counted another ten seconds as Bob maneuvered their bird into position for takeoff.

Dash Three began its roll as Bob ran up the engines to one hundred percent, pushing on the brakes so they wouldn't roll too soon. At the count of ten, Bob released the brakes and the Prowler began its takeoff roll. At about six thousand feet down the runway and at one-hundred-fifty-six knots, he rotated and the Prowler became airborne. Zach kept his eyes on Dash Three's lights.

"Dash Four's airborne," Zach said over the radio.

"Dash Three's eleven o'clock high," Zach said to Bob.

"Tally-ho," Bob answered and banked left to catch Dash Three.

Five minutes later, all four Prowlers were in formation, climbing for Flight Level two-zero-zero, heading for the break-off point.

Midnight — In a cabin south of Mount Mantap, North Korea

The large cement block cabin was built into the side of a hill, ten miles south of Mount Mantap, in eastern North Korea. Floor-to-ceiling windows made up the south wall, with sliding glass doors that opened onto a deck which jutted out from the hillside and looked out on the valley below.

Fifty soldiers were stationed around the perimeter of the property in camouflaged gazebos. Several gazebos pointing south had anti-aircraft artillery pieces hidden in them.

The soldiers lived in a barracks complex at the bottom of the hill. They were treated well. Three square meals a day, only two soldiers per bedroom, all the 'off-duty' alcohol they could handle, and night visits by women every weekend. But there was one drawback. They could never leave their barracks complex except to assume the duty in the gazebos.

Corporal Hu Sun Ming had been stationed at the complex for two years. Small and thin, he stayed in shape by doing yoga and running in place. He avoided the kickboxing matches his fellow soldiers so loved and he skipped the alcohol and women. Hu was a recluse. He loved being stationed at this mountain getaway because no one bothered him here. He had plenty of time to meditate and read. And with nothing to spend money on, he was able to send most of his salary home to his poverty-stricken mother in Wonsan.

On this particular night, he was at his post in a gazebo five miles east of the cabin, manning the AAA with another recluse soldier, Private Han Sing Mung. They went about their duties without even acknowledging each other's presence. Hu and Han knew that it was their solemn duty and privilege to protect Kim Jong Il and his sons. And so they agreed to stay ever-vigilant.

The cabin itself had well appointed rooms. Antique furniture and decorations from the Chinese Ming Dynasty decorated every room. There were five bedrooms. On this night, four were being used.

In the first bedroom lay Kim Jong Il. His nurse rested in a recliner beside the bed. The Dear Leader lay there with a ventilator feeding oxygen to his lungs. He also had a feeding tube down his throat. Kim had taken a turn for the worse the week before and was comatose.

He had been carried to his mountain retreat to die. Death could come at any moment.

In the bedroom next door lay Kim's oldest son, Kim Jong Nam. In his late thirties, Kim Jong Nam lived in a fantasy world. He loved theme parks and computer games. On this night, he was deeply into pornography. His fantasy life was in high gear as he watched the grotesque displays on his laptop.

In the bedroom across the hall from the Dear Leader was the number-two son, Kim Jong Chol. Jong Chol, in his mid-thirties, was practicing his acceptance speech. General Park had secretly picked him to replace his father as the leader of the Democratic People's Republic of Korea and had been preparing him for that eventuality should his father die. When Jong Chol had asked how this could be, since the Brilliant Comrade, his younger brother, had been chosen by his father for the job, Park had assured him that this would be their little secret and that, indeed, Jong Chol would be chosen over his younger brother. So Jong Chol was working on his acceptance speech, following Park's advice about losing the effeminate qualities in his voice and gestures.

Down the stairs in the back part of the house, the youngest brother, Kim Jong Un, sat in his bed. 'The Brilliant Comrade' was quite drunk. He had not been pleased with the woman his aide had brought him, and he gave her a beating. He would have killed her but his aide had rushed into the bedroom and rescued her. To appease Jong Un, the aide gave him an expensive bottle of brandy in exchange for the woman. The woman had now been gone for an hour and Jong Un was about to finish the brandy. He was not lying down because when he tried to lie back, the room started spinning. So he just sat there, willing himself to feel better as he took swigs directly from the bottle. He amused himself by thinking of all the things and people he would change when his father finally died and he as the Brilliant Comrade would rule all of Korea, both North and South.

0045, July 4th — Low level over the Sea of Japan

The flight of four Prowlers had reached twenty thousand feet thirty miles west of the Iwakuni. The lead two Prowlers, with the wing commander leading and Wally on his wing, then continued west while the other two Prowlers broke off and turned north. Bob and Zach refueled from the KC-10 as they proceeded north, and then followed their lead Prowler in a steep descent. When they were one hundred feet above the Korea Strait, their leader gave them the kiss-off and headed back to Iwakuni.

Now Bob and Zach were starting north at one hundred feet above the Sea of Japan. It was a moonlit night with very little turbulence even though they were flying so low to the water.

Four hundred fifty miles, Zach thought. *At this slow speed, we should get to the first target in about an hour and a half. That's about right. GPS predicts us on target at 0225. We may need to slow down as we get closer, or maybe do a three-sixty along the way. I'll need to monitor carefully.*

"Ya'll doin' your figurin', Zach?" Bob interrupted him. "Why ya'll need to do that? The GPS is tellin' us what we need to know."

"Backup planning, Bob," Zach replied. "Navigators are taught to figure all the angles and always have a backup plan."

"Yup. That makes sense. . . . Looks like we may need to slow down as we get closer, or maybe do a slow three-sixty along the way."

"Just thinking that same thing myself," Zach mused.

After fifteen minutes of silence, Bob came up on the intercom. "I'm gettin' bored if ya'll want to know the truth, Zach. Maybe I need a smoke."

"Are you kidding?" Zach looked across the cockpit at Bob. "We've got nukes aboard."

"Just messing with your brain, kid. Wanted to make sure ya'll are payin' attention. . . . How about jokes? Heard any good jokes lately?"

"Yeah, like I've been reading joke books the last month. . . . Okay, did you hear about the national chess convention? All the renowned chess champions from around the world met in a Las Vegas hotel for the big tournament. All they talked about was chess, chess, and more chess. As they sat in the hotel foyer late one night talking chess moves, the manager finally had enough of it. He kicked them out. Know why?"

"Here comes the punch line, right? I give up. Why'd the hotel manager kick 'em out of the foyer?"

"He didn't like *quote* chess nuts boasting in an open foyer *unquote.* . . . Get it?"

"Yeah," Bob deadpanned. "That's really funny. Sorry I asked. Now I'll be hummin' that stupid song for the rest of the night."

"How about this? How do we know God invented baseball?"

"I give up. How do we know God invented baseball?"

"Cause it says right in Genesis 1:1, 'In the big inning, God created the heavens and the earth.'"

"Stop! No more jokes."

"I could preach you a sermon. How about that?"

"Hey, here's a thought. I'll go back to bein' a bored pilot. And you can do yer navigator stuff."

0115, July 4th — P'yongyang

South Korean assassins Lee Ram-Ting, Kim Shin-Bong, and Pak Song-Ho walked down the street toward the building they sought. They were disguised as DPRK soldiers. Security guards for Premier Jang Song Thaek had alerted them by cell phone that Jang and General Park Rei Cho were in a secret meeting in a conference room on the fifth floor of the Foreign Trade Bank of North Korea Corporate Building on Nam'po Street.

When they got to the building, they walked around back and opened the door that had been left unlocked. Lee walked in first, followed five steps later by Kim and Pak. Once in, they pulled their forty-five caliber Slimlines from their pockets and attached silencers.

So far, so good, thought Lee, the team leader. *Now for the elevator.*

They approached the service elevator, walked in and hit the button for the fourth floor. As the elevator opened on four, Kim held down the 'Door Open' button and counted silently to five. Hearing nothing, Lee stepped out slowly, followed by Kim and Pak. They turned right and walked down the hall to the stairwell. Entering, they silently climbed to the fifth floor. Lee went over the scenario in his mind.

We turn left after entering the hall, walk twenty-five paces, then blow the door marked with red tape and shoot both men. Jang's bodyguards are on break on floor seven.

Reaching floor five and moving into the hall, Lee and Kim began pacing toward the marked door, with Pak hanging back in the stairwell. Just then General Park's personal bodyguard, not an agent of the South Korean government, who had just used the restroom, quietly stepped out of the restroom and surveyed the backs of the two assassins, noting that they were carrying pistols with silencers. Knowing what this meant, he unceremoniously pulled his pistol and shot them both dead in a millisecond.

The noise of the shots echoed through the hall. Jang and General Park heard the shots and dove under the conference table.

"Treachery, Park," Jang whispered as he watched the door, drawing his Glock. "It's good that we have security in the hall."

Park's bodyguard called Park on the cell phone. "Sir, I have just shot two assassins out here in the hall. Premier Jang's security guards are nowhere to be seen."

Park didn't speak. He instead thought about the solution.

The assassins were here to kill Jang or me or both. They may be South Koreans intent on doing us both in. But how would they know we are here? Or they could be working for Jang. They were probably here on Jang's orders to kill me, just as he has been planning all along. He can claim that South Koreans shot me. And without me here tomorrow, he'll launch the ICBM and ruin everything.

General Park Rei Cho pulled his service revolver and shot Premier Jang Song Thaek three times in the back.

He jumped up from under the table, ran to the door and swung it open. His bodyguard was standing there pointing his pistol at him. Recognizing Park, the guard ran into the room and found Jang on the floor, dead.

"Sun," Park said quickly. "You must corroborate my story. The assassins were sent by Premier Jang to kill me. But you found them in the hall and shot them. When you called me and told me what you had done, Jang pulled his Glock and tried to shoot me. Fortunately, you shot him before he shot me."

"Yes, sir," Sun replied. "It happened just as you said. Look. Premier Jang's Glock is right there beside his body. He tried to murder you in cold blood. I had just come into the room and shot him in the back before he shot you."

Just then, Jang's security men came running into the room, surprised to see Park alive and well. Park explained to them what had happened and then called his Chief of DPRK Security. As they ran for the waiting helicopter, South Korean assassin Pak, who had hung back in the stairwell for just such an incident as this, joined the fray, his DPRK uniform giving him perfect cover.

0200, July 4th — Low level over the Sea of Japan

"I'm doin' a three-sixty to kill time, Zach. How's it lookin'?"

Zach looked at his chart. "I can't turn the radar on yet. Too far to see anything at this altitude. But the GPS is showing that at this speed we'll hit the target at 0230. Too soon. Good idea to do a slow three-sixty."

Bob began a slow left orbit.

"In sixty miles," Zach continued, "we climb to two thousand and increase our speed to four-eighty. I turn on the 99 and the 113. Suddenly North Korea's world will go insane as their radar screens go berserk and their comm and data links go down. We can't get to that point until 0230, five minutes before we hit the target."

"Whatever," Bob said and nodded his head at Zach.

0210, July 4th — P'yongyang

General Park was barking orders at his aides who had quickly assembled at his office as soon as his helicopter touched down at his base.

"Shin, contact the cabinet members by coded phone. Then send men to get them out of their beds. We need an emergency meeting immediately.

"Bak, get me General Pak on the phone. . . . General Pak? This is General Park. Stand down on the ICBM launch. I repeat. Stand down on the ICBM launch. My authenticator is 22739C. I will explain it later. Stop the launch clock."

He punched in a number on his red phone.

"Da?" a voice answered.

"There has been a shooting here. Premier Jang is dead. I have halted the ICBM launch and called an emergency meeting of the cabinet. I have also dispatched a helicopter to pick up Kim Jong Chol." With that, Park hung up.

Holding the phone on the other end was none other than President Dmitri Medvedev. He picked up the other phone and punched in a number.

"Da?" came the stone cold voice. "What is it, Dmitri?"

"Vladimir," Medvedev said quickly as he addressed Putin. "Park is in control right now. Jang has been shot. Park has called off the ICBM strike on the Americans. And he is sending for Kim Jong Chol to prop him up as The Brilliant Leader."

"Do you think the Americans will find out before they attack DPRK?"

"I don't think so, unless they have a mole in P'yongyang's government that we don't know about."

"Good. Let the Americans bomb DPRK's nuclear facilities. One less hassle for us and it makes the Americans look bad. I will have our PR people draft up some press releases for you to look at."

"Mr. Putin," Medvedev formally addressed his mentor. "This will be the beginning of a whole new day in East Asia."

"Da," Putin responded and hung up.

0215, July 4th — The White House Situation Room

The President and his Security Council, augmented by his Chief of Staff and CIA Director Rogers, sat around the conference table in the situation room located in the basement under the West Wing of the White House. The hardened five-thousand-square-foot space was full of communications equipment and monitors.

This is a nightmare, Remington thought as intelligence information poured in on the boards. *I am actually going to engage in a nuclear attack on a nation I'm not even at war with. All to prevent that nation from engaging in a nuclear attack on us. It's the worst nightmare any president can have. But why me?*

"The President of South Korea's on the phone for you," whispered the Chief of Staff. "Says it is extremely urgent."

"What now?" Remington said as he picked up his extension. "I don't have time for this."

Speaking in a hurried voice, Remington answered his caller, "What's up, President Lee? I'm kind of busy right now."

"Good evening, Mr. President. Did you know that the North Koreans have called off their ICBM attack and are standing down?"

"What?" Remington waved for everyone in the situation room to shut up. "Mr. Lee, did you just say that the North Koreans are calling off their attack on us?"

The room grew immediately silent. Everyone stared at the President of the United States as he put the conversation on 'Speaker Phone.'

"Yes, Mr. President," President Lee continued. "There's been a coup in P'yongyang. The Premier has been assassinated and the General of the Armed Forces, General Park Rei Cho, has taken control of the country. His first act was to order the forces of the DPRK to stand down not only on the missile strike but on the buildup along the DMZ. . . . This is good news, Mr. President."

"If true, this is indeed good news, Mr. Lee," Remington replied cautiously. "Please don't think I'm insulting you, but may I ask how you know this?"

"I do not take your comment as an insult at all," Lee said slowly. "I would ask the same question if I were you. . . . In fact, we have infiltrated the DPRK Command Structure. I know that what I have told you is absolutely true. You might say our assassins have already been at work.

"One problem we have to overcome, however. Our assassination team that is bound for Kim Jong Il and his sons ran into difficulty getting to his house. Two of the five fell off a steep ledge and have been injured. The other three, after rendering first aid, have continued on. But they are now behind schedule. Our intelligence tells us that General Park has sent a helicopter to pick up one of the sons, and maybe kill all the others. The one son will be named the new leader of DPRK. We hope to get there before the helicopter, but it will be close."

"Uh, thank you so much, Mr. President," Remington responded. "On behalf of the United States of America, may I profoundly thank you for this information? Right now I have some work to do. But I'll call you back in one hour. Then we can coordinate our next actions as allies."

As Remington hung up the phone, he let out a cheer that almost deafened his heretofore silent staff. "We've done it! Ladies and gentlemen, we have averted a nuclear war."

Everyone cheered except General Rogers, who sat there silently writing a note.

"Call off the attacks by the Prowlers and do it immediately," Remington ordered Rogers.

"Yes sir," Rogers replied. "We'll have them return to base. They'll both have to refuel along the way back. We'll get tankers off the carriers to refuel them." Rogers turned to SECDEF, who nodded. Rogers and his aide walked into one of the small communication rooms, where he closed the door and got on the phone. SECDEF entered another of the rooms.

"Wow!" Remington was shouting to everyone in the room. "Just in the nick of time. Those Prowlers were only ten minutes from launching nukes at DPRK. This one will go down in the history books.

"Okay. We've got some quick work to do. Sandy, as quickly as you can, get me everything you've got on this General Park. Can we work with him? Who's he tilt toward?

"When I call President Lee back, I need to find out about Kim Jong Il and his heir-apparent son. Which son is it, and how does he tilt? I've heard that it's just a matter of days before Kim Jong Il kicks the bucket. What does that mean to this coup? And how does that work for General Park?"

He turned to his Chief of Staff. "I need to talk to the following in this order: Medvedev in Moscow, Hu in Beijing, Hatoyama in Japan, and finally Lee in Seoul. We've got to get our act together on how we handle this!"

Remington turned to his staff. "Ladies and gentlemen, relationships among lead nations win every time. We have just averted a world crisis. And now we can pick up the pieces in North Korea and forge a new reality."

0225, July 4th — Over the Sea of Japan

"We're at two thousand feet and four-hundred-eighty knots," Wally said as he scanned his Vertical Display Indicator and other gauges and indicators. He and Jerry were over Korea Bay just to the west of the North Korean mainland.

"We're already getting painted," Jerry said. "I'm switching on the 99 and the 113. . . . They're on. Come to three-four-zero and follow steering. I've got the first target on the radar. Going to infrared."

"Clambake Zero Five, Deer Slayer," came a voice over the secure radio.

"What in the world is that all about?" Wally glanced at Jerry. "See what they want. We're not supposed to get any comm except a mission abort order."

"Go ahead, Deer Slayer," Jerry responded on the transmitter. "I'm ready for your authenticator. But hurry up. I'm cooking here."

"Authenticator 299Charlie687. Respond."

"Valid authenticator. Mine is 3892537. Go ahead."

"Valid authenticator. Clambake Zero Five, this is a mission abort order. You are to abort the mission immediately and return to base. I say again. Abort the mission."

"You've got to be kidding," Jerry yelled. "I just zapped these guys with the 99 and the 113. They're sitting ducks!"

"Zero Five, abort the mission and return to base. We'll get a tanker up there to refuel you along the way. Read back."

Jerry shook his head at Wally. "Roger, Deer Slayer. We are aborting the mission and returning to base. Will head south while waiting for direction to tanker."

"Good day." General Rogers ended the transmission and dialed in another.

Across Korea, just to the east of the North Korean mainland, over the Sea of Japan, Bob and Zach were also at two thousand feet and four hundred eighty knots. They had also just blasted the North Korean radars and communications in their area.

"I've got Target One clearly defined on radar, Bob," Zach said as he gazed at his scope. "Take steering. Straight north. Going to infrared. Master arm's coming on. I'm switching into attack."

"That's a great big Roger," Bob said as he adjusted the stick to get on course.

"Clambake Zero Three. Deer Slayer, over." The same voice that had penetrated Wally and Jerry's cockpit now penetrated Bob and Zach's.

"What the. . . ?" Bob jumped in his seat. "Get that, will ya, Zach? I'm kind of busy on my side of the aircraft."

"It may be a trick, Bob," Zach said quietly as he concentrated on the attack.

"And it may be a mission abort order. Answer the dang call."

Zach kicked the transmit button on. "Go ahead Deer Slayer. Authenticate."

"Clambake Zero Three, my authenticator is 299Charlie687. Say yours."

"Valid authenticator. Mine is 649230," Zach responded, gazing into the infrared. "Go ahead, Deer Slayer. But make it quick."

"Valid authenticator. Clambake Zero Three, you are to stand down from Targets One and Two, effective immediately. You are instead directed to hit Target Three with your conventional missile only. Exit target as briefed. Read back, please?"

"Startin' another three-sixty till we get this figured out," Bob said to Zach over the intercom as he slowed the aircraft and went into a right bank.

"Copy, Deer Slayer," Zach said. "We are standing down from Targets One and Two, and will hit Target Three with our conventional missile. Exit as briefed."

"Your read back is correct. Good day."

"Master arm off," Zach said as he tried to reorient himself. "What the heck happened?"

"Beats me," Bob said. "Figure out how to get us to Target Three and give me a headin'."

At that moment — The White House Situation Room

Rogers' aide, John Brown, stood there listening to General Rogers as he commanded the nuclear mission abort and commanded the conventional strike.

Wait a minute. Wait a minute. President Remington just told the General to call off the missions. Do I dare confront him on this?

As General Rogers began to make another call, John Brown looked at him quizzically. "General, the President of the United States just gave you a direct order to abort those missions. What are you doing?"

"Look, son," Rogers said as he put the phone down and laid a hand on the aide's shoulder. "Sometimes we have to interpret orders. And that's what I'm doing now. The president wants to stop the attacks on the nuclear facilities. But he said nothing specific about not hitting Kim Jong Il's place."

That doesn't sound right to me, Brown thought. *I'm sure the president does not approve of what the General is doing.*

"But shouldn't you clarify that with the President?"

"Heck, no. He needs deniability on this. . . . Listen to me now. You just heard the President of South Korea say that their assassination team has been held up and won't get to that cabin before Kim Jong Il's rotten son, 'The Brilliant Comrade,' gets spirited off to P'yongyang to take over the country. We've got a chance to wipe out the whole Kim family. That's why we put that target in for a conventional attack in the first place. And we need to do it now or we'll regret it later.

"Son, I picked you to be my aide because of your intelligence and practical common sense. I hope to set you up to be one of the top leaders of the Central Intelligence Agency. So consider this one of the most important lessons you'll ever learn. Interpret orders with intelligence and common sense. That's what I'm doing now. So keep this to yourself. You understand?"

"Yes, sir," the aide said. But *I'm not convinced at all. Is this the way things run at the top?*

Rogers picked up the phone and dialed in the SECDEF waiting in the next room. "George, I've just called to abort the missions. Get those submarines moving south fast. They won't be needed for rescue except in an emergency."

"Yes, sir," SECDEF replied.

What? What's he doing now? Leaving that Marine crew to fend for itself?

"General," the aide said. "The sub on the east coast needs to be there to rescue the two crewmen! It can't move south yet."

Rogers looked into the eyes of Brown and put his hands on his hips. "Son, now you let me be the Director of the CIA and you go back to being my aide. Those two crewmen are going to sacrifice their lives for the good of our country. That's just the way it's got to be. For the president to have deniability on this, they have to disappear along with their airplane. Trust me on this. . . . They knew they might have to die when they took the assignment. And now they'll have to die."

This is a nightmare. If I blow the whistle on General Rogers, my career is cooked, and maybe even my life. But can I just stand here and let two Americans die because the general wants them dead. Perhaps I don't have the big picture here.

Brown looked solemnly at his boss. "Yes, sir. You know much more about this than I do." He quietly walked out of the room.

CHAPTER SIXTEEN

0236 — July 4th — Crossing the North Korean Coastline

"I'm at five hundred knots, five hundred feet, headin' three-four-zero," Bob said as he followed his VDI.

"So here's our route, Bob," Zach said as he checked his chart. "We're going feet dry right now ten miles east of Songjin. Come right to zero-one-zero."

"Zero-one-zero," Bob said as he banked right.

"In two minutes, we'll hang a left near Kilchu. See it on the scope? We'll head up the valley and I'll break out the target when we get in sight."

Two minutes later, Zach came up on the intercom.

"Approaching Kilchu. Come left to three-four-zero."

"Three-four-zero. Terrain Avoidance is on at one hundred feet," Bob replied as he pulled into a left turn.

"Now we'll go hey-diddle-diddle up the middle of this valley. I've got it on the scope and can give you manual heading changes. Mountains on both sides are up to six thousand feet. Okay, come left to three-three-zero."

"Three-three-zero."

0240 — July 4th — Camouflaged Gazebo

Corporal Hu Sun Ming sat in his lawn chair in the outpost, a small, square, concrete structure built into the side of the hill. It was open on the south side, allowing the twin thirty-seven-millimeter anti-aircraft artillery piece to point out at the valley. He was looking out over the valley.

This is boring, as usual. Less than four hours before we get relieved. And I'm tired. I just wish there was some way I could read. But the light would be seen for miles.

As he turned to his left, he heard heavy breathing coming from Private Han Sing Mung.

"Private Han?" Hu said softly. Hearing no answer, he said in a normal voice, "Private Han."

Still no response. Han's asleep on duty. That's a court-martial offense.

He walked over to the lawn chair in which Han was sitting and shook him. "Private Han, wake up! You're asleep on duty."

Private Han awoke with a start. He looked up and saw Corporal Hu pointing his rifle at him.

"Don't shoot, Corporal Hu! I profoundly apologize. I did not mean to fall asleep and was not even aware that I did."

"You goat! I should shoot you right now, but maybe I'll just bring you up on charges." Hu put the rifle down.

"Please, sir, don't bring me up on charges. I need to work at this job. I need the money for my family. What can I do to convince you that I won't fall asleep again?"

Hu glanced at him and then at the Triple A standing behind him.

"Okay. Go sit up there on the gunner seat. That will keep you awake. I am going to check on you every five minutes. Do you hear me?"

"Yes, sir. I will stay awake. Please don't punish me."

"I'll think about it, private."

0242 — P'yongyang

General Park Rei Cho threw the phone across the room and scowled. He was sitting in his office with two other generals and their aides.

"Communications down. Data link down. Radars down. What is going on here, Captain Rho?"

Captain Rho, his aide, glanced at him and then looked away. "I think we may be under satellite attack, General. Perhaps an enemy satellite has just zapped us."

"Does this mean I can't talk to anyone? Don't we have some backup communication plan in case our primary goes down?"

"I'm afraid there is no backup plan, sir," Captain Rho responded as he looked at the floor.

"Then how, captain, will I know if the helicopter has successfully picked up Kim Jong Chol?"

"I would not worry about it, General. The pilot of the helicopter is excellent. I know him well. He can fly without communications or radar assistance. He knows this country like the back of his hand. We will very soon see Mr. Kim Jong Chol walk through the door."

"I wish I had as much confidence as you have, captain." Park again scowled. "What about the cabinet? Are they all here yet? I want to start the meeting at Zero Three Hundred."

"We've picked up all but two, sir. There should be no problem starting the meeting in twenty minutes. I'll see that all is ready."

0245 — In the Valley aboard Clambake Zero Three

"We're crossing over Sumunnae," Zach said as the Prowler sliced through the valley.

"No Triple-A. Amazin'," Bob responded.

"Hey, they've got no radar and the people on the ground think we're one of theirs. They don't know we're coming."

"Sweet. How much time till target acquisition?"

"Another minute. . . . Okay, turn left into this valley — two-niner-five. Climb to a thousand feet."

"Two-niner-five. Climbin' to a thousand." Bob pulled hard left.

Okay, where's the target, Zach thought as he scanned and adjusted his radar. *It's supposed to be a building sticking out from a rock wall, facing south. Come to papa, building.*

"I have the target," Zach's voice went up an octave. "Going into attack. Master arm is on. Conventional weapon selected."

"Lookin' good," Bob replied. "I'm committin' to the attack."

"That target sticks out like a railroad car," Zach called. "Now I've got it on the infrared. It's a house built into the side of the sheer cliff. Don't know what or who's in there, but there's no way we'll miss that target."

"Sounds good to me. I don't like missin'." Bob concentrated on keeping the aircraft exactly on course.

"Detector head lock-on."

Suddenly the laser guided missile released from the wing and headed down toward the target.

"Weapon away," Zach called.

Bob pulled hard left and began his descent. As he approached one-two-zero, the missile hit the house dead on. Everyone and everything in the house were immediately vaporized.

0248 — Camouflaged Gazebo

Both Corporal Hu and Private Han heard the explosion. Han got on the radio to find out what happened but was surprised to find it dead. He also heard the loud whine of what sounded like an aircraft to their direct front.

"Han," Hu yelled. "I think the house has been bombed and there is an enemy aircraft in front of us. Fire! Fire!"

Private Han fired the twin thirty-sevens into the night, firing indiscriminately because he could see no enemy aircraft.

After thirty seconds of firing, he stopped and looked at Corporal Hu. "I hope for your sake, I didn't just shoot at one of our own airplanes. Because if we get into trouble for this, I will shout as loudly as I can that it was your idea, Corporal Hu. You did not have authorization to fire."

"It had to be an enemy aircraft, Han. Ours would not bomb the home of Kim Jong Il. The radios are down. That's why I didn't get authorization to fire. I did what I thought was the right thing. . . . I hope I did the right thing."

"When we get relieved, Hu, I am going to report you to the Sergeant Major."

Hu hung his head as they cleaned the gun. *I'm just not cut out for the military.*

Same Moment — Aboard the DPRK Helicopter

"Did you see that?" The pilot spoke over the intercom to his co-pilot. Helo One Eight Two Six was traveling northeast toward the mountain home of Kim Jong Il. They were scheduled to land on the roof in two minutes. DPRK assassins were to exit the aircraft and murder Kim Jong Ill and two of his sons. Others were to go in, grab Kim Jong Chol and get him on the helo for a quick return to P'yongyang.

The pilot continued, "The house just blew up. What is going on here? First the radios and nav aids go out. Now the house bursts into flame."

"Shall I take us on an orbit around the fire?" The co-pilot had control of the aircraft.

"No. There's nothing left. I can see that from here. The house was either bombed from outside or torched from inside. Nobody could live through that. Besides, there's no place for us to land. . . . Head back to P'yongyang, course two-two-zero. Let's make it snappy."

Same Moment — In Clambake Zero Three

As Bob got the Prowler back on the course of one-two-zero, the cockpit lit up like the Fourth of July.

"Tracers at ten o'clock!" Bob yelled and started to pull the Prowler into hard right climb.

Just then the canopy shattered and Bob's blood flew all over Zach. The wind was blowing everything around. The Prowler was spinning out of control. And Bob was slumped over the control stick.

"Bob!" *No. No.*

Zach pushed Bob's body back from the control stick and grabbed it. *Got to steady this aircraft up. . . . get control. . . . watch for mountains. . . . get out of here.*

With his heart rate now at hyper-speed and his breath coming in gasps, Zach righted the aircraft, steadied up, and began a gentle climb.

Gotta go for a thousand feet AGL. He watched the altimeter spoon up.

"Bob, can you hear me?" Zach tried the intercom. No response.

Reaching one thousand feet above the terrain, Zach turned on the autopilot, hit Terrain Avoidance and looked at his infrared.

He tried the scrambled frequency code on the radio. "Deer Slayer. Deer Slayer, Clambake Zero Three, over."

No joy.

He tried again, "Deer Slayer, this is Clambake Zero Three Bravo transmitting in the blind. Alpha has been hit. Repeat, Alpha has been hit. We're heading for the designated posit."

Gotta get us back down to Sumunnae. . . . There it is. Ten miles ahead. "I'm going to get us out of here, Bob. No sweat, G.I."

Just past Sumunnae, Zach hung a left turn, flew through a mountain pass, and then descended into a valley.

"Bob! Bob!" Zach called again over the intercom. Still no response. He felt Bob's neck for a pulse. Weak and intermittent, but it was there. He glanced at Bob's body.

Looks like he took a round to the left side of his body. Judging from the blood all over me and the cockpit, he's lost a lot of it.

I can't eject us over the water. Bob'll drown. I've got to eject us over land. With this aircraft in autopilot and Terrain Avoidance, it will fly by itself for a hundred miles before it runs out of fuel and sinks into the sea. . . . So I need to figure out where to eject us.

He looked at his chart.

There! Ten miles before we go feet wet. Some hills but not bad. And not a bad walk to the rescue point on the beach. "I'll get us out of this, Bob. Don't worry."

Lord God Almighty, protect us as we eject. I commend Bob's life to you. Please forgive him his sins and welcome him into your kingdom if he dies.

He tried the radio again, "Deer Slayer, Clambake Zero Three. Over."

Still no response.

"Deer Slayer, Clambake Zero Three. May Day. May Day. Both crew members ejecting."

I can't tell them where, or I'll pinpoint us for the enemy if for some reason they're monitoring.

As they neared the ejection point, Zach pushed Bob hard against the back of his seat. "Say goodbye, Marine," he yelled to Bob as he punched them out of the aircraft.

After what seemed like a lifetime, Zach found himself shooting up and out from the aircraft, dangling in the air for an instant, and bouncing hard as the chute opened and his ejection seat fell away.

So where's Bob? Zach swung around in his chute as he looked hard for his pilot. *There he is! A couple hundred yards north. I'll watch where he goes down so I can get to him when I hit the ground. Speaking of ground, where is it? There. I have some time. Thank you, Lord, for the safe ejection. Guide us down so we hit perfectly.*

As he descended, he oriented himself as to which way was the beach and what kind of vegetation he could expect when he landed. The bright moon was making it easier that it might have been on a cloudy night. He caught a last glance at Bob, who was a few seconds closer to the ground than he was.

And then Zach was down. Rolling several times, he released his chute and, lying there on the ground, did an inventory of his body.

Nothing broken or sprained, he thought as he got up. *Now let me get out of this harness, grab what I need from the survival kit and get over to Bob.*

He ran over the hill to his north. Since it was a moonlit night, he had no trouble navigating. They were in wilderness, with no lights or houses anywhere.

Five minutes later, Zach came upon Bob, lying in a culvert, gasping for breath. He tumbled down the culvert, reaching for Bob and grabbing him.

"Bob! Can you hear me?"

"What happened, kid?" Bob gasped as he looked up at Zach.

"We took a hit from Triple A. You got dinged on your left side. How are you feeling?"

"Like a. . . Mac truck. . . ran over. . . me. . . . I'm havin' trouble. . . breathin'."

Zach examined the wound on Bob's left side. There was no left side. It had been blown away. Blood was flowing like water.

How can Bob still be breathing? It looks like his lung has collapsed!

"We'll get you fixed up and out of here, Bob. Just hang tight."

"I'm not gonna. . . make it. . . Zach. . . . Lord, help me. . . I think. . . "

Bob's eyes closed. His breath stopped. Zach felt for a pulse. Nothing.

Bob's gone.

Zach took out his SAT phone and punched in the assigned number. No response.

Why am I getting no response from anyone?

Putting the phone back into his pocket, he did last rites for Bob, praying aloud, "Give rest, O Christ, to this your servant Bob, where sorrow and pain are no more. Into yours hands I commend my brother. Acknowledge him as a sheep of your own fold, a lamb of your own flock. Receive him into the arms of your mercy, Oh God, Father, Son and Holy Spirit. Amen."

After sitting with Bob for half an hour, Zach examined him again.

I've got to bury his body. He's definitely not coming back to life.

He took out Bob's trenching tool and dug a shallow grave. Placing Bob's body there, he conducted a short funeral service and then, saying goodbye a final time, headed east on foot.

0330 — P'yongyang

The cabinet members sat restlessly at the conference table as General Park Rei Cho told them of Premier Jang Song Thaek's treachery.

"Gentlemen, I think the loss of communications we were experiencing may have been part of Jang's attempted coup. I have received intelligence that the Chinese were behind him on this, as well as Kim Jong Il's own son, Kim Jong Un. Fortunately, I was able to save the day by defending myself against Jang. He is now dead and we can resolve this whole mess.

"Somehow the Dear Leader must have known of his youngest son's treachery because he has written to me a secret letter, which I have had authenticated, that his second son, Kim Jong Chol, is to succeed him. Since the Dear Leader is too ill to join us for this important meeting, I have sent for Kim Jong Chol to come to our meeting and assist me in filling in for the Dear Leader."

At that moment, Park's aide entered the room, whispered to Park, and left the room. Park's expression went blank.

"I have just received a communication that all three of the Dear Leader's sons have been murdered at their mountain cabin, probably at the hands of Jang's conspirators."

Every member of the cabinet gasped, almost in unison.

"Fortunately, the Dear Leader was not at the cabin," Park continued, lying through his teeth and looking from face to face. "He is in a hospital in Wonsan, and is very much alive. . . . Let us have a moment of silence in remembering these three valiant warriors. Then I shall send out soldiers to sweep up Jang's co-conspirators."

0400 — Marine Corps Air Station Iwakuni, Japan

Clambake Zero Five touched down at Iwakuni and immediately taxied to the hanger where the ground crew towed it into the hangar and shut the big doors. Wally and Jerry climbed down out of the cockpit, looked around, and walked to the Ready Room. Si was waiting for them.

"So when's Zero Three due in?" Wally looked at Si.

"Problem." Si was standing slouched at the lectern. "We haven't heard from them since they got the mission abort order."

"What?" Jerry yelled. "How can that be?"

"I don't know," Si said. "They acknowledged mission abort. But they never came up on the radio again. Didn't make the tanker, and didn't land. We thought we heard a couple voice transmissions at one point, but it was so garbled, our people couldn't make it out. We've swept the area with our radars. Vanished."

"Could they have been hit by enemy fire?"

"Hardly, man. The Koreans were without radar and comm. And Zero Three was too far out to sea to be hit by any North Korean ground fire. We're beginning to think they flew into the water. . . . They may have lost comm and just run out of gas. The sub is tracking south, listening for them."

Silence enveloped the room. Wally and Jerry bowed their heads in prayer.

Finally, Wally spoke. "We're going to get a cup of coffee in the supply building, Si. Let us know if anything happens."

"I will," Si replied. "But if we hear nothing by sun-up, we've got to start getting things together to return birds and bombs to CONUS."

"Roger that." Wally and Jerry walked slowly out of the Ready Room.

Two nights later, a KC-10 and a Prowler took off, headed for Area 51.

10 a.m. — P'yongyang

General Park Rei Cho stood before the microphones at the hastily arranged press conference, made up only of journalists from the Democratic People's Republic of Korea. A tall military officer stood beside him.

"And so, my dear countrymen, with the death of Premier Jang Song Thaek, we have thwarted this evil coup attempt. Unfortunately we were not able to prevent his assassination of all three of the Dear Leader's sons. We will have a state funeral for them on Tuesday.

"In the aftermath, we were able to interrogate some of Premier Jang's co-conspirators. We now know without a doubt that some senior leaders in the government of the People's Republic of China were in charge of Jang and were preparing to set him up as a puppet leader. Their attempt was to attack and kill not only me, not only the three sons of the Dear Leader, but to assassinate the Dear Leader himself! It was indeed fortunate that the Dear Leader had been taken to a hospital the very evening of the assassination attempt. I am happy to report to you that the Dear Leader has been apprised of the coup attempt and wishes to express his gratitude to the armed forces of DPRK for putting down the coup.

"The Dear Leader also told me that after some months of therapy, he feels confident that he will be able to return to P'yongyang and resume his day-to-day leadership. He has, in the interim, given me the authority to lead our beloved nation as your Premier. He has also announced that Vice Marshall Han Fo Chi will serve as my Vice Premier. Vice Premier Han, I welcome you to your new position."

Applause could be heard in the room. The cameras panned the cheering and clapping reporters as Vice Premier Han stepped to the microphones.

"It is an honor to be named by the Dear Leader to be the Vice Premier. I take it as my solemn duty to protect the Democratic People's Republic of Korea at all costs. And in doing so, we will move in some new directions.

"Number One. We must re-assess our relationship with the People's Republic of China. The fact that some people high up in the leadership in Beijing have fomented this trouble will be a determining factor in how we relate to our neighbor to the north. We are not stepping away from our ally, but we must reassess what that alliance means to our safety. We must survey the damage that has resulted from their attempted dominance of our land.

"Number Two. We must reassess our relationship with the Russian Federation. Behind-the-scenes negotiations give us assurance that Moscow wishes to be of support to us. We feel that our two nations can assist each other in a number of ways. Within the next week, I will lead a delegation to Moscow for serious discussions on how our two nations might renew old friendships.

"Number Three. We must reassess our relationship with the Republic of Korea. President Lee has, for the last several years, been very open to serious trade negotiations. It is now time to discuss our differences and see if it is possible for our two nations to live peacefully on the same peninsula. This morning, we have already been in contact with the leadership of the South, and will start high-level talks in the next weeks.

"And Number Four. We must reassess our relationship with the United States of America. We acknowledge that much of our concern has been the massive number of American troops gathered to our south whose presence continually threatens our well being. If we can reach some agreements with the Americans regarding troop withdrawals from the Korean Peninsula, it is our belief that the need for nuclear weapons will decline. Therefore, we are opening the door for the Americans to enter. In this regard, President Medvedev has agreed to allow Moscow to join us in a new series of 'Three-Party Talks' whereby the American presence to our south decreases and our need to defend ourselves from them also decreases.

"Premier Park and I say to the world: Let's open the windows and let the pleasant breeze of nations trusting nations begin to blow through."

Thunderous applause lit up the morning as the press conference was broadcast around the world.

10:10 a.m. — Office of the Chairman, Beijing

"Treachery," President Hu said, uncharacteristically pounding his fist on his desk. He was seated at the desk, with Vice President Xi and his intelligence chief, Wang Wat Fer, seated on straight-back chairs in front of his desk. They had been watching the P'yongyang press conference.

"How did this happen? I thought you had it all arranged, Vice President Xi."

Vice President Xi hung his head and did not make eye contact with Hu. "I have disgraced us, sir. But I had no idea that Jang would botch it so badly. He gave every indication of having the situation well in hand. . . . I suspect there were collaborators from other countries involved."

"Collaborators?" Hu looked from his vice president to his intelligence chief. "What can you tell us, Minister Wang?"

"Mr. Chairman, I can tell you much." Wang was an old party hack who had risen to the top of the intelligence chain because he knew how to negotiate the waters of inter-party politics. He was sixty-five and fit, taller than most Chinese, and spoke thirteen different dialects of Chinese. Today he was speaking perfect Mandarin. "First of all, we know that no one from our country had anything to do with this purported coup attempt. What has happened is not Vice President Xi's fault. He is very intelligent but he is still young and naïve."

Vice president Xi grimaced and adjusted himself uncomfortably in his chair.

Wang turned to look at Xi. "No offense meant, Mr. Vice President. But I must be candid here. Our country is threatened. You will be an excellent Chairman of the Party some day. But not today. You were just not ready to manage the operation."

Turning back to the President, Wang continued. "The Russians did this. My intelligence people in P'yongyang knew something was up but they couldn't get it figured out quickly enough. I have now put it together. It is Putin and his lackey Medvedev who have done this. They obviously worked closely with General Park, including the assassinations of the sons of Kim Jong Il. . . and Kim Jong Il himself—"

"Kim Jong Il?" Hu interrupted. "He's dead?"

"Even this morning, our intelligence people have learned that Kim Jong Il was killed by the Russian assassins. One of our people heard the military leaders at the site of the attack state that fact. What Park will do is use Kim's double on important State occasions for several more years, until Kim 'dies' of cancer. By that time, Park will be well established. . . . and deeply in debt to Putin and Medvedev."

"So," Hu said as he sat looking out the window. "Our adversaries the Russians are re-establishing hegemony in the region. What shall we do about that?"

"Park's days are limited, sir. We have had snipers in Korea for some time for just such a contingency. In a few months, when the fright is gone and Park becomes complacent, we'll place a well-aimed round into his brain. We'll also even the score with his lieutenant, Vice Marshall Han Fo Chi. He tilts toward the South and the Americans. Meanwhile, we will work on a scenario to gain DPRK back from Russian domination."

"Mr. Chairman," Xi said, regaining his composure. "We should hold a press conference, denying Park's assertion that we had anything to do with the failed coup. And we should make diplomatic approaches with the Republic of Korea's President Lee. Trade negotiations. That's what we need to do. It's the old shell game. We'll let the world see us as keen traders with the South and with the Americans, while with our other hand we are re-establishing ourselves as the dominant military power in East Asia."

Hu looked at Xi for a full minute. "That's a good idea, Xi. See to it. . . . And until I say otherwise, I want to see you each morning to talk over your duties."

Same time — Moscow

"What a dance this has been," President Medvedev yelled to Premier Putin as they sat in Medvedev's office, watching the press conference coming from P'yongyang. "Instead of winning two potatoes, we at least got one."

"We can work with this, my friend," Putin replied. "True, the Americans have not been discredited as we had wished. They have just been rendered irrelevant. With us leading the negotiations, they will save face by agreeing to an ordered withdrawal of the Peninsula. Since the nuclear arsenal is still in place, we can use it to our advantage. And the Chinese have one big black eye this morning. . . . Dmitri, East Asia is ours!"

Both men laughed and toasted each other with their Stoli vodka.

Same Time — The Oval Office

"We did it!" President Russell Remington sat at his desk, with Vice President John Vernowsky, CIA Director Forrest Rogers and Director of National Intelligence Sandra Lindquist seated facing him. "We averted a nuclear war! Forrest, your little Prowler caper wasn't even needed, but it did give me the courage to play it all out. No nukes dropped. North Korea ready to play ball with us. This is sweet."

Miss Lindquist glanced at the president with a playful smile. "You did it, Mr. President. You are phenomenal—"

"There's a problem, Mr. President," Vernowsky said, cutting in. "Did you notice Vice Premier Han Fo Chi's comments regarding Russia? The North is proposing not the 'Six Party Talks' we've been insisting on, but 'Three Party Talks,' with Moscow, directed by Putin, leading the action. This was pre-arranged. You can bet on that. We'll now be in for a tough time with Moscow."

"Whatever, John," Remington mumbled. *Worry wart! I'm not going to let his comments spoil this for me.* "Tell you what. You and Forrest here work up a brief for me so I can see it in a week. And Sandy, why don't you and I work with the writing staff and come up with a good press conference?"

"That's a fine idea, Russ, er, I mean Mr. President." Sandy let the edge of her dress climb above her knee as she sat there facing him.

"Well, Mr. President," General Rogers said curtly as he glanced from the President to Miss Lindquist. "Vice President Vernowsky and I will prepare a briefing immediately. We hope to get on your calendar tomorrow. Not next week."

With that, he rose, bowed slightly and walked out of the office, followed by a confused Vice President Vernowsky.

CHAPTER SEVENTEEN

1100, July 4th — In the hills, within sight of the Sea of Japan

Zach awoke with a start. He was lying under a bush, and the sun was beating down on him between the branches. Rising slowly, he looked around. From his position on the side of a hill, he could see the sea some miles away.

Where am I? Let me see. I left Bob's grave and stumbled east. How far did I go before I just couldn't go anymore? That's got to be the Sea of Japan right there. Looks like I'm about five miles from it.

He pulled his cell phone from his flight suit pocket and hit the number. No answer. Nothing.

He hit the GPS function.

Ten miles northeast. I'll start that way. No houses around up here on the hill. Think I'll just head northeast, staying up in the hills. Then I'll head down to the beach when I'm abeam of the safe location.

He took a power bar out of his pocket and munched on it. Then he took a swig of water from his flask.

After he finished his morning prayers, he started northeast.

Same Time — CIA Headquarters, Langley, Virginia

Deputy CIA Director Bobbie Turline strolled into the office of CIA Director General Forrest Rogers and sat down in front of the desk. It was late.

That's unusual behavior for Turline, Rogers thought as he looked up from his computer monitor. *He's got something important to say, obviously.*

"Why are you here so late, Robert? And even more puzzling, why are you sitting in my office without being invited?"

"We got the terrorist cells that were going to blow up our nuclear facilities, General," Bobbie Turline said with a smile on his face. "I just got word from my counterpart over at the Bureau. FBI agents nabbed both teams. Just hours before they were to go into action."

"Whew. That was close." Rogers smiled back at Turline. "Tell me about it."

"Satchel nukes. They were going to blow us up with satchel nukes. We don't know how they got them into the country."

"Probably in ship containers. Probably came in at various ports. Maybe Long Beach. Or Seattle. Or maybe even Baltimore. So give me the scoop."

"The South Koreans gave us everything we needed," Turline continued. "They've got one heck of an intelligence network, boss.

"Here's what we pieced together. There were two teams of North Koreans. All of them have been here for years, sleepers. One team on the east coast was to blow up the Indian Point Nuclear Station near Peekskill, New York. That would have taken out two hundred thousand Americans! The other team was to blow up the San Onofre nuclear generating station near San Clemente, California. They were supposed to have blown them both at the same time, and just after the North Korean ICBM hit our territory."

"Whoa!" Rogers slapped his thigh. "That would have devastated us and sent panic throughout the country. If they had succeeded, public opinion would have forced us to immediately pull our troops off the Korean Peninsula or pulverize North Korea. . . . or both, most likely."

"You might say we dodged a bullet on this one, General."

"We dodged a lot more than a bullet, Robert. . . . All right, we need to get our Russian experts in here first thing in the morning. We've got to figure out this new reality in North Korea. I judge that the Russkies have iced the Chinese out of North Korea and will try to establish hegemony over the entire region, South Korea included."

"So that's what the DPRK's new Vice Premier was talking about when he announced that Moscow will now broker a new peace initiative between us and the North?"

"Precisely. We've got to have our facts together so I can brief the President. Since he's my brother-in-law, I know him all too well. He'll accept, without limitations, the Russians' offer, thinking it'll make him look like an international player.

"And he'll give away the farm in the process. We've got to convince him that we must have limitations on the talks. If we precipitously pull our troops off the Peninsula in exchange for the North Koreans doing away with their nuclear weapons program, we will have been had. Even with new leadership, chances are they'll just continue their nuke program underground while on the surface they'll smile and say they're nuke-free. Meanwhile, the Russians will slowly but surely work North Korean dominance over the South. In two years, we'll be right back where we started, with a belligerent North, this time under the thumb of the Russians rather than the Chinese.

"To convince Russell 'R-Cubed' Remington of anything, we need to have overwhelming evidence. And we have to convince him that he'll look like a two-bit Boston ambulance chaser if he doesn't follow our advice."

"Sounds like we've got our work cut out for us."

"Indeed."

Okay, Rogers thought. *Time to drop the John Brown promotion idea on Turline and see what he does with it. If I can get John Brown out of here, I'll feel a lot better. And by promoting him, I can further convince him to keep his mouth shut about those two crewmen who had to die for their country.*

"Robert, before you go, I want to run something by you."

"Shoot."

"My aide, John Brown. He has done an absolutely colossal job supporting us in this operation. I want to get him promoted...."

"And your point is?"

"I want to bump him up to a Fourteen and send him to Thailand to be Number One in the embassy."

"General?" Turline looked at Rogers with a quizzical expression on his face. "John Brown is, if I'm not mistaken, a Ten. You want to bump him up four grades? He can't be more than thirty years old.... What's really going on here, General?"

Turline's getting suspicious. I've got to win him over to this idea.

"You know how things work here better than I do, Robert. That's why I'm running it by you first.... Look. I have no ulterior motive. I just see great potential for Brown. He's destined to reach the very top. So I want to do what we call in the armed forces a below-the-zone promotion. Way below the zone. Promoting Brown like this may send a wave of hope through the heart of every junior operative in the Central Intelligence Agency. Every last one of them will suddenly start working at one hundred ten percent, hoping they might get such a promotion."

"Yeah. And it will send a wave of resentment into the heart of every senior operative, wondering if you've got to be an aide to the director to get special treatment.... General, what you're proposing is a definite break with protocol. It's going to be hard for a lot of people to swallow, a lot of senior people who can make your life miserable if they lose respect for you."

"I appreciate your candor, Robert." Rogers shifted in his chair and gazed at Turline. *Now I'll let him know I appreciate what he's saying and let him know what I really want to do.*

"Yes, you're right, I guess. That's why I'm so glad to have you as my Number Two. You know how to read the tea leaves here.

"But I really do want to reward John Brown for his ingenuity and common sense. How do you think the establishment would react if I promoted him to a Twelve, jumping him over Eleven, and assigned him to a less desirable spot. Maybe Bangui, Central African Republic, as number two in that embassy?"

Turline sat silently for a moment. "I think I may be able to sell that, General. It's not that nobody likes Brown. They do. It's just that we have to make everything look fair here, promotions based on one's abilities rather than any favoritism.... Yes, I think bumping him up two promotions but assigning him to a minor nation in Africa might be doable."

"Fine, Robert. Thank you. Would you see to that tomorrow please?"

Turline rose from the chair and began to leave. "Yes, sir. I'll get on that tomorrow."

July 5th — In the Hills of Eastern North Korea

I've got to get out of this flight suit and get some clothes that help me blend in. If I'm seen in this flight suit, I'll be caught. And I need food. My power bars are gone and I haven't seen any game to shoot.

Zach was walking through the wooded hills. The weather was warm and sunny. He'd had a good rest and was moving along with vigilance toward the safe spot. He'd tried his cell phone a number of times. No response.

I'll head down the hill and look for a farm. Maybe I can steal some stuff.

He spent an hour making his way down through the trees. At some points, the way down was steep. Once he slipped and fell about thirty feet. Jumping up, he wiped himself off, felt for injuries, and continued down.

Coming out in a field, he smelled something like rotten cabbage.

Kimshee. I'm near a house!

Then he saw the house in the distance. In the field, a man and woman worked their scythes, cutting wheat. Zach carefully walked around the field, staying in the trees.

There's the house. Now I need to carefully sneak up and listen for any sign of people.

The house was a small, unpainted, wooden structure. In the back yard was a clothesline, with several sets of clothes drying in the sun.

I hate stealing from these people. They're obviously poor. But I have no choice. . . . Let's see. That black outfit should fit me.

He took the clothes he needed off the line and then walked to the back door. Lifting the latch carefully, he opened the door and looked in. No one. He walked in. On the table in the kitchen were various vegetables and a pot of the infamous kimshee. He stayed away from the strong, pungent kimshee, grabbed several squash-looking objects and wrapped them in his stolen outfit. He opened the cabinet and found cans of food. Putting them in his makeshift pack, he found a can opener. That went in the pack. He found a box of matches and put it in his pocket. He also grabbed a pan off the wall. And a straw hat on the table — he grabbed that. Seeing nothing else he could use, he quietly stepped out the back door, walked across the yard and disappeared into the trees.

That night, back up in the hills, Zach found a gully in which to camp. Gathering wood, he built a fire. He used his survival knife to chop up the vegetable and threw the pieces into the pan. He opened a can of food. Beans. He poured them in the pan, added water from the stream, and cooked the concoction over the fire.

This is absolutely the best meal I have ever enjoyed. Lord, you are good. You provide what I need, when I need it. Please also provide for that poor Korean family as well. I don't like stealing things, Lord. But if I'm going to survive, I have to live off the land. Please forgive me.

After evening prayers, he curled up on the ground, wearing his new outfit and using his flight suit as a blanket. Sleep came easier now that he had a full stomach.

At daybreak, he was on his way through the hills, heading for his destination. Another try on the cell phone yielded no results. But the GPS was working and he was closing in on his objective.

Scanning the coast from the hill he occupied, he looked at the map on his GPS and compared it to the topography.

The town there on the coast is listed as Samp'o-dong. Yeah, I remember that. And there to the south, there's the promontory. That's my spot!

Zach walked carefully down the hill. In an hour, he reached a narrow paved road. Slowly he crawled out of the trees and approached the road. He looked left. Nothing. He looked right. Nothing. Picking himself up, he ran across the road and into the trees on the other side. Along the way, he could always tell where houses were because he could smell kimshee.

He followed the GPS instructions, walking for another hour. The terrain became flat. Trees gave way to sand.

I feel vulnerable out here. Even though I haven't seen a soul. Wait a minute! There's someone walking over there.

About two hundred yards away, a man was walking across the sand. Zach froze in his tracks and watched the man. Dressed in gray pants and a brown shirt, and wearing a straw hat, he looked to Zach like a local farmer. And he was walking away from Zach, not seeing him.

Zach began to walk in what he judged was a farmer's manner, imitating the man he had just watched. Head slightly bowed, taking quick, short steps, he headed for the trees on the other side of the small field of sand.

He reached the trees and sat down.

I'm about a mile from the promontory. If I can get to those trees, I can make it over the hill and down to the beach.

To the woods he went, seeing no one. Up the hill of the promontory and over the other side. He descended down through the trees, reaching the edge of the beach. The GPS showed he had arrived at his destination. He stood there looking out to sea. Several boats sat out in the bay to his left, fishermen hard at work.

Let's see. Protocol calls for the sub rescue team to show up here at twenty-three hundred every night. Still no joy on the cell phone. Guess I'll just take a nap, since I may be up all night when that sub rescue crew gets here.

That night after eating his beans, Zach waited and watched. He looked out to sea, hoping to see something. The fishing boats were gone. And he waited and watched some more. He watched the darkness descend. He now watched and listened. By midnight, he began to think that they were late. By one, he knew they were not coming. He sat there all night, trying to keep awake just in case.

Next morning, he said his prayers, took care of his personal hygiene and ate more beans. He was getting tired of beans. Then he slept for four hours.

At about noon, he awoke and did some calisthenics. All afternoon, he sat and watched the fishing boats come and go. By early evening, he was again tired. So he slept for three hours.

His dinner was beans. He had only three cans left.

Three more days of rations. Hope that sub crew gets here soon.

That night was exactly like the last. No sub rescue crew arrived. Zach sat up all night waiting and watching.

After breakfast, he did some mental calculations.

Something's suspicious. I couldn't reach anyone on the Prowler radio before we had to eject. I haven't been able to reach anyone on this cell phone. And the sub rescue team is not coming. That may mean they think Bob and I are dead. It's possible the carrier radar saw the Prowler crash at sea and now they think Bob and I went down with it. They may have searched the water and didn't find us. . . . But why would they have shut down the cell phone connection so quickly? They should have left it on just in case we ejected over land. That was the backup protocol.

Unless they wanted us to die. . . . Could that be possible? I don't know whom or what we attacked when we bombed that cliff house. But suppose we assassinated somebody. Maybe a high ranking North Korean. Kim Jong Il? What if whoever was directing us wanted us to kill him or somebody else without anyone knowing it was the USA that did it? Suppose it was just easier for them to make sure we never came back. What if the sub was never there in the first place? We would have ejected over the sea and died in our life rafts from exposure. Am I getting paranoid?

One thing I can do. The Russian border is about a hundred miles from here. If I can get into Russia, I can get home to Yanrakinnot! Bethany and I can get lost in the wilds of the Chukotka Peninsula. . . . Bethany and Tomas, I'm coming for you.

Disappointed and angry, with tears streaming down his cheeks, Zach started his trek toward Russia.

July 8th — Mys Shmidta

Secret agent Dmitri Plovnic stepped off the ship in Mys Shmidta harbor and looked around.

Another decaying port city on the Chukchi Sea, Plovnic thought as he made his way down the gangplank. *Why don't we just bomb these places and put everyone out of their misery? Now, let me search this filthy village for Mrs. Bethany Savage.*

Plovnic walked up the street to the shopping area, drifting through shops, keeping an eye out for Bethany. Soon he would wander over to the Magistrate's Office and do some interrogating.

If this woman is hiding here, someone will have seen her. I'll start with the police. They get paid to know who comes in and out of town.

As Plovnic walked slowly along the street, he was noticed. Leonid, standing in one of the stores, saw him and recognized him from Yanrakinnot. Leonid ducked his head and walked quickly out the back door of the store.

A slight knock at the door. Bethany froze.

Leonid? Or someone I don't want to see.

She waited silently. Then came Leonid's coded knock.

Opening the door, she became immediately afraid when Leonid rushed in, his moonface showing anguish.

"What's happened, Leonid?" She looked into his eyes.

"That man is here. The one I knocked out back in Yanrakinnot. He got off a ship an hour ago."

"Oh, no," Bethany exclaimed. "How could he find us here?"

"He may not have found us, Matushka. I think he is maybe stopping at all the port cities and searching for you. He is probably going to the Magistrate's Office to find out if a woman matching your description came here recently. He'll show them your picture. Since we have disguised you, you look more like a *babushka* than Matushka, but the police will tell him who has recently come into the village. And as much as we tried to keep you here in the apartment and away from the public, you have been seen by some. He will come here to check you out."

"So what do we do now?" Bethany walked over to Tomas, who was crawling on the floor playing with a toy truck, and picked him up.

"We must execute our escape plan immediately, before this man knows for sure that you are here. Please gather everything together. I have two all terrain vehicles with trailers for our use."

"Where will we go, Leonid?"

"Amguema. It is a Chukchi village many kilometers south of here. I have people there."

"Will we be safe there?"

Leonid smiled. "Yes. The Chukchi love me. And they will love you and Tomas. They will protect us with their lives."

Bethany shifted uncomfortably. "Leonid, how will Father Zacharios find us there?"

"Matushka, you need not worry. Peter knows that if we cannot stay in Mys Smidta, we will be in Amguema. Don't worry. Peter will tell Father when he comes back.

"Now, what you must do is dress and act as a man for the trip. I've brought some clothes that will fit you."

"I'll feed Tomas, change into these clothes and we can be on our way, Leonid." She took Zach's cross down from the wall and walked to the kitchen counter. "Will you go and thank the doctor for caring for us while we were here? Here is a pastry I made. Please give it to him."

An hour later, the three of them headed south, Leonid driving the lead ATV, with Bethany following. She wore black rubber boots, brown pants, a brown deer-fur jacket, and a flopping hat over her short dark hair. She looked every bit a man. Tomas dozed in the trailer she pulled, covered with blankets.

They headed south along a narrow paved road, encountering a few trucks and other ATVs. When the pavement ended, they continued along the dirt road to where the bridge was washed out by a river. Leonid led them across the shallow stream to the road on the other side. Remembering Peter's instructions, he stopped frequently so that Bethany could change Tomas' diapers and feed him. Leonid had learned by now to disappear when Bethany said it was time to feed Tomas. After his feeding, Bethany would call Leonid and ask if he would hold Tomas. As she disappeared into the woods for a few minutes, Leonid held little Tomas tightly, praying for him.

That night, they camped in the woods, sharing some pork Leonid had bought at the market that day. They slept in their survival tents.

Next day they were back at it. As they traveled southeast, they left the highway and followed a trail.

Leonid seems to have an internal GPS, Bethany thought as she followed him mile after mile. *How can he possibly know where we're going? There are no roads or road signs. Just these trails and the mountains to our right. He must be following the mountains.*

And he was. He followed the Siberian Mountain range southeast until they came to a pass. He took them through the pass and then headed southeast again, following the river. That night, they stayed in a stand of trees beside the river.

And on Day Three, they arrived at the village of Amguema. As they drove in, Bethany took notice of the village on the flats, just above the Amguema River. Mountains towered around them. To the east of the village, she saw reindeer grazing, herds of them, tending by their Chukchi masters. In the village, she observed new single-story, multi-colored, wooden houses lined up row by row. As they passed the houses, she saw people walking to and fro from house to house. They all glanced up at Leonid and Bethany as they rode past.

So this is to be my village for awhile. How will the people accept me? Or will they at all? I just have to trust Leonid. I have no other choice.

They stopped in front of one of the homes. Leonid motioned for Bethany to pick up Tomas and join him. They walked to the front door and Leonid knocked loudly. A tall Chukchi came to the door, recognized Leonid and invited them in.

They were ushered into a large living room/kitchen. Reindeer fur lined everything — the seats, the table, the floor. As they sat down at the table, the lady of the house, wearing a deerskin skirt and blouse, laid a cup of coffee in front of them, and a loaf of brown bread. Bethany noticed that she was maybe fifty, chubby, with graying hair. She had a pleasant smile.

Her husband looked about the same age. Bethany thought they looked like twins. Leonid had introduced them as Tug and Valeria. Tug was serving as the village chief and magistrate.

Valeria asked if she might hold Tomas so Bethany could use the bathroom. Bethany was amazed as she opened the door to the bathroom.

This home has running water and a flush toilet!

She used the bathroom and came back to the table, allowing Valeria to snuggle Tomas, who was smiling back at Valeria and cooing at her.

"Tug, Matushka and I have come here to ask your protection," Leonid said slowly. "Matushka's husband, Father Zacharios, has been sent back to Moscow by the bishop on a project. But while he's been gone, some bad men have been chasing us. They claim to be government people. They're Russians. We don't trust them."

Tug smiled at Bethany, then shifted his gaze back to Leonid. "How long have you been on the run, Leonid?"

"Over a month. We spent some time in Mys Shmidta. But they came looking for us there. Our backup plan was to find you. Uncle Peter sends his blessing to you."

"You are most welcome here, brother," Tug said. "And Matushka, you are most welcome here also. By the way, we are in need of another teacher at our school. Is it possible you might help us until it is time for you to go?"

Valeria cut in. "Matushka, we have a boarding school here in Amguema. People from surrounding villages send their older children here to pursue their education. We need another teacher. If you could help us, it would be appreciated."

"I'd love to help," Bethany said hesitantly. "I will help. But I'll have to figure out how to take care of Tomas and teach at the same time."

"That should not be a problem, Matushka," Valeria said, beaming. "Our school girls will love to entertain him while you teach. And we also have a child-care room. You see, some of our girls are already mothers. We have to have a place for their babies while we teach them."

"I'll start whenever you wish. But I have to warn you I may not be here very long. As soon as my husband comes, we'll have to be going."

"Any help you can give will be appreciated, Matushka," Tug broke in with his winning smile. "Now for arrangements. We have a guest house next door. Valeria manages it. We have several empty rooms. Would you be willing to stay with us at the guest house?"

"We would be most honored to stay in the guest house," Leonid said in a formal voice. "We would count it an honor, dear Brother."

Thus began a stay that would prove longer than Bethany could have imagined.

CHAPTER EIGHTEEN

July 10th — On the road in North Korea

*L**et's see. I've been heading toward Russia for two days now. And we ejected six days ago. Eight days on the run!*

Zach was walking up a coastal road, dressed like a Korean and trying to walk like one. He had actually passed several other Koreans, who had simply nodded at him as they walked by. He kept his hat down over his face and simply nodded back. He had broken into another farm house and taken more canned food and clothing. In the evenings, he would walk back into the woods and camp without a fire. Jumping into a stream and using the soap he'd stolen provided some cleanliness. And he was able to shave, using a razor he had stolen.

On the third day, he was walking along the road about noon, when, all of a sudden, something stopped him. Something felt strange inside.

What is it? What's up with this feeling?

He carefully slipped back into the trees and peeked down the road.

A white cargo truck sitting on the side of the road. Front driver side jacked up. Someone is removing the tire. . . . Good gosh! It's a Caucasian. And that's a Russian truck, a ZIL 5301 if I'm not mistaken. Think I'll ease closer and check this guy out.

Zach inched closer, staying in the trees. As he drew even with the truck, he crawled up to the edge of the road and stood behind a tree, not more than ten feet from the man.

Maybe six feet tall. Slim. Brown hair and beard. Russian looking clothes. Could this guy be Russian?

Then he heard the man singing a Russian Christian hymn as he lifted the flat tire off the rim and began to put the spare on.

Okay. Got to be careful here. Don't get my hopes up. Lord, lead me to do the right thing.

With that, Zach laid his pack down, stepped out from behind the tree and walked up behind the man. In Russian, he said, "Can you use some help, comrade?"

The man jumped up and turned around.

Silence.

"If you'll excuse me," the man answered in Russian. "It's a bit of a surprise to meet another Russian here in the Korean countryside. . . ."

"Yes. That's curious, isn't it? How about if I help you with this tire while I explain?"

"Very well. What's your name?"

What will I use? Got to think fast.

Zach picked up the flat and began to place it in the spare tire rack of the truck. "Zacharios Shatinski. Yours?"

The man began twisting the lug nuts, securing the rim to the axle. "Janos. Janos Flourik."

"Janos Flourik. That sounds Baltic." Zach began to let the jack down.

"Latvian actually, though my family has lived in St. Petersburg for years."

"Well, Mr. Flourik. What are you doing with a flat tire in the middle of the Korean countryside?"

"I'm an aid worker, Mr. . . . What did you say your name is?"

"Shatinski. Zacharios Shatinski."

"I'm here on a contract to supply medical equipment, food, and other items to the villages, Mr. Shatinski. I work out of Ch'ongjin."

Ch'ongjin! That was one of my targets!

"I see." Zach put the jack in the truck. "Well, all set now."

"How about you?" Janos Flourik said. "What is it that brings you into the countryside with no car? Dressed as a Korean farmer?"

Hmm. . . . I should have thought of a story before now.

"To be honest, I'm on the run, Janos. . . . Something tells me I can trust you. I'm a Russian agent on a secret mission that went wrong. North Korean Intelligence is hunting me down. I'm charged by my superiors with getting back to Russia on my own. Can you hold this in confidence? If you can't, I may have to commandeer your vehicle."

Zach pulled the Yargin out of his pocket. *Seeing this Russian weapon should help convince him.*

Janos put his hands on his hips. "That won't be necessary, Mr. Shatinski or whatever your name is. I'm assuming that if you steal my truck you'll be able to get across the heavily guarded Tumen River? You can't drive across from Korea to Russia. No bridge. . . ."

"I have a plan." Zach lied and it showed.

"Perhaps you'd like my help, Zacharios? I know how to get you across. If you'll agree not to steal my truck or shoot me, I'll help you get back home to your headquarters. Do we have a deal?"

Got to trust this guy to get me to Russia. "Sure. That's a deal. What do we do?"

"My friend, we jump into this truck and head north to my office. I'll fill you in on the way."

The two bumped along the narrow road, heading north. On their right the Sea of Japan washed up on the beaches and on their left were towering mountains.

"So how are you going to help me get across the border?" Zach said, glancing at Janos.

"We'll go to my office in Ch'ongjin, have some food, and wait until dark. I know some of the guards who patrol the river. You see, I provide them things they can't buy. Western clothes, jeans, appliances. And so they help me when they can. Once in a while, I need to get something across the border. This afternoon, I'll contact the guards. When we get to the river tonight, they'll be nowhere to be seen. You'll get into your little rubber ducky and paddle across to Russia."

"What about the Russian guards on the other side of the river?"

"Simple. They are few and most of them don't care. They know the Korean guards won't let anyone leave Korea. And the Russian guards know that no one in their right mind would want to leave Russia for Korea. You'll get across without even being seen tonight. And then you can head wherever you choose."

"I really appreciate this, Janos."

How do I ask him about the Russian Christian hymn he was singing when I met him? How could this guy be a believer in Christ rather than Marx?

"Say, when I approached you, Janos, you were humming a tune I think maybe I've heard before. Maybe one my mother used to hum. What is it?"

Janos glanced at Zach and quickly returned his gaze to the road ahead. "It's an old song my mother taught me. I only know some of the words."

Zach put a finger to the windshield where Janos could see it. And he made the sign of a fish, the secret code for Christianity.

Janos slowed momentarily.

He's going to stop and throw me out. Or report me to the police. I need to be ready to run.

"I know the fish you just drew," Janos said slowly as he regained speed. "And I'm not sure what to say. . . . I can draw the same sign."

"Then you are a believer as am I."

Silence.

"Zacharios, you are a Russian agent. And you are a believer?"

"There are many like me, Janos. Many who have become believers in Jesus. . . . Does this surprise you?"

Janos kept his eyes glued to the road as he was obviously in thought. "Dear Lord God," he finally said aloud. "Thank you for bringing a Christian believer to me just when I needed one. Amen."

Zach watched a farmer out in his field. "Apparently the Lord has done the same for both of us. I also needed a Christian believer.

An hour later, Zach noticed that there were large factory buildings on both sides of the road.

"What have we here, Janos?"

"We're just south of my city, Ch'ongjin. This is the East Sea Light Electric Factory. It's actually a weapons factory. It's rumored that nuclear weapons are developed and tested here. See the high wire fences all around?"

"Oh," was all Zach said.

I know this factory, Zach thought. *This weapons complex was to be our second target! Holy Smokes, if we had fired our nuclear missile into this complex, everything for miles would have been blown away, including Janos and all the people who live around here."*

"Tell me about Ch'ongjin, Janos."

"Not much to tell, actually. It is the third largest city in DPRK, about a half million residents. But the city has come upon hard times. Lack of resources has led to the shutdown of many factories. You'll see their rusted carcasses as we get closer in. It has a seaport which once flourished but is now a shadow of its former self. And an airport, which is now under the control of the military.

"Let's see. Ch'ongjin has several universities. And it has the privilege of having both Russian and Chinese Consular Offices. And unfortunately, even with so many people, there is virtually no Christian presence. The government only allows Christian churches in P'yongyang, and with that, only churches it completely controls. The only Christian presence here in Ch'ongjin is a secret underground Korean congregation. They won't let me in because they don't trust me."

"That's quite a rundown. Thanks, Janos."

Zach became silent. *My missile could have killed up to a half million people! Si didn't tell us that. He just said that a few thousand people lived in the area and that collateral damage would be minimal. A half million people is not minimal!*

Of course. He had to lie to us in order to make the mission sound attractive. . . . Si, why did you do that to me? You almost caused me to kill a half million people. . . . Lord, why do humans have to do this to one another? In their efforts to defend national security, they rationalize immoral behavior and then pulverize one another. And innocent civilians often bear the brunt of it all. I know, I know, Lord. 'There will be wars and rumors of wars until you come again.' I've got that. And I know we actually do have national security issues. I do believe that the government of North Korea had every intention of blowing the USA away and killing millions of us in order to assert itself as a world power. The fact that I've heard nothing of a nuclear attack by North Korea tells me that we somehow foiled their attempt.

I just wish I didn't have to be part of our national security, Lord. Can't I just go back to my mission work in Siberia, bring up a family, and eventually go to heaven to be with you in a closer presence?

Speaking of North Korea not launching an attack, maybe I can get some information from Janos.

"Janos, one of the reasons for my secret mission here was to inhibit the Korean government from launching nuclear missiles. Since my part of the mission went bad, I'm out of communication right now. Maybe you've heard something in the news?"

Janos smiled at Zach. "You have been under a rock, haven't you? There's been a change in government, Zacharios. A coup by moderates. Your mission worked! New leadership has taken hold of the government and is tilting toward us, toward Russia. The nuclear threat is receding as we speak. I listen carefully to the state-run media, but I also listen to the short wave radio.

"The USA has been put firmly in its place by our dear Mr. Putin. They will have to reduce their forces in the Republic of Korea in order to get assurances from Putin that DPRK is disassembling their nuclear arsenal.

"Even more important from my standpoint? DPRK will take a more tolerant view toward religion. That means Christians from the South will flood into the North. Yes. I'm quite optimistic regarding the future of this country. Thank you for your part in all this. . . . Ah, here we are."

Janos pulled into the parking lot of a gray, cement block warehouse. Zach noticed an old broken down truck beside the building, but no other vehicles in the lot. Janos backed the truck up to the platform and motioned for Zach to get out. Then he opened the huge garage door and they walked into the warehouse.

Whoa! Look at this, Zach thought as he surveyed rows and rows of furniture, foodstuffs, and medical supplies.

"Storing up for a rainy day, Janos?" Zach waved his hand in front of the supplies.

"I'm a distributor for a major relief organization called Refrinograf. All these supplies have recently come in by air from Vladivostok. In fact, I've just completed my first distribution run. For the next two weeks, I'll be very busy each day, loading in the early morning, carrying materials to a distribution location, dropping them off, and returning here in the evening. . . . Too bad you can't stay. I could use the help."

Zach unconsciously backed away. "Much as I'd like to stay and help, Janos, I've got to get back to my headquarters and report in. When I get to Russia tomorrow morning, I need to find the nearest Orthodox Church. That's our conduit for communication. You know of a church near the border?"

"Let's get some dinner," Janos said. "We can talk about it as we eat. I think I can help you with that."

They walked through a door and entered Janos' apartment. The smell of pork chops and frying onions greeted him.

How long has it been since I've had a home-cooked meal?

Mouth watering, he looked around. He saw a very simple apartment. A kitchen/dining room/living room all spread out in the former large storage area. An open door led into what looked to be a bedroom. The walls were all gray concrete, as was the floor. Various carpets and scatter rugs dotted the floor. Nothing covered the walls. Overhead warehouse lights high up on the concrete ceiling gave Zach a feeling of impersonal institutionalism.

How can Janos live this way? No wonder he's lonesome and depressed. No color. No character. I should know. I lived this way for nearly eighteen years when I was trapped in the gulag.

When he glanced into the kitchen portion of the room, he noticed a Russian babushka at the stove. She was short and squat, with gray hair tied in a bun. Her long brown dress was covered with a white apron. As she worked on the pork chops, onions, and potatoes in the large frying pan, the babushka looked Zach up and down without saying anything.

"Marisa, this is my friend Zacharios. Thank you for making us dinner. When will it be ready?"

"Ten minutes," was all she said. She opened the oven and pulled out a sheet with four potatoes halved and filled with what looked like eggs.

"Okay, let's go into my bedroom. My office is there."

They walked through the door, which Zach noticed Janos closed after they were through it. He saw a small bed and bureau against one wall. On the other wall was a desk, a computer and monitor, and several chairs.

"If you need to use the bathroom, it's outside through that door, Zacharios. Please sit down."

Zach sat in one of the wooden chairs while Janos took his chair in front of the computer monitor.

Swinging around to face Zach, he began. "Zacharios, let me ask a question which may insult your intelligence. Do you have any identification on you?"

"'Fraid not. Protocol called for me to bring no ID in at all. Why?"

"You're going to need some ID in case you get caught in the river. If you've got Russian papers, you'll have a good chance of getting through. But if you have no ID, it's going to be much harder on you if you get nabbed by any Korean guards who chance to see you."

"So. . . . Are you saying that you can get me some papers?"

"I not only can. I will. One of the perks of this job is that I know a lot of people. I even know smugglers. If you approve, I'll call one of my contacts. He'll come over, take your picture, and get you some official looking Russian identification."

"You are amazing, Janos! You can just snap your finger and get anything done?"

"Pretty much. So is it okay to get you some ID?"

"Yes. But you need to know that I have no money with me. I can wire you some when I get back to headquarters."

"I don't need your money right now. But if you'd like to wire me some later, I would appreciate that. I'll have to pay my contact for his service."

With that, Janos got on his phone and talked in Korean to someone. As he finished the conversation, babushka knocked on the door. Dinner was ready. The smell was almost intoxicating for Zach.

Dinner was more than Zach could have imagined. Shredded cabbage salad, borscht, brown bread, fried pork chops covered with fried onions and potatoes, broiled potatoes and eggs, cake and strong tea. *A meal fit for a king!*

He ate slowly, savoring every bite. Janos seemed to know that talking would be a distraction, so he quietly ate his meal and said nothing. Babushka picked up the plates and silverware as soon as they finished, placed them in a bin, and took them somewhere out of the apartment.

Dinner over, the two went back into Janos's office/bedroom.

"So how's this escape going to work, Janos?" Zach and Janos were back in their chairs enjoying another cup of tea.

"Here's my plan. In an hour, my contact will come, photograph you, make your ID and leave. Then we'll drive several hours to the border town of Namjungsan-dong. It's right on the Tumen River. As you know, in Russian we call it the Tumannaya River. Remember that name in case you get picked up by Russian guards.

"I'll park the truck behind a warehouse and escort you to the river. Then we'll put your lifejacket on and you'll swim across. It's not wide at that point.

"Once in Russia, walk up the bank, climb over the fence and duck into the woods. Get rid of your lifejacket, throw away your Korean clothes, take the dry, western clothes out of the plastic bag, put them on, and turn right. Walk through the woods parallel to the river. Do not walk on the road. Too dangerous. Just stay in the woods. Eventually you'll come to the railroad tracks. You should come out right near a building with a red roof. It used to be a train station.

"If you should get stopped at any point by Russian guards, show them your papers and claim that you're a guest of Father Nicholas. The guards all know Father. He serves as their chaplain. They may even give you a lift to his house.

"If you're not caught, lie down somewhere in the woods and rest. At ten o'clock tomorrow morning, come out and stand in front of the building. Father Nicholas will meet you and take you to his house."

Zach searched Janos' face. "You know Father Nicholas?"

"Yes, I know him. I don't trust him, but I know him. Rumor is he's a spy. Since your conduit is the Orthodox Church, he's your man. I've already called him. He says he'll pick you up at ten o'clock tomorrow morning."

A knock on the door.

"Zacharios, I'm going to suggest that you climb the stairs to the upper storeroom and hide while I see who's at the door. If it's my contact, I'll call you back down."

Zach climbed the stairs and hid behind a box in the darkened room.

Hopefully it's the contact. But I didn't like the look on the babushka's face. Could she be an informant?

"Zacharios?"

Janos' voice. Must be the contact.

Zach walked back down the stairs and was greeted by the contact, a North Korean. As Janos had advertised, the contact took Zach's photo and fingerprints and conferred with Janos in Korean about bogus information to put on the ID card and passport. In an hour, he presented Zach with two sets of papers, one set showing DPRK permanent residence, and one showing Russian citizenship and visa. The results were pleasing to Zach and he showed it. Janos gave the contact a bundle of paper money and the contact bowed and left.

July 13th — Area 51

Si Longstreet stood at the podium in the Ready Room in Hangar Three at Area 51. It was eight o'clock in the morning. The whole team — both

Ramoses, the aircrew, and the ground crew — were stuffed into the room.

"Gentlemen, today at 1600, you will stand relieved of duty. On behalf of the President of the United States, I commend each one of you for your part in this successful mission. In a moment, I'm going to present Captain Wally and Commander Jerry with Distinguished Flying Crosses, and then Captain Wally will present all of you with the Bronze Star Medal. Of course, no one can ever know of your participation in the mission. But you have my assurance that what you did caused the breakthrough we are experiencing on the Korean Peninsula."

Wally stood up and spoke. "Si, what's the latest on Bob and Zach? Is the search still on?"

"Nothing has been discovered," Si said slowly. "They've vanished off the side of the earth. Other than maybe two muted radio calls which we've not been able to decipher, we've heard nothing from them. Satellite, ship and air searches have turned up nothing. No debris. No survival radio calls. We can only assume that they experienced some sort of emergency, did not have time to yell a Mayday, and flew into the sea. We'll keep their files open in the remote chance that somehow one or both of them are floating around the Sea of Japan in a raft without being seen. We're also entertaining the slight possibility that they may have been close enough to land that they are now wandering around North Korea somewhere. We've inserted some South Korean troops who will blend in and look for them on the ground. They'll be snooping around for a week and then get picked up. That's all we can do. Meanwhile, we need to just go about our business."

"Well, there's one thing we can do." Wally put his hands on his hips. "We can have a prayer service for those guys where we can both ask for their rescue and pray for their souls. Let's get together here after noon chow.

"Master Sergeant Washington, you served as Colonel Zach's assistant chaplain. You and Jerry wanna put together a service for all hands?"

"Yes, sir," both said.

"Okay then," Si took charge again. "Captain Wally, you want to present the decorations?"

Wally and Jerry were given Distinguished Flying Crosses. Then Wally gave the men their awards. Si also gave each man a hefty financial bonus.

The rest of the morning was spent getting gear together and packing. After lunch and the worship service, they got on a bus and started the journey to Las Vegas. Within hours, they would disperse all over the world, getting back to their lives. But none would ever be the same.

CHAPTER NINETEEN

July 14th — On the border of DPRK and the Russian Federation.

*J*anos and Zach arrived in the city of Namjungsan-dong at about one in the morning. After Janos parked the truck behind a warehouse, they walked to the railway station. Crossing the tracks in the dark, they proceeded through the trees, across a guard road and onto the sand. There were no guards. Janos' conversation with the North Korean Officer-of-the-Day had paid off. The guards had been carefully deployed farther north, leaving this path to the river completely unguarded. They reached the river bank.

"With this overcast sky, we can't see across the river tonight, Zacharios. Once you're in the water, just head that way. You'll see the bank after a few minutes. Let me pray for you."

Janos gave a short prayer for protection and helped Zach put his lifejacket on.

Zach shook Janos' hand, smiled, and walked into the river.

This water smells to high heaven, Zach thought as he paddled along. *I feel like I'm swimming through a sewer.*

After four minutes of swimming, he saw the other bank. All was dark; there were no lights. Arriving at the bank, Zach scurried up, climbed over the fence, crossed the path and disappeared into the woods. Again he saw no guards. Ditching his lifejacket and his Korean clothes, he dressed as a Russian with a black turtleneck sweater and baggy, brown pants. Placing his weapons and identification carefully in his pockets, he started out through the woods, walking parallel to the river.

What's that? I hear someone.

He crouched down and looked through the trees. Walking down the path not more than ten feet away was a Russian guard, wearing what appeared to Zach to be night vision goggles. Zach's heart stopped.

I can't move. I can't breathe until he goes by. Then I'll make sure there's not another accompanying him.

The guard passed by. Sure enough, ten paces behind, another guard followed, wearing the same type goggles and looking from side to side, first to the river then to the woods. Zach froze in place, hoping he wasn't seen.

He wasn't. The guards continued their walk up the path.

After five minutes, Zach again started his journey, this time deeper into the woods. After an hour of walking, stopping, looking, listening, and walking again, Zach arrived at the railroad tracks. Aware that other guards might be using night vision goggles, he did not approach the tracks, which were in the open. Seeing the old railroad station, Zach faded back into the woods and found a place where he could fall asleep.

Back in Ch'ongjin, Janos arrived at his warehouse early next morning, walked in and was greeted by a squad of soldiers.

"Where have you been, Mr. Flourik?" The sergeant stood face to face with Janos while his squad members surrounded him.

"I had to pick up a load of furniture from Namjungsan'dong. Would you like to look in the truck to confirm that? Here's the paperwork." Janos handed a bill of lading to the sergeant.

The sergeant looked at the paperwork and then threw it on the floor. "And did you drop off a parcel? A person?"

They know, Janos thought as he felt his body tense up. *Someone has alerted the police. Was it the babushka? She's been acting nasty lately.*

"Yes. I did drop off a person there. I met him on the road yesterday. He said he was a secret agent of the Russian government, and that he was trying to get back to Russia. I gave him some food and dropped him off in Namjungsan-dong, since I was going up there anyway. That's all there is to it. I've done nothing wrong."

The sergeant put his face about an inch from Janos's face. "It is forbidden to do that. You must report strangers to the police. You are in big trouble, Mr. Flourik. I must take you into the station for further questioning."

"I know nothing, sergeant," Janos said, trying to back away. A guard behind him shoved him back toward the sergeant. "And if I have to go to the station or be incarcerated, there will be no one who knows how to distribute these much-needed supplies around here. . . . Please do not take me to the station."

"You have lied. There is much you can tell us. My soldiers will distribute your supplies. Now, let's go to the station."

They all marched out of the warehouse in a circle with Janos in the middle. As they approached the police vehicle, a military jet broke the sound barrier, drawing everyone's attention to the sky. Janos, noticing that, made a run for it. Shoving one of the soldiers aside, he broke into a run, heading for the corner of the warehouse. The sergeant raised his rifle, took careful aim, and put two rounds through Janos' back.

"Pick him up and load him in the van," the sergeant grunted to his squad. To his assistant squad leader, he whispered, "This is better than I thought it would be. The stupid Russian resisted arrest. Now he's dead. And you and I will have to deal with his supplies. We are rich, corporal." They smiled at each other.

Someone else was smiling. The babushka looked on from across the street. She had done her duty and would be paid off handsomely by the sergeant.

Zach awoke about nine, washed in a stream, and did his morning devotions. At ten, he went to the train station.

I feel really exposed out here. A guard could come by at any time. Maybe I'd better wait in the trees.

But just as Zach stood up to leave, a little white ZAZ Slavuta pulled up driven by the biggest Russian he had ever seen.

"Get in, get in," the Russian said as he pulled to a stop.

Zach noticed that the man was dressed as a priest, so he jumped into the passenger seat. No sooner was he seated than the little car was bouncing along, picking up speed.

"I am Father Nicholas. You would be Zacharios?"

"Yes, I am, Father. Thank you for collecting me."

"I owe a favor to Janos Flourik. You are the favor. But what's this about you being a Russian secret agent? And what's this about your claim that you work through the Orthodox Church? I know this to be a lie, comrade. Punishable by death. . . . What do you have to say for yourself?"

How do I play this? Do I pull my Yargin and commandeer the car? Or do I play my 'fellow priest' card?

"Yes, that is a lie. Father, I must tell you who I really am. I'm a fellow priest, from the Diocese of Anadyr, on special missionary assignment. I beg your confidentiality on this."

As Father Nicholas looked closely at Zach, sizing him up, Zach saw a car coming toward them head-on. "Watch out, Father!"

The priest smashed on his brakes and swerved to the right. The move smashed Zach against the door, which sprang open. Zach went sprawling out onto the ground, banging his head. The lights went out for Zach Savage.

Zach awoke kicking and screaming. "Don't hit me again, you beast! I've told you all I know! Leave me alone!"

He opened his eyes and looked around. *It was just a nightmare from my gulag days.* He saw that he was lying in a bed. At first, he didn't remember where he might be.

"Bethany?" He called her name and looked around for her. But then he realized he was not in their home in Yanrakinnot. He noticed that he was in a small room with a plush oriental rug on the floor, clean wallpaper with an Orthodox cross on one wall and an icon of Jesus, Mary, and Joseph on the other. Then he saw Father Nicholas sitting in a rocking chair on the other side of the room.

"Nightmare, Father? Welcome back to the world of reality," Nicholas said, smiling at Zach. "You've been out cold for two days. I was beginning to wonder whether you might ever wake up."

"What. . . what happened?"

"Let me see. You told me you were a priest rather than a secret agent. I was so surprised that I almost ran into an oncoming car. In the confusion, you fell out of my car and hit your head on a pole. You've been mumbling something about Bethany for several hours. . . . Is Bethany your wife, Father?"

Zach sat up in the bed. Nicholas handed him a cup of tea, which he gulped down in spite of its hot temperature.

"What time is it?" Zach looked at his wrist and found that his Seiko was missing.

"It's one in the afternoon on Sunday. You slept through Divine Liturgy! And now it's time for dinner. My matushka has everything ready. Do you think you can walk?"

Zach slowly climbed out of bed and tried to stand. He was only able to stand by leaning on the bedpost.

"Let me help you out to the dining room, Father."

The big priest picked up Zach like a sack of flour and carried him to the table, where he helped him sit down.

"Father, this is Matushka Natalia," Nicholas said, pointing to his wife. "I'm afraid I did not get your real name, Father."

Zach bowed to Natalia. *Nice lady. Short and squat. Dark hair bunched in a bun. Brown dress.*

"My name is Janos Zacharios, Matushka. My matushka is Anastasia. I am the priest at a mission church in Chukotka, Diocese of Anadyr. I am pleased to make your acquaintance."

Natalia nodded her head and smiled as Nicholas said the meal prayer and they began to eat. Cabbage salad, heavy vegetable soup, chicken, potatoes, squash, brown bread, and strong tea. They ate in silence, Zach once again savoring every bite.

As they sat eating cake, Nicholas began the conversation. "So tell me, Janos, why are you here and why were you in Korea? What does it all have to do with the Diocese of Anadyr and its crazy bishop?"

"That's the point, isn't it?" Zach swallowed a bite of cake. "Our Bishop Diomid is considered crazy and out of step with Moscow. What better person to run the secret Catholic missions of Korea? Nicholas and Natalia, I must ask for your strictest confidence. I have been on assignment in the Democratic Peoples' Republic of Korea, visiting the underground missions on behalf of the bishop. We, of course, could never get permission from the DPRK government to do this, so I was smuggled in three weeks ago.

"While I was in Ch'ongjim, someone informed on me and I had to escape immediately. Janos Flourik got me out. But he couldn't tell you who I really was, lest someone might be listening."

"Very foolish plan," Nicholas said as he stirred his tea. "It's fortunate that the guards are my parishioners or you would be toast by now. I've tried to contact Janos Flourik but get no answer on his phone. . . . What happens to you now?"

"Can you get me to Vladivostok? And can you loan me some money? I can catch a flight from Vlad to Anadyr."

"I can drive you to Vladivostok. It's only one hundred kilometers from here. But I surely don't have the money to get you a ticket to Anadyr. . . . However, the dean of the Cathedral of St. Nicholas might give a fellow priest the money. Especially if I vouch for you."

"That would be wonderful, Nicholas. When can we go?"

"Let's see how you are feeling tomorrow. If you're up to traveling, we'll head out in the morning. Matushka would like to visit the Dean's matushka and do some shopping. We don't get up to Vladivostok as often as we'd like. Petrol is so expensive."

On Monday, Zach said he felt well enough to travel, so they started out in the little car, Nicholas and Zach in the front seat, Natalia bundled up in the back seat. Up and down hills they drove, the little ZAZ slowing to almost a stop going up the hills and then running almost out of control down the hills. They were in Vladivostok by noon, slowly chugging along in the heavy traffic.

What a beautiful city this is, thought Zach. *A city in the hills with crystal harbors. Look. There's a great big cruise ship parked at the port!*

Nicholas pulled up in front of the Cathedral of St. Nicholas. Built on the side of a hill, it took Zach's breath away. The building was ornate and well cared for. They got out of the car and walked into the deanery offices. The dean greeted them and took them to his apartment where they had tea. Zach met the matushka and gave her greetings on behalf of Bethany. He noticed that both the dean and his wife were short and portly, and that they were at least twenty years older than Nicholas and Natalia. *Clergy mentors?*

The dean was not surprised at all to hear that Zach was from the diocese of Anadyr. He was careful to correct Nicholas, "That is the Diocese of Anadyr and Chukotka, Nicholas. Not the Diocese of Anadyr. And Bishop Diomid is a folk hero. Please give him my regards, Janos. I've been a secret admirer of the good bishop for some years, and am not surprised that he has the duty of providing for the underground church in Korea. I commend you on your dangerous work and will keep this in confidence as I'm sure Nicholas will."

Zach nodded. *Do I believe this guy? Will Nicholas let his government contact know about this? I have no choice, though. I've just got to trust that the Lord is guiding me.*

"I wish I could introduce you to our own bishop, Archbishop Theotokos," the Dean continued. "But he is back in Moscow for a meeting. Archbishop Theotokos is of the same personality and leanings as Bishop Diomid — strong, opinionated, and very holy—"

"Would you please excuse me, Dean?" Nicholas interrupted. "Janos has to get back to Anadyr but has lost his wallet. He has no money. Could you buy him an air ticket?"

The Dean immediately walked to his wall safe, spun the dial a few times, and opened the safe. He pulled out a stack of paper money and walked over to Zach. "Please accept this as a gift to you from the Cathedral of St. Nicholas. We appreciate your missionary activity and are happy to be a part of your work."

Zach rose and bowed deeply as he accepted the money. "Thank you, Mr. Dean. I will convey your greetings to the bishop and tell him how kind you have been to me."

"All right," the Dean said resolutely. "It's time for the matushkas to go shopping, and time for me to show Janos around our beautiful city. Tomorrow, early, we'll escort you to the airport. The flight leaves at eight. You'll have to stop a few times. It is a journey of three thousand kilometers. With good weather, you should be in Anadyr by tomorrow night."

It was with a light heart that Zach boarded the Antonov the next morning. The Dean was able to get him through the documents desk with just a glance at his passport. Two hours after takeoff from the Vladivostok Airport, he arrived in Chabarovsk, where he waited in the cramped terminal for two hours. Matushka had prepared some chicken sandwiches for him, which he ate while he waited.

Then followed a slow, five-hour flight to Magadan, much of it over the Sea of Okhotsk. It was a bumpy ride, causing some of the passengers to throw up. By the time they reached Magadan, the passenger compartment smelled like a bar-room bathroom. Zach was glad to just get out of the airplane and catch some fresh air.

Due to delays and weather, he got no further that day. A ramshackle hotel near the airport sufficed for the night. Dirty and small, with a most uncomfortably thin mattress that smelled of sweat, the room caused Zach to get very little sleep.

I can't sleep in this hellhole. And I'm also keyed up about arriving in Anadyr tomorrow. One step closer to Bethany and Tomas! First thing will be to report in with Bishop Diomid. Then it will be on to Yanrakinnot.

After a fitful night of sleep, Zach boarded the Antonov for the final leg of the journey, a four-hour jaunt over eastern Siberia before finally touching down at the Anadyr Airport at one in the afternoon.

Zach leaped onto the launch to go across the bay. He was almost giddy as he watched the city of Anadyr get closer and closer. Once the launch was at the dock, he ran off it and jogged all the way to the bishop's residence on Partizan Street.

He knocked enthusiastically with the large door knocker. Father Dmitri opened the door, recognized him, and invited him in.

"Come in, Father," Dmitri said casually as he ushered him along the hallway to Bishop Diomid's office. "We have missed you. I hope your time in Moscow and St. Petersburg went well."

Does Dmitri not know where I've been? Has Bishop Diomid kept him in the dark on this? Or is he just playing it cool?

"Quite successful. Thank you for asking, Father Dmitri. How have things been here?"

"We've managed. . . . Ah, here we are. Please wait for a moment, Father."

Father Dmitri walked into Bishop Diomid's office, leaving Zach standing in the vestibule. Zach waited, swaying from one foot to the other.

Hurry up, Dmitri. Just tell him I'm here, for gosh sakes. . . . What if the bishop doesn't want to see me? What if something's happened? What is taking so long?

After several minutes, Father Dmitri opened the door and waved Zach in. Zach walked quickly into the room and approached the bishop, who was standing in the middle of the room.

The bishop looks sad. What can be wrong? Bowing, Zach did the protocol greeting. "Would you bless me, my Father?"

Official greeting over, the bishop asked Zach to have a seat as he himself sat in the chair right next to his rather than behind his desk. *Something's definitely wrong. Why else would he sit right beside me?*

"Father Dmitri, tea, please for us both. And some of those delicious pastries. . . . Now, Zacharios, you are most welcome back. I think I should thank you for what you may have been involved with in what happened in Korea?"

"My Bishop, is everything all right in Yanrakinnot?"

Bishop Diomid hesitated. "Things are all right there. But first, tell me about your mission. Was it a success?"

Zach spent the next fifteen minutes filling the bishop in on the last three months of his life, stopping only when Father Dmitri came in carrying pastry and tea.

"So," Zach wound up after telling his story and enjoying the pastry and tea. "I can't figure out whether my government knows I'm alive or not. But I have a deep suspicion that we were set up by someone. I think that if I showed up in America right now, people in my own government would try to bump me off. It's just not worth it, my Lord. I've come back to take up my ministry in your diocese.

"But I've been thinking, my Lord. It may not be wise for me to continue at Yanrakinnot. Too much chance that if people in my government are looking for me, they may track me down there. I'm wondering if my matushka and I might be assigned to another location."

"Of course I will re-assign you," Bishop Diomid said as he lay his hand on Zach's leg. "Father, I must tell you something that may be hard for you to accept." The bishop looked into Zach's eyes. "Your matushka and your son are missing."

"What?" Zach began to shake. "What happened?"

"Father Dema has been reporting to me. Your matushka, your baby son, and Leonid left Yanrakinnot suddenly on June 8th, over a month ago—"

"Where did they go?" Zach, still shaking, stared at the bishop.

Bishop Diomid shifted in his chair, removing his hand from Zach's leg and crossing his arms. "Dr. Peter told everyone that your matushka had been summoned to Anadyr by me because I wanted her to join you in St. Petersburg. He also told everyone that he had scheduled Leonid to get some mechanical schooling in Magadan after he dropped her and the baby off here in Anadyr.

"Zacharios, what Dr. Peter said was not true. I did not summon your matushka, and she never showed up here in Anadyr. . . . I wondered what was really up, so I sent a secret message up to the good doctor to explain himself. But he never got the message.

"Dr. Peter disappeared on June 22, Zacharios. He vanished. No explanation to anyone. No goodbyes. No note. The whole village went out searching for him. No results. His ATV was still parked at his office. His house was left as if he would be returning shortly. But it has now been three weeks and Father Dema wired yesterday that there is still no sign of him."

Zach sat quietly, obviously in thought. He slowly poured himself another cup of tea. *I've got to get hold of myself before I do something stupid. I've got to think through what this means.*

"My Lord, I can only conclude that someone came into the village to take Bethany. That can be the only explanation as to why she would disappear. I think Peter must have had a plan for Leonid to take my wife and child to a safe place, and he put the plan into action. He had to fabricate a story to explain their departure. And I have to assume they are somewhere in the interior waiting for me—"

"That would make sense," the bishop interrupted Zach. "But what about Dr. Peter's disappearance?"

"Very curious," Zach replied. "There are several possibilities. "One. He may have left to be with them. But if he did, he would have left some explanation for that. A note maybe.

"Two. He may have tangled with whoever tried to grab my wife. And he could have been captured and tortured for information about her. He may be incarcerated somewhere right now.

"Three. And I don't want to think about his. He may have been murdered by whoever tried to grab my wife."

Bishop Diomid stood. "We need to pray about it. It is possible that you will need to do some detective work on this. And I can put the word out to our mission stations and churches to be on the lookout for your matushka."

"Don't do that yet, please. Let me search around first. I'll get back to you on what I find out. Do you have someone you trust who might travel with me and help? Someone who can be a fellow detective?"

"Let me pray first." The bishop placed his hands on Zach's head and said a long prayer of protection for Zach as he investigated, and a plea that Bethany and Tomas would be found safe.

Prayer over, the bishop called his assistant. "Father Dmitri, come here please."

Father Dmitri scurried into the room. "Yes, my Lord?"

"Father Dmitri, you will take a trip with Father Zacharios. He will explain everything. Take many rubles with you. Wherever Father Zacharios thinks you both should go, you go and pay for whatever is needed. And get out of your priest clothes. Dress like Father Zacharios. Do you understand me?"

Father Dmitri perked up. "Yes, my Lord."

"Father Zacharios," the bishop said, turning to Zach. "I am giving you Father Dmitri. He's big and smart and he loves reading mysteries. He'll be of good assistance to you. . . . Bring him back safe, Father."

"Yes, my Lord," was all Zach could say.

Zach and Dmitri then left the bishop's office. Bishop Diomid went to his prayer desk, knelt down and prayed fervently.

CHAPTER TWENTY

July 20th — Provideniya

*T*he Antonov touched down at the Provideniya Airport at seven in the evening. Zach and Dmitri climbed down the ladder and looked around.

Lots of sun. Trees in leaf. The distant mountains with some snow on the peaks. This place has changed since I left it two months ago. It's a veritable paradise today! Hope I can get a lead on Bethany. Lord, guide me.

They got a ride around the bay and entered the village. They walked up to the apartment building on Chabarova Street and climbed the stairs to Apartment 327. Zach did his coded knock.

"Muk! Great to see you again," Zach said in Yupik as he was greeted by his friend. "This is my friend Dmitri."

"Good to meet you," Muk said in broken Russian. Then returning to the Yupik language, he spoke to Zach. "Father, I am so glad to see you again. There's enough food for the three of us."

This is like coming home, Zach thought as he walked into the sitting room and sat down in his favorite chair. He took the old apartment in — its dirty floor and walls, its worn-out furniture, its moldy smell.

I love this place!

Dmitri followed him in and sat on the sofa, turning up his nose as he sat down.

"It's okay, Dmitri," Zach said, noticing his discomfort. "This place may not look or smell like much, but a lot's happened here for me over the last few years. It's like home to me."

"It does have a lived-in feel," said Dmitri drily.

"Father, I have a cold dinner planned," Muk said, coming out of the kitchen with tea. "Cold reindeer meats, cheese, brown bread. We can sit down and eat as soon as you wish."

After prayer, they sat at the table and made sandwiches, washing them down with strong, black tea.

"What have you heard about all the happenings in Yanrakinnot while I've been gone, Muk?" Zach sat back in his chair and enjoyed his tea. "Speak in Russian so that Father Dmitri can understand."

"On June 10th, Dr. Peter came to see me here in Provideniya." Muk began the briefing, speaking in a low monotone, which was the typical way a Yupik passed on important information. "He said that a bad man had come in on the cruise ship and had tried to grab Matushka. Leonid shot him. So then Dr. Peter knew that Matushka must leave. He sent Matushka and the baby with Leonid. He said to tell you that he sent them to Mys Shmidta. He gave me the name of the doctor there who will know where they are. And if they cannot stay there, they are to go to his kinsmen in Amguema.

"When Dr. Peter left, that's the last I saw him. I heard that on June 22, he disappeared. Maybe he followed Leonid. But if he had decided to do that, he would have let me know. I fear that something bad has happened to him, Father. . . . I have now told you all I know." Muk bowed his head and frowned.

Zach sat quietly, thinking.

I know where Mys Shmidta is, but I've never heard of Amguema. Maybe Muk can help me with that. But I'm also concerned about Peter. He wouldn't purposely leave without notifying Muk. I'd better sneak into Yanrakinnot and check his house.

"Muk, tomorrow Father Dmitri and I will head up to Yanrakinnot to search Dr. Peter's house. You want to come with us?"

"If you want me to come, I will come," Muk said.

"And Muk, I think you should move out of here as soon as possible. Surely you realize we've got some foreign intrigue going on here. I don't know whether Simon Longstreet is on our side or not. There's no way I can be sure. But if he's not on our side, it's just a matter of time before he comes looking for me. And since he spent so much time in this apartment talking to me, the first person he's going to look for is you in this apartment.

"Also, if the bad man Dr. Peter spoke of was working for someone else, and if that someone else got hold of Dr. Peter, he may have tortured him to get information about me. He may know about you by now and may come after you in order to find out where I am. . . . You've got to get out of here, Muk. You have somebody who can take this apartment from you?"

"Yes. I can do that. I know someone. But where will I go, Father?"

"You want to move with me? When we find Matushka, Tomas, Leonid, and maybe Peter, we can all be together somewhere in Chukotka."

"Yes, Father," Muk said, smiling. "I will go with you. And I will live with you and work for you. Leonid is like a brother to me. I was with him when his wife died. I would like to be closely associated with your family and with Leonid and Dr. Peter."

"Okay," Zach said with resolution in his voice. "Find that person you're going to leave this apartment with. We'll head out in two hours rather than tomorrow morning. And we'll drive in the dark. You and I know the way in the dark as well as in the light. You know where we can get our hands on three ATVs?"

"How many rubles do you have?"

"All you need," Dmitri responded.

"Give me some. I'll go now and be back in two hours with the keys to three ATVs."

That night at about ten, the sun still up, they headed north for Yanrakinnot. The three drove on as the sun began to set at one in the morning. By three, there was some darkness and they were on the edge of Yanrakinnot. Parking their ATVs in a gulley, they walked through the woods to the outskirts of the village.

"We've got about one hour before the sun starts to come up. Muk, where is Father Dema living, Peter's house or mine?"

"He lives in your house since Matushka and the baby left, Father."

"Okay then," Zach said as he changed direction. "Let's get over to Peter's house and see what we can find. Got the flashlights, Muk?"

"Yes, Father, I have the flashlights."

They walked down the street that led to the doctor's house and walked around to the back door. Zach tried the door. It was locked. He felt around the ledge over the doorway and found the key. Unlocking the door, they walked in.

"What are we looking for, Father Zacharios?" Dmitri looked around the kitchen.

"I'm thinking Peter left me a note. He once showed me the spot where he kept his secret papers and money."

Zach led them upstairs to Peter's bedroom, pulled down the shade, pulled the curtains together and switched on his flashlight.

"Look," Zach said, shining the flashlight around. "All his clothes are still here. He didn't pack for a trip. And his bed's not made. He would have done that if he were going on a trip. He's either been killed or captured. That's for sure. Let's see if his stuff is gone."

Zach looked down at the wooden floor. He pushed on a loose board and it flipped up, revealing two boxes under the floor. Zach pulled both of them out and laid them on the bed. He opened the first and found an envelope on top of the pile of papers. It had 'Zach' written on it, in Bethany's writing. Zach tore open the envelope, took out two letters and read them. The first was from Peter.

My Dear Zachary,

I pray that your mission has been successful. If you have found this letter, it means that something has happened to me. On June 8th, a Russian came off the cruise ship and tried to break into your house. Leonid shot him. When I looked him over, I could tell that he was an agent, either of the Russian government or a crime syndicate. Zachary, I fear that your mission has gained the attention of the Russians who kept you cooped up in the gulag for all those years. I think their plan was to find you by maybe torturing the truth out of Bethany. So I sent Leonid with Bethany and Tomas to a safe place. I sent them to Mys Shmidta, where my friend Dr. Ivan Opinsky can watch over them. If for some reason they can't stay in Mys Shmidta, Leonid is to take them to our kinsmen in Amguema deep in the interior. You will find them in one place or the other. I've alerted Muk to all this. As for me: as I said, if you are reading this note, something has happened to me. My resolve was to remain here until your return. If I am still alive, I will find you. Meanwhile, go with God, my son. Find your wife and child and be a blessing to all whom God calls you to minister.*

Peter

Tears ran down Zach's cheeks as he read the note. He didn't try to hide the tears. Dmitri and Muk stood there shifting from one foot to the other.

Finally Zach handed the letter to Muk and took up the other. This letter was from Bethany.

My dearest Zach,

How Tomas and I have missed you! Zach, someone tried to grab me here in Yanrakinnot. I don't know who, but Peter felt that the only safe thing to do was to disappear. So Tomas and I have fled with Leonid. I've told Peter that as soon as you find him, he's to give you this letter. I'll be waiting for you, Zach, my love. Soon we'll be together again and can start over somewhere safe. I hope to see you soon. I love you, Zach.

Bethany

Zach read the letter twice through as tears continued down his cheeks. *Lord God, help me find my family. Please.*

He reached for the other box and opened it. It was filled with rubles. He picked up half the rubles from the box, put them in his pocket, tucked the letters into his other pocket, and put both boxes back in their hiding place.

"Muk," Zach said, glancing at his friend. "We may or may not see Dr. Peter again. He would want us to have half his money. If he comes back, he'll need the other half. . . . Now, we need to get back to Provideniya and book ship passage to Mys Shmidta.

"Dmitri, I won't be needing your assistance any longer. Once we get back to Provideniya, please report back to the bishop all you've seen and heard. If he has an assignment for me, he can get word to me in one of those two places — Mys Shmidta or Amguema. . . . Now, let's get out of here."

They walked back to their ATV's and drove for two hours until they were so tired they couldn't go any farther. Pulling into a gulley, they bundled themselves up and slept for four hours.

July 21st — CIA Headquarters, Virginia

Simon Longstreet walked into the office of Curtis Mitchell, director of the CIA's National Clandestine Service (D/NCS), and flopped down in an easy chair. They had been working together for years and were old friends.

Mitchell got up from his desk and walked over to where Si was slouched. "Thanks for the good work, rabbi," he said as he punched him in the arm. "We avoided a nuclear catastrophe and a lot of it had to do with your aircrews being there if needed. That gave the president enough courage to press the mission."

Mitchell sat down in a chair beside Si.

"I appreciate that, boss. Both the aircrews and the ground crews did an extremely professional job, but I consider it a personal failure that I lost one of the aircrews. We still can't figure out what happened."

"Well, I wouldn't take it too personally, Si. What they did was dangerous and they knew it. It wasn't your fault. You did everything you could to make the mission just as safe as it could be. Any sign of the crew?"

"Nah. We've checked out every speck in the sea, man. We sent in some South Koreans to do a land check. Nothin'. . . . I think they flew into the water, Curt. No other explanation. And it's been three weeks. If they were alive, they would've turned up by now. . . . We need to close the case. The pilot had no family, so we don't have to notify anybody except maybe send a note from him to his postmistress in Montana, telling her he's had to make a quick move to Alabama and to send his stuff to him.

"I feel badly about the bombardier-navigator, though. He's got a wife and baby back in Siberia. We've got to somehow let her know her husband's not coming back. Make a lump sum payment to her. I'll work on that next week after I get some other things caught up."

"I'm afraid next week will be too late, Si," Curt said, looking at him with a frown. "You're being given a permanent change of assignment, starting in three days."

"What?" Si sat up. "I just got home! What's this about an assignment?"

"Afraid so. This is from the top. The director has personally picked you for it. He says he was so impressed with your work on this last assignment, he needs you right away for a new one overseas, one that will take two to three years."

"You've got to be kidding," Si said as he threw up his arms. "I don't want a permanent assignment overseas. I want to rest from the last one and then be available for a new CONUS assignment. . . . Where is the new assignment, by the way?"

"You'll be based out of Nairobi. Subject is Somali pirates. The job comes with a promotion."

"Curt, please. Can you get me out of it?"

"Look at the positive side, Si. You're one step higher on the ladder. You've got a mission that will possibly solve the pirate problem. And you can come home to a plush assignment in three years. . . . Look, I'd get you out of this if I could. But the director is determined that you will be the man."

"But what do I do about notifying the lady in Siberia? We have a responsibility to let her know about her husband, and to give her his money."

"Give me the contact information for your man out there. I'll get someone on it right away."

And with that, General Rogers, Director of the CIA, got rid of the only other person who could have blown the cover off the fact that he had tried to kill two patriotic Americans, all for the greater good, of course.

July 25th — Uelen, Russian Federation

The ship pulled into Uelen's small port in the early afternoon on Sunday. Zach and Muk had boarded the *Stanislaw* three days earlier. *Stanislaw* was actually just a large boat, fifty feet long, which carried people and supplies to and from the ports between Anadyr and Pevek. They had made a stop at Lavrentiya and were now making the next stop on their journey to Mys Shmidta.

Uelen, Zach thought as he looked at the village built along a spit of land jutting into the Chukchi Sea. *The easternmost settlement in Russia, closest village to the United States of America. Wonder if I'll ever get back to my home country. Well, that's in the Lord's hands. My primary mission is to find Bethany and Tomas and then to continue my ministry in Chukotka.*

Zach and Muk celebrated the Divine Liturgy in their room early in the morning, and since there was to be a three hour layover, decided to walk around the village. Little wooden houses greeted them. Beaten by the wind and blizzards, these houses had little paint left on them. Huskies inhabited every yard, chained to each house. Residents paid them no mind, assuming they were off the ship and would soon be back on the ship.

As they rounded a corner, Zach glanced up and stopped dead in his tracks.

I recognize that man coming our way. He was the sergeant who accompanied the crazy Colonel Strasdie that morning in Anadyr two years ago. He helped kill the colonel before the colonel killed me. Only one conclusion: that man works for Dolgoprudnenskaya, the crime syndicate. I think he may be here looking for Bethany!

Zach put his head down and turned back around the corner. Muk, noting his quick turn, did the same thing. The two began walking casually back toward the ship.

"What is it, Father? What's wrong?"

"Muk, I just recognized a bad man, one who would hurt Matushka and me. We must make it back to the ship before he sees us. Glance over your shoulder and see if a Russian in a long black coat is following us."

Muk glanced over his shoulder. "The man is continuing down the street. It does not look like he is interested in us."

"Praise God. Let's hurry back to the ship before he comes upon us."

The two picked up the pace and boarded their ship. From behind an oil drum on the main deck, Zach sat and watched. He watched as the man walked down to the port and got on another ship. He watched as the other ship pulled away from the dock.

As one of the sailors walked by, Zach stopped him. "Comrade, where is that ship bound?"

The sailor looked at it closely. "That is the *Stalin* and it is bound for Anadyr right now."

A wave of relief swept over Zach.

That tells me that this man hasn't found Bethany. So he must have looked around Mys Shmidta on his way from Pevek. She's still safe.

An hour later, the *Stanislaw* pulled out of Uelen, bound for its next port of call, Alyatki.

July 26th — Moscow

Dmitri Medvedev and Vladimir Putin sat in Medvedev's office sipping strong tea. They were sitting in front of the fireplace, which was burning due to unexpected cold weather. Medvedev loved the smell of pine logs burning. It reminded him of his childhood when he lived in the little one room home in his village so many kilometers from Moscow. His father always had a fire going, and he always burned pine logs. Medvedev thought back to those carefree days.

Not carefree now. If I do one thing out of line, my mentor here will have me banished to eastern Siberia.

"So, Mr. Prime Minister," Medvedev said, smiling. "We now have the conference scheduled between representatives of the American State Department and the new Vice Premier of DPRK. And the foolish American president has agreed to have the conference here in Moscow, with you as the broker. Is he totally stupid or just under the control of left-wing advisers?"

"We do have a few people in the White House," Putin responded. "And one who is close to him. The president is a frightened man, intent on being re-elected. His advisers are telling him that he needs to play ball with us in order to get re-elected, that if he turns down our offer of negotiations, he'll incur the wrath of his leftist base. His base will then sabotage him. So he has no choice but to play our game."

"So you will negotiate the USA off the Korean Peninsula?"

"In good time, my friend. In good time."

"There's a loose end," Medvedev said as he glanced at his mentor. "As you know, I don't like loose ends. . . . Who killed Kim Jong Il's sons?"

"Ah, this is not just a loose end, Dmitri. This is the mother of all loose ends.

"Here's what we know: It was not just Kim Jong Il's sons who were killed. Kim Jong Il himself was killed, perhaps just days before he would have died a natural death—"

"So the appearance of Kim Jong Il sitting up in a hospital bed on the newscast yesterday was not Kim Jong Il?"

"The DPRK Premier, our man General Park, believes it is necessary to keep Kim alive for the next year, so what we will be seeing on the newscasts will be Kim's double. He is paid well to impersonate the Dear Leader. And he does a good job of it.

"In a year, when Park's government is well established, Kim will suffer another stroke and die. Then there will be a magnificent state funeral with much grieving. The double, by the way, will also suffer a grave illness, lead to the head! But he doesn't know that.

"But back to the assassinations. Our sources in Seoul tell us that it was not a South Korean assassination team that did the killings. They in fact were on their way to the mountain house to assassinate everyone when they ran into some problems and were delayed. When they were in range of the house, they saw it explode. So we can eliminate Seoul.

"General Park's assassination team also got to the house after the explosion. The pilots saw the house blow up, and so turned back to P'yongyang. So we can eliminate Park.

"The Chinese would have had no reason to assassinate the Kim family. They were in fact backing that regime."

"Then who did it?" Medvedev stood and stirred the logs in the fireplace, then sat back down.

"We have pieced something together. Our intelligence people put a Russian team in there two days after the blast. They interrogated the guards, they inspected the blast area, and they brought back some samples. Here is what they found.

"On the night of the explosion, two guards were manning an anti-aircraft gun when the explosion occurred. The senior guard reported hearing a jet engine and ordered the other to fire his guns. The guard who fired the guns said that he heard no airplane but fired out of obedience to his senior guard. The senior said there was an airplane; the junior said there was none. But suppose there was an aircraft which fired a missile into the house. And suppose the guard who fired his guns hit that aircraft. Whose aircraft was it? And if it was hit, where did it go down?

"Then our people analyzed the material the team brought back from the house. It was a missile fired from an aircraft, Dmitri, that hit the house and killed Kim Jong Il and his sons. This we now know.

"So an aircraft from which nation? Not from DPRK. They don't have such missiles. Not from us. Not from Japan. They've stayed out of the confrontation between DPRK and the USA. Maybe Seoul? Highly unlikely. They were using an assassination team. Remember?"

"That leaves. . . America," Medvedev said slowly.

"Yes. America. Remember that the American CIA sent two aircraft to make a clandestine nuclear attack on DPRK's nuclear weapon sites? As you know, the coup took place in P'yongyang just before those aircraft were to make their strikes. They had already begun jamming DPRK's radars and communications in preparation for the strike.

Our intelligence states that the aircrews were commanded to call off the strike and return to their base. Now listen to this, Dmitri. One of the aircraft did not come back. Our intel team at Iwakuni counted only one returning Prowler.

"The CIA people are saying among themselves that the other Prowler flew into the Sea of Japan, just off the east coast of DPRK. Do you think a well-experienced aircrew would just fly into the water? Suppose, instead, that the aircraft had another mission so secret that not even our highly placed intelligence people in Washington knew about it. Suppose that aircrew had a mission to blow the Kim family off the map. That aircraft would have flown low-level into the radar and communication jammed DPRK, fired its missile into the house, and then escaped back over the Sea of Japan.

"Now suppose that the aircraft got hit by the guard's anti-aircraft artillery but not enough to bring it down immediately. It could have flown for a while before crashing. Those mountains in Northeast DPRK are desolate. An aircraft could crash there without anyone hearing it. The aircrew could have ejected into the mountains and may be wandering around out there as we speak. Or the aircraft might have gotten out over the Sea of Japan and then crashed into the sea."

"So many unanswered questions, Mr. Prime Minister. More loose ends."

"Yes. Loose ends we can tie up. Here's what we will do:

"One. We'll do some satellite photography of those mountains. Perhaps we might find the crashed American aircraft.

"Two. We'll send some teams to look through those mountains and interrogate people. Did anyone see or hear anything suspicious? Any flying clothing or equipment found? We'll talk to the police in all the precincts of northeastern DPRK. Do they have any evidence of Americans or Europeans wandering around?

"Three. We'll go into a surge with our intelligence in Washington. Surely someone in the CIA must know something. We'll see if we can find out what happened.

"Four. I need to follow up on a hunch. Several years ago, an American pilot who had been secretly incarcerated in one of our criminal work camps near Chukotka escaped. We had a chase for him but in the end he got away. We heard later that he was to be one of the crewmen who attacked Iran on that clandestine mission. Before we could get to him in the USA, he escaped again. Then we heard this spring that he was now a religious man somewhere in Chukotka and that he was recruited by the CIA to participate in the raid on DPRK.

"Now suppose, Dimitri, that he was one of the crewmen that struck the Kim house, that he and his crewmate ejected, and are on their way to Russia! Suppose he and his crewmate are returning home to Chukotka to be with his wife! If we can catch them, we can get the truth out of them and use it as a bargaining chip with the Americans. Do you see the possibilities here?"

"So you'll check the border between DPRK and the Russian Federation?"

"We will, my friend. But we won't commit huge resources to the project. I've just been talking in broad suppositions. I could write action adventure thrillers, could I not? The facts are that we know that the Americans killed the Kim family and we can be thankful for that!"

"We can, indeed, Mr. Prime Minister. It is a job well done by all concerned. We are now back in charge in Eastern Asia."

CHAPTER TWENTY-ONE

July 26th — Mys Shmidta

*7*he *Stanislaw* pulled into Mys Shmidta at noon on a sunny Monday. Zach and Muk walked down the gangplank and started the short trek up into the city.

"How do we proceed, Father?" Muk walked beside Zach, looking from one side to the other.

"We ask for the office of Dr. Ivan Opinsky and then we go see him. Since you're a Yupik, you can get farther in asking for him. Less suspicion that way."

"Yes, Father."

They walked into the shopping district and into a store where an elderly native woman was working as cashier. Muk listened to her speak to others for a moment, and then brought a flannel shirt to the counter.

"Good day," he said in Chukchi. She responded in kind as she rang up his shirt.

"Madam, can you tell me where I can find Dr. Ivan Opinsky? He is an old friend whom I have not seen in a long time."

The woman looked at Muk for a moment. "Where did you know him? He's been here for years."

"Anadyr. When I was a boy, he was our family doctor. And my uncle and Dr. Opinsky were in practice together there."

"Yes, he did move here from Anadyr. . . . You go up the street to Korsakov, two blocks up. Turn right and you will find his office in the second building on the left."

"Thank you, madam. And may God bless you."

She hesitated and then smiled. "God bless you also," she said so softly that only he could hear her.

Zach and Muk walked up to Korsakov Street, turned right and found the second building on the left, a three-story concrete structure that looked like it had been the victim of a bombing attack. The concrete was discolored. Some of the windows on the second and third floors were broken. The front window on the first floor was boarded up. A sign in the door said, 'Dr. Opinksy — Walk-ins welcome Monday through Friday from 10 to 2.'

They walked into the office, a small room with some patients sitting on benches, and a desk and chair with an older Russian woman sitting in it. As they walked in, she greeted them in Russian. "Welcome. How may I help you?"

Muk responded. "I am an old friend of the doctor and have just come into town. May I see him?"

The woman hesitated, so Muk spoke again, this time quietly. "Tell him I am a friend of Dr. Peter. Tell him Muk Toranjuta is here."

The woman got up and walked into the inner office. Zach and Muk waited patiently. One minute went by. Then two minutes.

Is she notifying the authorities? Zach thought. *Do we need to run?*

Just as he was about to suggest to Muk that they leave, the woman came out of the doctor's office. She handed Muk a note.

"Thank you for coming," she said. And then she called the next patient.

Confused, Zach and Muk walked out of the building. Muk read the note and then showed it to Zach.

Greetings, Dear Muk. It is good to know you are here. I may have some information you need. Please stop by my apartment for tea at two. 24 Paraski Street, number 271.

"Okay, Muk. We lie low for two hours. I'll buy you lunch." They walked back down to the shopping district, found an out-of-the-way diner, and ate a leisurely lunch.

At two o'clock, they knocked at the door of the apartment. An old Russian answered. Short and thin, with no hair on his head. Zach judged him to be in his mid-eighties. He was dressed in a gray suit with a dark tie.

Very trim and very proper, Zach mused.

"Come in, Muk, come in," the doctor said, waving them in. "It's so good to see you after all these years."

They walked into a small one room apartment, with the typical worn wallpaper, cracked linoleum, and worn-out furniture that were so common in the old apartment buildings of Chukotka.

Motioning them to be seated, he proceeded to pour tea into the cups he already had ready on the kitchen table.

"Doctor, this is my friend Father Zacharios."

The doctor smiled at Zach. "It's good to make your acquaintance, Father. It seems I know your wife and baby quite well. Your matushka is wonderful. She was so good to me."

Was? She was good to him? That sounds like she's no longer here. Good Lord, help me.

The doctor finished pouring the tea and, placing a plate of pastries in the center of the table, sat down with the two men.

"Thank you, doctor," Zach said. "It is about my matushka that we have come. I've come to take her home."

"That will be difficult right now, Father," the doctor said, taking a sip of his tea. "She's not here—"

"Please, doctor," Muk cut into the conversation. "Can you tell us what happened? Dr. Peter told us Leonid brought her here, to you."

"Yes." The doctor sighed. "I so enjoyed her. . . . It was tragic when Leonid came to me and said they had to leave."

"Why did they have to leave?" Zach was growing impatient.

"Father," the doctor said, looking into his eyes. "Someone, a Russian, came to town looking for her. Leonid seemed to know him. He told me it was too dangerous for them to stay here another moment. They left that same day, only an hour after he told me they needed to leave."

"When was that?" Zach looked intently back at the doctor.

"That was July 8th, almost three weeks ago. Leonid didn't tell me where they were going. He said it would be safer for me if I did not know."

"Thanks for the info. But did anyone come to you asking for information?"

"A Russian came by my office late that afternoon and asked about any new women in town. My nurse told him I was on an extended trip back to Moscow and that she didn't know anything about a new woman spending time here in Mys Shmidta. It seemed to satisfy him. He never returned. . . . By the way, Father, Leonid left a letter with me for you, in case you came to Mys Shmidta."

The doctor went to his sofa, pulled a cushion out and pulled the letter from the lining. "Here it is."

Zach tore the letter open and read it. Then he spoke to Muk.

"This letter is exactly what we need, Muk. We've got to get going. . . . Doctor, thank you for looking after my family. I would tell you the whole story but it would put your life in danger."

Exchanging farewells, Zach and Muk left the apartment building and walked down the street.

"What was in the letter, Father?"

Zach handed him the letter. "Directions to Amguema. Look pretty complicated to me and I'm a navigator!"

Muk looked at the directions. "Not too complicated. I know much of this territory. We'll need two ATVs and trailers to carry petrol, and camping supplies for three days of travel."

Zach handed Muk a roll of money. "You'd better buy what we need, Muk. I stick out here in town. Go ahead and buy a couple of used ATVs and all the camping supplies we need. I'll hang out down by the docks. At nine tonight, meet me in front of the doctor's office. I'll go with you to where you have the ATVs and we'll start out. We may get only three or four hours in tonight before we have to stop, but at least we'll be out of town and out of sight."

That night, they put up their tents in the semi-darkness and got four hours sleep. Next morning found them driving down old washed out roads and trails, following Leonid's directions.

On the third day, they came over a rise and saw it — Amguema. Zach's heart began to race. They drove down into the village, heading for the house Leonid had written in his directions. Zach scanned the street as he drove.

Suddenly there she was, walking down the street carrying Tomas. She was wearing a deerskin jacket and long brown dress. Her hair was now dark and short and straight, but Zach recognized her immediately. She was the most beautiful woman he had ever seen.

He drove up beside her and stopped. She glanced up, then did a double-take. Suddenly he was off the ATV and she was in his arms, kissing him and holding him. Zach kissed her and then looked down and kissed Tomas, who cooed back at him. Tears running down both their cheeks and mingling, Zach and Bethany just stood there holding each other and savoring the moment.

"Zach, oh, Zach," she said between sobs. "You're back and safe. Thank you, dear Lord, for answering my prayers and bringing my Zach back to me."

"There's so much to tell you, Bethany. So much. . . ."

Muk pulled up beside them and sat there silently. Bethany finally broke the silence.

"Hi, Muk. Thanks for delivering Father back to me safely. If you go to that house right over there, you'll find Leonid. He was just talking this morning about how soon you might get here."

"Thank you, Matushka." Muk gunned his engine and headed toward the house.

Zach and Bethany walked hand in hand toward the house, with Zach now holding Tomas.

"I was beginning to be afraid I wouldn't find you, Bethany. But thanks to Peter's planning, it happened. By the way, is Peter here?"

Bethany stopped and looked at Zach. The blood seemed to drain from her face. "Isn't he in Yanrakinnot?"

"He's vanished. Left no directions as to where he might be. Just left me a note with directions to get to you. And your wonderful letter. And money. I've got a bad feeling about what may have happened to him."

"Well. . . ." Bethany seemed caught between jubilation at Zach's return and fright at what might have happened to Peter. She started walking slowly. "I don't know what to say. We'll have to have a family powwow about it. . . . Meanwhile, come in and meet our hosts. They've been so good to Leonid and me. Gave me a job teaching school until you got back. I'm staying in the guest house. . . . My room has a double bed!"

Zach giggled. "Much as I'd like to accompany you there right now, we'd best conform to custom and greet your hosts."

"Oh. I forgot," Bethany said, freeing her hand from his and reaching into her pocket. "A Father Dmitri from Bishop Diomid's staff was here a few days ago on his way to a visitation to the church in Mys Shmidta. He said you might be coming soon and that if you got here, I was to give you this letter right away." She handed it to him.

Zach opened the letter and read it.

My Dear Father Zacharios, Father Dmitri tells me that you are out searching for your matushka and baby. He told me where you might be and so I have sent him with this letter for you. Actually two letters which say the same thing. Hopefully you will get one of them. If you are in Mys Shmidta, you are to report to the priest at St Stanislaus, Father Ivan, to assist him in the work there until such time as I give you a new assignment. If you are in Amguema, congratulations. You are the vicar of a new church plant — Church of the Transfiguration, Amguema. I hereby commission you to this work. Once you are set up there, come down to Anadyr with your dear wife and I will quietly but properly ordain you. And I will give you some funds to begin building a church. Pray for me daily as I do for you. Your Servant in Christ, The Most Reverend Diomid Anadyr, Third Bishop of Anadyr and Chukotka

"Looks like you'll keep that teaching job," Zach said as he handed her the letter. "I think we have a new home."

She quickly read the letter. "Oh, Zach. The people of Amguema are lovely. What a gift the bishop is giving us! Tug, our host, was just saying yesterday how good it would be if you could be assigned here. They're ready for a church. Leonid will be happy to hear this. He can be your pastoral assistant again."

"Yes. We'll start over here. I'll plant a church and Leonid and Muk will help me do that. And possibly Peter will join us later."

Bethany stopped and looked into Zach's eyes. "But one thing before we go into the house, Zach. Will we be safe here? Or will we be hunted down?"

"I wish I could answer that question, Bethany. I don't want to sugar-coat this. The man who was searching for you is an agent of the major crime syndicate here in the Russian Federation. I've had dealings with him and his group in the past. Somehow they got wind that I was alive and well here in Chukotka. I think their plan was to get to you so they could get to me.

"I'll fill you in on the details later, but I think word will get out among the intelligence networks that I'm dead. When the syndicate gets this information, which they will very soon, I'm pretty sure they'll call off their search. If we make it through this autumn here without an incident, I believe we'll be safe for the duration. Meanwhile we'll be vigilant. Okay?"

Bethany reached up and kissed Zach on the lips. They lingered there, until Tomas started to cry. Then they walked slowly into the house.

August 15th — Pevek, Far East Command HQ

Dmitri Plovnic sat at his desk eating sour cream and berries. He was on the phone with his superior in Moscow.

"I have found no trace of this Bethany Savage. After checking all the port villages along the Chukchi and Bering Seas, and no one having seen her, I can only conclude that she has escaped to one of the Chukchi villages in the interior. It might be almost impossible to find her there."

"Major Plovnic, I have instructions for you," came the response over the phone. "We have pretty reliable intelligence that her husband, Zachary Savage, may be dead. He probably died when his aircraft crashed on July 4th.

"But there is a possibility that he still lives. Some North Korean police said they knew of a Russian illegally crossing the border into Russia. Could be our man. Or it could have been a smuggler.

"If it is our man, he may be returning or may have already returned to Chukotka to be reunited with his family. That is a very slight possibility, major, but it is a possibility. My superiors instruct you to be on the lookout but not to spend much in resources in doing so."

"Spend much in resources I don't have, colonel," Plovnic said as he put another spoon of cream and berries in his mouth. "How about if I just close the case altogether and keep our normal vigilance?"

"Don't close the case. Keep it open. But don't spend a lot of time and money on searching for her and her husband. If by chance you do find him, he would be a prize for us."

"Yes, sir. Since it's mid-August, it's already getting cold and snowy in the interior. I think what I'll do is to wait until next spring when the weather warms up again. Then I will send some agents through the interior villages, those we can find. If we happen upon the wife, we can interrogate her. She may know something we can use. If we find her man, we'll turn him over to you immediately. But as you suggest, I will not put a lot of effort into it."

"That sounds like a good plan, major. Keep me informed."

May 10, 2011 — Amguema

Spring was in the air. The snow was melting day by day. Father Zacharios sat in his office, looking out the window at the mountains to the east.

So much has happened in the last nine months, Father, Zach prayed silently. *So much to be thankful for. Let me count my blessings. The quiet ordination by Bishop Diomid in September. The commissioning of the new church plant, St. Nicholas Orthodox Church. This new building put up by the villagers. The many villagers who have given their lives to Jesus and joined the congregation. The wonderful help Leonid and Muk give me everyday both in caring for the property and looking after the villagers. So many blessings, Father. But I'm beginning to think that I won't see Peter again until I join you in Heaven. Maybe we'll never know what happened to him, not this side of Heaven. I commend him to your care—"*

The door burst open and Leonid flew in, interrupting Zacharios' prayer.

"Father, come quickly. Matushka needs you right now!"

Father Zacharios grabbed his coat and threw it on as he followed Leonid out of the church and toward the house. They flew into the house and into the bedroom. Muk was holding Tomas, cooing with him. Matushka lay on the bed, holding the new baby.

"It's a girl!" The midwife said to Father. "She's healthy. Congratulations."

"Zach," Bethany said as she looked up at him. "God has given us a baby in our old age. A beautiful baby. Shall we call her Grace?"

"Grace," Zach said as he looked at the baby. "A beautiful name. God's grace in our lives. Yes. Let's call her Grace."